Why does your heart keep secrets

Miranda Jones has kept quiet about her past.
Her close friends know she comes from privilege, but she's asked them to keep her secret. Who is she now? A painter with growing success who focuses on wildlife, landscapes, and the environmental issues that mean so much to her.

But now it seems other people in her life are keeping their own secrets. Is Zack Calvin who he claims to be? How long can she keep her interest in Cornelius secret? What is it about the Clarke house that seems so out of place? Why is Meredith, her own sister, suddenly so interested in Milford-Haven? And how can she demand others reveal their secrets, when she won't reveal her own?

California's Central Coast is growing explosively.
Now, in the late 1990s, tourism is up, but so are environmental regulations. Housing is on the rise, but so are water restrictions. Gambling is limited, but the Chumash tribe lobbies for a gaming casino. Crime is low on the quiet Central Coast, but a murder born of greed has yet to come to light. The stock market is booming, the upwardly mobile are pouring out of Los Angeles in search of a fresh start or a weekend getaway. In these affluent, pre-9/11 days, it's a time of infinite possibilities.

Milford-Haven is a town full of characters.
Escapees from San Francisco and Los Angeles, New York and Arkansas, Montreal, Australia and South Africa, have come here with their own hopes and expectations, agendas and shadowed pasts. The stakes are high: create a new life from scratch. The opportunities are dazzling: own a piece of the California dream.

It's a town of buried secrets and a dangerous mystery, quaint shops and breathtaking vistas, peaceful solitude and spontaneous conversations.

What draws people here is the sense that—in their heart of hearts—they know there's something they've always wanted to do. But once they see the sign to **Milford-Haven,** pull off Highway 1, and find this coastal treasure, they'd like to keep the place a secret.

Come discover for yourself . . . ***Why Hearts Keep Secrets.***

THE PRESS PRAISES MARA PURL'S
MILFORD-HAVEN NOVELS

Book Three – *Why Hearts Keep Secrets*

"[In *Why Hearts Keep Secrets*] Purl has expertly interwoven her characters' lives into a colorful, fascinating tapestry of mystery, romance, and suspense. The writing flows easily and the characters are compelling. . . . Readers will find it fun to pass the time with the inhabitants of Milford-Haven, and will want to know more about their fates."   *— ForeWord Reviews*

"*Why Hearts Keep Secrets* by Mara Purl is a compelling romance that draws readers into a world of mystery, suspense and intrigue. Set in the coastal town of Milford-Haven, Miranda Jones' story continues as buried secrets and hidden agendas combine to create an electrifying plot that will keep readers on the edge of their seats. Readers will fall in love with Purl's masterful plotline and stunning use of descriptive imagery. In addition, the characters are memorable, original and believable, with unique, well-developed backstories. An interesting, engaging read that could be read as part of the series or as a standalone."   *— Maincrest Media Reviews*

"I found this continuation of Mara Purl's Milford-Haven series to be every bit as captivating and revealing as all the others. This one is really Miranda's story and without giving too much away, I can say that we learn she does find the happiness she's been searching for. Then there's Delmar Johnson – the only Black officer and investigator on the police force and he's determined to learn what happened to Christine Christian. The way Purl composes her novels, this series could go on for a long, long time. And true to form, the last chapter is another bit from Samantha Hugo's journal. Purl uses this journal to tie the story all together and it works well. Another wonderful read."
— Linda Thompson, Host of https://TheAuthorsShow.com

Book Two – *Where the Heart Lives*

"In *Where the Heart Lives,* Mara Purl strategically presents a glamorous alternative to big city vibrancy. In the second installment of her already popular Milford-Haven series, the California Central Coast is once again the locale for her magnetic cast of characters. Purl's success is based on her ability to appeal to readers on a more elevated level than traditional romance fiction generally prescribes. Though she never loses the common touch in her storytelling instincts, in every potential stereotype emerges a well-developed character with a standout personality."   *— ForeWord Reviews*

"[In] the second volume of this ongoing saga . . . Purl returns to picturesque Milford-Haven. The town is filled with back stories—dark secrets, hidden agendas, failed romances and budding love, not to mention the unsolved mystery. Skillfully interspersing the moment-to-moment thoughts of her characters with their actions and dialogue, Purl effortlessly moves from one personal story to another. Like visiting friends and catching up. . . ."
— Kirkus Review

"Part small-town confidential, part mystery, part romance, the story is cozy in the best sense of the word. Steeped in California charm, the setting plays host to a wide variety of characters from across the social spectrum. High society rubs shoulders with artists and diner cooks, providing a snap shot of an up-scale village. Despite the town's air of quaint charm, the people are refreshingly realistic."   — *Bookwire*

"[In] the second Milford-Haven novel, award-winning writer Mara Purl deepens the intrigue in this captivating window into the little battles, victories, successes, and failings of ordinary people in [the] complicated world [of] Milford-Haven."   — *Midwest Book Review*

Book One – *What the Heart Knows*

"Former *Days of Our Lives* star Purl presents the first novel in her Milford-Haven series, which . . . features a setting of unadulterated beauty—the small coastal town of Milford-Haven, CA in the prosperous mid-'90s—and a cast of successful, sexy, sometimes quirkily independent characters. . . . Readers will find details galore . . . and the novel's many inner monologues reveal scheming, secretly confused, or flawed personalities. . . . Milford-Haven offers depictions of daily life, hints of possible future romance, the threat of scandal, and carefully parsed out mystery. . . . the novel is poised to convince readers to continue with the series."   — *Publishers Weekly*

"Former *Days of Our Lives* actress Purl imbues her soap opera finesse into the fictional setting of Milford-Haven, a sleepy California coastal town. This may be Apple Pie, USA, but hearts are on the line, professions are at stake and a possible murder has tainted the landscape. A whirlwind of juicy drama with dangling-carrot closure."   — *Kirkus Review*

"*What the Heart Knows* is an upbeat novel . . . the first book of Milford-Haven. The book opens powerfully . . . Purl does not use external paraphernalia to bring her characters to life. Multiple love stories, friendships, crushes. . . . Purl's characters are well-traveled, educated, and street smart."
                                                        — *ForeWord Magazine*

". . . in Mara Purl's enchanting novel *What the Heart Knows* . . . although the picturesque, seaside setting of Milford-Haven plays an important role in the novel, the cast of interesting and eccentric characters is what really draws the reader into the book."   — *BookWire*

"Mara Purl's *What the Heart Knows* is a first class novel by a very talented writer with strong believable characters, a rapid pace delivery of story, and very tight writing that make this novel such a delight to read. I look forward to seeing other titles in this impressive series."
                           — *Gary Roen, Nationally Syndicated Bookreviewer*

"I read Mara Purl's *What the Heart Knows* and loved the book—just devoured it, in fact—and can't wait to read the next installment."
— *Anne L. Holmes, APR, National Association of Baby Boomer Women*

"You can't escape the pull of Milford-Haven, the setting for *Days of Our Lives* actress and award-winning author Mara Purl's enticing new novel *What the Heart Knows*. This fictional, coastal California town offers a simpler life. . . . My kind of romance, this [is a] juicy, take-me- away-from-it-all read . . . plus, the inviting story makes you think." *— Charlotte Hill, Boomer Brief*

The Milford-Haven Novels Series

"In Mara Purl's books the writing is crisp and clean, the dialogue realistic, the scenes well described. I salute her ingenuity." *— Bob Johnson,*
Former Managing Editor, The Associated Press

"Every reader who enjoys book series about small town life has a treat to anticipate in . . . Mara Purl's Milford-Haven Novels." *— Dee Ann Ray,*
The Clinton Daily News

"Mara Purl's characters have become old friends and I keep expecting one of them to give me a call!" *— Nanci Cone, Ventura Breeze*

". . . an intrigu[ing] cast of diverse characters."
— Fred Klein, Santa Barbara News Press

ENDORSEMENTS FROM OTHER AUTHORS

"Mara Purl is a skillful storyteller who has written a charming and tantalizing saga about the ways in which lives can intersect and be forever changed. The first novel in the saga is not-to-be-missed." *—Margaret Coel*
New York Times Best-Selling author

"I found a kinship with . . . your heart for character . . . and with your truly fine unveiling of story events." *—Jane Kirkpatrick, Author*
Wrangler Award, Willa Award

"I so admire Mara Purl's writing style. The pictures she paints are just glorious, her characters and attention to detail inspiring." *—Sheri Anderson*
Emmy Award-winning writer, Days of Our Lives

AWARDS FOR *WHY HEARTS KEEP SECRETS*

American Fiction Award
Finalist – Women's Fiction

Book Excellence Award
Finalist - Women's Fiction

ForeWord Book of the Year Award
Finalist – Fiction: Romance

Global EBook Award
Winner - Women's Fiction
Winner - Legacy Award

Hollywood Book Festival Book Award
Silver - Sequel

Independent Press Award
Finalist - Women's Fiction

International Book Award
Finalist - Women's Fiction: Romance

Los Angeles Book Festival Book Award
Winner - Regional Literature

Maincrest Media Award
Winner – Fiction: Romance

National Indie Excellence Award
Winner – Fiction: Romance

Pinnacle Book Award
Winner - Women's Fiction

Southern California Book Award
Winner – Regional Literature

USA Book News Best Book Award
Winner – Fiction: Romance

AWARDS FOR *the Author*
The Authors Show Top Female Author – Fiction
Los Angeles County Commission for Women – Woman of the Year

Why Hearts Keep Secrets

Also by MARA PURL

Fiction

When the Heart Listens (Prequel)

What the Heart Knows (Book One)

Where the Heart Lives (Book Two)

Why Hearts Keep Secrets (Book Three)

Whose Hearts Align (Novel Four)

Milford-Haven Wildlife Adventure Novellas & Novelettes

When Hummers Dream

When Whales Watch

When Otters Play

Milford-Haven Paranormal Novellas

What the Soul Suspects

Where the Soul Journeys

Milford-Haven Holiday Novellas & Novelettes

When Angels Paint

Where an Angel's On a Rope

Whose Angel Key Ring

Mystery Sleigh Ride – YA Holiday Story
(with Kengington Norfleet)

Non-Fiction

Act Right: A Manual for the On-Camera Actor
(with Erin Gray)

Kenneth Leventhal & Co.:
A History of the Firm

S.T.A.R –Student Theatre & Radio
High School Curriculum; College Curriculum

Plays	**Radio Plays**	**S.T.A.R.**
Mary Shelley–	*Milford-Haven, U.S.A*	**Radio Plays**
In Her Own Words	(100 episodes)	*America the Beautiful*
(with Sydney Swire)		*Ashton Valley*
	Green Valley	*Boom*
Dracula's Last Tour		*Caught in a Web*
	Haven Ten	*Changes*
Screenplays &		*Cruising*
Teleplays	**S.T.A.R.**	*The Curse of*
The Meridian Factor	**Teleplay**	*Santa Florida*
(with Verne Nobles)	*Only A Test*	*Deep Freeze*
		Fountain Hills Mall
Welcome to		*Friendz*
Milford-Haven		*Frozen Hearts*
(with Katherine		*The Game*
Doughtie Nolan)		*Going Somewhere*
		In or Out
Guiding Light		*The Journal*
		K-RAP
		Love Child
		Love Resolutions
		The New Girl
		The Peak Mystery
		San Feliz
		Secretos
		Tokyo Time Travel
		Toxicity
		Westland High
		Wrong Way

Mara Purl

Why Hearts Keep Secrets

Book Three
A Milford-Haven Novel

Milford-Haven PUBLISHING, RECORDING & BROADCASTING HISTORY
This book is based in part upon the original radio drama Milford-Haven ©1987 by Mara Purl, Library of Congress numbers SR188828, SR190790, SR194010; and upon the original radio drama Milford-Haven, U.S.A. ©1992 by Mara Purl, Library of Congress number SR232-483, broadcast by the British Broadcasting Company's BBC Radio 5 Network, and which is also currently in release in audio formats as Milford-Haven, U.S.A. ©1992 by Mara Purl. Portions of this material also appear on the Milford-Haven Web Site, http://www.MilfordHaven.com © by Mara Purl.

The Library of Congress has catalogued this book as follows:
Purl, Mara.
Why Hearts Keep Secrets/ Mara Purl.
p. ; cm. — (A Milford-Haven novel ; bk. 3)

Based in part upon the original radio dramas Milford-Haven and Milford-Haven U.S.A., broadcast by BBC Radio 5 Network.
Portions also appear on the World Wide Web at http://www.milfordhaven.com and were published in early editions.
ISBN: 978-1-936878-23-9
1. Women painters—California—Fiction. 2. California—Fiction. 3. Mystery fiction. I. Title. II. Title: Milford-Haven U.S.A. (Radio program) III. Title: Milford-Haven (Radio program)
PS3566.U75 W45 2022
813/.6

Published in the U.S. by Bellekeep Books, New York www.BellekeepBooks.com
Distributed by Ingram

10 9 8 7 6 5 4 3

Printed in the United States of America

*This book is dedicated to
my readers
and to the transformative power
of releasing the secrets of your own hearts.*

Acknowledgments

Thanks to my publishers: Patrice Samara, Kara Johnson and Tara Goff at BelleKeep Books. Thanks to my gifted editorial team: Vicki Hessel Werkley, editor; Derra Moyers, editor & proofreader. Thanks to Mary Helsaple for exquisite watercolors for my book covers, to Reya Patton for cover concept, and to Rebecca Finkel for superb interior design and cover adjustments.

Thanks to my marketing team: Jonatha King at King Communications in Santa Barbara for PR and marketing; Don McCauley for PR distribution; Kelly Johnson and Sky Esser for internet design and wizardry. Thanks to Judith Briles for marketing programs and events.

Thanks to those who provide expertise during my research: to artists Mary Helsaple, Caren Pearson for inspiration and depth of detail; to Dr. Laurence Doyle for astronomical specifics; to Pilulaw Khus for Chumash wisdom and for her book *Earth Wisdom* co-written with Yolanda Broyles-Gonzalez. Thanks, always, to the SLO County Sheriff's Department.

The fictional mural in Lompoc is based on a real mural in Lompoc, California, titled "The Lighthouse at Point Conception." Its master artists were Vicki Andersen and Linda Gooch, and it's located at 131 South H Street. It was part of the Lompoc Mural Society's Mural in a Weekend program and was painted in 2018.

Thanks to dear friends in Cambria who've supported Milford-Haven for many years with such enthusiasm, including Elaine Travel Evans, Kathe Tanner, Susan & Brent Berry, Judy Salamacha and Dennis Eamon Young. Thanks to Verne Nobles, and to Frank Abatemarco for clear vision and passionate commitment to the Milford-Haven Television project.

Thanks for special events: to dynamic organizations in several parts of the country for working with me to produce the community-based Milford-Haven Socie-Teas® (Possibili-Teas, Generosi-Teas, Hospitali-Teas, Creativi-Teas, and our list continues!) And to Unique Soap Boutique for the wonderful *Days Of Our Lives* events.

Thanks for organization support: WWW (Women Writing the West), CLAS (California Literary Arts Society), IBPA (Independent Book Publishing Association), SLO NightWriters, Sisters in Crime, the Author's Guild and Author U/Author You, Colorado Authors Hall of Fame, and Publishing at Sea.

Thanks to many independent bookstores who participated in my program #SendIndieBookGift during the Pandemic. It was wonderful supporting you and reaching new readers all over the U.S.

Thanks to Bill Berkuta and all at Haven Books Audio for award-winning audio books. Thanks to my mentor Louis L'Amour, who believed in my project and told me to keep going with it.

And most important of all—thanks to you, my readers! I'm thrilled to welcome those of you who are new to my books. And I extend a special heartfelt thanks to the core group of readers who began with the novels' early editions. I appreciate your steadfast support during my publishing journey.

The Radio Drama

Milford-Haven had its first air date in 1987, and my thanks go to KOTR, in Cambria, California, our first radio home. In its next incarnation *Milford-Haven, U.S.A.* was broadcast on the BBC, thanks Ms. Pat Ewing, Director of Radio 5—a maverick network that launched a maverick show, and celebrated with us when we reached 4.5 million listeners.

Before there were any shows to broadcast, there were the cast members, and my thanks go to both the original cast of *Milford-Haven* and to the cast of *Milford-Haven, U.S.A.,* seasoned professionals who brought my characters so vividly to life that their work is inextricably woven into the fabric of the characters themselves.

Before there were cast members to record, there had to be a studio, and my thanks go to Engineer Bill Berkuta whose Afterhours Recording Company became our studio home, a workshop in which we created one hundred episodes of the first show and sixty of the second, and where we now create audio books of the novels.

Thanks to the late great David L. Krebs, our foley master, a gifted sound artist who created our aural reality. Thanks to Marilyn Harris and Mark Wolfram, who composed the haunting *Milford-Haven* theme and all the music cues that support the emotional ebb and flow of the story. Thanks to Warren Talcott for the intriguing *Milford-Haven* poster, and to Caren Pearson for the compelling *Milford-Haven* logo art—each of which gave our town its visual reality.

Before I created my own soap opera, there was *Days of Our Lives* and my thanks go to the producers, writers, directors and fellow cast members with whom I worked, and from whom I learned so much.

And before there was a *Milford-Haven,* there was a young woman who had always lived in cities—Tokyo, New York, Los Angeles. I spent a summer performing in a play at Jim and Olga Buckley's Pewter Plough Playhouse in Cambria, and became fascinated with the life in and of a small town. With Elaine Traxel Evans's help, I immersed myself in this new culture— admittedly seeing it through the eyes of an environmentalist—and began to realize that it was not only a local drama that was being played out in its quiet streets, but a universal one as well.

Listeners in the U.S. and in the U.K. agreed, writing to me about their own lives, their own towns, and the commonality of the situations we face globally. My thanks go to my listeners everywhere. Several years later the link with listeners was to be vividly demonstrated, when the original Milford Haven in Wales embraced me as an honorary citizen and showed me those same streets, those same dramas, uncannily alike in the multi-cultural parallel universes we all inhabit. Thanks to Bruce Henrickson of the Belhaven House Hotel. Special thanks to Jim and Anne Hughes, who shared my vision even before we met, who welcomed me into their home, and with whom I continue to forge a unique town-to-town relationship.

My thanks go to my family and friends—helpful, discerning and, above all, supportive—Ray Purl, Marshie Purl, Linda Purl, Larry Norfleet, Erin Gray, Miranda Kenrick, Vickie and Bob Zoellner.

And finally my thanks go to my characters, among whom are—Jack, Zack, Miranda, Cornelius, Samantha, Rune, Meredith, Connie, Rick, Emily, Kevin, Joseph, Sally, Tony, Zelda, Notes, Susan and Cynthia, who are building, buying, painting, observing, planning, rehearsing, flirting, traveling, dealing, reporting, cogitating, dominating, dishing, healing, conniving, playing, sneaking and seducing, respectively.

Dear Reader,

Welcome back to Milford-Haven! And if this is your first visit—it is my pleasure to introduce you to my favorite little town and to its many residents, all of whom are described in the Cast of Characters at the back of the book.

All of us have secrets. Indeed, we might prefer to classify certain things as "private." Sometimes we're planning a surprise, or we have some other benevolent reason for keeping quiet. On the other hand, withholding important information can damage relationships. Most malicious of all is requiring someone else to stay silent about a known evil.

The interweavings of lives forms a rich tapestry in Milford-Haven. Relationships include colleagues and competitors, collaborators and conspirators. But mostly they include dear friendships and the coming to fruition of vivid, if sometimes complex, romances.

For my protagonist Miranda, her head has commanded her not to reveal her deepest feelings. But in this book, her *heart* at last overrides this limitation and her sentiments flow out—at the right time and to the right person. This is a joy for her, for me as her author, and I hope for you as a reader who's been waiting for this eventuality.

You may read these books out of sequence, but I think you'll enjoy them most reading them as I wrote them. *Why Hearts Keep Secrets* is the third novel, with novellas and novelettes expanding and enhancing the saga.

Through the novels, each Prologue proceeds with the investigation of journalist Chris Christian's disappearance. The heart of the story is seen through the artist-eyes of Miranda Jones. And each novel's themes are concluded by environ-mentalist Samantha Hugo in her ongoing journals.

In each novel, we leave Milford-Haven to follow Miranda Jones to destinations that fascinate her painter's eye and her restless heart. This novel takes her—and you—to the Deschutes State Recreation Area, a beautiful region of Oregon. But then it brings her back to a deeper sense of home than she has ever known, one her heart recognized from a drawing done much earlier—a home she will share forever in Milford-Haven.

As the story unfolds, follow my footsteps over the inter-connected pathways of those who inhabit Milford-Haven, and come to understand. . . why hearts keep secrets.

Mara Purl

"The two most important days in your life
are the day you are born and the day you
find out why."

—Mark Twain

"A woman's heart is a deep ocean of secrets."

—Gloria Stuart

"Everything vital about someone's soul can
be found locked in what they hold closest,
hidden sometimes even from themselves.
Perhaps this is why hearts keep secrets."

—from Samantha Hugo's Journal

Prologue

Senior Deputy Delmar Johnson had a date with a ghost.

Nervously, he glanced at the empty chair across the table from where he sat in the conference room. A shiver ran down his spine. *Does it matter if my date is no longer among the living?*

No matter how many times he denied the absurd notion, some unmistakable presence seemed to haunt him. The worst part of it was the recurring nightmare. No, the worst part was that he couldn't tell whether he was dreaming or not. He never knew until he awoke, usually in a cold sweat.

He shook his head as though to clear away the tendrils of the eerie dream and force his mind into its usual, methodical approach to his cases. Though broadcast journalist Christine Christian's body had never turned up, a gnawing intuition told him the missing woman would not be found alive.

Del touched the table as though to convince himself he was awake. But am I? *Does a dreamer ever know he's dreaming?*

The alternate reality that seemed to grip his mind also brought its own sense of time. Was he remembering something that had happened? Or was this a foreshadowing? A strange lethargy pulled at him, preventing him from consulting the calendar on his desk down the corridor.

Del looked across the table, watching as Christine Christian arrived, taking the chair opposite.

"Nice of you to show up for our date," he said, his tone more acerbic than he'd intended.

She looked confused, then asked politely, "Uh . . . sorry. Am I late?"

"Not really a date. An appointment, let's say," he amended. Into the awkward silence she said, "So . . . looks like you already reviewed the first episode in the series and you're at the end of episode two."

Del glanced at the television screen on which he'd been reviewing VCR tapes of her special report on adoption. "I better watch this again."

"Really? I'm flattered." Her face suffused with a slight blush. He watched the second segment, and before starting the third, decided he needed a restroom break and a coffee. When he returned, he carried two mugs and set one in front of her.

"Thanks," she said.

"Such as it is," he replied. "You know, cop coffee."

They both laughed.

Del ran a hand over his hair, then over his face. "I have . . . I have so many questions. Not sure where to start."

Confused, Chris asked, "About adoption?"

"No! No," he countered. "I enjoyed watching your series. Actually, it could help me with another case. You're good at what you do. Great, in fact."

"That means a lot. I like the digging, you know? The investigating, peeling back the layers."

"Exactly!" Del leaned in, his forearms on the table. "That's what I like, what drew me to this career."

"Same here. Well, not the same career, but there are similarities, I guess."

Del nodded. "More than I realized. So . . . okay . . . the most obvious question is, where have you been?"

Dismissively, Chris replied, "I got caught up in a story I was researching."

"Yeah, but where? I mean, people have been worried. I've been worried. You go to the Clarke house. Then what?"

Chris leaned back in her chair. "My contact is a no-show. I walk around the house. It's dark, kind of spooky. I wait for a while. I mean, this guy promised key information, so I didn't want to miss him. And then I fall."

"Fall?"

"There was a hole in front of the fireplace, where the hearth will go. Didn't see it in the dark. I fell, hit my head. I've still got a nasty bump." She felt for it, then dropped her hand in her lap. "I have no idea how long I was down there. I woke up in the pitch black, felt my way till I found stairs, climbed out."

Del observed, "You said there was a hole when you fell, so no stairs. But then when you climbed out, there were stairs?"

Chris thought for a moment. "Yeah. That doesn't quite make sense.

"Any chance you had help with that fall?"

"Help?"

"I'm saying . . . is it possible someone pushed you?"

"I . . . there's . . ." Chris began to shudder. "Honestly, I can't quite remember. I've had some trouble, lately, since that head injury. There are some gaps. At least . . . I finally . . . got out of there alive."

Very quietly, Del replied, "Chris, I'm not sure you did."

Part I

Confessions

"Confession of errors is like a broom
which sweeps away the dirt and leaves the surface
brighter and clearer."

—Mahatma Gandhi

Chapter 1

Fog settled over Milford-Haven like a thick comforter, snugging its damp weight against the hills on the last cool night before spring.

A traveler driving Highway 1 along California's Central Coast might not even notice the village shrouded in mist, its identity a well-kept secret.

Miranda Jones lay in bed and pulled the comforter higher as though it might help her hold onto the bits and pieces of incomplete dreams adrift in the haze of memory.

She recalled a moment in her artist's studio upstairs, when Cookie the lioness walked through the room, stepping delicately on huge paws till she stood in front of the portrait of herself and her mate, inspecting it for accuracy. Miranda smiled at that image, and then was pulled toward another memory, that of a bobcat sitting just outside the studio window, peering in curiously. *Both animals, both in my studio.*

Finally, a mocking bird appeared in the dream she suddenly remembered, perched atop her highest shelf, its piercing cry sounding out a demand— no, a warning—communicated in that secret language of sight and sound.

The dream-bird's insistent song seemed intentional, as though its purpose was to call her attention to something important. Heeding these animal signs, something generally dismissed in modern culture, was nonetheless a valued message she'd learned to trust. She'd even made a start at learning to read these signs, thanks to her friend, Chumash elder Kuyama. *I'll do more reading about mockingbirds and perhaps call my friend later. We're overdue for a call anyway.*

For now, however, Miranda longed so much for another few hours of sleep that she tried to ignore the dream messages. She turned over yet again, careful not to crush her kitty.

"Meh," her adolescent cat, Shadow, complained, being jostled for the fifth time in as many minutes. *A very clear animal message!*

The kitty settled, but Miranda couldn't seem to do so. Wind rattled her window. *A spring storm brewing?* Her roving thoughts rolled right along with the clouds she imagined must be scudding over the coastal hills.

Remnants of another dream began to surface, and she knew she must've been processing her recent encounters with Zack Calvin. Again.

Why couldn't she just let it go? It's not like they'd had a real relationship. It'd started out with the loud drumbeat of potential, then quickly dissolved into awkward silence. It'd picked up again with an almost steady rhythm when he'd invited her to the Doobie Brothers Concert.

Now that was some *real* drumming! What incredible music!And what a thrill it'd been to be there, dancing along with the thousands at the Hollywood Bowl, then congratulating the band members backstage afterward.

But by then Zack—overwhelmed with his producing duties—had been nothing more than courteous. Well, to be more accurate, he'd seemed to blow hot and cold, or maybe tepid and cool. He couldn't have been more complimentary, but he always seemed to hesitate when it came to following through.

She tried to summon his handsome face, but strangely, it was the image of another man that popped into her mind. She'd seen him that very first time she'd come to Milford-Haven, before she moved here, and was just exploring possibilities. Twelve months ago.

She'd stopped at the local self-serve car wash, where she'd met Kevin, now a good local friend. There'd been a man just leaving, and he'd called a greeting to Kevin. She'd barely even seen his face, except for a glance. But something about his dark hair, his muscular build, and the warmth in his voice. *No. It wasn't all that. It was his eyes.* Their gaze had caught for a long, haunting moment. And she'd heard his name when Kevin said it: Cornelius.

Then last Christmas Eve he'd come into the gallery. She'd backed right into him. They'd both been startled, made their apologies. She'd turned to be caught again by those eyes, so much closer this time.

They'd awkwardly introduced themselves, but when she reached to shake his hand, he'd winced. She apologized, and couldn't stop herself from turning his hand over, startled to see a livid rope burn across his palm.

He'd revealed the same injury on his other hand, muttering, "Yeah, I had an adventure today."

Miranda had known in an instant that his adventure, whatever it'd been, was not only connected to the small painting she'd done the day before, but the very reason for it. What a strange experience that'd been for her—a compulsion to paint an image she'd neither seen nor photographed, a steep, rugged mountainside with a climbing rope draped down the escarpment. And now, a virtual stranger came into the gallery with rope burns across both hands.

She thought back to that moment. Had there actually been a spark when the touched? She'd tried to dismiss it as reaction to the burns, or even as static electricity in the dry, cool weather. But it wasn't that. It was science—like molecular alignment skin to skin. And it was art—like finding the right color of blue to match the sky.

It'd struck her as being far beyond a personal connection. Instead, it was as though the universe had used her for its own purposes and a life had been touched, perhaps even saved, as a result. She could take no responsibility for such an event, nor could she dare to taint it with personal feelings. Awestruck by the mighty power of this force for good that'd somehow worked through her, she had taken a step back emotionally. Grateful beyond words that he was safe, she had handed him back to the Great Spirit from whence he'd come. And it'd been Christmas. She'd flown to New York the next day, consigning the moment in the gallery to the magic of the season, then being swept up in her family reunion.

Since then, life had stayed busy. Ironically, she'd been in Zack's hometown without seeing him. In Santa Barbara to fulfill two mural commissions—the sea otters outside and her representative Zelda McIntyre's condo inside—she'd stayed focused. Her calendar showed more work, more travel, a full schedule. And now it was March.

Didn't this prove that being an artist was a full-time job? Could there ever be room in her life for a relationship? What had happened—or not happened—with Zack could be consigned to the proverbial missed opportunity. And what'd happened with Cornelius those many weeks ago was really nothing personal. She didn't know him. She could only wish him well. And she'd appreciate it if he'd stay out of her head, whether asleep or awake.

Irritation began to give way to drowsiness. Her consciousness sank just beneath the surface of full awareness, like a sea otter floating in the kelp and buffeted by the tide.

A new dream tried to drag her down, a quasi-nightmare of missed chances and lost opportunities. A man that meant something, until he didn't; a promise implied but unfulfilled; an urge to breathe that dangerously ignored the sea water.

Miranda gasped awake, threw back the covers and caused Shadow to leap straight up off the duvet, too startled even to make a sound. To calm the rapid beating of her own heart, and that of her pet's, she caught the kitty and held her in a gentle embrace, stroking her sleek black fur.

"So sorry, Pookaloo, didn't mean to frighten you," she soothed.

As if sensing her human's distress, Shadow reached a paw forward to touch her cheek. Miranda and her pet exchanged tiny, delicate kisses, and soon the kitty was purring and settling back for a few more minutes of nap time.

But the surge of adrenaline had brought Miranda too awake to try for sleep again, yet still unwilling to get out of bed. She decided to consider the animals who'd visited her dream. *Maybe I'll get some insights.*

The beautiful pair of lions names Cookie and Lionel were easy to understand. The painting was her newest commission, and the reason for last week's visit to the L.A. Zoo, where she'd taken the photos she needed.

What do lions represent? Courage, of course. And, unlike other big cats, lions were social, so they represented family. And though no big feline could ever be considered "tame," these rescued cats did live in captivity. So in the language of dream-symbols, they seemed to represent bravery and family.

Beautiful, she thought, feeling that occasional longing toward love, marriage, and a family of her own, even though she felt incapable of achieving any of it.

She pulled away from the depressing thought. *What about the bobcat?* Mysterious, solitary, intense. Those were the qualities that came to mind. Several weeks earlier, during a walk on the Coastal Trail, she'd glanced across a ravine to see a bobcat observing her. *That impish face with the "I dare you" attitude.* They'd stared at one another for a long moment before the cat bounded away.

How long had the bobcat been watching me? Ah, she remembered. *They're known for patience.* But there's some-thing else. Secrets. "You invoke the spirit of the bobcat when you need to uncover secrets," Kuyama had said.

Miranda lay there quietly considering. She'd been work-ing on this "secrets" theme in her paintings. *Was something more trying to surface?* Everyone had secrets, of course. But many could be better described as information not yet ready to be shared. Real secrecy carried more weight, either for benevolent or malevolent purposes. She couldn't think of anything in either category. But she determined to switch on her mental radar.

She'd more or less deciphered what the lion and the bobcat might signify. That left the mockingbird about whom she'd had that vivid dream. She considered it a kind of whimsical reminder that she was about to work on a bird project—a commission to paint the Oregon state bird. During the course of her preparatory research about avians, she'd learned more about the "mocker."

This species' patterns of behavior were more complex than most people suspected. According to what she'd read, these birds defined their territory aurally. If they saw or heard a cricket, for example, they would mimic the cricket's sound, as if to say, "I hear you, I know you're there, and you're in my neck of the woods."

Such a clever way to express that territorial imperative. But this didn't seem pertinent. *What else?*

Sleep was obviously not an option tonight. *Maybe working through the night is the best way of observing the Vernal Equinox.* She slid carefully away from her still-slumbering cat.

Miranda felt the chill of cool night air and closed her bedroom window. She shouldered into the dark green velour top that matched the drawstring pants she'd pulled on. Twirling her hair into a loose circle, she fastened the long strands with a barrette and climbed the stairs to her studio, then turned on her desk lamp.

The moment she did, the wall of windows seemed to turn into dark mirrors, making it impossible to see the view outside. The familiar space suddenly took on a spooky aspect, as though she could be seen by some imagined voyeur lurking in the trees. *Absurd!* Nonetheless, she lowered the wooden blinds and twisted them closed, restoring the coziness she seemed to need tonight. *Besides, if the storm cracks a window, the blinds will minimize broken glass in the studio.*

Her discomfort now held in abeyance, she reached up to her reference shelf to grab a favorite book about the meanings of animal communication. Its lovely photographs and lists of symbolic meanings were arranged alphabetically, and she thumbed through until she found the listing she wanted.

"Are you striving for self-expression? Mockingbird can speak to you as your Spirit Animal." *Self-expression. I suppose that's my whole career.* "Mockingbird sings for you to help you discover your voice," the text continued.

Miranda stopped reading, sensing the importance of this message. "Finding your voice" was what every artist worked on, listened for, and strove to perfect. This was the essence of the journey itself. Whether painter or author, composer or sculptor, indeed any sort of creator, the process was to study and learn from mentors, but then pull away into your own unique way of seeing, hearing, expressing.

Okay, this was worth getting up for. But I need a cup of tea. She padded across the living room, into the adjacent kitchen, filled her electric kettle, and switched it on. While she waited, she thought of her Grandma Dorothy. *She loves birds. Maybe she'd have an insight about this one.* Her grandmother lived on the East Coast in a town called Milford, ironically. When Miranda had first moved here, they'd shared a moment of recognizing the synchronicity. *I'll call her later today. It'll be good to hear her voice.*

A few moments later, Miranda carried a crockery mug fragrant with hot Earl Gray tea back into her studio. She gazed across her workspace. Facing her from the easel was the now-completed portrait of Lionel and Cookie. The majestic pair of African lions stared regally out from their perch. Yet there was a slight tilt that brought their heads close, showing their natural affinity with one another.

They'd been rescued along with thousands of other exotic animals by the Waystation in the mountains just north of Los Angeles. She suspected they were destined to become favorites at the popular zoo in Griffith Park. They'd certainly become two of hers, when she'd met them last week. Dignified and regal, they were also openly affectionate with one another and playful at times. Clearly, they were soul mates, and she hoped the portrait reflected these qualities.

She'd made another quick trip south in February to attend the San Diego Zoo gala with its "I Heart Wild Animals" theme. It'd been quite an evening. She'd been honored for her painting of Lia the cheetah, who lived in the zoo's Wild Animal Park area. Her painting had fetched a handsome sum during the fund-raising auction, and she'd been delighted her work served to raise needed funds for her beloved big cats. Seated at her table had been the L.A. Zoo director, and that'd led to this most recent commission.

Miranda looked up at the shelf that held her HandBook notebooks. She'd used Sharpies to write on the spines CAT: Commissioned Art Tracking, as she used these to track the progress of all her commissioned works, always amused that the acronym spelled the name of her favorite creatures.

Each was a different color, and the first notebook was actually titled CAT Cat, and featured her Large Feline series. The second notebook was titled CAT Land for landscape; the next CAT Birds, then CAT Critters, for the other species she painted. One final notebook held her postcard series, CAT Cards.

As works were completed, she painted small watercolor drafts and pasted them in the notebooks to remind her of the finished piece. They also contained business cards taped onto pages, hand-written phone numbers, instructions from the client, and anything else pertinent to the job.

She took a few minutes to thumb through the recently completed and planned work, then thought about projects on her immediate horizon. First would be her trip to Oregon, scheduled for the day after tomorrow. She'd been commissioned by the state to paint the meadowlark, and she'd done a fair amount of homework to prepare to photograph the birds from a blind, then to paint once she was back in her studio. Weather or circumstances permitting, she'd also do some *plein air* painting, which meant she'd need her portable easel, which had gotten damaged. *Gotta remember to take it to the hardware store today, see if Mr. Hargraves can repair it.*

Almost immediately upon her return from her four days in Oregon, she'd be driving south to a town near Santa Maria. Lompoc, situated on the peninsula jutting westward from Santa Barbara, had become known as a town of outdoor art, thanks to the Lompoc Mural Projects founded in 1988 by Gene and Judy Stevens.

The civic mural projects tended to be created almost as performance art: planned well in advance, but painted quickly and in public view, often attracting local audiences. Sometimes these were even done as coordinated group efforts, with artists self-assigned to complete certain sections of the image. The murals were painted on the sides of large one-story buildings, providing a perfect landscape aspect ratio, and, in some cases, giving an almost *trompe l'oeil* illusion of being actual scenery,

Having perfected her own skill at precisely this kind of mural in several locations, Miranda was thrilled to have been invited to contribute to this one. She'd be painting with three other artists, and their assigned subject was the lighthouse and grounds at Point Conception, twenty-five miles from Lompoc. Though once open to the public, this lighthouse was now shrouded in mystery.

Point Conception marked the clash of two major ocean currents, making it one of the most dangerous areas to maritime navigation. To be visible below the low fog that sometimes clung to the rugged landscape, the light stood midway down a steep mountainous escarpment that plunged into the sea. The property still belonged to the U.S. government, and its maintenance was administered by the Coast Guard. But access to the light was now surrounded by a private ranch that considered all visitors to be trespassers.

Wish I could see it in person, take my own photos. But, since that would not be possible, Miranda and her colleagues had contented themselves with historical photos provided by the Lompoc Valley Chamber of Commerce. Miranda had been elected to do the scale drawing and would paint whatever she was assigned. They'd chosen spring as the time of year, because it would allow them to include the vivid wildflowers that covered the hillsides.

The foreground of the image depicted a curving beach, which had brought back a sweet childhood memory of building a sandcastle with her father. *It's been a long time since I felt close to dad.* To honor that memory, or perhaps to add an iconic touch of playfulness, she'd drawn one in. It seemed to work, and the team had approved.

Miranda reached for her day planner, looking at the month-view. Three weeks from tonight, she'd be at her art show at the local gallery right here in Milford-Haven. On one hand, this made her more nervous than any of her other work. She'd be on display as a local artist with nowhere to hide.

On the other hand, she felt excited about the show itself, Over the past year, she'd experimented with placing hidden elements in some of her non-commissioned paintings. In one, a mountain lion crouched behind a boulder, his eyes just visible above it; in another, an osprey hunkered in her nest; and one pictured a doe blended cleverly into the brown leaves where she stood.

Miranda glanced up and noticed her young kitty lurking in a shadow at the edge of her desk. As if playing along with this game, the cat sat quietly, gold eyes blinking.

"I wondered where you were," she said in a gentle voice. "You just love to hide. No wonder I named you Shadow!"

The cat let out a soft "Meh," which made Miranda laugh. It also brought her thoughts back to that moment with the bobcat. When she'd done her painting, she'd placed the creature out in the open rather than partially obscured. But the combination of the cat's camouflaging coat and its absolute stillness in dappled light had made it hard to see. *Makes sense the bobcat represents the concept of secrecy.*

It'd been that painting that'd brought the show's theme into focus. She and Nicole, manager of Finder's Gallery, had met to brainstorm ideas. Nicole had noticed the almost playful aspect of creatures partially hiding from view. And when she heard about the bobcat, she'd suggested "Find the Secret" as the title of the show.

Since all the pieces had this theme, Nicole had decided that customers who found the hidden elements would earn a discount off the purchase of one painting. It seemed a clever gimmick, and Miranda's representative Zelda McIntyre had approved.

A gust of wind dashed what must have been a branch against the studio window, startling both Miranda and her kitty. Nothing broken, *but that storm is getting stronger.* It was just as well she'd decided to get up. She'd never have been able to sleep through the increasingly turbulent wind and the rattling of the trees.

Trying to focus again, she looked at the array of notebooks now spread out on her desk, noticing the notebook labeled "Cards," and realizing it was time to get to work on her next miniature. These were seasonal, so the next one would depict spring. *Wildflowers. Though not yellow, because I already did those. Pink ice plant covers the lighthouse hillside.*

As she reviewed her mural sketch, she realized that a small portrait version of part of the image could become her next postcard. It would tie in to her previous postcard, a map of the Central Coast that showed its lighthouses. And the new image with the wildflowers would perfectly represent spring.

Thinking about postcards brought her thoughts back to Cornelius and the surprising notion that he'd sent her some. That was the last thing she'd expected, yet she found herself charmed by his efforts. *I suppose he might've seen my painted postcards at the gallery.*

She'd received his first one last January, a Central Coast tourist card with a thoughtful message, thanking her for the painting of the rope on the mountain. She'd thought it a nice courtesy and stashed it in a carved keepsake box.

The bigger surprise came when she received another one from a place called the Milford Sound in New Zealand. A beautiful photo on the card made it seem exotic, while the name made it seem familiar. But of greater interest was the fact that he seemed to like sending postcards, just as she did.

So nice of him. But I haven't written back. Once again, she asked herself why. Then a realization struck her. *I've been doing a good job of finding my professional voice. What about my personal one?*

The next moment, the crash of something breaking resounded through the night. Miranda jerked to a standing position, then stood listening for some further noise but heard only the blustering wind. The sound seemed to have come from her deck. Heart pounding, she flipped on the exterior light, then parted two blinds with her fingers to peer out. Sure enough, there on the planks were the pieces of a mug she'd left on the railing. Opening the sliding door a crack, she stepped outside to retrieve the remainders. *It's the one I painted for Zack but never gave him. Why didn't I?*

After coming inside, wiping her feet, and discarding the shards, Miranda returned to her desk. *I need to get to the bottom of this.*

From the first, Zack had seemed an impressive guy. Last autumn he'd rolled up to her door unannounced, with his flashy car and good looks. She'd done her best to look past the eye candy, particularly when he'd expressed interest in her work. He'd gone so far as to state his intention to commission a work from her, but then he never followed through.

That wasn't exactly a red flag. He had every right to change his mind. But he'd never actually said as much. Next, he'd gone silent, then reappeared with the rather extravagant invitation to join him backstage at that fabulous concert. But then he'd been too busy to spend any time with her. *A master at the grand gesture.*

He still calls intermittently, always courteous. But he always seems to be withholding something. Yes, that was it. These gaps in communication . . . what did they mean? Why had she never heard more about his work?

Most recently, he'd said he and his father planned to attend her art show. *Another grand gesture?* He'd left a message saying they'd stay at the Belhaven, where he'd stayed before. But there were no additional plans. This time, she'd be busy herself—greeting local friends and whomever Zelda had invited, and afterward visiting with her sister—certainly not exactly able to entertain the Calvins. Assuming they did come, what did Zack expect?

The storm seemed to quiet down, and she thought again of the mockingbird in her dream. *He certainly found his voice. It's time to find mine.*

Miranda took a hard look at her own behavior. It was easy enough to play the blame game. Indeed, all this time, she'd been blaming Zack for their lack of communication. But had she ever expressed her feelings to him? She could have shared her doubts, her frustration when he didn't call, her confusion about his career—but she hadn't. *Why? Because she hadn't yet found her voice.*

Now Cornelius was trying to communicate with her, yet she hadn't responded to him either. *But I want to.*

When it came to Zack, she'd felt either intimidated or annoyed. On the outside, he seemed a great match. Yet inwardly, they were out of sync. And how did she feel about Cornelius? Though they had yet to spend time together, already she felt curious and even excited at the prospect of getting to know him better.

She reached for the carved box and lifted out the cards Cornelius had sent, somewhat ashamed she'd been ignoring him. *I don't have to ignore him anymore.*

Twisting open the blinds, she looked through her window and could just make out dark silhouettes of the pine trees standing tall against the sky. The mockingbird trilled a familiar melody.

As the first hint of light touched the sky, the reticence that had silenced her voice began to ebb away as gently as the shadows that were giving way to the coming dawn.

Chapter 2

Cornelius Smith sighed with relief as his Dodge Durango began to speed north on the relatively empty 405 freeway. His twelve-hour flight from Amsterdam to Los Angeles had landed at 6:00 a.m., and with no checked baggage, he'd been able to walk directly to the parking structure where his vehicle had been parked for four nights.

His drive to the Central Coast would take him about four hours, including a brief stop to refuel the car. It might take a little longer, given intermittent raindrops were hitting his windshield. As he drove the Sepulveda Pass into the San Fernando Valley and prepared to transition to the 101, he calculated the time change. *It's about 7 a.m. here, meaning it's 4 p.m. there. I'm okay now, but the jet lag will likely hit me later.*

Later this morning he'd arrive at his parents' home in Milford-Haven, where he hoped a good brunch awaited. His mom was used to the upside-down schedule of her astronomer son—often up all night and in need of a meal before resting during the day.

Though technically his own home was in northern California, he'd grown up in Milford-Haven, and had plans to live there again full time—soon, if all went according to plan. This would please his parents tremendously. And, as their only offspring, he felt responsible for their well-being as they got older. *This visit, I'll be in time to help Mom as she switches out her decor from winter to spring. And Pop and I can take my EV for a spin or too.*

Just last Christmas, Cornelius had bought the GM EV 1. Its sleek silver body would likely be tucked in the garage beside its home charging unit, paddle plugged into the hood—unless his dad had left it shining in the driveway, showing off to the neighbors.

Despite being technologically advanced, the car had a limited range, so he'd bought it for his folks to use for local errands. He drove it himself when he came to visit, which cut down on emissions. Much as he enjoyed his Durango and needed it to reach the mountain observatories he frequented for work, he was eager to get away from combustion engines. His folks knew perfectly well that he'd secretly bought the car for himself. But they didn't mind at all being his excuse, and his dad always enjoyed their tech conversations and debates.

Glad to be driving in the opposite direction as the commuters streaming into the city, he made good time to Santa Barbara. As he glanced left to catch glimpses of its beaches and marina, he thought back to Amsterdam, which was also a coastal city. His event had concluded the night before last. He'd been presenting at the ICAASS, the International Conference on Astronomy, Astrophysics and Space Science.

As always, he'd met or reconnected with several colleagues and enjoyed hearing the latest news about their various projects. Preparing talks about his own work helped to keep him sharp.

And most importantly, he felt it was critical to keep his finger on the pulse of innovations and trends in his field.

Held at the Anton Pennekoek Institute for Astronomy, only fifteen miles from Airport Schiphol, the institute was also close to the city's waterfront and several fine dining establishments, according to colleagues who'd arranged a dinner excursion. It'd been a lovely evening, with the moon waxing Gibbous. *Seems so much longer than just two nights ago.* He'd seen the full moon out the window of his plane, but it'd set at 4:39 a.m. California time, no longer showing in the sky.

By the time he reached San Luis Obispo, he could feel the nostalgia that always tugged at him as he neared his alma mater, California Polytechnic State University, locally known as Cal Poly. Mental snapshots flashed through his mind: his first dorm room, the observatory, his classmate Jameson, his physics professor, his girlfriend Sara.

He took the familiar exit 203B on Toro Street to blend onto Highway 1 North, doing his best not to accelerate too much. Climbing the hill just beyond Cal Poly, he glanced left toward the Cuesta College campus, where'd he'd also attended classes. Another favorite place. Both institutions did an excellent job of keeping abreast of latest developments in the sciences. He himself liked to keep one finger on the pulse of local meteorological events too, as evidence of climate change began to mount.

His acquaintance Maury Roos, Chief Hydrologist at the California Department of Water Resources in Sacramento, had said he was preparing a presentation on the recent New Year's flood of 1997 that'd occurred in northern California, from the Oregon border down to the southern end of the Sierra. Horrific flooding had swamped many communities and had extended into the Sierra's eastern slope, affecting Tahoe, Carson, and other communities there.

Over the past winter, these regions had suffered the wettest back-to-back months of the century, though other parts of California had been spared. *But no region is immune, he thought.*

He passed Hollister Peak, one of the twenty-two-million-year-old Nine Sisters, a chain of volcanic outcroppings that formed a cordillera known as the Santa Lucia Range. The first of them was the famous Morro Rock that would come into view soon. *And Hollister was once sacred to the Chumash. Now it's private property, something the ancients wouldn't have understood, nor condoned.*

He passed Morro Bay, Cayucos, and Cambria, then approached Milford-Haven. Though he'd taken this turnoff so many times over the years, now it held a special significance. At this corner he'd first caught a glimpse of Miranda. He'd pieced it together later, realizing it was she who drove that dark green Mustang.

Last Christmas when he'd been here, he hadn't known he'd meet her at the gallery, or that it was she who'd somehow pulled out of the ether that image of the rope hanging down the mountain escarpment. His own spiritual journey had taught him to trust his intuition. But she'd helped him learn to trust help that might come from an unknown or unexpected source.

That would've been enough to cause an upwelling of gratitude and possible friendship. But once he'd felt that voltaic charge when they'd touched, he'd known immediately there was something more. *What to do about it?* He was taking it as slow as he could. But he also didn't want to miss his chance with her. So he'd started sending postcards.Since his future plans included moving back to Milford-Haven, he'd established a P.O. box, giving him a local address.

No response yet, but that's okay. He'd keep sending them. If he was wrong and she truly wasn't interested, he'd find out soon enough.

Cornelius had expected to have breakfast with his parents. That was their custom, and he always enjoyed both his mother's cooking and his folks' constant interest in the events of his life, whatever they happened to be.

He'd been surprised to discover they were out when he arrived at their home. A note explained they'd taken the EV to SLO for shopping and an afternoon movie. That seemed a good choice, given it looked like rain would continue on and off all day.

It was all too seldom he had the chance to come home. Sure, his rental house up north was serviceable. And it was good to be near NASA Ames, where his project list was so long he could never hope to complete in several lifetimes. Mostly it was useful work, the hours filled with scientific inquiry, mathematical calculation, and—when he could get it—time on a decent telescope.

It had all started when he was a kid lying in a field looking at naked stars right here above this little coastal town. For him, this would always be home. And thanks to plenty of encouragement from Mom and Pop, he'd finally realized this Central Coast location, with its low level of ambient light and its nearby mountain range, was an ideal setting for his future observatory.

Cornelius started up the Durango again, his stomach rumbling in concert with the car's engine. As it turned out, this morning would be a good time to try that new little corner restaurant. Well, it'd be new for him since it was only open in the daylight hours when he was either away or catching up on sleep. It'd opened a few years ago and always looked so inviting with its cheery windows.

As he drove, he reflected that it was odd he knew so few of the contemporary shops in town. He could point out where every single store had been twenty years earlier, when he'd ridden his bike or been driven by his parents up and down Main Street. But since leaving for college, and then the start of his career, he'd focused only on his parents' home, or helping them with their errands. *I should get reacquainted, since I'm gonna live here again sooner than later.*

Chapter 3

Sally O'Mally was good at keeping secrets—if she didn't have to keep them too long. The question was how long she'd be able to keep this one.

She lay in the pale light of dawn and stared at her ceiling, doing her best to keep anxiety and anguish at bay, not wanting them to affect the child. But submerged, the pain of Jack Sawyer's desertion lurked like an underwater reef, sharp-edged and ready to rake holes in her boat. The intermittent morning sickness added insult to injury.

During the day, she was distracted by persistent, nagging disappointment. Usually it manifested as something missing: the yeast was left out of a batch of biscuits; the address was left off an envelope. But it was hardest after work. No longer did she prepare evening meals for Jack. No longer did she busy herself with the banter they'd once enjoyed—however one-sided it had eventually become. Now the evenings were adrift in inertia, or awash in guilt.

She reviewed and examined her own actions relentlessly. Jack had been selfish and cruel, but that was for him to live with. Whatever had possessed her to sail into such treacherous waters? She'd never have left the dock had she known she was sailing with a pirate.

Perhaps the worst thing she'd done was to sail away from her own sense of self. His charisma had disarmed her, and his strong personality had pulled her away from tending her own thoughts. She'd never imagined a relationship would be a day at the beach. But now she'd ignored her own hopes and dreams, delayed her own goals and deadlines, and allowed the once-sturdy vessel of her own life to run aground on shoals of neglect.

What I need is a lighthouse. That's what Miranda would say. Her friend liked to paint them. *Yes. Something to guide me back on course.*

The thought of Tony Fiorentino flashed into her mind. Absent from her life for so many years, Tony had suddenly surfaced last December, inviting her to a Doobie Brothers concert when the band had played the nearby Central Coast Bowl. And what a concert it'd been—a benefit for Vietnam veterans, with Tony the guest of honor.

She'd been honored too, just to be there. *And just as taken with the man as I ever was,* she now admitted to herself. Terrified she wouldn't know what to say when she saw him in a wheelchair, she'd practiced all kinds of opening lines. They'd flown out of her head the moment she'd seen him, losing herself in his chocolate-brown eyes, coming back to herself when he'd touched her hand.

Once, when he was young, he'd been tall as a mast, lean and athletic, bright and irreverent—and in love with her. But then came time and distance, war and tragedy. For years she hadn't known he came home a paraplegic and moved back to

New York to be near his mother. Now she sensed he was the same Tony he'd always been. *Yet he's different too.*

A favorite painting by her friend came to mind, one she'd seen hanging in the gallery. The Mukilteo Lighthouse near Seattle seemed as much a home as it was a light station: a lovely wood-frame Victorian house attached to a matching tower. Where most lighthouses were tall, solitary structures, this one looked as though it had sat down companionably next to the home, the top of its tower only twice the height of the house. Painted a dazzling white, it had a rich burgundy-colored roof that matched the blooming tree by its front door.

It might not be the tallest lighthouse, but it appealed to her more than anything. It wasn't so much the height as it was the substance. *Like Tony,* she thought. *He used to move around too much to be a beacon. Now he's steady as a rock.*

The Mukilteo still had as bright a light as ever, but it came with a home and a garden. *That's what I need. A place that gives a steady light. A place to grow things.*

The garden image brought her to a new metaphor. If her evenings were now spent weeding the garden, her days were occupied with planting new seeds. Sometime in these last few weeks she'd made a life-altering decision, and she'd made it alone.

The fact of her pregnancy hummed in the background like the tuneless tune she so often sang to herself. It had neither lyrics nor stanzas, but it was music nonetheless—the morning song the universe sang to itself as it awakened to new life.

Enough of this poetic foolishness, she thought and threw her legs over the side of the bed. But as she walked down the hallway, the metaphors continued. *Kind of like music being played on some distant radio station, with plenty of static mixed in, she decided. No point foolin' with the dial. Station's still too far away.*

But she knew as she continued down the road, the signal would get stronger and the tune of motherhood more unmistakable.

How many weeks along am I now? She glanced at her kitchen calendar. Thursday, March 21st. But knowing today's date didn't give her a fix on when she'd conceived. She thought back. *Sixteen or seventeen weeks, prob'ly.*

She padded down the hall to the bathroom and stood in front of the long mirror on the back of the door, pulled her nightshirt taut across her abdomen and checked her profile. She was still barely showing. Her body was so fit, her posture so good, it was likely she wouldn't show for a while yet, particularly at work where she wore an apron. But there were other signs, and some women were pretty good at reading them. The fact that she could still hardly stand the thought of breakfast was one. She'd probably have no choice but to tell June, but at least her long-time colleague and employee at the diner was trustworthy.

As she flung the nightshirt over the hook above the mirror and flipped the shower dial to hot, Sally considered how long she could delay confiding in June Magliati.

Early customers at Sally's were quietly enjoying their copies of the Milford-Haven News and sipping freshly filled mugs of hot coffee.

"Biscuits are ready," June said as she headed for the freezer.

"Oh, do you mind taking them out?" Sally asked.

June looked at her. "You sho-wa?" she asked in her distinctive Brooklyn accent. Though their regular cook handled most orders, it was always Sally who pulled out her sheets of biscuits.

"If you don't mind." Sally tried to keep her tone nonchalant, but she could tell right then and there that June knew something was up. Sally returned to wiping the long countertop, nodding at Mr. Hargraves as he came in to take his customary seat. "Morning," she said. "I'll get your coffee, and the biscuits are just coming out."

"No hurry," Mr. Hargraves said. It was what he'd said every morning for as many years as he'd been a regular customer. But they both knew his daily ritual was timed so his arrival coincided perfectly with the presentation of her fresh biscuits. Their aroma was all the invitation anyone needed, but today it was almost more than Sally could bear. As June brought in a basketful of the piping hot delicacies wrapped in a cheerful yellow-and-white checked napkin, the aroma filled Sally's nostrils, and she hurried from the room.

June watched Deputy Delmar Johnson amble in and take his favorite stool at the long, polished counter. Before he'd had time to settle, she asked, "Cawfee, Deputy?" At his nod, she poured a deep splash of fresh, hot java into a gleaming white mug. He nodded his thanks and glanced around, probably looking for a sight of Sally, apparently surprised not to see her during the morning rush.

Sally had retreated to the deep recesses of the kitchen, sped past the busboy, and opened the back door for a gulp of fresh air. She collected herself after a few deep breaths and got busy at the sink. Normally she'd have a running count of customers and orders in her head. But this morning she felt as though she were outside herself, looking down at her own body.

She stood differently now. She'd worn comfortable rubber-soled professional shoes intermittently before, but now she wore them every day and practiced standing with her knees bent, reckoning that in future days it would release the tension in the small of her back. All her life she'd always kept her stomach flat. It had, in fact, been something of an obsession, so much so that she'd bought Burn It Off, the local aerobics studio. With no time to build her second business, she had only a small number of loyal attendees. In fact, she'd become her own best customer, her long workout sessions arduous but satisfying. Now she noticed the slight bulge of her abdomen and accepted the altering shape without resistance.

She thought about the changes taking place in her body. There were times she wanted to shout: "I'm pregnant! I'm having a baby, and the whole world is going to be different now!" She couldn't prevent a smile from lifting the corners of her mouth. And yet the moment the smile came, tears welled. She'd been so sure of Jack's reaction, and she'd been so wrong! The moment joy arrived, so did sorrow.

I've gotta push all this self-pitying folderol from my mind and get myself back to work. With a final inhalation of refreshing sea air, she closed the back door, smoothed her apron, and headed back to the front lines.

The carefully made-up face of Nicole Champagne was the first one Sally saw as she arrived back at her long counter. Nicole was, as usual, carrying her *Melior*. She claimed "café filtre'" was the very best, though as far as Sally could tell, *all* coffee was filtered. Nicole swore by her special little pot with its screen-plunger.

Sally smiled at her, took the glass pot, measured out four heaping teaspoons of double-roast French. "You're sure, now. No paper, no nothin'?"

"*Mais non!*" Nicole insisted, offering to demonstrate her contraption for the umpteenth time. "This way the coffee and the water, they meet, they mix, it is better, no?"

Sally laughed and poured scalding water over the grounds. "Customer's always right!" she chimed. "Gettin' all set for Miranda's show over there at Finder's Gall'ry?"

"*Oui.* It will be beautiful, all the animals, all the nature scenario. You are coming to the opening?"

Nicole's accent made everything sound so elegant, she'd have wanted to go even if Miranda wasn't her friend. "Hope to be there." Accepting Nicole's dollar bill, Sally smiled at her, and Nicole turned to leave, her short, sassy hair falling over one eye, her body tightly contained in a black turtleneck and mini skirt. Every man in the restaurant watching, she walked out the front door wearing the only high heels in town.

"Always wonder how she walks in those things," remarked Mr. Hargraves from his seat at the counter.

"She makes it look easy, wouldn't ya say?" Sally retorted. "I'm not touching that." Del sat at the last stool, a smile tugging at his mouth.

"Mornin', Dep'ty," Sally said, reading the look in his eye. "Got somethin' you wanna ask me? Awful early. Give me a minute." She walked quickly away.

Delmar Johnson stared after her, having had no chance to respond to her question. *What would be the use anyway? She seems to have a built-in intention detector.* Studying the menu as though it might contain an overlooked clue, Del decided to vary his usual fare this morning. When Sally returned, he said, "Get me a short stack, will you, Sally? And a side of bacon?"

Sally lifted an eyebrow and glanced up at him. "Been up all night, haven't you," she asked, though it was more of a statement. "What was it you needed to ask me?"

Del replied quickly. "Two things I need this morning, Sally. One's a big breakfast. The other's your help."

"Oh, fiddle." A frown creased her brow. "I don't like the sound of that." She walked a round trip length of the counter, refilling cups for other customers. "I suppose it's about that stranger who asked for Ms. Christian."

"Right again, Sally." *How is it she always knows?* "I want to thank you again for working with our sketch artist last fall. You're the only one who noticed this guy, talked to him."

Sally nodded.

He hated to ask for more help but pressed on. "I don't suppose there's anything else that's come back to you in the meantime? A phrase, a gesture? Any detail might help."

She thought for a moment, then pursed her lips. "Nothin', Dep'ty. But I could look back through my journal."

Del looked up sharply. "Didn't know you kept one. That'd be great."

"I'd like to do somethin' useful this week."

"Thanks," he said. Sally referred to her journal as though it were a matter of course that she wrote in it regularly. He wondered if her journal-writing helped with her keen powers of observation. He figured it was mostly women who kept journals. If so, he wondered how many others in town followed the practice.

Cornelius Smith pulled into one of the parking spots in front of Sally's and walked in. A pert waitress caught his eye, but her attention was drawn back to another customer, so he chose a corner table where the light was good and settled himself. From his jeans jacket he withdrew a report, which he unfurled and smoothed. With the new grant, his professional focus would finally be shifting toward his favorite field of study: finding planets. The sooner he knew the parameters of the project, the better. Forgetting his growling stomach for the moment, he read:

> The number of planets one might expect to detect in any microlensing program is quite dependent on the assumptions about the planetary systems, e.g., Gould and Loeb (1992).

We indicate sample results from a hypothetical microlensing survey where 3000 events are assumed to have been followed with high time resolution, 1% photometry, and with 50%average coverage (Peale, 1996, in preparation). A 5%perturbation of the otherwise smooth light curve of the source sometime during the lensing event will be assumed detectable. About half of these events will have lenses that are members of binary or higher order systems, although only a fraction will reveal their binary nature.

Cornelius moved his elbow and inadvertently swept his knife to the floor. The clattering interrupted his reading, and he bent down to retrieve the cutlery. As he was about to pick it up, the sight of its location stopped him. *Incredible,* he thought. *What are the odds?* The knife lay perfectly perpendicular across one of the wide wooden planks of the floor. *This simplifies Buffon's Needle Problem since the length of the knife and the width of the floor strips will cancel out!*

He couldn't resist pursuing his experiment. The odds were, in fact, astronomical. Chuckling at his joke, he moved off his chair, knelt for a better view, and picked up the knife, then dropped it again to see at what angle it would land.

If I drop this knife over and over again, I can see how many times the knife will lie across a strip, compared to how often it will not cross any strips. By dropping the knife at a fairly extravagant multiple, the number of times the knife crosses a border between planks divided by the total number of drops, this will give me the probability that the knife will fall across an edge. If I divide this probability number into 2, this should actually converge onto the number pi, 3.14. . . .

Cornelius, oblivious to the discomfort of kneeling on the hard wood floor, continued dropping the knife. He did begin to notice a knocking sound overhead. Ignoring it, he continued his train of thought. *Deriving the value of pi this way would be interesting. But it would take at least a thousand knife drops to start to get pi.*

Now the knocking resumed, and a voice seemed to be speaking to him. "Ahem. Sir, uh, excuse me," it said loudly. "Uh, sir, did you want to order something?"

Sensible shoes appeared in front of his view as though waiting for an answer. *This must be the waitress and she's gonna think I'm nuts.* It seemed some sort of explanation was appropriate, so he peered out from under the table and looked up. "You see," he began, "it all started when I dropped my knife."

"Well, Sir, I would be very happy to bring you another knife." It was the pert waitress speaking to him.

"Oh no," he answered quickly, "whatever you do, don't do that. I'll be down here all day." He gave her a broad smile, thinking she'd understand the joke.

But the waitress put her hands on her hips. "Sir, it's perfectly okay with me if you prefer to stay down there under the table, only if you want to order something, I am going to serve it on top of the table. Just so we get the rules straight here."

"I'll come up," he responded, bumping his head as he did. "Ow!" he muttered. "Should have seen that coming."

"Ooooh!" the waitress echoed. "Are you okay?"

"Yes." Cornelius stood, noticing how diminutive the woman seemed. She was looking up at him with concern, so he continued his explanation. "Sorry, I like math and, uh, I got sidetracked. You see, if I had dropped the knife, let's say, in the middle of a plank that first time, it would never have happened."

"It wouldn't?"

"But once it fell across the tile the first time, it was just irresistible. There was nothing I could do, you see, but perform geometric probability."

He watched as lines began to form across the waitress's forehead and she asked, "You were doing a performance under there?"

Cornelius suppressed a laugh and tried again. "No. You see by continuing to drop the knife and to calculate the number of times it did and did not cross the plank, I was attempting to derive the value of pi." Surely *that* would make it clear to her.

Sure enough, relief washed over her face. "The value of pie? Land sakes, I could have told you that! It's two dollars and fifty cents. Says so right on my menu."

"No, no," he protested. "Pi, as in a *circle*, you know, something perfectly round."

"Well, I beg your pardon, Sir, but my pies *are* perfectly round. So is that what you want then, a piece of pie?"

"A piece of pie. Sounds wonderful! I've been up all night." "You and ever'body else around here. We have apple today. That be all right?"

"Excellent!" As if in agreement, Cornelius's stomach issued a loud rumbling.

"I'll get it right away," the waitress said.

He took his seat and looked at the blackboard where other offerings were colorfully listed.

She was back before he finished his perusal. Placing the plated pie and a cup of coffee in front of him, she said, "Thought you might like some coffee to go with it. Do you mind if I ask where you're from?"

"Thanks! I would. And I'm from Milford-Haven."

"Milford-Haven? I've never ever seen you before. You work around here?"

"Yes, I'll be working at the observatory. *On* the observatory, I should say."

"The observatory? You mean where people look at stars? You mean you're one of those astrologers?"

"Astro-*no-mer*."

"Right, astro-no-mer. But I didn't know there was one of those observing places in Milford-Haven."

"Well, there isn't, yet. But I'm going to build one." As if complaining, his stomach growled again. But he was gratified someone took an interest in his project.

"Hope you like the pie," she said, the non sequitur seeming to give him permission to dig in, which he did. "Say, what's your name?"

Struggling to swallow, he managed to reply, "Cornelius Smith."

"I'm Sally."

He was just tipping hot coffee into his mouth but made an attempt to stand.

"No, no, sit, sit," she protested. "Corn-lee-us? What kind of a name is that?"

"Biblical," he answered between bites.

She squinted, as if trying to remember the reference, then said, "Oh. Well, I surely do hope you're hungry, Corn-lius, 'cause at my restaurant we serve a healthy portion of pie."

"I can see that, and it's delicious! And excuse me, but it's Cor-nee-lius. And yes, I could definitely enjoy surrounding a large number of its molecules," smiling at her again.

Sally laughed. "Some what? I don't think we serve any of those!" She walked away then, still amused.

He was glad he'd been able to make her laugh. The prospect of new friends in his hometown delighted him almost as much as the pie. And he'd be back soon for more of Sally's home cooking.

Chapter 4

Samantha Hugo unlocked the door of the Environmental Planning Commission Friday morning, strode across the outer room, entered her private office, and sat heavily. During her brief morning drive to work, she'd seen clouds gather at the horizon: anvils forming as though ready to pound the coastline. They seemed to echo perfectly the headache that hammered at her temples as she looked at the piles on her desk, each seeming to clamor for attention.

Scooting her chair closer, Sam attempted to neaten the stacks and review her list of priorities. Once again, she noticed, her assistant Susan Winslow had failed to sort the mail correctly. Magazines intended for the waiting area were mixed in with research journals, which needed to be placed on shelves chronologically after she'd given them a quick perusal.

Scientific American and the *Amicus Journal* belonged in both categories: first they were public reading material; then when the next issue appeared, the previous one would be archived. Since the concept was simple, Samantha felt baffled that Susan seemed incapable of grasping it. Sighing, Sam began making new stacks: bills here, journals there, until the latest *World Wildlife Fund* mailer surfaced. The glossy cover photo captivated her—a cub with its lioness mother hovering protectively. She saw this kind of image every day. But now, it triggered feelings that took her back.

Samantha pulled at the downy folds of the blue blanket, its softness almost rough compared with his skin. She was fighting a losing battle with the blanket, as the baby was determined to kick and fuss. "Lambie lamb," she comforted, "it's okay. Yes . . . it's okay."

"Bbbbbb," he cooed, as some of the flailing stopped.

"That's right, darling, everything's all right." She held a tiny foot and felt it wiggle.

"Gheeee!"

"Gheeee," she repeated, though she was unable to match his bubble technique.

"Bbbbb." That seemed to be one of his favorite sentences.

"Bbbbb," she agreed. Real conversation! *she thought.*

"Gheeee," he gurgled, and she matched him tone for tone, her emotion running as high as if she'd made contact with another species. He looked away suddenly, briefly, telling her as clearly as though he had words, that he desired a pause. She waited, her face hovering over his tiny body. In the time it took to catch her next breath, he turned his baby-blue eyes back to hers and erupted into a stream of burblings any mother would understand. "Hee hee, Mommy! I can look away any time I like, and you're still here with me!"

"Yes, darling boy, I'm here. I'm here," she said as her heart sang. Her boy had already taught her his own secret language.

Sam forced herself back to the present and grabbed the scientific journal from the top of her stack to turn to the article she'd marked last week with a sticky note. The topic was coastal tides, which she looked forward to understanding better.

Reading with the concentration she'd cultivated for so many years, she absorbed data hungrily. She read about amphidromic points, where there would be almost no vertical water movement. She learned that high tides occur twelve hours and twenty-four minutes apart—the twelve hours a result of Earth's rotation, the twenty-four minutes of the Moon's orbit.

Absorbed in her study, she ignored the office phone the first two times it rang. Then, realizing Susan must be late again, she pursed her lips, picked up the receiver, and spoke a greeting.

"Answering your own phone this morning, Sam? How commendable." The gruff voice was unmistakable.

"What can I do for you, Jack?" Samantha asked with no hint of cordiality.

"As little as possible."

Sam let out a sigh of exasperation. "I beg your pardon?"

"You heard me. Don't *do* anything. Don't get in my way on the shopping center."

She paused long enough to take a breath. "Jack, if you don't work with us and the Town Council, you won't have a single ally in this town. Is that what you want?"

"I couldn't care less," replied Jack with more than his usual degree of callousness. "What've my so-called allies ever gotten me? Up to my neck in useless regulations. Thanks for nothing."

"How a man your age can be as immature as you are is a constant bafflement to me," Sam huffed. "I can just see it now: everyone on the Town Council choosing their regulations carefully so Jack Sawyer doesn't have to go out of his way."

"You don't know what you're talking about, Sam. You never did."

"And just what the hell is that supposed to mean?"

"These regulations you claim are the law of the land—they're not. They're just suggestions you, our high and mighty Queen of Ecology, has come up with to slow down the growth of this town so much it'll die on the vine. You're playing with people's lives here. That's what you don't realize."

"And you're *not?* You're tampering with the soil they build their houses on, taking away the trees that give them the oxygen they breathe. Why do you think people come up here to live, Jack? If they want freeways and billboards, there's a big place just a few hours south called Los Angeles."

"What you can't get through your thick skull, Samantha, is that people need to eat. To do that, they need jobs. And when they have jobs, they take their paychecks and go to the market to buy food for their families. They do this novel thing called shopping. To go shopping, they need a market!"

"We have markets at both ends of town now, Jack, which have served perfectly well for as long as—"

"Can you park at these markets? No. Can you fit a shopping cart down the aisle? No. Can you ever find anything you need without driving to San Luis Obispo for it? No. People need things, Sam. It's a fact of life. We're building a shopping center. Get used to it."

"You'll build if and when our environmental study is completed, Jack."

"I don't have to justify myself to you. We're not married anymore. I'm hanging up."

Jack Sawyer did so, banging the phone down with enough force to enjoy himself. *I bet that sound bounced her out of her chair,* he thought with relish.

Alone in his own office at Sawyer Construction, Jack tugged at his mustache and felt a slow smile creep across his face. *She's still an easy woman to manipulate, always has been.* And all it took was one call. She'd go after the shopping center with a vengeance now. And that would leave him plenty of elbow room at the Clarke house.

Sam chewed her lip and did her best not to break her handset as she slammed it into its cradle. A list of regulations applicable to this proposed shopping center began ticking off in her mind, and she grabbed pen and yellow pad, making note of movers and shakers in town who'd be sympathetic to ecological priorities.

She glanced at her watch, wondering why she had yet to hear the unmistakable clomping of her assistant's shoes in the outer office.

Even after a full year as the EPC's only other employee, Susan Winslow remained an enigma to Sam. She'd hired her from the local Chumash Reservation office—one part good deed, two parts practicality.

It'd been smart to hire someone who seemed capable and promising whose salary would squeeze within the narrow parameters of the local government budget. And the young woman sometimes showed tremendous promise. Sam paid for some classes at the local college and gave her plenty of on-the-job training. Yet her efforts at mentoring often fell on deaf ears and left Samantha feeling like a misunderstood stepmother.

After her conversation with Jack, she was in no mood for Susan, and everything about her was likely to cause irritation: the Doc Marten shoes that hammered the wood floors, the surly attitude that almost rivaled Jack's, and more importantly, the sense that a smart mind with its youthful energy was being wasted.

When Susan's loud soles ricocheted off the outer office floor, Samantha stood at her window taking long pulls on her bottle of water, hoping it would cool her down. Nothing could make her blood boil faster than Jack's insults and insinuations. She'd been making an effort to internalize her anger, but was about to externalize it.

"Susan, you're late," she said, her voice projecting while she watched the arrival of her tardy charge.

Susan, unaware she was being observed, shrugged out of her leather jacket and mouthed, "You're late!" while contorting her face. She was poised to stick out her tongue but stopped when she caught a glimpse of Samantha.

"Susan, turn on your computer," Sam demanded from the open doorway. "Get *Eco Net* up and running. Do it now."

Knowing Susan would, in fact, do nothing while being watched, Sam turned her back and strode to her own desk. She found the notes she'd scribbled on a notepad, tore them off, and walked purposefully to Susan's desk. The dial tone, rapid dial and pulsing static of the modem sounded as Sam dropped her notes next to Susan's keyboard.

"Okay, go to the search site I showed you," Sam said absently, her eye scanning the screen over Susan's shoulder. Susan's hand failed to move. "You'll need to use the mouse, Susan, and then point the little arrow up there at the Search button. You should know how to do this by now!"

"Whatever," replied Susan. This seemed to be her standard answer to all uncomfortable requests.

"No, Susan, not *whatever. Search!*" Still no compliance. "You must still be asleep. Get yourself a cup of coffee, and I'll start it myself."

Bouncing out of her chair, Susan pounded across to the coffee pot. Sam sat in front of the screen, tempted to do a quick search of her own before getting started with her daily review of coastal developments. "Chernak," she almost typed in, and "missing children." But there'd be time enough for her private homework after Susan had left for the day, which, judging by her attitude, might be soon.

Having poured herself a mug full of coffee, Susan flounced back to her desk. After clicking through the preliminary search commands, Sam slid out of the chair just as Susan slammed back into it, sloshing liquid dangerously close to the keyboard.

Sam clenched her teeth, deciding to say nothing about the spilled liquid. "We're tracking two developments today," she explained. "One is offshore oil rigs. There's probably nothing new, but I want to be sure."

She looked at her assistant whose blank expression was not reassuring. "Then we need to track the coastal issue we've been working on. Try 'Coastal Commission' for starters. After that try 'Proposition 70,' 'Coastal Protection Act,' 'Chumash Tribal Council,' 'Hearst Corporation,'—you get the idea." *I hope*, she said to herself as she returned to her own desk.

Half an hour later, Sam called out from her office, "How are you doing with that search?"

"Not that great," Susan called back.

"Try the Boolean features to narrow it down," Sam called back.

"What's that?"

Exasperated, Sam yelled, "If you can't remember my instructions, take notes. And if you can't handle the job, there are others who can."

Susan Winslow stuck her tongue out at the wall between them. She mumbled, "I'll show you your stupid boo-boolian features." Jabbing angrily at the keyboard, she added, "Maybe I *can* handle the job, Samantha. How would you like *that?*"

The office phone rang, and Susan answered in her usual terse style. "She's on another line. Wanna leave a message?" She scribbled the message down, then returned her attention to the ever-mysterious computer screen. *Entries found: 71,524,* it said. "Like that's *so* helpful," Susan muttered back to the screen.

"Who was that, Susan?" Sam's voice yelled from the next room.

"Connie!"

"Travers? From Constant Travel?"

"Who else?"

"Thank you," Sam said, her tone oozing sarcasm.

"You're welcome," Susan said under her breath, matching her tone. "You stupid thing." This last comment was addressed to the computer, whose screen was presenting her with pop-up advertisements for a new job—adding insult to injury.

Pressing a *More Like This* option, she tried connecting to a site that would yield results about California coastal issues. The maddening little hourglass appeared, dancing across the screen as she moved the mouse. The system was taking so long, Susan assumed something was wrong. She clicked the Back button. Still nothing happened. "Okay," she mumbled to herself. "If I remember right, this X in the upper right corner closes the program."

A fatal error has occurred in module 00:45:99:333, announced the screen.

"Shit!" Susan muttered, pressing the power button.

Just then the phone rang again, and Susan answered gruffly. The caller said, "It's Paul Herzog, A.P."

Unable to recognize what sort of degree an "A.P." was, Susan hesitated.

"The reporter from the Associated Press. I called last week. Is Ms. Hugo available?"

"Oh! Yeah. I mean, hold for a moment, please."

Susan pushed the hold button, banged down her phone and yelled, "It's that reporter guy again." She listened as Sam lifted her receiver, apologizing for the delay, and began answering the questions asked by a professional interviewer.

Susan punched the computer's power button and sat in a computer-induced limbo waiting for the whining and whirring of the booting-up process to finish, all the while overhearing Samantha's comments to the reporter.

"Yes, but there's a difference. The Gulf of Mexico has rigs ninety miles from shore. Here in California, we're blessed—or cursed—with a narrow continental shelf. Any drilling would by necessity be close to sensitive coastal areas and wildlife habitats."

Now Susan knew why Samantha'd asked for the Internet search on offshore oil rigs. She kept eavesdropping.

"Well, it's not just the platforms that bother us. They bring with them a host of undesirable environmental impacts most people don't think of. The diesel generators bring air pollution, the drilling muds bring toxins, and of course, there's the ever -present danger of a spill."

Susan thought Samantha was doing pretty well improvising, since she didn't really have all the information. *Tough!* Susan thought. *If she'd asked nicely maybe I would have gotten it in time!*

Was it really her fault? She couldn't help it if she didn't understand how the stupid computer worked. And anyway, since the reporter'd already called, chances were Samantha probably wouldn't need that search anymore.

If you can't do the job, there are others who can. Samantha's words taunted. It was obvious her boss didn't want her to succeed. She was always criticizing her, undermining her confidence.

Well, screw you! Susan mouthed. *I'll get good at using the dumb computer if I want to!*

With a new-found focus, Susan again tried her hand at the maddening process of an Internet search. From the other room, she heard Samantha hang up the phone and place another call.

Samantha hung up her phone and rubbed her ear. Her call with the reporter finished, she placed a return call to Connie, whose company name—Constant Travel—was a little too cute, but who was quite an expert at her business.

"Connie of Constant Travel," answered the overly cheerful voice.

"It's Sam, Connie. You called?"

"Yup. Thanks for getting back to me so fast. Got a minute or two?"

"Got one exactly."

"Okay. Wanna help me design an eco-travel package for Milford-Haven?"

Sam paused a moment. "Hmm, sounds interesting. What does it mean exactly?"

"Organize nature walks with a botanist or somebody; have a marine biologist describe what's going on in the tidepools down by the landing; show them cliffs with coastal run-off and stuff like that."

"Well, Connie, you're speaking my language, but do you think anyone but another environmentalist is going to take an interest?"

"Oh, yeah, if we do stuff like free coupons for breakfast at Sally's, and a special rate at the Belhaven Inn, and free drinks at Wing Ding's—you know . . . sort of jazz it up."

"You're a smart lady, Connie. What do you need from me?"

"Well, like um . . . ooh, can you hold on a sec?"

"Not really, Connie, I— "

"Okay, I'm back."

"You were gone?"

"So just, you know, like lists of stuff you think would be cool to do, and who I should contact in town that really knows their stuff."

Sam scribbled notes in her phone log. "Got it. This is good. I'll give it some thought."

"Ooh, that's my other line. . . ."

"Call me next week," Sam said, hanging up the phone. Now *there* was a go-getter. How she'd love to have someone with *that* kind of energy working for her. But, of course, someone with that energy would be working for herself, just as Connie did. With a sigh, Sam stood to check on Susan's progress. "Got a print-out for me yet, Susan?" she asked, walking to the coffeepot.

"What?"

"The Internet search, Susan. Have you printed out any materials from the websites you've found?"

"Like . . . I haven't actually found any sites yet."

"Really? Too many to choose from?"

"Well, yeah, like 72,000 or something."

Samantha sighed. "Susan, that was before you narrowed the parameters, surely. Let's see what you've got." Sam walked to Susan's desk and looked over her shoulder. "Susan, you're not signed on."

"Yeah, well, whatever."

"Why aren't you still signed on? Did the system crash? Did you have to reboot?"

Susan stared straight ahead at the miserable machine and said nothing.

"Are you listening to me?" Samantha was beginning to raise her voice. Susan remained silent. "Susan!"

"What?!" Susan erupted out her chair, nearly knocking over her coffee mug. "Why are you shouting at me? I'm right in front of you!"

"You weren't answering! And you're not doing your job!"

"Oh, yeah? And who answers the phone every damn time it rings, and who does all the filing and the stupid cataloging and the deliveries and the invoices? Who d'you think's really saving the planet in this office?!"

Taking a deep breath, Samantha looked at her reluctant protégé, noticing how red her face had become. "Susan, I know you're feeling beleaguered."

"Whatever."

Sam clenched her teeth. "Let me just ask you one more question. Have you actually gone to any of the computer classes I've paid for?"

"Whatever, Samantha."

"You keep saying that, and I don't find that to be a meaningful expression, so I wish you'd stop using it."

"I don't have to take this." Susan pushed away from her desk and reached for her leather jacket.

Sam stopped her. "You're not going anywhere, Susan. I am." And with that, Sam grabbed her purse, flung open the door of the EPC, and rushed down the three steps to the sidewalk.

Sam let the screen door at Sally's slam behind her, enjoying the jarring sound for once. Taking a moment to catch her breath, she noticed Deputy Johnson just settling himself at the long counter. Deciding she'd prefer the counter herself today, she left a polite distance and chose a stool one removed from his.

Del nodded his head at her and turned upright the clean white mug of heavy china in front of him. "Ms. Hugo."

"Deputy." She nodded back.

"Cawfee?" June offered, holding a full carafe as she walked in from the kitchen.

"Sure," Del replied.

"Yes," Sam echoed.

"Cawfee fo' the two o' yas," June confirmed, then turned back toward the kitchen.

Sam reached for the cream, her hand still shaking, poured a generous splash and stirred, staring into the hot mud-colored drink.

Delmar Johnson had returned to the restaurant at Sally's request, and now waited politely, hoping for some of the white stuff himself. Clearing his throat after a silence, he said, "Sorry, could I?"

"Oh! Sorry, sorry," apologized Sam. "I seem to be in a . . . I'm rather— "

"Yes, I can see that."

Del looked at his dining neighbor, noticing her sheepish expression and slightly pinked cheeks.

"Working on an environmental problem?" he asked, trying to strike up a conversation. He didn't know Samantha Hugo well, but she was a mover and shaker in this town. Beyond the expediency of making connections in high places, something about her appealed. But as he looked at her face, despite her light and natural-looking makeup, there was slight darkness under her eyes and tension around her mouth.

"Hmph. Not that lucky. Stuck with a computer problem." She took a sip. "Or an assistant problem. I'm not sure which."

"Ah," Del said. "Well, the assistant problem is all yours, but if you need computer help, just let me know."

She gave him a skeptical glance. "You're joking, right?"

"Not at all."

"You . . . you know anything about Internet searches?"

Del chortled. "Yeah, you could say."

"Meaning?"

"Sorry, it's just . . . it's one of my hobbies. I've been known to click away the hours."

Sam looked at him as though he'd spoken the words of the prophet. "Truly?"

"You don't think I have these bags under my eyes all the time, do you?" He paused. "Don't answer that. It's just that I was visiting cyberspace all night. What's your project?"

"Well, I'm trying to do a little background on this particular company."

"Eco scofflaw?"

"No. This is kind of a special project of my own."

Del took a long sip of coffee and considered the ramifications of that statement. *Is she using company hours and company assets for personal projects? Pursuing an environmental bad boy the Town Council had warned her to leave alone?*

Setting his speculations aside for the moment, he looked circumspectly at Samantha to see if she'd share anything more. As though he could see the wheels turning in her head, he sensed a shift in her before she spoke again.

"This is a personal project, Deputy. If I ask for your help, I'll also have to ask for your confidentiality. If that's a problem for you, I'll just ask for a computer lesson. But either way, your assistance would be welcome."

Del trained his eyes on hers. "Doing confidential work comes with the territory. Is this regarding the matter we spoke about back in December?"

She glanced around the restaurant to make sure no one was within earshot. "It's the adoption," she confirmed.

"Interestingly enough, another case I'm working touches on the subject too. You're not adverse to adding some time to your Friday workday, are you?"

Samantha snorted. "Friday's the end of a tough week. Why not improve it a little?"

Chuckling, Del lifted his napkin and wiped the corner of his mouth. "Come by my office after four p.m. I'll be happy to help you out."

"That's the best offer I've had all day." Sam gave him a smile. "You're in the Forestry Office building, right?"

"Right."

Del noticed Sally poke her head out of her office to give him a nod. With a final swig of his coffee, he swung his boots off the rail and stood, hitching up his snug uniform pants. "See you then, Ms. Hugo."

Chapter 5

Susan Winslow slunk out of the EPC office the moment her employer's footsteps faded. Yanking her leather jacket around herself against the strong winds typical of the Central Coast in spring, she pounded down the sidewalk to her decrepit VW bug, and once in her vehicle, sped toward the Landing.

The wind was angry today—the trees withstanding blasts, the surf roiling, the otters apparently in hiding. *This has to be the smallest, stupidest State Beach in California.* But it was deserted today, so she'd have it to herself. Angling her car carelessly into the row of empty parking spaces, she slammed her car door behind her and headed down steep, muddy banks to the rocky shoreline.

During childhood she'd heard as much screaming as she ever needed to hear, and she damn well wasn't going to take any more of it from Samantha Hugo.

Dinner's ready!" The front door slammed behind Susan, and she overheard her mother's call.

"Not hungry anymore," her father growled. "Been waiting an hour."

"Fine!" Mommy yelled back.

The TV blared: the squeaks of rubber-soled shoes, the roar of the crowd, the basketball hitting the hardwood—Daddy's favorite show.

Something banged in the kitchen; she went to check on Mommy. At age seven Susan was already her mother's unofficial guardian. Mommy was mad and was trying to push the broiled chicken leg from Daddy's plate to hers. But it slipped between the plates, fell to the floor, and rolled on the sticky linoleum.

Susan picked it up, went to the sink, stepped up on her own little stool to wash the chicken leg. But Mommy grabbed it away and dumped the ruined piece of chicken into the top of the garbage bucket.

The TV now blasted a beer commercial. Daddy didn't need any more beer. He'd been drinking it all afternoon. "Where is it?" her father's voice shouted from the other room.

Uh-oh, *thought Susan.* Daddy changed his mind again.

Mommy, too, seemed to sense the imminent disaster.

"It's half-time. Where the hell's my food?!" The voice grew louder as Daddy entered the room. His glance took in the discarded chicken. His hand grasped a hank of Mommy's hair and pulled downward, yanking her to the ground. "Stupid cow!" he bellowed. "I work hard all day, and you throw away my food?"

"You said you weren't hungry!" Mommy shouted back up at him, her eyes angry, her face red.

"I don't eat when you say!" he yelled. "I eat when I say!" He lifted the chicken from the garbage, bent over to wag it in Mom-my's face.

"No, Daddy," Susan yelled, "I threw it away, not Mommy!"

Daddy's huge hand shoved little Susan, and she staggered back. Yanking Mommy to a standing position, he let go of her hair and tried to push the chicken into her mouth. She took a bite, spit it in his face.

He shouted at her again, threw the chicken across the room, then hauled back to hit her. Wham! The heel of his open hand connected with Mommy's nose. Her head snapped back and she fell. She didn't get up. She didn't move at all.

Susan remembered reaching for the big telephone on the wall. She remembered the paramedics, the tears her father cried. What she couldn't remember was feeling anything. Ever since that night, a part of her had been numb.

She'd been the only witness. Lots of people had asked her questions until her version of the events was seared into her memory. Now she had a private movie that wanted to play over and over again in her head. But at least no one else could see it.

She would go far away someday. Meanwhile she became a child with a secret. She wanted to keep it that way forever.

Susan tried not to fall as her Doc Martens sank into the dense black sand of Touchstone Beach. Driftwood lay strewn where surging waves deposited it, untidy and treacherous underfoot.

Moving past the sand to the promontory, she walked slowly, careful not to turn an ankle on the slick rock. Water filled the tidepools, then disappeared as the next gathering wave sucked it back, leaving behind a clutter of urchins and sea stars and a clatter of colliding stones, the sounds echoing a few moments after her as she trod a weaving path through debris.

The beauty of surf and sand, rock and feather, seemed to add insult to injury. In her sullen mood, she wanted to paint the landscape in the gray of her frustration. But on the ridges along the shore, blooming ice plant tendrils danced heavily in the breezes, and sea birds spoke to each other of hidden treasures.

How dare you be so beautiful, she thought. Looking only from one step to the next, Susan continued until her path ended at a long pile of rocks jutting into the sea. Unable to go farther, she hunched down, gripped her knees, and let tears sting her wind-burned face.

There wasn't a moment of peace anywhere, no matter how she battled. Samantha hated her. Fine. She hated Samantha too. So what if she'd paid for school and given her a job? It was a prison, that job, and she was damn well going to find a way to free herself.

Susan knew she could do great things one day. But first, someone would have to see something good in her, something dynamic and exciting, something to take her away from this empty, useless town, so full of environmental correctness it made her want to puke.

Somewhere rock stars were sharing laughter and music on the road, movies were being made, photographers were capturing magic moments with super-models, and she—Susan, surely just as exciting as the next girl—was stuck in a backwater that fancied itself the center of creation. In her misery, she sat at the edge of the universe, waiting to be discovered.

Dimly, she thought of her ancestors—those keepers of Native wisdom who were supposed to be guarding and guiding her. Where were they when she needed them? *Nowhere,* she thought, *because they don't even exist.* And if they ever had, what had they to do with her? At best, they were irrelevant. At worst, they were a dangerous superstition that only kept people from getting on with real life, here and now.

Her hands like ice, she tucked them in her armpits, trying to warm them. Rocking back and forth on her haunches, she allowed her gaze to drift from the distant horizon till it rested in a shallow tidepool scooped from the flat rock on which she crouched. Through the pool—as clear as a perfect lens—she could see the bottom was filled with stones.

As if sensing her attention, the spirit of the tiny pond replied by inviting her to join it there, promising to reveal a secret if she did. Unaware of the conversation her own soul was having with the pond-spirit, Susan sat transfixed, her gaze sinking into the pond, mesmerized by its clarity. It seemed deeper now than it had at first, its bottom a mosaic of precious jewels. Susan touched the surface of the still water, reached down, and felt the lovely smooth rocks lining its depth. Feeling each stone in turn, she watched as jade and jasper, onyx and tourmaline danced under water. Her hand numb from the cold, Susan drew it back, and found resting in her palm, one perfect piece of jade, its shape a fat triangle smoothed by its many journeys on the tides.

The pond-spirit released her then, allowing her to keep her treasure. As though awakening from a dream, Susan stood and shook her head. It was time to get back to work, and besides, she was shivering now. Looking at her palm, she considered the small green stone.

Should I toss it back?

"Whatever," Susan mumbled to herself, and dropped it into the pocket of her worn leather jacket.

Kevin Ransom had gone directly to one of the Sawyer job sites early this morning, rather than stopping by the office. Hot, sweaty, and dirty from the muddy construction zone, he'd headed home to clean up before going to the office. Jack would want him for something and might even expect Kevin to join him for lunch.

Jack was no easy employer to work for. But he'd been good to Kevin, paid a fair wage, and offered challenges that'd allowed him to learn new skills. Kevin was no fan of conflict, though, and always did what he could to avoid it.

After a shower and a change of clothes, Kevin stepped out onto his deck for a breath of fresh air. The only time he could get his outer and inner worlds to match up was when he was working with machines or talking to animals. *I wish I had an animal to talk to now.* As though summoned, an opossum stuck his head out from under some bushes far below.

Kevin stilled his own movements, all except his eyes, which tracked the awkward creature as it ambled into the sunlight, looked around, and began to clamber up the nearest tree. Watching, fascinated at the clumsy yet steadfast progress of his visitor, Kevin was still afraid to move lest he frighten the creature away.

The only North American marsupial, he remembered from a recent Discovery Channel program. He loved how they were sleek-bodied with heart-shaped faces and big ears. Though he'd never had a chance to see a female carry young in its pouch, he'd always enjoyed the wide-eyed gazes of this tree-dweller and considered any encounter to contain a special significance.

"What are you trying to tell me, little fellow?" he intoned softly. His companion had climbed to the level of Kevin's deck. Eye to eye across a ten-foot chasm, creature regarded creature in perfect stillness. Perched in their respective havens, it seemed to Kevin that they each tried to outguess the other in a silent communing.

"Well, I don't know about you, but I'm hungry," said Kevin, a little louder than before. Slowly moving away from his railing, he turned to go into his kitchen, where he retrieved the bag of nuts he kept for his squirrel. Returning to the deck, he pulled at the rubber band holding the plastic bag closed, annoyed when it suddenly snapped out of his hand. Looking up, he saw the animal react, and realized the rubber band must have hurtled all the way to the tree. *I should have been more careful!* He looked away for a moment, considering ways he might check to make sure the animal wasn't injured. When he looked back at the tree, the critter was nowhere to be found.

"Where are you, little fella?" he called gently. Clutching the railing, Kevin trained his gaze to follow the line of tree trunk all the way down. To his horror, the opossum had apparently fallen and lay collapsed in a heap, unmoving.

Terrified he'd caused the critter's demise, Kevin dashed inside and leapt down the stairs, then ran outside. Ignoring the impulse to retrieve a pair of protective work gloves from the garage, he reached for the creature, touching its fur lightly, praying for signs of life.

Full of self-recrimination, feeling helpless and forlorn, Kevin looked at the animal. *Maybe a little water would revive him somehow!* Kevin dashed back up to the garage, filled a large metal dish, and brought it back, keeping his eyes on the dish, careful not to spill as he walked.

He looked up. *Gone!* Standing still for a moment, Kevin checked his position. No, here were the footprints he'd made himself only a moment earlier. And then he remembered. *Of course!* The clever little critter had "played possum"—and convincingly too.

Laughing so hard he sloshed water out of his dish, Kevin looked around the corner of the state forest he called his back yard. *Not a sign of him, but he has to be close.* Placing the dish on the ground, Kevin left it for his elusive friend and headed back upstairs to his main floor.

Chuckling as he gathered his tool belt, he climbed into his truck and headed for Sawyer Construction.

Chapter 6

Sally O'Mally had finished her private talk with Deputy Del, and he'd hurried back to his office. The only thing she'd been able to tell him was that the stranger who'd asked for Chris Christian had been tall, blond, and well-dressed. *A cityslicker if I ever did see one.* Hadn't she mentioned that before? Del said she hadn't, and that it might help. It'd certainly struck her as odd at the time—that an obviously professional type had been looking for her in a restaurant, not at the reporter's place of work. *But what do I know about how journalists work?*

Sally hadn't been in the mood for a restaurant full of breakfast customers a few hours earlier. She felt even less enthusiastic about serving lunch. It wasn't the cooking she minded. That actually helped to calm her thoughts and steady her nerves. Though the cook would handle special orders that came in, her own stew simmered now; the hamburger meat was browned for today's special; and the lettuce for salads had been washed and was crisping in the fridge.

Already, early lunch customers were arriving, but June was handling them, and Sally couldn't resist the temptation to stay another few minutes in her tiny office. Her huge, comfortable chair —threadbare though it was—enveloped her, and her feet rested on the needlepoint stool Mama had stitched for her. She took another few deep breaths and moved her thumbs across her forehead as though she were kneading dough. Try as she might, she couldn't wrench Jack from her mind.

If only he'd been born ugly, maybe that'd help. But such was not the case, at least from her perspective. Though he could stand to lose a few pounds, the man was strong and solid, quick on his feet, and ruggedly handsome. Salt-and-pepper hair, piercing blue eyes and a few character lines on his face just added to his appeal.

But the fact that she liked Jack Sawyer, and understood him better than anyone this side of Little Rock, seemed to count for nothing; certainly, it meant nothing to *him*. She saw in him the need to become husband and father, the need to nurture and create. It was what he did all day long, nurturing and creating one project after another. And yet he wouldn't admit to it. She'd assumed this was a verbal failing, not a psychological one— that he'd been the strong silent type who likes to *do*, not talk. She knew she was right about that too. But the obstinacy of the man had proven too stubborn even for the universal solvent of old-fashioned loving.

In fact, the love she'd shared with him these last few years had served not to soften him, but rather to harden his resolve. He'd grown in self-importance rather than in gratitude. *I've spoiled him!* she thought. And, like milk left too long in a warm barn, it had soured what had once been sweet.

She was right that he'd be upset about any progeny of his own. What she hadn't counted on was that Samantha had beaten her to the punch. *That woman has a way of ruining things for other folks.*

Samantha was a taker, and a holier-than-thou do-gooder to boot. She was one of those people who put ideals before human beings, and when her ideals steamrolled the people in her life, she gave herself credit for being noble enough to overcome emotions with "principles." Samantha talked about the "hard choices" in the high-and-mighty environmental speeches she was forever giving. *Well, it's a lotta tripe as far as I'm concerned!* It had cost Jack his first chance at being a father all those years ago—and now might be costing him his last chance as well.

Sally rarely indulged in condemnation. Guilt began swirling into the mix of her thoughts, like a touch of purple food dye in white icing. There must be a reason why Miranda thought highly of Samantha, she thought, but then dismissed the notion. *No, that's just Miranda's own pure nature.*

Her thoughts again strayed back to Jack. He'd been born with too much energy, and he'd always had to put it somewhere. She knew she'd brought him a measure of peace for the first time, grounding his electrical surges before they burnt him out. Now his grounding seemed to be gone, his circuits overloaded as he obsessed about finding his long-lost son.

Why can't he see the wisdom of lettin' the past alone, see it would be better for him—and for the son—to continue with their own lives, rather than enduring the disruption?

His utter rejection of her was causing her feelings to curdle like that sour milk. Depression was something she'd been aware of during her adult life, but generally from a distance. Like a dark cloud, it would sometimes appear at the far horizon. She'd seen others suffer and felt compassion, and occasionally the cloud had moved closer to her own terrain. But she knew depression as one knew a headache—annoying, but hardly threatening. At least with a headache, if it got bad enough, there was always aspirin.

The depression that threatened to take her over now was something else entirely. It was more like a tornado, dreadful in its scope, terrifying in its pinpoint accuracy, devastating in its destructive power. She watched, helpless as the thing tore through the landscape of her hopes and expectations.

Just when I finally have it all, Sally grieved. *At last I have the joy of the deep confirmation every woman desires in some way—I conceived!*

She was fertile, functional, and now, perhaps, a new purpose for her life was going to reveal itself. It was a primordial urge she was fulfilling, and with it came the power of primal imagery: an orderly home, time to muse and dream about the coming changes, a sense of newness, a great renewal of spirit, a perfect sense of safety in a haven set apart.

And yet now, there was the nagging presence of rejection that continued to swirl and suck up her hopes like fragments of worthless debris. It was bad enough that he'd refused everything she was—and everything she had to give. But he'd done more. He'd said to a human being not yet born that he or she was worthless, unwanted, and unwelcome. It was as though he'd cut the child's lifeline and left it spinning, enveloped in a vortex of rejection, which had now become the life-threatening storm itself.

So she would become Warrior Woman, have the child against all odds, commit to being a single parent, scrounge to find appropriate male energy and role-modeling for her child, but keep herself from connecting with any man fully because the child came first. She figured she might have to give up her business —unless she could find someone else to run it for or with her. A full-time restaurant owner and a full-time mom sounded like two different people.

Now that a child was on the way, it would have to come first. Sally had roots now in Milford-Haven and knew this would be a wholesome atmosphere. If she had to let go of her restaurant, she'd find a job of some kind, one that would allow her to be with the child as many hours of the day as she could. *Mama'd want me to move back to Arkansas. Or . . . maybe she'd move here to be with us.*

She knew once she'd given birth to her own flesh and blood, she'd never be able to send her child into the void, where roots were lost and love was uncertain. *No*, she promised herself. *No adoption.*

Weeks ago, there'd been that fleeting, other, unthinkable option—now too late to implement. She'd let go by the chance to slice herself out from under her new burden and try to return to the life she'd had before. Though she made no judgment for others, this was the only way forward for her, and though scared, she embraced the new life and how it would transform her world.

Ralph Hargraves bent over the boxes that had arrived with his latest order, his glasses slipping down his nose. His store, which he'd loved running with his late wife, had become too much for him, and he'd finally admitted it.

"Well, glory be," his wife would've said if she were still here. But she wasn't. That gal Sally who ran the place next door was sweet as the pies she made and kind as a daughter might be. He'd eat his breakfast at her counter and lunch most days, and she often sent him home with a boxed-up dinner.

Hearing the phone ring, he winced as he straightened his back and shuffled to his front counter. "Hargraves Hardware," he answered in a well-practiced tone.

"Uh, yes, Mr. Hargraves, it's Tony Fiorentino."

"Who?"

"It's Tony, from New York."

"Tony from New York! Yessir! How's the weather there?"

"Not too bad, not too bad, sir. A little rain yesterday."

"Oh, yes, well, that's just the thing, you know."

"Just the thing, sir?"

"To make the spring flowers grow! We're getting a few of those here too, don't you know."

"That's good," said Tony with a chuckle in his voice. "I'll have to get over to the Park and have a look."

"Too much concrete over in those parts for me. Gotta have my flowers." Mr. Hargraves noticed a spot of dried paint on his wooden countertop and worked on it with his thumbnail.

"Have to agree with you there," said Tony.

"Got your check. Put it in my account," Hargraves declared.

"Yes, sir. My accountant mentioned it'd gone through."

Ralph pulled his tall stool closer and sat down. "Long as you're satisfied, then I am too, young fellow. I think you'll do just fine with the store." He paused for a moment, listening to the silence, and let the news sink in. "Now, I'm not publishin' this forth just yet. Thought we'd ease folks into it."

"Yes, that's how I'd like to do it," Tony agreed. "I'm gonna need to be your apprentice for a while, learn the ropes, you know."

"Smart fellow like you, won't take long. Even after you take the reins, I don't plan to be moving anywhere. I'll still be in town. Expect to see you soon, then?"

"Yeah . . . yes. I have a few more things to close up here. And I've got a realtor looking for a place for me in Milford-Haven."

"Nothin' but nice places here," Mr. Hargraves said with conviction. A customer walked into the hardware store, ringing the door chime. "Gotta run now—got somebody browsing."

"All right, sir. I . . . I want to thank you—"

"No need."

"I . . . I'm looking forward to—" Tony tried to continue.

"Just holler when you get here." Mr. Hargraves hung up the phone. "Be right with you," he said to his new customer. Walking to the storeroom, he reached deep into his back pocket for his oversized handkerchief and dabbed a tear from his eye.

Sally could sense Jack's presence the moment he entered her restaurant, and her heart began to race. Whether out of anger or anxiety, she couldn't say, but with every passing minute, she grew more agitated.

As usual, he arrived with architectural plans under his arm, and his loyal employee Kevin Ransom in tow. They scanned the room for a place to sit. She considered fleeing to the kitchen and staying out of sight for the duration of their meal but dismissed that notion out of both pride and practicality. Instead, she busied herself with a rag and pretended not to notice him and his cohort—though she had no quarrel with Kevin. Their customary table was occupied by some tourists, and she took a small delight in the scowl that crossed Jack's face.

"Here, this table will do," she overheard him say to Kevin.

"Okay, Boss." Kevin looked up and bid a friendly, "Hi there, Sally."

Having no wish to ignore Kevin, she grabbed the handles of two mugs and her coffee pot, then walked the short distance to their table. "Hey there yourself, Kevin. What can I get for you?" It took effort to keep her hand from shaking as she poured their coffees.

"What's the special today?" Kevin was tall enough that, even sitting, he was close to Sally's eye level.

"Today it's Sloppy Joes." Sally kept her gaze fixed on her order pad.

"That sounds great! I'll have one of those." Putting down his menu, Kevin gave Sally a warm smile.

"That's fine for me too, Sally," Jack growled.

"I'm sorry, Jack. All I have left is enough for one. And that one's just been spoken for. My, my, what a shame." Her sarcasm rang out like an improvised song, surprising even herself.

Refusing to look up, Jack replied, "Well, give me a turkey on rye, will you?"

"I'll give you something wry, all right. Like how about, we don't serve turkeys in here. It's my new policy."

Jack and Kevin looked up, each stunned by the unaccustomed bite in Sally's tone. Jack spoke slowly. "Let's don't continue our little argument, shall we? Let's just get to the business at hand, namely lunch."

Kevin cringed at the all-too-familiar threat in Jack's voice. Sally, however, seemed almost cheerful. "Oh, by all means, Jack. We can get to the biz'ness at hand right away. Why don't you just let me bring you something appropriate, okay?"

"Yes, fine." Jack was visibly relieved. Sally hummed as she retreated to the kitchen. Jack gave Kevin a sidelong glance, nodded toward the drawings and tried to keep the edge out of his voice. "How're you coming with the plans for the Clarke house?"

"Fine, Boss. Those Environmental Planning Commission rules are strict, but it's only so it'll be safer for everyone."

Jack snorted. "The safety of that house has nothing whatsoever to do with the damn EPC rules, Kevin. They wouldn't know an unsafe from a safe building practice if it bit them in the—" He broke off for a sip of coffee before resuming. "How do you think the houses I've built all over town have stood the test of time till now? I know what I'm doing here—always have. I follow my own rules."

Sally returned with their food, sparing Kevin from having to make further comment. "Well, here we are, folks. Here's your Sloppy Joe, Kevin, and here's a little green salad on the side— that's good for you, you know?" Her words were considerate, but brittle. Kevin looked at her with concern.

Jack noticed the fragrant, oozing sauce on Kevin's plate with some concern and reached for the drawings, moving them to an empty chair to avoid any stains. While he leaned away, Sally set a wide, flat bowl of her stew at his place without a word. As Jack straightened, his elbow caught the edge of his bowl, upending it neatly into his lap. The burning sensation brought Jack to his feet with a yelp.

"Ah! That's hot!" Grabbing for his napkin, he began stabbing at his groin. Through clenched teeth he muttered at her, "What in blazes do you think you're doing, Sally?"

Her shoulders shook slightly, and she seemed to be suppressing a chuckle. "We do have a sayin' in my rest'urnt, Jack. 'Lunch is on you!'" With that, the laugh began to squeeze up her throat.

"There's really something wrong with you, Sally," Jack intoned with menace, "Laughing at someone else's pain. You're not fit to run a business—or anything else."

The accusation silenced Sally's mirth and made her lip tremble.

Kevin came to his feet as if trapped in their interminable silence. The three of them stood there hovering over the ruined lunch, Kevin's eyes downcast, Sally and Jack locked in a hateful stare.

Then, apparently too proud to stay on the premises even long enough to clean himself, Jack spun and marched to the entrance, banging open the screen door with vehemence. Kevin looked back and forth between Jack's retreating figure and Sally, momentarily torn between conflicting loyalties. Then he bolted after Jack, his quick reflexes the only thing that prevented him from taking the rebounding screen door squarely on the forehead.

The restaurant lay in hushed silence, all eyes fixed on Sally. Looking around at her patrons, Sally tossed her dish towel over her shoulder. "Just go on back to eatin', folks. It was just an accident, and we'll get it all cleaned up." With determined cheer, she picked up the spilled plate and stacked it with those on the table. Then she used her rag to wipe the floor and headed to the kitchen with a bounce in her step.

Out of sight of her customers, she put down the dirty dishes, hurried to open her back door, and gulped fresh air. Her hands still shook from her confrontation, and now her head was beginning to throb.

June breezed into the kitchen and refilled her coffeepot. "Nice goin', Sal. I can never think of the smart comeback till later. I couldn't tell if the customers were gonna break into a round of applause or what!"

Sally took another gulp of air. "Sounds like they're returning to normal in there," she said. "This'll run 'cross town like wildfire."

"Prob'ly give us the biggest lunch crowd we'll get all year," June added cheerfully. "You doin' okay?"

Sally turned to face her trusted employee and friend. "Wa-yil, ye-yus. But I'm thinkin' I'll go pay Mama a visit. Been a while."

"She okay?" June asked, her tone laced with concern.

"She says so, and I do b'lieve her and all, but it's just . . . somethin' in her voice, ya know? I've been puttin' off a visit with her. And plus, I could stand to get away for a minute myself."

"You really could, Sal."

"So then, you be all right on your own if I leave for a long weekend?"

"Shu-wah!" June drew the word *sure* out in her Brooklynese. "Not a problem. You know that, Sal." Without another question asked, June spun backward through the kitchen door and returned to the waiting throng.

As Sally untied her apron and headed for her office to collect a few things before going home to pack, she replayed the comment she'd overheard Jack mumble to Kevin. He did, indeed, make his own rules. That being the case, she was beginning to wonder who else he was hurting.

Chapter 7

Sally rose so early on Saturday morning that it was still night. She opened the door that led from the kitchen to the driveway and peered toward the horizon, where the bright, full orb was still visible. "Moon in the mornin'," she said aloud. Since this was one of her mama's favorite expressions, she took it as a good sign and smiled to herself.

With her faded but sturdy tapestry suitcase already packed and loaded into her car, Sally locked the house door behind her, then drove to her restaurant. She'd asked the airport shuttle to pick her up there, as it was much easier for the driver to find than her small house, located up a windy hill. She could park her vintage yellow Chevy Chevette in the parking lot she shared with Hargraves' Hardware during her trip.

Her tires made a soft, crunching sound in the gravel behind the store. She doused her headlights, climbed out, and retrieved her suitcase and purse. Unable to resist one last look around the restaurant before leaving town for her long weekend, she unlocked the back door and carried her things inside. *I'll see the driver when he arrives at the front and go out that way.*

Her eyes swept over the kitchen, its stainless steel counters spotless, its sturdy white dishes gleaming on their shelves. Checking the washing machine, she discovered a final load of towels lying damply in the bottom of the round drum. She put them in the dryer, ratcheted the dial to "cotton sturdy" and pressed the Start button. *By the time June has those towels folded and put away, I'll be sipping tomato juice on the flight to Little Rock.*

Kevin Ransom rolled out of bed early, as usual. He stepped onto his deck to deposit a nut along the railing for the squirrel who inhabited his backyard forest.

Though he almost always woke up happy in Milford-Haven, today he felt especially glad, because he felt useful and needed. His good friend had asked him for two favors. The first was to cat-sit Shadow while she was away. He always enjoyed the black cat's company. The second was that she'd asked him for a ride to the San Luis Obispo airport.

Kevin didn't own a car. But the truck he owned was his pride and joy. Granted, it was ten years old. Well, eleven, now. And granted, the heater still didn't work. That was next on his list of repairs. But since that time last winter when he'd taken Susan to the Doobie Brothers concert—worried the whole time that his vehicle might not make the round trip—he'd worked on it with the help of his friend Art, who owned the best local garage.

The 1986 faded red Ford F-150, also known as the Ranger, was a classic as far as he was concerned. This model had been introduced in 1975 but then went through several generations, no doubt because of its tremendous popularity.

At 6-foot-8, Kevin was a big man, and he'd had to have a couple of modifications made to the truck. The seat now slid back a bit farther and was situated a bit lower than factory standard. Otherwise, it had the standard features, like the traditional Ford "blue oval" affixed to the center of the front grille and the name "FORD" embossed on the rear drop panel. He'd bought some aftermarket seat covers and added cup holders to the interior.

The 4-wheel-drive vehicle was as hardworking as he was himself, hauling construction materials all over town and beyond. In honor of today's guest, he'd given the truck a good wash. He'd have had to anyway, given the muddy conditions at his job sites. But yesterday he'd also vacuumed the interior.

At 7:00 a.m., Miranda's Mustang pulled into the empty lot next to Kevin's house, which he used for parking. While she climbed out of her car, he reached into the passenger's side to retrieve the cat carrier and took it inside, holding the front door open for Miranda.

The moment she unfastened the lid to the carrier, Shadow leapt gracefully out and walked to the pair of guest cat bowls, in which she found the fresh water and kibble Kevin had already set out for her.

"I think she's just as happy here as she is at home," Miranda commented.

Kevin beamed. "Hope so. I want her to be comfortable."

"Oh, she always is. I know she loves me, cuz I'm Mom. But I think she has a crush on you."

Kevin felt himself blush. "Well," he said, "the feeling is mutual."

"Shall we?" Miranda asked.

"Yup," Kevin agreed. "This is for you," he added, handing her a thermos. "Hot tea for the drive."

Miranda shook her head. "There is just no one as thoughtful as you, Kevin."

During the hour-long drive to the airport, they sat in companionable quiet part of the way, enjoying the light show as dawn streaked the sky with vivid color.

Then Kevin would break the silence with some outrageous episode from a construction project, usually involving the difficult and domineering Jack Sawyer. But as they neared the destination, they were sharing funny cat stories that had them both laughing out loud.

After lifting her luggage from the truck bed where he'd had it secured and depositing it on the terminal sidewalk, Kevin promised to pick her up when she returned. "Just let me know when," he said. Then he waved to his friend as he drove away, happy he could help and even happier to be entrusted with her previous pet.

Cornelius called his good friend Jameson Raymond, who answered on the first ring.

"Hey!" he said in cheerful welcome. "You in town?"

"I am."

"Great. Have time for lunch?"

Cornelius thought for a moment. "Tell you what. If you'll give me a couple of hours this afternoon, I'll buy you dinner."

"Best offer of the month, since Susan's busy this evening. What are we doing for the two hours before we eat?"

"I have a property I'd like you to walk with me."

"Aha! Thought you'd never ask!"

Jameson had been Cornelius' classmate at Cal Poly and, in the years since graduation, had become a leading architect in the Central Coast. This was home territory for both men, who'd actually been friends since childhood. They always shared a love of environmental science and had learned that studies in ecology inevitably led to a review of history—how the land had been used, how those uses had impacted local systems.

The original inhabitants of Milford-Haven and its immediate neighbors, Cambria and San Simeon, were the Salinan and the Chumash tribes, and detection of artifacts had been part of the men's Cal Poly course work. Long before that, as young boys they'd loved to examine the real estate Cornelius had in mind. Long deserted, the property had been the source of speculation, rumor, and even fear, and the boys were often told not to go there.

That'd never stopped the intrepid explorers, who'd constructed a rickety fort near the crumbling seawall and even dared to climb into the deserted mansion and the fake lighthouse the owners had once built. While that property had been the stuff of childhood adventures, it'd also spun into grown-up dreams for Cornelius.

For the past several years, each time he'd visited his folks, he'd taken some time to research local history and land ownership. For the longest time, that strip of coastal property remained in limbo. It'd been inherited by a group of siblings who didn't live locally, had no desire to take up residence, no plan for repairs, and apparently no agreement on what to do with the decaying remains of a once-glamorous site. Not being Californians, they evidently had no concept of how valuable a slice of coastal land could be.

Eventually, it'd come to the attention of the Environmental Planning Commission. The director Samantha Hugo, a friend of his parents, had warned that some sort of action should be taken before a developer like Jack Sawyer put his eye on it. So, Cornelius had done some more homework.

He found that an adjacent lot was under protection by the Central Coast Council. After checking with them, he figured that whoever might want to buy the property from the heirs would have to ask for the Cultural Resources Survey and Impact Assessment the Council would require.

Accordingly, he commissioned the report from a local archeological firm and discovered that adjacent protected areas were not included in the property itself. When he brought this to the EPC, Samantha was thrilled someone responsible wanted to take the next steps. Both she and Cornelius were delighted there seemed no impediment to proceeding. Well, except for two more factors: getting the heirs to agree to a sale and coming up with the money.

Like most scientists, Cornelius had been living from grant to grant throughout his career. Some of his proposals got funded, some did not, but enough were approved that he'd always had a steady, if modest, paycheck.

One of his favorite ideas had received neither approval nor funding from NASA. But because it seemed so simple to him and so easy to launch through his own friends and followers, he'd pursued it.

Everyone who owned a personal computer tended to leave it on most of the time, which necessitated a screensaver, so no permanent image would be etched into the monitor screen. Cornelius designed one that showed shifting skyscapes, beautiful images of stars and galaxies. He charged $10.00 a year for a subscription, with a promise to provide updated images on a regular basis.

What was running in the background made the program infinitely more interesting, particularly to the nerds who followed him. Invisible to users, but running in the background, would be an ongoing search through star data to process location and behavior of distant stars. If, for example, a star seemed to grow dim, this was an indication that it had a planet in orbit. NASA had claimed Cornelius' project would require a supercomputer. This was a way of "creating" a supercomputer by having, he hoped, hundreds of individual computers all contributing to the calculations.

He named his project exactly what it was: PlanetQuest. For amateur astronomers, the chance to be beta testers in this project had become irresistible, and he'd had not hundreds, but thousands of participants sign up. But he'd discovered that a whole different group—the arts-and-visual community—had also discovered the program. They, in turn, had shared it with others until the whole endeavor achieved "liftoff." He'd grossed six million his first quarter.

He'd kept quiet about his unexpected fortune. And it turned out, he'd be spending quite a bit of it to get this property project launched. As he did more homework on it, he discovered that unpaid taxes had caused foreclosure, and also that coastal erosion had caused damage that would have to be repaired. He'd signed paperwork agreeing to pay the taxes and to pay for whatever might be needed to support the substructure of the coastal escarpment. These satisfied both the heirs and the county authorities.

There were more hoops through which he'd had to jump. The property contained a rock mound with proven remains of kitchen midden from Chumash use thousands of years earlier. He'd have to preserve it, rather than building over or removing it. And he'd had to agree to restore the faux lighthouse, now a local landmark, but that'd been part of his goal anyway.

Over the previous two years, his work on this project had been ongoing, balanced with his workload at NASA. Though replete with red tape, it'd seemed almost uncanny to him that the possibility of moving forward with owning this cherished land had arisen simultaneously with the means to complete it. As confirmation that he lived in a benevolent universe, the experience was unparalleled. The purchase went through, and he was now the proud owner of his favorite piece of land.

Cornelius glanced up into his rearview mirror to see Jameson pull up and park behind him. He was already talking as they both exited their vehicles.

"You've gotta be kidding me," Jameson called out.

"Surprise!" Cornelius said with a grin.

"When you asked me to meet, I assumed you meant you'd bought a piece of land or—"

"I did."

"You don't mean—"

"Oh, but I do."

The two men stood eye to eye, Jameson's straw-colored hair as unruly as ever, his build and fitness similar to his own. Cornelius watched as a series of revelations shone through his friend's face. "Oh, my God!" he exclaimed after a long moment.

"Yup!" Cornelius couldn't help but laugh out loud.

Jameson slapped a hand against his shoulder and gave him a grin. "Well, I guess we have our work cut out for us."

No one would understand better than Jameson the scope of a project like this. "That we do," he confirmed.

They headed into the property, taking care not to trip over tangled undergrowth. They stood with hands on hips glancing past weeds and buildings to the sparkle of ocean winking through the trees.

"Hope you have a big budget," Jameson quipped.

"Yeah. Well, enough to get started, anyway," Cornelius offered. *Who knows how long my screensaver will last? Right now, it's a hot commodity, but it could be eclipsed by something else one of these days.*

"Wow," Jameson said, interrupting his worries. "Good for you. Okay, well the first invoice to pay will be to a landscaping company to clear the underbrush."

"Right," Cornelius agreed, following his friend to the sea wall.

"Then, if I were you, I'd get a quote from a mason about repairing this. Some of it looks pretty good, but some of it . . . well, you don't want anything dangerous."

Cornelius grabbed a pen from his shirt pocket and a memo pad from inside his jacket. He jotted some notes. "Got it."

Then they took several minutes to walk the entire property. While they did, Cornelius wrote further memos to himself.

They passed a ruined pool, its foundation cracked; a small clapboard guesthouse probably beyond repair; and a mansion whose style didn't appeal, and which, also, likely would be beyond repair.

But when they came to the small, stone lighthouse they'd once gleefully climbed in boyhood, they paused. "Let me ask you," Jameson said. "What do you think of as the center of this property?"

"The lighthouse, for sure. This was what drew me here," Cornelius said.

"And this is where we start," Jameson confirmed. "The whole property emanates from here. It's a reflection of the forces that are coming together."

Cornelius had nodded his head. "Must be why it was built here in the first place."

"Okay, then this is where we start. I mean, the landscape cleanout and the wall repair can start as soon as you like. But from the perspective of design, the lighthouse will determine the flow. So, tell me how you feel about this building."

Cornelius thought for a moment. "Well, there's the navigational sense of it. So even though this isn't an authentic lighthouse, it's got that metaphor going for it."

"It does. Once some of the tangle is removed, it'll be more visible from both land and sea too," Jameson observed.

"Yeah. But from standing right here, there's something else." Cornelius looked upward, taking in the structure, its rounded walls, its position at the edge of the sea, standing sentinel for the whole property. "*A l'erte,*" he said, which means 'in the watchtower.'"

"Etymology buff, eh? I might've guessed," Jameson remarked. "You're right, it is a watchtower. So, this is a place to keep safe. To keep others safe."

"Colleagues. Friends. A family, someday." Cornelius looked at his friend and saw the light of understanding in his eyes. *No surprise that he understands exactly what I mean. He and Susan have been together for a while now.* The two men stood in silent communion for a long moment.

"I kind of see the whole place as a campus, really," Cornelius continued. "Multiple spaces for different activities. I want a small planetarium."

"Awesome!"

"And of course, a functional main house. Not sure what else, yet."

"Yeah, it'll evolve. But your home, your campus, needs to grow from here. The base will have to be expanded. You could do the master on the next level, but this, the ground floor, will have to be kitchen, great room."

"And maybe an outdoor deck," Cornelius added.

"This part of the coastline slants northwest, so we've got a southwest ocean view. Sun coming from the south is important," James had said. "We'll want windows to bring in that light. And the street side of the property should be private. No need for passersby to be able to see into the buildings. So, what about your workspace?"

"Separate building," Cornelius said without hesitation.

"Got it. Okay, so the lighthouse will be the heart, the personal space, the restore-your-soul place."

"Exactly!" Cornelius enthused.

"The base is round, so the expansion footprint would be fan-shaped."

"I love that!" Cornelius said. "Though it's kind of a lot for a bachelor."

"If you build it, they will come," quoted Jameson.

The two friends stood in the sea breeze, vines and weeds rattling, tall pines vibrating. Neither had families yet. But both stood on the threshold of the next great adventure.

This is what Joseph Campbell would call the "Hero's Journey Begins," Cornelius considered. *Like a portal opening.* His trusted friend would help him create space for living, sharing, growing. It felt like a silent pact, one that would soon be formalized with documents and funding.

Chapter 8

Miranda sat on her deck wearing a fleece jacket, legs wrapped in a throw, as the chill of early spring dawn stung the air.

She inhaled, grateful to be home. *Even though it's a rental, I do think of it as home.* The view of ocean through the pines, both from here on the deck and from inside her studio, always brought a sense of peace. Inside, the high angles and rich wood paneling made her feel she was, indeed, living in the trees.

Her flight yesterday had been uneventful, even if the trip itself had not been. Between visiting with her art professor, spending a night camping in the meadowlark habitat, running into "Mrs. Lime"—of all people—and then more or less rescuing the woman . . . well, it'd been an adventure. She smiled to herself. *And adventure is one of the things I love about my life.*

Kevin had picked her up as promised, and she'd been reunited with Shadow, who now reclined on the railing. When Miranda looked into her amber eyes, the kitty gave her an approving blink and a soft, "Mow." *I hope she won't be too upset when I take her back to Kevin's tomorrow.*

~~Smiling,~~ Miranda zipped her fleece higher and inhaled a deep breath of ocean air, grateful, ~~too,~~ at having found such an ideal place to lease. *I'm in no position to buy this yet, but maybe someday.* Though technically her absentee landlord used the adjacent house to rent to vacationers, it was usually empty.

The design of the structure—two matching buildings offset from one another and partially attached—had driveways and entrances on the main level with bedrooms below, following the contour down the hill. Miranda's side sat farther west, with its large deck unobstructed. The deck on the other unit faced south, providing privacy for both dwellings.

She went to her kitchen to spoon some oatmeal from her crock pot into a bowl, then brought it back to the deck. Warming her hands on the bowl, she watched steam rise from its surface. The blue jay who shared the property with her called raucously from a nearby pine, threatening to swoop down on her breakfast.

Shadow was, as usual, incensed at the jay's presumption. Responding with her own exclamations, the cat bared her fangs, issued a series of staccato warnings, and only stopped short of hissing. Receiving no acknowledgment, Shadow turned her head to Miranda, said a curt "Meh" and—head held high—stalked back inside.

Miranda chuckled, savoring this brief time. Watching the jay swoop from tree to tree with the morning light filtering through the branches made her feel as though she were inside one of her own paintings.

Her weekend photographs of the meadowlark in Oregon would need to be processed and reviewed. *I'll drop the film off at the photo shop today.*

While doing her errands, she'd have liked to stop by Sally's Restaurant to discuss the mural her friend wanted done. The drawing, long since complete, depicted a farm scene reminiscent of Sally's original home in Arkansas. The image, which would show rolling green hills and white fencing, would fill the right and left walls behind tables and chairs, then follow along behind the long bar where some of her customers preferred to eat.

Sally herself had delayed the project, explaining to Miranda that she was now pregnant, with future plans somewhat up in the air. Things were a little complicated. The man she'd been seeing—and the baby's father—had broken up with her; a new man was on the horizon, but nothing was settled yet. And for now, the whole thing was a secret.

Miranda shook her head, thinking of her friend. Strong, capable, and determined, Sally would make an outstanding mother, whatever her circumstances. And if the mural ever did get started, Miranda now planned to add a "cow jumping over the moon" to the image. But since a childlike image might lead to speculation, for now, Miranda agreed the project should be on hold.

Miranda would, however, stop in at the shell shop, probably on her way home from Atascadero. She'd been painting one shell each season for her friend Shelly Larrup. They enjoyed their discussions about which shell it should be. Synchronicity always played a role in these conversations, and she smiled at the prospect of recognizing related ideas as they surfaced. *I keep thinking a scallop shell would be a beautiful one to paint, but I'm not sure yet what the relevance would be.*

And that brought her to the next thing on her agenda: a trip to Kuyama's. These visits were all too rare, and she always looked forward to meeting with this woman who was both friend and mentor. Though casual on one level, their meetings always seemed to hold special significance. Miranda finished her cereal and headed inside to dress for the day.

Miranda had been spending a productive morning in her studio.

After a quick shower and a change into jeans and a T-shirt, she'd ordered things on her desk, putting postcards as a priority.

First, she'd quickly done three versions of her next miniature, using the idea that'd come to her during her sleepless night. The huge mural she'd soon be doing in Lompoc was already sketched and outlined, so creating a small, cropped version had been easier than the previous "mini" images had been.

Keeping one of the three for Zelda to duplicate, she'd then used the other two to write messages. Once the watercolor dried, she'd carefully turned the three cards over and used her ruler to draw lines separating the message from the address.

Then, to get warmed up, she wrote one to Meredith first. The message was simple, but she liked sending one each of these miniatures to her sister. *To prove I'm being prolific? To encourage her to visit? Maybe a little of each.* But once her sister's card was complete, she decided against sending it. *I should wait and send her one of the printed versions. It'll have the gallery info and look professional. That'll matter more to her.*

For Cornelius, however, she liked the idea of a completely handmade card. She held it in her hands for several minutes as she considered what she wanted to say.

> Dear Cornelius,
>
> Happy first day of spring! Thank you for your postcards. Thought you might like to have one of mine. This is a miniature of a big mural I'll be painting in Lompoc. Maybe you'll see it sometime.
> Best to you, Miranda

After placing one of her lighthouse stamps on the back, and using his local P.O. box address, she walked out her front door to put it in her mailbox, wondering whether she'd already missed today's pickup. When she opened the box, she saw that a couple of fliers and a catalogue had arrived. And wedged in between them was yet another postcard from Cornelius.

Smiling, she looked at the slightly tattered edges of a beautiful image of Amsterdam. *Well, now he'll receive at least one from me.*

Miranda glanced at the clock on her kitchen wall. *It's already eleven? I still have to finish packing!* Not only that, she still had to run to the hardware store to get her easel repaired.

She felt hungry. *Is there time for a quick bowl of soup at Sally's counter?* Probably. But then she and Sally would wind up talking and Miranda would delay herself. Instead, she spread some chunky peanut butter on a couple of chilled celery sticks, chomped them quickly, then washed them down with a tall glass of iced tea from the pitcher she kept on hand in her fridge.

She loaded her damaged easel into the back seat of her car, since riding her bike with it would be awkward. Then she climbed into the car and took off down the hill toward Main Street.

Trying not to communicate her sense of panic, she carried it inside and walked directly toward the back of the hardware store, where Mr. Hargraves kept his work desk and register.

"Well, hello there, Miss Miranda," Hargraves said. "Whatcha got there?"

"Oh, I broke this on my last trip. And I need it tomorrow because I'm heading out of town again. I apologize for the short notice!"

"Well, let's see what we can do. If it's a simple repair, I might be able to do it right now."

"Oh, that'd be great. This is my field easel, and this hinge tore off, so it won't stand correctly anymore." She pointed to the hole in the wood.

"I see that. You've got the other side out of alignment too. Looks like it would be smart to replace both hinges."

The sound of a male voice quietly counting drifted toward them from an aisle or two over. Seeing Miranda's inquisitive look, Hargraves said. "That's a customer and his nails. Apparently, he's very particular."

Miranda smiled and nodded, too distracted to respond further. She glanced at her watch.

His attention back on the easel, Hargraves continued, "I'm wondering if it would work to move the hinges down the leg slightly and put them here."

"Why?"

"Well, this wood is so soft, they'd probably tear out again if we used the old holes. Either that, or we can do a little fill with wood cement."

"Whatever you think would make it stronger."

"Both, I'd say. Do the fill. Then the drill. Into new holes."

Miranda smiled at the little poem. "Sounds good. And you're sure you have time for all this?"

He glanced up at Miranda. "It shouldn't take long. I think I can do it for you now while you wait."

"Really? I'd appreciate it!"

"You got it. Back in just a few minutes." After lifting the easel from the counter, Mr. Hargraves disappeared into his back room. In a moment, Miranda heard the drill and, still in the background, that other man's voice counting.

Glancing around, she decided her best use of time was to check through the aisles to see if something struck her as indispensable for her trip to Lompoq. Even though she'd be working primarily on murals, she wanted to have the easel in case she had time for a little *plein air* painting. *You never know when just the right thing might show up.* The first thing that caught her eye was a small apple-green teapot, and she picked it off the shelf. *It does plug in,* she considered. *But I don't really need it the next time I go camping.* She placed it carefully back on the shelf and walked farther down the aisle.

She noticed a submersible coil for heating water and wondered if this might be more practical. *But I really like that little teapot.* Stepping backward to look at it again, she collided heavily with someone, and the sound of boxes of nails crashing to the floor filled the room.

"Oh!"

"No!"

Miranda spun around to survey the damage. "Oh, I'm sorry! There must be a thousand nails on the floor!"

"Two hundred twenty-seven, actually."

That voice . . . could that be—? Miranda looked up into the intense dark blue eyes of Cornelius. "I'm very, very sorry."

"We have to stop doing this," he said, humor lighting up his face.

"You're right," Miranda agreed, feeling her cheeks heat, whether from embarrassment or shyness, she wasn't sure. To cover it, she squatted and began picking up nails. "That'll teach me! Not looking where I was going," she mumbled.

Squatting himself, Cornelius joined her in picking up nails, his hand brushing against hers. The touch, almost familiar, calmed her.

"So you just got back—" she began.

"I heard you say you're leaving—" he said at the same time. "Sorry, you first."

"Everything okay out here?" Mr. Hargraves called out. "Thought I heard a . . . oh, brother."

Looking up, Miranda said, "It was all my fault. I backed into him, and the nails went everywhere. I'll clean it up."

"Not a problem. I got me a magnetic wand I've been wanting to try. Just leave everything. I'll do it later," Mr. Hargraves said as he walked away. "Oh," he added over his shoulder, "In case you haven't met, that's Milford-Haven's astronomer, Cornelius Smith."

"Yes, we . . . uh, met," she said quietly. Still embarrassed, she added, "Thanks for your postcards."

"Glad you received them."

"I wrote you back. It's in the mail."

He continued to stare into her eyes. "I'm in town for a little while now. How long will you be away?"

"Just for a long weekend. I have a job in Lompoc, have to leave day after tomorrow." *I'm blathering on.*

"I've got your easel ready!" Mr. Hargrave's voice rang out.

"Go," Cornelius said. "I'll find you next week."

As they stood, she gave Cornelius a smile and replied, "Thanks. I'm sorry, I'm sort of in a hurry." As she walked to the back counter, she said to Mr. Hargraves, "You got it fixed already?"

"Yup."

When she arrived, he presented it to Miranda. "I think this should do the trick."

Inspecting it, she grinned. "It's brilliant, Mr. Hargraves. Fantastic. What do I owe you?"

He thought for a moment. "A picture."

"What?"

"A small one, or, you know, a drawing, or something. No hurry. Just, when the spirit moves."

Smiling, Miranda said, "You got it. Maybe I can sketch some-thing for you while I'm away. And you know, I'll be having an art show at the gallery next week. Maybe you could come and pick something you like."

"Grand. You travel safe, now, and we'll see you when you get home. And I'll come to your show!"

Cornelius finally rounded up all the nails, then added the box to his long rolling cart that held some precut shelves and metal wall supports toward Mr. Hargraves counter.

"Let's see watcha ya got there, young fellow," the owner said, leaning over the counter.

Cornelius smiled at being called "young"—something he hadn't heard in a while, since he was now pushing forty. *You are not!* He could hear his mother say. *You're only thirty-seven!*

Hargraves interrupted his thoughts with a question. "You buildin' shelves?"

"Yeah, my mom needs more storage in the garage for her silk flowers."

Hargraves pursed his lips. "According to George, Phyllis could just about open her own silk flower store by now."

Cornelius laughed out loud. "Dad might've told *you*, but he wouldn't dare say that aloud at home."

"I imagine not," Hargraves agreed. "How's that observing project of your coming along?"

Trust this dear man to remember. "Thanks for asking! Things have taken a turn for the better, as a matter of fact. One of my projects started to pay off, finally, and it looks like I've gotten the properties I wanted."

"Well, now, ain't that the best news in a month of Sundays!"

"It is! I think it'll be good for the community."

"I bet your folks are pleased as punch!"

Cornelius paused for a moment. "I, uh, haven't even had the chance to tell them yet. I just got back this morning, and they're out for the day. So would you mind—"

"I won't say a word, till you give me the all clear," the older man said. "They'll get lit up like a Christmas tree when you tell 'em, though."

Cornelius grinned, and said quietly, "Yes, I imagine they will."

"Now, you said properties with an "s." There's more than one?"

"Sure you want to get me started on this?"

Hargraves glanced down the long aisle toward his front door. "Don't see any other customer beggin' for my help right at the moment."

"Okay. Well, the observatory needs to be way up a hillside. Otherwise fog and other atmospheric elements would interfere. Last winter, I did a star party up in Mendocino. While I was there, I visited a remote site where there was an observatory years ago. Helped me figure out the best location here in the Central Coast."

Cornelius saw Hargraves eyes start to glaze over. "Uh-huh," he managed.

"Long story short, lack of turbulent air makes for observing. So I found a site up the 46 that'll be perfect. It'll take a while, though, before we can start on that."

"Okay. And the other property . . . it's something in town, right?"

"Yes," Cornelius confirmed. "It's that site on the other side of the 1, with the little lighthouse you can barely see?"

Hargraves raised his eyebrows. "You mean, that old, deserted place that's all tangled up in weeds?"

"That's the one!" Cornelius said, feeling excitement rise. "I finally got the heirs to agree to sell."

Hargraves nodded. "Those kids never did live here after their folks passed, never did know what to do with it."

"Right. They seemed glad to get it off their hands. My pal Jameson has agreed to walk it with me, start to make plans."

Hargraves nodded again. "If Jameson is gonna help, you'll be in good hands." The man grinned. "You two young fellas are gonna have quite a project on your hands!"

"We sure are!"

Hargraves shook his head. "And you want me to keep quiet about all this? You're gonna have to go ahead and tell your folks right soon. Otherwise, I might bust a gut!"

Cornelius laughed. "I promise, I'll sit down with them this weekend. So, what do I owe you?"

"Guess I can't ask you for a painting, like I did Miranda," he remarked, ringing up the sale.

Chuckling, Cornelius reached for his wallet and replied, "You wouldn't want anything I painted."

"Her works are right pretty. Not near as pretty as she is herself, though."

Cornelius felt his face grow warm.

"Saw a couple of sparks back there when those nails went flyin'," Hargraves offered.

There is no such thing as privacy in Milford-Haven. I'll have to remember that! "That so?"

It was Hargraves' turn to chuckle. "I'm an old man now, but I ain't dead yet."

Cornelius gave the man his warmest smile, remembering that his wife of decades had passed on a few years earlier. "Indeed, not," he said. "Well, thanks a million, Mr. H. Always good to see you."

"Back atcha, C. Be seein' ya around.

As Cornelius pushed his cart out the front door, he thought for a moment about how life would be once he moved back home. *Less privacy. More support.* Based on his exchange with his parents' long-time friend the hardware store owner, that about summed it up.

As he loaded the shelving materials into the back of his SUV, he thought about the immediate future. Miranda was away now, and he had a chunk of work to get done—both his own and his folks' projects. But one thing he'd already decided: he wouldn't be leaving town again until after Miranda's art show next week. That was one event he did not want to miss.

Chapter 9

Delmar Johnson sat at his computer, wrestling with a new dilemma. He'd promised to help Samantha Hugo with her adoption search, but now he was afraid he'd be steering uncomfortably close to a breach of confidentiality.

He'd even mentioned he was working on the issue of adoption for his own purposes. *Why did I ever offer to help her?* He wished, now, he'd kept his mouth shut. It wasn't his job to help citizens with their Internet searches. Yet, as a law enforcement officer, it *was* his job to be of service. And it was his inclination to be helpful.

Besides her role as a prominent local citizen, Samantha Hugo was—from what he could tell—a hellova nice woman. Because of her position as Director of the Environmental Planning Commission, she'd probably forgotten more about the Central Coast than Del would ever know. He looked forward to cultivating her as a mentor. Doing her a minor favor seemed an excellent place to start.

It was hard to get to know people on a personal basis while wearing the mantle of law-enforcement. Given his technical interests, he also wasn't a great match with this town full of artists and artisans. But, as was sometimes the case, his computer ability had gotten him access to this still-new connection with Ms. Hugo. He used his Internet researching skill to great advantage on the job and kept at it long past working hours because he loved it. *I should just admit it,* he chided himself. *I'm addicted.* Be that as it may, now that he'd come across this valuable piece of data regarding Ms. Hugo, he'd have to tread carefully lest he break the law.

Evidently, Ms. Hugo had decided to look for the son she'd given up. According to Chris Christian's television report on adoption, this was a fairly commonplace occurrence these days. But there was a system in place and a prescribed series of steps to be taken. Though cumbersome, these regulations were meant to protect all parties—adoptees, adoptive parents, and birthparents.

Because he had the special access of a law enforcement practitioner, he'd been able to penetrate sealed records. He'd discovered some intriguing information, including that Samantha Hugo's baby son had been adopted in Santa Barbara. With a little more digging he felt confident he'd be able to unearth the name of the family who'd adopted him.

But telling her even as much as he knew was not only premature, it was illegal because the records were sealed. So instead, he planned to take her through some more rudimentary steps in the search process. *Was her decision a hasty one? Was it a knee-jerk reaction to something that had happened to her recently? Had she watched Chris Christian's special reports on television? Had that sparked this decision?* It was his intention to find out more during their time together today.

He also looked forward to probing as tactfully as possible in hope of discovering what she might or might not already know herself.

Samantha reached the turn off Highway 1 just as the sun was sinking into storm clouds. She pushed the gas pedal of her Jeep Grand Cherokee, accelerating to make it up the incline leading to the California Department of Forestry and the SLO County Sheriff's Department where Deputy Johnson shared office space. The double glass door was still unlocked, and she pulled it open, inhaling faint traces of fresh paint and new carpeting. Had she been in a better frame of mind, she'd have enjoyed the sleek redwood structure with the last of the day's sunlight glinting through its tall windows. As it was, she read the posted roster of office numbers and hurried upstairs.

The deputy sat alone in his office, and he glanced up, watching Sam over the top of his computer monitor as she approached. "Come in, Ms. Hugo." He stood, offering, "I'll pull up a chair for you." He placed it where she'd be able to see the computer screen.

Swinging her bag to the floor, she nodded appreciatively. "Please call me Sam. Everyone does."

"And I'm Del." His voice held sudden warmth.

Smiling back at him, she asked, "Short for Delmar, right?"

"Right." He sat and returned his attention to his screen. "Just closing up a few things here." Turning to her, he continued, "Now, how can I help?"

She sighed. "I suppose what I really need is a computer lesson so I could do this kind of thing myself," With a nervous laugh she added, "Not that I'd want to waste your time with such a mundane matter as computer lessons."

"My time today's my own, and so's the computer, by the way."

"Ah." Sam nodded. "I was wondering what would make a county agency spring for such a sleek-looking machine."

"Yeah," admitted Del. "It's state-of-the-art now, but of course six months from now, it'll seem like a dinosaur." They shared a chuckle but then slipped into an awkward silence.

"Del, I—" Sam began.

"Sam, there's—" Del said simultaneously, then apologized with a quick, "Sorry."

"No, I just . . . first of all, I'm not used to asking for favors. Second, I don't want to put you in an awkward position."

With relief Del answered, "I appreciate your saying that. In fact, all I was going to say is that there are certain restrictions in terms of what I can divulge. Some information is considered secret or proprietary I should say. I'll tell you what I can, but I'm going to be strict about staying within legal boundaries."

"Of course." Sam nodded.

"That said, a lay person can gather a tremendous amount of information. And I can show you how to do that."

"Perfect." Sam smiled. "I'll be a good student. And uh, there's something else I should say. You know the information I'm looking for is . . . well, it's touchy. For me, I mean. I guess what I'm saying is, I'm not sure yet how far I really want to go with this search."

"Okay," Del said. "We'll take it one step at a time. Want to get started?"

Sam nodded.

Del rolled his chair closer to his desk, and she did the same. "So, you've already tried some preliminary web searches, right? What kind of problems did you have?"

Sam thought for a moment about the issues both she and Susan had encountered. "When you do a search, how do you keep it from providing thousands of irrelevant answers?"

"You have to narrow your parameters by using search limiters like quotation marks and plus signs."

She reached for her bag, pulled out a notepad and rummaged for a pencil.

He asked, "What did you want to look for first?"

"Missing children," she answered.

C-h-i-l-d-r-e-n his fleet fingers typed, then he added *f-i-n-d*. "You want to use search words that will narrow the field."

"Okay, well, that's not quite right. Actually, it has to do with children who were adopted."

Turning his head, he looked at her. "As I mentioned, I've been doing a little research on this myself, it turns out."

"Really? Why?" Sam seemed skeptical—or tense.

"Because of a case I'm working. A reporter is missing, and she did a TV series on adoption."

"On KOST?"

"Yeah, that's right."

"I saw that," Sam said.

Nodding, Del hit the back space a few times, then typed *a-d-o-p-t-e-d*.

In seconds, the screen filled with information about adoption. *Category matches*, it said, *1-16*. "Oh, that's not so bad," Sam said, "only sixteen."

"But that's categories," Del pointed out.

He watched her read, *Society and Culture; Families; Parenting; Adoption,* then Business and Economy; Companies; Children; Adoption; and the list went on and on as Del continued to hit his Down Arrow.

At last choosing a category, Del clicked on *Net Events, Adoption,* and up popped a screen called *Adoptions Evermore.* The organization was "certified by the IRS as a 501(c)(3)," promised the description, and "welcomes your tax-deductible contributions!"

Del felt Sam watching at his shoulder as images appeared— an oval photo held a picture of twins, their heads touching, their outfits in matching pink. Sam's hand darted forward to touch the screen when a coastal image appeared—a square photo of a lovely beach where a baby boy played with a bucket. Then she yanked her hand away.

A better idea occurred to him and he said, "Yahoo."

"Good news?" She asked excitedly.

"No," Del said, suppressing a laugh. "I've decided to switch to a different search engine. It's called *Yahoo.*"

"Really." Samantha Hugo sat back in her chair, clasped her hands, and tried not to fidget, watching as Del continued to wield his mouse expertly.

What popped onto the screen as a result of this search was *AdoptionAgencies.Org*, where a list of children's I.D. numbers appeared. *Gender: M, Birth date: 2/9/98, Race: Caucasian, Eye Color: Hazel*, and so it continued.

All these children, she thought. *Are they all lost?* Though their pictures weren't shown, Samantha began to imagine each shining eye, each set of fat cheeks, every pouty little mouth. As though facing a sea of bobbing babies' heads, all waiting for homes, each one cuter and more appealing than the next, Samantha's eyes glazed over, and she lost track of time.

"This isn't quite right, is it? Current adoption possibilities?" Del asked.

"What? No, no, that's not what I was looking for," she answered, pulling herself from her stupor. "It's more like a lost child."

L-o-s-t, typed Del, and a series of choices appeared. *Bereaved parents—for those who have lost a child,* said one, then *Lost child —a resource for locating abducted or runaway children.*

"No, no that's not it either," she said with a sigh.

"It would help," Del said gently, "if you could tell me what you really want to find."

Samantha looked down at her hands, turned them over, then over again, and looked into his dark eyes. "What if a child—an adult child—were looking for a parent he'd lost years before? Or what if a parent were looking for a child?"

"A child given up for adoption, right?"

She nodded.

Turning back to the screen, Del paused, his fingers poised over the keyboard. "I've found sometimes second-guessing the search function doesn't work so well. Let's try going direct." With that he typed *Find my* . . . "Son, right?"

"Son." Inhaling sharply, she did her best to remain calm. The idea that she could sit here—at a desk, watching someone type the very words that rolled over and over in her mind . . . through the fiber of the dreams that now woke her each morning with a silent shout . . . the idea that someone could type these words and that her son might appear on this screen—was almost more than she could bear.

She wanted to leap up and run out of the office, but she also wanted to stay, to hover closer to Del's shoulder, to touch the screen, to step—like Alice through the looking glass—into this virtual world that held the secrets of her life.

After the tiny "please wait" hourglass finally disappeared, several choices sprang to the screen, each of them seemingly irrelevant, until Del chose one and clicked. *Found At Last*, the headline read. And the two new friends sat in silence as they read the story of a man who, obsessed with finding the first-born he'd never known, pursued clues till he found him. A picture with two smiling—and strikingly similar—faces appeared.

"Something like that?" asked Del.

"Yes, something like that," said Samantha, breathless. Could such a glowing reunion await her in some golden future? *Don't even think about it!* She tried stanching the flow of her feelings, but it was like standing helplessly in a mudslide, watching a bluff shift its massive weight in her direction. Her hand rose to her throat as though she were choking, but she dropped it back in her lap when Del turned to her with a question.

"So, do we want to put in some actual parameters here? What are the names?"

"Try Hugo," she suggested.

Delmar Johnson typed in the name, discomforted by his own duplicity. Of course, he had already *done* this search for himself and now had to pretend he hadn't. He already knew Samantha Hugo was the mother of a live-born son. The tidbit he'd found so intriguing was that Jack Sawyer was listed as the father. Further, the child named Gregory was listed as "legitimate," indicating Samantha and Jack had been married at the time. *You never know how many connections exist in a small town,* he thought. *Will she tell me, or will she want to keep this a secret?*

What the "Hugo" search returned was an encoded page that required legal or law enforcement clearance. "I've got something here," he explained, "but the record is sealed."

"I see," she said. He watched as she chewed her lip, reading the warning on the screen. "Okay, let's try something else," she said. "I have been getting some other help. Try the name Chernak."

Even as Del tried to keep surprise out of his expression, he noticed that Sam looked suddenly clammy and pale. "Care for some water?" he asked. "I could use some."

Gotta buy myself a couple of minutes. While his own mind raced to process the alarm of recognition set off by the familiar name, Del stepped to the water cooler. He pulled two clean paper cups from the holder. *The woman I met at Clarke Shipping. Is she the adoptive mother? But if Samantha already knew the name, why is she still looking? Has to be some other connection.*

Del returned to his desk, handed her one of the cups, and took his seat. Keeping his voice neutral, he asked, "That's the father's last name?"

"No, no, actually it's the name of an agency I've spoken to. They purport to provide this kind of service. And they told me something rather startling. They said my son was adopted in Santa Barbara."

"That's interesting," Del said, keeping any inflection out of his tone. *So that's it.* Del's fingers flew again, and soon *The Chernak Agency* appeared as a headline at the top of the screen. "Nothing much but an opening page, except at least they bought a domain. Not bad for a small private agency."

"What's a domain?" Sam asked.

"Just means they bought the name to use as their website." The site seemed to consist mostly of photos and testimonials of happily reunited family members. "No way to check the accuracy of these stories," he continued. "They didn't add any links, didn't give specific locations." The site was signed by Stacey and her husband. *We are the Chernaks,* it said. *We believe in your right to be a family. Let us help you.*

"Legitimate enough, I suppose," Sam mumbled almost to herself.

"Seems that way." Del leaned back in his chair, making a show of appearing unconcerned. But what he saw were pieces of a puzzle that didn't fit. *Who are these people? If the agency is legit, and viable, why is one of the principals working a temp job? And why is she putting up with an abusive spouse? How ironic the agency claims to believe in "the right to be a family."*

"Deputy Johnson—Del—I've taken enough of your time." Samantha stood suddenly, hoisting her heavy bag to her shoulder. Agitation was written all over her. "I really want to thank you."

Standing to face her, he rested his hands on his hips and smiled. "No problem. Hope it helped."

"Yes, it did. I learned a little more about computer searches. And I found out this agency was for real. Didn't want to get my hopes up if they weren't."

"You're smart to check it out," he reassured her.

"I'll see myself out. Hope your weekend is good."

"Thanks, Sam. Yours too."

She tossed him a smile. "No rest for the wicked," she said as she left the room and headed for the stairs.

Del watched her go, then returned to his computer desk. Though he generally trusted his own ability to read people, he now wished he had Sally O'Mally's higher degree of intuition. He quickly catalogued some of Samantha's reactions: from elation and expectation to fear and apprehension—she'd run the gamut. Clearly, she had her suspicions about this Chernak agency, despite her apparent reassurance. And now, he had suspicions of his own.

Quickly, he looked up the sealed record and confirmed for himself that the child had been adopted in Santa Barbara. *But how did the Chernak Agency discover this?* They would have no legitimate way to penetrate a sealed record. Therefore, their source could only be via some sort of black market for information, indicating there was a corrupt source somewhere and that the Chernaks had access to it.

It wouldn't take long to run "Chernak" through the NCIC database to see if the name popped up through the National Crime Information Center. Besides, the office was now technically closed for the day. If he had to, he could pull another all-nighter.

Part II

Admissions

"Though silence is not necessarily an admission,
it is not a denial, either."

—Marcus Tullius Cicero

Chapter 10

Sally O'Mally had endured the crowded fight to Little Rock on Saturday uncomplaining, since she'd grabbed the last available seat.

Night had fallen soft in Arkansas. The crickets were deep into their evening song as the rental car's tires crunched gravel to the end Mama's driveway. Sally opened her car door, lifted her arms in a satisfying stretch, and inhaled deeply of the warm, humid evening.

She'd smiled to herself at seeing the glow of the homestead's yellow porch light. It would be on all night. Her mother Glenda O'Mally would insist on it. *For those who know their way, and those who don't*, she'd say.

The soft creak of a porch swing carried easily in the night air. "There you are, Mama!" Sally hefted her bag to the front porch, dropped it, and leaned down to give her mother a long hug. "I didn't see you sittin' out here watchin' the traffic."

"Well, girl, I ain't watchin' the traffic, I'm lookin' at the moon."

Sally smiled.

"Take a load off, girl. Not that what you carry on that little frame is what I'd call a load."

As Mama moved over to make room, Sally sat down next to her on the swing, the gentle creaking adding peacefully to the night sounds.

"Sorry for the short notice," Sally said quietly.

"No trouble, Sally Girl. Let's go in for a nice cup of tea. Saved you a piece of chocolate cream pie."

"You said the magic word, Mama. Chocolate!"

While Mama chuckled, Sally lifted her bag and watched her mother open the screen door. Sally'd been waiting for that screech. More than any other sight or sound, it made her feel she was home.

Delmar Johnson had set aside tonight for the review of the Chris Christian VCR tapes.

He'd made special arrangements with the missing reporter's former television station to gain access to her most recent broadcast tapes. Whatever stories she'd been working on at the time might provide some clues to her disappearance. At the very least, he'd get a sense of who she was. He'd picked up the tapes himself from KOST-TV, and they had to be returned in a timely fashion. But not before he gave them a thorough viewing. *Tonight's the night.*

Technically, he shouldn't be racking up overtime on a Saturday night, but it didn't matter, as he'd be doing this on his own time. When a case wouldn't let him alone, he often found the best time to work was into the wee hours, when phones didn't ring and colleagues didn't interrupt. He justified his marginal breach of protocol by reassuring himself he could catch up on his other cases, starting tomorrow.

On his list was a visit to Morro Bay to follow up on Stacey Chernak. His friend Gladys Wilson worked with her at Clarke

Shipping, but also volunteered at a local domestic violence shelter and had mentioned Mrs. Chernak as a possible victim. Clarke Shipping itself was a company whose name had come up regarding another matter, so a stop there might prove useful for several reasons. He might also drive farther south to Santa Barbara to follow up on that sea otter killing that'd happened there. Though investigation of an animal death was hardly within his job description, this time the otter had been shot, and the local wildlife authorities had agreed to keeping him informed should ballistics indicate any connection to human crimes.

Though still relatively new to the SLO County Sheriff's Department Special Projects Unit, already he had a reputation as a maverick. Under orders from his supervisor Detective Rogers, Delmar had interviewed Mr. Joseph Calvin three months earlier. Calvin had been a friend of Ms. Christian, eventually concerned about her unexplained absence. Del had conducted the interview at Calvin's estate in Santa Barbara. But then he'd taken it upon himself to meet Calvin in Santa Maria, because he'd promised access to Chris Christian's condo, to which Calvin had a key.

This was unusual, as the woman wasn't yet officially missing. Captain Sandoval had said that had taken matters too far. And though nothing official had been inserted in Del's personnel jacket, the verbal admonition still stung.

Had the slight reprimand been racially motivated? Del didn't think so. But, as the only African American officer in the unit, he had no choice but to hold himself to a more rigorous standard than his fellows. He'd heard that complaint from female colleagues in Los Angeles, but there were no women in the SPU.

Perhaps to distract himself—or maybe just to give himself something pleasant to offset the sour residue of the professional slap—Del had decided to have an early dinner at the Lighthouse Tavern. He'd only heard about it since moving here but had no firsthand experience.

There were several real lighthouses on the Central Coast: Point Hueneme at Oxnard, Point Conception in Santa Barbara, and Point San Luis in Avila Beach, all to the south; and Point Sur near Monterey farther north. Between them stood the Piedras Blancas light just north of Milford-Haven—the closest local lighthouse, now automated and inaccessible to visitors.

He'd been curious as to why Milford-Haven had only this pseudo-light . . . realistic enough to fool the eye, but without the powerful beam that would be visible from the sea. So, after a long morning run and a session at the gym down in Morro Bay, he'd gone home to shower, shave, and dress in some pressed khaki chinos and a dark brown blazer. Then, out of uniform for once, he'd driven to the Tavern to introduce himself.

As he'd pulled into the parking lot, he'd been unsure whether he'd find a tourist trap or a quaint coastal gem. As it turned out, he liked the place and its owner. Michael Owen looked him straight in the eye when he talked and seemed devoted to the culinary craft, sharing details of the special he was preparing for this evening's menu. Owen was also apparently a successful businessman, as his restaurant had the reputation of drawing both tourists and locals.

Though Del was officially off duty, he'd be in the Sheriff's offices later, so he ordered a plain soda.

"Ice and slice?" Michael asked.

"Please." Sitting at the bar would give him a view into the kitchen, so he took a seat at one of the comfortable high stools. He ordered fish-and-chips, apparently a regular item here and a favorite of his. After ordering, he inquired about the history of the building, wondering why what appeared to be a real light-house was not being used as such.

Michael delivered Del's drink and, rag in hand, automatically wiped down the gleaming bar. Then, picking a clean, dry cloth, he began polishing a glass. "Odd thing is, there are actually *two* 'unreal' lighthouses here in Milford-Haven."

"Is that right?" Del asked, taking a sip of the chilled soda. He might occasionally have a beer at home, but he seldom drank while out, and never drank alcohol while on call, which was pretty much always, given his job.

"Well, this one's not really a fake. It's real enough. Just never got commissioned."

According to the story Michael recounted, if Aberthol Sayer—an entrepreneur from Milford Haven, Wales, in the 1880s—had succeeded with his ambitious plan, the American Milford-Haven would've had its own lighthouse.

Sayer had moved to California in 1875, the successful owner of a small shipping firm. Taking stock of developments on the Central Coast, he couldn't help but notice what a bustling export center the Piedras peninsula had become for the region. Convinced that Milford-Haven's smaller point of land slightly farther south posed a treacherous obstacle for fishermen, Sayer had believed that by having its own light, the area could develop a profitable fishing industry. He'd thus gone to the trouble and expense of having a defunct lighthouse on the coast of Wales dismantled and transported on one of his ships across the Atlantic, then cross-country by rail from New York to California.

Certain he'd receive the appropriate commission from the U.S. Lighthouse Board, which had been established in 1852, he'd reassembled the structure at Milford-Haven. He even had his public relations slogan ready to use: "The first lighthouse to shine on two oceans." But because he failed to receive the requisite approval, he was never allowed to install a working Fresnel in the tower. He did install a lesser light, but nothing bright enough to "confuse navigation," as the Board had admonished.

"So, when you took it over, you converted it into the Tavern?" Del asked.

"Yup. Big job. This adjacent building is the restaurant. Next door on the actual lighthouse ground floor, we have a mini-museum shop. T-shirts, mugs, keychains, that sort of thing. We've got an office up on the next floor, up the spiral stairs. Then a small sleeping room above that, which comes in handy some-times. Nothing much above that except the light itself—a replica that doesn't put out a seaworthy signal. I mean, it's blacked out on the ocean side, per Coast Guard regulations. But it casts a short beam toward land so our customers can find us."

"Ingenious," Del said. "And, obviously, successful."

"Touch wood," Michael replied, putting his palm on the gleaming wooden bar.

"So where's this other fake located?"

"Farther north, toward San Simeon. But it's deserted."

"Oh, okay, that's what I've glimpsed in passing. If the build-ing's unused, I guess it's always dark," Del surmised.

"Right. It's hard to see because it's on private land, way out on a promontory, where it's lower than Highway 1 and shrouded by the coastal pines that've grown much taller since the building was first erected."

"Who owns it?" Del inquired.

"Family heirs who don't live here. There've been rumors of a resort going in."

"That would make a big change, shift the character of things in Milford-Haven," Del remarked.

"Yeah, but every time *that* notion rears its ugly head, the town fathers and mothers go nuts. Not really a worry, though. Between the coastal commission, the historic preservationists, and the heirs' inability to make any decisions, it'll never happen."

Del took a sip of his soda. "Ever been inside?"

"Naw. I don't know anyone who has. Heard a lot of stories, though," Michael admitted. "Damnedest thing. Don't know why they built it. I mean, from what I understand, it's just a look-alike shell."

"At a glance, pretty realistic," Del commented.

"From the outside, yeah," Michael agreed. "The original owners built it back in the 1950s."

"Looks like it's attached to a mansion. Must have a cost a fortune, even then."

Michael laughed. "Yeah. Well, nothing on the level of the Hearst property farther north."

"The Hearst Castle? No, I guess not."

"Still," Michael went on, "the owners were a wealthy couple, private almost to the point of secrecy. They had traveled, collected treasures, and this was what they built to enjoy it all, so they say."

"I guess if you have that kind of money, you can do whatever you like," Del reflected. "What were their names?"

"Well, it was something like Joan."

"No, I meant the last name," Del clarified.

"Yeah, that *is* the last name. I mean, I never saw it written down, just heard stories. 'J' pronounced 'Y'."

"Hispanic?" Del asked.

"Naw. Welsh is what I heard."

"Welsh? Hmm, not familiar. Might be fun to research."

"If you like that sort of thing," Michael said, finishing with the glassware.

A waiter delivered Del's plate—crisp, piping hot, lightly breaded fish, french fries, coleslaw, and a big wedge of lemon. "Man, this looks great," he said, salivating while he slipped the napkin onto his lap.

"Good, good," the restauranteur said. "Whatever happens to that old estate, I hope it stays private, and never becomes some huge tourist thing. People move here to get away from that kind of thing, you know? We all need to make a living, but we like it peaceful."

"I hear that," Del agreed.

"Enjoy!" Michael exhorted, leaving his customer to his meal.

Del sank his teeth into his first bite, savoring the fresh flavor. As he continued to relish his meal, he thought further about the moribund old lighthouse. He imagined it was only a matter of time before someone bought it. Perhaps it'd be a creative type, since Milford-Haven was full of artists and "makers" of all kinds. But for now, some forty-plus years later, the lighthouse stood quietly in the shadow of trees and rugged coastline, apparently content to remain concealed and keep its secrets, whatever they might be.

As he waited for his check after an excellent meal, Del took a final sip of coffee and pressed the napkin to his lips. He turned his gaze toward the restaurant's window to marvel again at the view—a sweep of coastal scenery that would have few equals—all the more spectacular at close of day, with sunset painting vivid streaks across low-hanging clouds.

After paying his bill and thanking Michael again, Del stepped outside into the March evening. The sun had sunk into the water, the sky overhead just beginning to deepen to a Prussian blue. *Nice the days aren't quite as short as they were a few weeks ago.*

The signs of early spring were everywhere on the Central Coast. Though mornings were still often foggy, rains were no longer the steady pummelings of winter but had shifted to blustery, intermittent storms. Tiny buds dotted the deciduous trees, and just yesterday he'd seen rows of huge ice plant flowers blooming along the beach at the Cove. Now a faint trace of lavender hung in the air like the perfume of a woman who'd passed by and disappeared. *Ironic that in this season of renewal, the life of a young woman has almost certainly been cut short.*

Chapter 11

Del's SUV rumbled to life, and he made the forty-minute drive down Highway 1 to his workplace, glancing at a darkening sky where he could just see storm clouds hanging offshore. He suspected they'd soon overtake the coast just as his own looming angst about the case seemed certain to swamp his mood.

He parked his truck and, before locking it, lifted out the box of borrowed tapes. After climbing the stairs to the front entrance and unlocking the double-glass doors he stepped into the darkened offices shared by the North Coast branch of the County Sheriff's Department and the California Department of Forestry. His footsteps rang into the quiet hallways until he stepped into the conference room and fired up the television and VCR. After loading the first cassette, he squinted in the flickering illumination from the video screen, doing his best to read the button designations of the VCR remote control.

He was hoping no one from Forestry had the same idea about using the conference room any time tonight. It'd been a matter of economic necessity, placing the San Luis Obispo County Sheriff's off-site offices in shared space. The new building lacked the charm of the old-California stucco municipal structures, but Del had settled in comfortably and—thanks to his computer expertise—enjoyed being regarded as the technical hot-shot.

At the moment, he wasn't so sure he deserved the title. He squinted again at the VCR. Certain he'd finally discerned the difference between Fast Forward and Search, he pressed something, and the blue screen sprang to life with the rapidly talking figure of a blond woman standing in a playground. Horizontal lines of static stood still as the figure raced through her story and Del struggled to find the Stop button.

I better watch this again, he thought. Rewinding the tape, he started it again by hitting Play, deciding to be more patient with the opening designations. White letters on a field of royal blue read:

KOST-TV NEWS FILE

KOST SUNDAY NEWS MAGAZINE

REPORTER: CHRIS CHRISTIAN

ARCHIVE NUMBER: 0395749:0CC889A

SUBJECT: ADOPTION [THREE-PART SERIES]

SEGMENT ONE:

"WILL THIS LOVE LAST?:

IF I ADOPT THIS BABY, WILL SHE BE MINE FOREVER?"

A second or two after the writing faded, Chris Christian appeared. Del gulped air, the sight of her animated form causing his breath to come in sudden jerks. *Nice of you to show up for our date . . . even if you are a ghost.*

Del hit the pause button. *Get a grip, man!*

He hit Play again, willing himself to catalog the details of her appearance. *Blond hair, tan blazer, white blouse, black slacks. Flawless on-camera makeup. Professional appearance and calm demeanor inspires confidence, as does speaking with authority.*

While the camera lens pulled back to reveal a playground, Chris advanced, clasped her hands, looked down, then up at the camera, all the while introducing the topic of her show. If Del remembered his broadcast terminology, this would be what they called the Teaser.

"Adoption," said Chris in a news-voice. "It's one of the most consuming interests among Americans today." She stepped toward a swing and sat carefully in its leather strap. "Approximately three thousand five hundred children are adopted annually in the United States, with the trend rising more than 80 percent since 1990, the year November was named National Adoption Month. And the rules have changed."

Del hit the Pause button again. Ghostly light reflected onto the slatted blinds in the closed room. The image of the reporter —crisp, animated, and *alive*—disturbed him. To give himself a few seconds' break, he glanced at the pale gray walls offset by black trim and looked up at the unilluminated bulbs that stared back like glassy, unseeing eyes. He turned back to the TV, hit Play, and watched the screen as the camera zoomed in on Chris's face.

"Adoption used to be a private and irrevocable matter. If you, as a parent, gave up your child for adoption, you knew you would never see that child again. You also knew it would be better for the child not to suffer the confusion of meeting a parent he or she had never known.

"Each state has its own laws regarding adoption, and, as a general rule, records were not legally sealed but were kept strictly confidential by a 'gentlemen's agreement'—which would now be considered an antiquated euphemism.

"While in most cases it's still difficult to find missing parents—or a long-lost child—recently developed websites mean that frustrating searches now take weeks or months, rather than years, and the Internet is brimming with information concerning all aspects of adoption. No matter how valuable adoptive parents may have been in the life of a child, as a nation, we seem consumed with uncovering our biological connections.

"Tonight we take you on the first of a three-part journey into the mysteries and emotional turmoil of adoption. If you adopt a child, will it truly be yours forever?"

After a brief pause, and a flash of white letters reading INSERT COMMERCIAL A, the program resumed. "A child of five is taken one day from the only home she's ever known," said Chris's voice-over. Del watched the screen as a wailing child held her arms out, yelling, "Mommy! Daddy!" while the adoptive parents stood paralyzed, tears streaming down their faces. On the far side of a police car, the couple—apparently birthparents—stood waiting to reclaim the child they'd given up several years earlier.

Three more three-minute reports followed, interviews with both sets of parents, interviews with Child Service professionals, and a wrap-up by Chris. Pressing Rewind, Del sat in the darkened room, deeply affected by the raw emotion he'd just witnessed. *Everyone in the story had rights; but no one seemed to have achieved a happy ending.*

Del realized he was getting drawn into the story, losing track of his own goal, which was to research the reporter. *Must mean she's doing a good job*, he acknowledged. Determined to keep an objective perspective, he hit Play and began the tape again from the beginning. This time it was details he was after — not details of the story, but of the journalist and her surroundings. *That playground . . . Miller Street Elementary in Santa Maria? I can check the photo file. Makes sense—shooting the footage close to home.*

As the segment played through, he looked at the background, pausing the tape intermittently to jot down notes or to see if he recognized the face of a passerby. *But nothing seems remarkable. I need to take an inning stretch.* He ejected the tape and held it in his hands for a moment. *Who else did I see on this tape and not recognize? Was it someone hiding in plain sight who wished you harm?*

Del started up the machine again, the blue screen and white letters now familiar.

KOST-TV NEWS FILE
REPORTER: CHRIS CHRISTIAN
ARCHIVE NUMBER: 0395749:0CC889B
SUBJECT: ADOPTION [THREE-PART SERIES]
PART TWO:
"FINDING MY ROOTS:
SEARCHING FOR THE PARENTS I NEVER KNEW"

He watched as the blue screen gave way to Chris Christian, standing once again in the playground. She began her second report with the same opening sentence. "Adoption: it's one of the most consuming interests among Americans today."

Then she introduced the topic of her second segment. "Many adopted children grow up in stable and happy homes, never giving much thought to the fact that their adoptive parents are not blood relations. It is they who are there for them day in and day out. It is they who are there from the first skinned knee to the achievement of graduation, with everything good and bad that happens in between. In every meaningful sense of the word, these people are family, the parents who cared enough to rear the child. Why is it, then, that increasing numbers of adopted individuals begin a search for their birthparents? Find out in tonight's segment, Part Two, 'Finding My Roots: Searching for the Parents I Never Knew.'"

Glued to the screen in the small, dark room, Del took in story after story of young people who felt increasingly unsettled until they went through the sometimes long and frustrating search for original parents. "These people feel they have 'rights,'" explained Chris's voice-over. "The right to know their own physical history, the right to confront birthparents." Chris's coverage revealed a young woman who begins her search and finds a mother who'd been raped as a teenager. The mother wants nothing to do with the child she'd tried to forget; the father's still in jail, serving out his sentence. Was the young woman happier for knowing the details of her birth? *Can't see how.*

But another story turns out very differently: a young man is himself a new father, and the baby suffers from a rare disease. By tracking down his genetic parents, he uncovers needed information about his child's health, and begins a slow—but apparently fulfilling—process of healing.

Pressing Stop, Del stood and stretched, jotting down a few more notes, then exited to the corridor to retrieve a cup of instant coffee from the break room. His hot drink in hand, he returned to the video room and resumed his screening session. The white letters said:

KOST-TV NEWS FILE

REPORTER: CHRIS CHRISTIAN

ARCHIVE NUMBER: 0395749:0CC889B

SUBJECT: ADOPTION [THREE-PART SERIES]

PART THREE:

"A CHANGE OF HEART:

FINDING A CHILD GIVEN UP FOR ADOPTION"

Chris again began her segment in the same location, with the same words, then continued with: "Say you found out you were pregnant at the age of sixteen. Your family threatened to disown you if you kept the child. You were not yet out of high school, and your only hope of employment was waitressing, but the restaurants that offered to hire you would not allow you to work while you were pregnant. You decide to have the baby anyway—and then realize it's more than you can handle.

"What if twenty years have gone by and you've decided it's time to find the long-lost child? Get the answer in tonight's special report: 'A Change of Heart: Finding a Child Given Up for Adoption.'"

Del fast-forwarded through the next blank spot in the tape and pressed Play when he saw Chris talking again. "Tonight, in Part Three of our series, we look at adoption from the point of view of a parent who gave up a child years earlier and now wants to reconnect. Of all the difficult aspects of adoption, this one is perhaps the most emotionally charged."

Over images of a middle-aged man walking from his mailbox to his front door, Chris narrated. "We begin our story with this man—we'll call him Edward—who was told only last year that he has a son: a son who by now is twenty-five years old."

Inside the house, the man opened an envelope and began to read as Chris's voice-over continued. "After months of persistent effort, he receives news. A search firm has located the boy he'd never known existed." Tears welled and the man wiped his eyes.

A quick cut took the viewer to an airport scene where father and son—the physical resemblance unmistakable— shook hands, then embraced, the mutual bear hug lasting for several seconds.

Chris's narration continued. "Now Edward and his son have been reunited. Although this was a joyous reunion, it has made life for both men more complicated. Both have other families; both have anger about the opportunity denied them by the boy's mother, who long ago decided to conceal the fact that another family member existed. Since she died several years ago, no one has the option of asking her burning questions, nor does she have the option of explaining her choice.

"Complex as this can be for men, in many ways it's even more so for women." The story continued as Chris, now in a different outfit in footage shot on a different day, was followed by the camera into someone's office. "A woman now in her fifties agreed to meet with us, to explain some of her sorrow and some of her pain. But she's not just any woman; she's Dean of Students at Coronado Community College. Today we meet with Dr. Sheila Swain, PhD." Del noticed Chris Christian's voice was still unwaveringly authoritative but perhaps more empathic than in the previous interview. She was, after all, not any more immune to these stories than he was, watching from the safe distance of videotape.

After introductions, the attractive, well-spoken African American woman began her story. "I was just seventeen when I found out I was pregnant," explained Sheila. "My mother'd reared us alone, and getting rid of the baby wasn't even discussed."

"So you gave birth even though you weren't married?"

"Yes. There wasn't going to be a marriage with the father of my child. He was just a child himself really, though, of course, I couldn't see that at the time. He wasn't ready for the responsibilities of fatherhood and made himself scarce."

"So it was you and your mother."

Dr. Swain looked away, then back at her interviewer. "You see, it was, in fact, the wrong paradigm to be working with, but we had no means to change it, or so we thought."

"Explain what you mean by 'wrong paradigm,'" Chris said, the camera angled over her shoulder.

Drawing herself up till her posture was perfect, Dr. Swain briefly squinted her almond-shaped eyes, tension pursing her full lips. "Well, the assumption in the black community was that the father would not be there. It'd happened so often through our history, beginning with the enforced breaking up of black families during the time of slavery and continuing with the systemic exclusion of bread-winning fathers from subsidized housing, that it became a consistent part of our heritage."

Her voice husky with emotion held in check, her diction flawless and dignified, she continued. "Therefore, the only father figures young black children grew up with were the local preachers, and it was the churches that became the centers of the community. It was in the churches that families got everything from a reason to dress right to a good square meal."

Flashing back to his own childhood in South-Central Los Angeles, Del thought about Sundays with his mother. Scrunching his face, he'd endure the endless rituals of hair-combing and tie-tying. His shoes polished, his coat brushed, his hands and face scrubbed almost raw, he'd slide as low as possible down the wide front seat of their third-hand car, as it rattled off to church, hoping his friends didn't see him in his newly cleaned state. Mother'd been one of the pillars of the AME Church just a few blocks away; Sundays were the highpoint of her week, especially when it was her turn to cook.

As services droned on, he'd puzzle with God's justice and the vengeance he saw on his streets, trying to reconcile the irreconcilable, jumping up whenever the music started, singing and swaying with the congregation.

But best of all were the smells coming up through the old wooden floorboards. The cooks in the basement kitchen knew what they were doing, tantalizing the sinners to repent and promising the faithful a foretaste of heaven. Fried chicken, grits, fresh cornbread, warm salted gravy, greens, lemon pie—all were being prepared by the mothers, clad in their starched aprons to protect their Sunday outfits. To disobey these formidable women meant severe punishment, but they rewarded obedience with mouth-watering, soul-satisfying victuals exquisite enough to provide a lifetime of culinary memories.

Del realized he'd lost track of the tape as it had played through, and he pressed Rewind. Rubbing his eyes, he resumed near where he'd left off. " . . . good square meal." Yes, those were the words that had touched off his brief reverie.

Sheila continued, "As a young woman I had no expectation of creating a nuclear family. My concept of extended family was excellent—there were aunts, neighbors, friends of all ages, coming and going through a busy household. But generally, the women were a constant, and the men were transient."

"So you intended to rear your child with the help of your mother and your aunts?" asked Chris.

"Yes. And for a while everything was more or less normal. I managed to go back to school part time. Mother worked part time, but then she fell ill and didn't live."

"Your mother . . . died."

"Yes. I wasn't able to keep the house. For a while I lived with my aunt, but that didn't work out for long. I was offered a college scholarship but would have been disqualified had I not attended school full time. Eventually, I had to give my child up for adoption."

The scene shifted to Sheila Swain performing her various duties, counseling students, meeting with parents. Chris's voice-over said, "Dr. Swain's academic accomplishments are considerable. After graduating from Howard University summa cum laude, she received her PhD from Harvard and has built a life helping students of color—particularly the underprivileged—to reach their own goals."

The camera followed as Chris joined Sheila Swain on a walk across campus. Chris asked, "Dr. Swain, do you have a final word for our viewers?"

Stopping, the Dean turned, her expression growing even more thoughtful than usual. "I never have found my daughter, though I did try for several years." Maintaining her elegant bearing, she bowed her head slightly, then lifted it. "I would say to young women today, consider carefully putting yourself in a position to conceive a child. The soul that touches yours will leave you forever changed. The child you abandon will, in some ways, never abandon you."

Del stopped the tape, shaken. This woman, with her dignity and power, could be his own mother. Yet Ruby Johnson had held onto him, sacrificing every opportunity for advancement to make sure he got ahead instead. If only she'd received the education she should have, she might have looked and sounded like this Dr. Swain, an expert in her field, a woman with means and the respect of her peers.

His mom had always been beautiful to *him* no matter what. But he knew Ruby had been a real beauty. She was sought after by men, admired by women. Ample-figured, long-limbed, and big-hearted, Ruby had the largest kitchen in the neighborhood, and her table was always set. Children of every age gravitated there, where they'd received food for body, mind, and soul.

Del remembered one boy half his age, who—on the verge of sinking his teeth into a piece of hot cornbread—had been asked by Ruby, "How do you spell *watershed?*" Because he'd tried to spell the word, he'd gotten a double portion of home-made pea soup that day. When he joined a gang a few years later, Ruby had asked him, "How do you spell *stupid?*" Had anyone else stood up to him, he or she would've been killed. In front of Ruby, he averted his eyes, looked down and walked out, issuing orders to his henchmen to leave Ruby's house alone.

With a new appreciation for what his mother had done, Del once again pressed Play. Perhaps, after all, Ruby did have part of what Dr. Swain had: the respect of her community. And if he could ask his mother now, he knew she'd count the riches of Spirit to be far more estimable than those of this world.

Del peered out the window of the still-darkened room, watching starlight dance on the shallow coastal waters. The scene failed to make its usual impression, as his mind was filled with images from the videotapes.

His reaction to Chris Christian's television series on adoption was intellectual, true. Her intelligence and insight were impressive, drawing the viewer into the issue she wanted to illuminate. But he was aware another reaction gripped him too, something visceral and emotional. He couldn't seem to disentangle any one part of his response, and all of it roiled together through his gut like an undigested mass.

Compelling in its depth and honesty, the reports revealed a great deal about the emotional landscape of the nation and the increasingly complex web of society. *This reporter was doing good work,* he thought, *before she disappeared.* More than ever, he was determined to find her, discover her fate.

Thin though it was, he'd come up with one possible connection, and that was the name "Clarke" written more than once in her diary. He'd found it jotted on a page from several months earlier, unfortunately not in connection with anything else. No appointment was written, and the name didn't show up in other notes she'd kept on pending articles. More recently, he'd seen it again, this time circled several times, as though she'd been on the phone doodling or had realized something and decided to pursue it.

With its less-usual spelling, the name "Clarke" had been easy to find in the Central Coast directory. Clarke Shipping was located in Morro Bay. Of course, it didn't mean this was *the* Clarke, but it seemed a place to start. His idea was to appear in the offices of Clarke Shipping during the lunch hour. Presumably, few people would be available, and he'd be less conspicuous. With any luck, he'd find a receptionist or secretary who might say something to him casually without bosses looking on.

What trail was Chris Christian following, and where did it lead her? Del knew from reviewing her work schedule that she was a "roving" reporter, often out of town for several days, weeks, or even months, working on a story. She'd also racked up plenty of overtime and had vacation days coming. These elements—plus the facts that no family members had filed a Missing Persons report and no body had turned up—conspired to keep her case sidelined. As a member of Special Projects Unit, Del had inherited the case. He was now sufficiently intrigued that he knew he wouldn't have had to be assigned this case; he'd have *asked* for it.

Del ejected the final videocassette and stacked it carefully with the others, knowing he might want to review one or more of them yet again. Turning off the VCR and television, he grabbed his coffee cup, returned it to the small kitchenette down the hall before exiting the building and locking it for the night.

Night had closed in by now, and he knew the moon wouldn't rise till 1:47 a.m. He liked keeping track of small details like sunrise and sunset, temperatures and prevailing winds. They could become markers in the cases he tracked, and it'd long been a habit he'd nurtured, though only since moving to the Central Coast had high and low tides been added to his list.

As he glanced around the parking lot and pressed his SUV's remote, he noticed the momentary silence of the crickets in response to its chirp, but they soon resumed their evening song. The intoxicating aroma of orange blossoms wafted past as he climbed into the driver's seat, and again he thought of the fragrance of a ghostly woman who wasn't there.

Chris Christian had been working hard to shed light on various subjects of use and of interest to the public. Her reports were deep and thoughtful, not the usual three-minute news features that only skimmed the surface.

Here she'd been tracking the twisting eddies and currents of childhoods where children were born into troubled circumstances. He wanted to think that all children were born into the sunshine of a lovely and loving world complete with tender protection. Instead, she'd shown her audience a shadowy realm where the only light that reached the children was deflected, like sunlight that reached the Earth by bouncing off the moon. It left these lives to form in the shadows, influenced by things they couldn't see, struggling against invisible forces.

Her thorough thoughtfulness had enrolled him, Del realized. They were in league now, Del and his absent Chris, holding hands across an empty void, but equally determined to shine a bright light where it might do the most good.

The hour was late. Deputy Delmar Johnson had a big day ahead.

Chapter 12

Jack Sawyer had slept poorly, and Sunday morning had found him lying spread-eagled under sweaty sheets, staring at the drooping cottage-cheese ceiling and thinking about his long-departed mother.

How had she managed, alone for all those months and years? The military had been his father's taskmaster, an exacting mistress jealous of wives and families. Some dependents followed their leaders from country to country. But not in wartime. And not against the father's wishes. It'd been important to Dad to know his wife and child were safe in the States, out of harm's way. It'd never occurred to him a boy might need his father to grow up right.

If Jack still carried any childhood longing, he dismissed it now. Swinging his legs out from the rumpled mass of sheets, he trudged down the hall and performed his morning ritual of reheating coffee in his battered soup pan.

As the bitter brew began hissing around the edges of the heating pan, he decided today was the perfect time to cheat on himself and steal a smoke. He'd resume his battle to be a non-smoker tomorrow. For now, he reached into the cabinet high over his refrigerator and pulled out the leftover box of Camels he'd flung there a month earlier.

Stepping onto his weather-beaten balcony, he settled into the one remaining deck chair. Decrepit though it was, its faded fabric would still hold his weight. Leaning back, he put his bare feet up on the railing and winced at a splinter. He took a sip of the hot, acrid liquid in his chipped mug, then lit a cigarette and scowled at its stale taste.

Daylight savings had just ruined the clock again, and Jack found himself sitting in the dark at six a.m. In a way, the blackness suited him. *Soon enough, light will burst over the horizon and the hassles of the day will start.* Meanwhile, he had a moment of peace.

The day would bring its share of annoyances, each one of which he'd take personally, since that was the only way he knew how to take anything. Now that he was ignoring Sally and her little problem, his personal life had virtually no content, and his thoughts moved him back to his work. His various building projects were going well enough—both the honest and the questionable—though only the ones in which his own schemes were intertwined were of any real interest to him.

The Clarke house—its proportions huge, its design dynamic —nagged at him like a dull, intermittent toothache. *It's not really that thrilling a piece of architecture,* he told himself. *Nothing I couldn't have come up with before, if I'd chosen to.* Yet secretly, the design excited him more than any project he'd undertaken in ages. Years ago, he'd buried his talent for marrying structure to site. At long last it was surfacing—thanks to a gutsy client and a decent budget. With license to "be creative," Jack saw this job as a gateway to the next level.

The client did have his eccentricities. The reinforced sub-terranean room without windows was one; the hidden area tucked in the rafters was another. But Jack told himself these were just a billionaire's quirks.

What did *he* care if someone wanted to have a secret room? The very words conjured up childhood fantasies. Indeed, as a child, what wouldn't he, himself, have given for a secret room of his own? A private, inviolate place, where grownups were admonished not to enter and where friends were invited only by clandestine pact after being sworn to secrecy.

How long would Mother have put up with that? he wondered. *What kind of a boy was I? What was it like raising me largely on her own?* He had fleeting memories of his insistence on having his way, of his mother's tolerance with his aggressions, and of her high spirits during their moments alone.

Jack and his mother'd had to move after Dad's death, no longer welcome in the Army housing. Mother had found a new house for them, promising they'd have a puppy, a garden, and a swing. But till the furniture arrived, they had those magical days and nights in the empty house.

"I wanna play Lincoln Logs!" he demanded the first night.

"Our toys didn't come yet, honey."

"Let's go outside!"

"No, it's dark and very cold outside, Jack."

Jack lifted his eyes to the mantel and saw the photos Mommy always moved from house to house. There in a small silver frame was Mommy as a child, sporting a pink tutu, proudly showing off her costume. Jack's fertile mind then arrived at the perfect solution.

"Dance, Mommy!"

Standing, she put her hands on her hips for a moment, mimicking the photo of herself. Then she launched into ballet movements—a turn here, a twist there, arms lifted gracefully, her lithe figure spinning the perimeter of the room. When he stood to join her, she grasped his arms, swung him wide in the empty room, his squeals of delight echoing against the bare walls.

Jack had never been given the chance to know his son. He'd have done anything to be with his own boy. But Samantha had shattered his chance at fatherhood, betraying him not once, but twice. She'd had a child without his knowledge. Later she'd given him up for adoption. The depth of the betrayal staggered him, the woman's brazen disregard sending shock waves to his bruised ego. *How could any woman dare to keep such a thing from a man?* he wondered. *How could she not see her responsibility, take her place, do her duty?*

Consumed with playing the role of the injured party, Jack ignored the irony that Fate, in her wisdom, had chosen to present him with another child.

The hopes he'd planted in Sally O'Mally's heart for so long had been driven from his mind like blackbirds scared away from a grain-field. And in the faint beams of early dawn, his second chance at fatherhood was slipping away even more silently than had his first.

He thought back to his former wife—the woman he'd fallen for so hard he'd never again breathed the same. He'd always imagined having a child with her, had tasted only the dregs of bitterness when that dream had drained away with Samantha's desertion.

Yet now for the first time, he wondered—and would never know—what it must have been like for Samantha to bring a child into the world all alone.

Samantha had prepared herself for this moment for months, determined to do it alone. No one knew. She'd told her father she was going on a long-overdue vacation during spring break.

"How long will you be gone?" he'd asked.

"A month."

"Must be nice!" He'd paused. "No, really—you deserve it, kid. Have a ball."

Have a ball. Have a baby. She was having a baby! Part of her was so excited—so proud—she wanted to share it with someone. There was no sister. No brother. No mother. And she was adamant about not notifying Jack.

She'd gone to the hospital alone. "Father's name?" The nurse's voice lifted at the end of the question as she filled in yet another form.

"There's no father," Sam said.

The nurse looked at her over the top of her glasses as if to ask if she believed in immaculate conception.

"I mean—the father is not known. He . . . he doesn't want to know." Sam bit her lip in confusion and embarrassment.

The nurse's look softened. "You'll need to put it on the birth certificate, dearie," she said.

"Jack Sawyer," Samantha whispered.

"Jack Lawyer?"

"Sawyer," Sam corrected, clutching the edges of her chair.

"Oh, as in Tom." The nurse continued writing on the form.

Sam's face contorted in her next contraction. "No . . . Jack!"

"Just rest easy, dearie. Don't get your knickers in a twist. You're gonna need your strength."

Sam refrained from pointing out she wasn't wearing any knickers.

By later that day, the nurse was proven right. "Squeeze my hand, dearie!" she said. Nurse Bowen, her name was. Miss Bowen. Sam's own private godsend.

"Let's see how far along you are." Gentle with her patient, Nurse Bowen briefly examined her: dilated to six centimeters and growing more uncomfortable by the minute. "You're doing just fine, dearie. Let me go and give Doctor a call."

"No . . . no . . . " Sam panted.

"I'll be right back!" Nurse Bowen hurried from the room and stepped to the nurses' station to use the phone.

"Doctor Ware, our Miss Hugo's at six centimeters. The head is well-applied to the cervix. The membranes ruptured sponta- neously fifteen minutes ago. I think she's going to need some help getting through transition."

"Sounds like it's time to administer our Special Cocktail," Dr. Ware ordered. "Let's use standard protocol. Call me when you think we're close."

"Yes, Doctor," she responded. Using her key to open the locked narcotic cabinet, she reached for the scopolamine and pursed her lips, ambivalent about the amnestic. Used only on its own, it induced loss of memory, but it tended to send most patients out of control—ranting and yelling, screaming and thrashing—a handful for any nurse. Damn good thing the patient doesn't re-member that, *she thought.*

Mercifully, it could be used in conjunction with an analgesic —usually morphine—which removed the pain from the patient. .. or the patient from the pain. The trick was to find the correct balance for each patient: not enough morphine, and the patient would babble; too much, and she'd be in respiratory depression.

In the right dosages, the two drugs together were referred to as "twilight sleep," though Dr. Ware always called the concoction his "special cocktail." He intended his patients to remain comfort- able, by which he meant semiconscious.

Nurse Bowen had extraordinary expertise with the needle —Sam hardly felt it going in. Now hovering in a state of partial awareness, Samantha wakened to pain, then receded into dis- jointed dreams between contractions. Eight endless hours later, she realized the voice she heard was directed at her.

"Push!" the doctor was saying. "Miss Hugo, it's time to push. Push hard now!"

She pushed with all her might. She pushed until she feared she would cause every organ in her body to exit through this strangely expanding new opening. It was unimaginable. She could think only of survival.

"Don't forget to breathe, dearie." Miss Bowen was saying. "Take a breath. That's it. Take a breath!" Sam heard her through a screen of internal noise: the roar of blood careening through her veins and arteries, the exaggerated sound of her own yells.

"I can't do this!" Sam's voice erupted into a plea with the universe. "It has to stop now! I can't do this anymore!"

"You're doing just fine, dearie, just breathe . . . you can do it —you are doing it. You're almost there."

And then the voices, the yells, the roaring, and the pain receded and ceased, fading like white sand meeting a white sky in a soft and distant landscape.

Now she was floating, like a buoy in a shallow blue lagoon. She was holding something. It was smooth and perfect, like a beach ball. It glowed with an inner light, and as it shone more brightly, it gently lifted her from sleep. It's a baby, *she thought as she crossed the threshold into consciousness.*

Awareness overtook her like dawn bursting over the horizon, and she awoke to the cold, clear light of a hospital room. Her heart throbbed in her chest as she tried to orient herself. In that ambiguous cusp between waking and sleeping, panic spun her like a top. Where's my baby? *The thought surged through her,* filling her with an involuntary longing to hold and nurture her child. Reflexively, she reached for the buzzer beside her bed.

In a moment, Nurse Bowen's crisp white cap appeared, haloing her beaming face. Her wide frame at first concealed the tiny bundle she carried. "He's got all his toes and fingers, dearie, and he's ready to meet his mama."

"He? He?"

"Oh, yes, dearie, you have yourself a healthy son." The good nurse placed the tiny person in her waiting arms.

Her son looked up at her, his soul seeming to unfold like a rose opening in sunlight. As she gazed into those blue depths, she *felt herself link to life as she never had before. Samantha touched his cheek, soft as a hummingbird's feathers, and watched his rosebud mouth open. Instinctively, she put him to her breast.*

While he suckled, she worried. What if I don't have enough milk for you? *And then a deeper fear seemed to grip her.* How will I ever have enough of *all* you'll need in life? How will I ever have enough?

Sally called out, "Be back in about an hour, Mama!" Not hearing a reply, Sally listened for the screen door as it banged shut behind her. *She's gettin' ready for church. I already told her I wasn't goin' with her today.*

As the morning waned, spring rose fragrant on the Arkansas farm country. Her footsteps made a satisfying crunch as she stepped onto the gravel driveway. Turning down the long, country lane, she picked up her pace.

Though she'd slept well, a peculiar dream hung at the edges of her mind, leaving her with a vague dread. In the dream, she'd planted a garden, but every plant had grown enormous, far beyond her ability to tend or even harvest. *It was a Jack-in-the-Bean-stalk nightmare.* The name suddenly struck her. *Jack . . . trying to climb out of the garden I'm growing?* Made sense in a way.

At another point in the dream, she'd been floating high above her restaurant looking down at herself, her employees, her customers . . . an image that seemed to suggest detachment or loss, or even her own death.

Shaking off the bizarre images as best she could, she breathed deeply and tried to take in the pleasures of the loamy farmland air. Her thoughts were not long her own. Jack had a way of intruding even here. Anger welled up first—a healthy sign, she decided. Better than the awful sadness and disappointment that sometimes swamped her.

It was easier, in a way, to focus on his problems than on her own. The more she thought about it, the more she realized Jack was in serious trouble. *When a bull gets himself wounded, he gets ornery; if that wound never does heal, he gets nasty.*

What you *didn't* do to a wounded bull was scare him. And that's what she'd done with her news about the pregnancy: scared him enough to charge, horns first. *But what's confusin' as pumpkins in springtime is we* talked *about the possibility of a child several times.* Jack had never seemed wildly happy about the idea. But he'd never seemed scared or angry either. He'd said things like, "I leave domestic arrangements to you."

There was something to this old-wound theory. She knew instinctively that this predated their own relationship by many years. So the next logical conclusion was that it had something to do with Samantha. He'd been particularly angry—irrationally angry—when Sally mentioned his first child, the mystery-child of Samantha's.

Had Samantha deceived him while they were married? Had she been unfaithful? Was this the source of his constant irritation at Samantha? *Of course, being irritated at her comes naturally to anyone who has any sense*, Sally thought. *Except for Miranda, who thinks she's great. But Miranda's just too nice. If a snake bit her, she'd apologize and ask if the snake had a toothache!*

It would be just like Jack to let a thing gnaw at him for years. It could be that he was still ruminating over some incident that took place during his former marriage, a real down-and-dirty affair. Or, Sally had to admit, some imagined liaison between Samantha and a man of whom Jack was jealous. Then, too, she doubted Jack himself was lily-white in the fidelity department. Probably he'd glanced at another woman himself, once or twice, and maybe more than that.

And what if he'd taken a fancy to someone and given her up to be with Samantha, only to lose them both? Now, *that* would stick in his craw. Still, there was one thing wrong with that picture: *the size of Jack's reaction to my news the other night.*

It was out of all proportion to the event, as far as she could tell. Granted, being confronted with a pregnancy was big stuff. Even so, Jack had just about lost it. She'd watched the blood rush up his neck, turn his face bright red. She'd watched him hyperventilate. He'd almost passed out. He'd been out of control. Sally's instinct told her whatever was grabbing Jack Sawyer by the throat had to be something even farther back.

Something in childhood? Something hammered into Jack when he was a little boy, something he could never forget? Perhaps his reaction was involuntary, causing him as much pain as it was causing her. Perhaps she should talk to him, tell him she understood, that she'd wait while he sorted out his feelings.

Like hell! Her own anger starting to run freely. *I'm all through being a ninnyhammer!* What she really felt like doing right this very minute was running for all she was worth, sprinting as she'd once done for her high school track team. Even though her pregnancy was still in its early stages, it didn't seem the right thing, to run now. But as the sun climbed overhead, Sally learned she could burn just as many mad-calories by walking as fast as her legs would carry her.

Sally emerged from a hot shower and changed into a long cotton dress, a pair of white socks with flat canvas shoes, and pulled on a comfortable blue cardigan.

Here in Arkansas, the main meal on weekends was served in early afternoon. Glad to be here, where her own routine was broken, she slipped easily into Mama's, joining her in the kitchen where cornbread batter was about to be poured into the hot cast iron skillet.

"Let me do that, Mama."

Glenda transferred hot gravy into a little pitcher. The two women worked in silence, as salted beans, cut corn, and mashed potatoes were placed in friendly old bowls on the well-worn kitchen table.

"Chicken's just about ready," Mama said. Sally's mouth was already starting to water, and she wondered if her appetite was changing. Reaching into the fridge for the milk container, she poured herself a full glass of the cold liquid, some remnant of the dream trailing through her mind.

Even with her back turned, Glenda seemed to notice. "Somebody walkin' on your soul?" she asked, expertly wielding tongs to lift a sizzling chicken breast from hot grease.

Taking a sip of her milk, Sally shook her head and sat down quietly, her chair scraping the linoleum floor. "Just a dream I had."

"What sort o' dream?"

"Just sorta . . . weird, like I was floatin' and then I was growin' these tomatoes—you wouldn't believe how big."

"Oh, that's not so unusual—time like this." Humming a little tune, she placed a final hot drumstick on paper towels to soak up some of the grease, then brought a plate full of perfectly browned chicken to the table.

Mama often said things that sounded enigmatic. But in her simple comment, Sally began to suspect her mother'd guessed her secret. Deciding against acknowledging it for now, Sally bided her time while her parent served their dinner. Then she closed her eyes and sank her teeth into Mama's delicious home cooking.

"Mmm . . . oooeee, I never can get it to taste this good, no matter what I do, Mama."

Chuckling contentedly, Glenda wiped her mouth. "Just takes practice, Sally girl. You'll get there."

They ate in silence while early evening sun still streamed in through the windows. Crickets began to sing, and a light breeze teased the curtains. Between bites, Sally found herself talking. "Got a decision to make, Mama."

"Mmm-hmm," she answered. "What about?"

"'Bout this man, customer o' mine."

"That Jack Sawyer man?"

Sally looked up sharply, then calmed herself with a sip of milk. "Overheard him planning' something in the rest'urnt the other day. Set me to thinkin'."

"Best not think about it at all, if it's not your bizness."

Familiar table sounds filled the room for several seconds. "Think I gotta make this my bizness. People might could get hurt."

"That does make it difficult, then."

"Comes a time a person has to speak up."

"Only your heart knows when."

Rising from the table, Sally poured more milk for both of them, then scooped some more corn onto their plates.

"What's he done, then?" Mama asked.

"Scooted right around the edges of 'vironmental rules with his buildin's." Sally chewed for a moment. "Seems to me like he mighta scooted around a few more things too."

Glenda savored another bite of chicken, mopped up gravy with a final piece of cornbread, and rose to clear the dishes. Running water into the sink, she asked, "He know you know?"

"He doesn't realize. Either that, or he thinks I'd never say."

"You ready to make an enemy?"

"Might be too late to ask that question." Sally rubbed her hands along her thighs. "Don't know what to do. Gotta decide."

Glenda looked at her. "Seems to me you already have, Sally girl. You want my permission to rat on a conniving no-good-nik? You got it."

A smile started to pull at the edges of Sally's mouth, but the impulse faded quickly as she considered the ramifications of turning Jack over to the authorities.

"That makes it easier, Mama. And harder too."

Chapter 13

Stacey Chernak feared Sundays more than she did any other day of the week.

Before dawn, she had lain perfectly still in bed, listening for the slightest sound. Her husband Wilhelm had just left, as he did every Sunday morning, driving south from their Morro Bay apartment to Santa Barbara for some undisclosed reason. After she'd fixed him a bowl of muesli, she'd seen him off. He'd instructed her to lock the door after him and return to bed for one hour. She'd obeyed and lain here since.

Only the clock told her when the hour had passed. Through the window she saw nothing but gray on gray—low fog swirling into the clouds, one indistinguishable from the other. The dimmed sky left her rooms semi-dark, shrouding them in gloom.

Daring to swing her legs out of the high bed, she tiptoed to the front door. *Everything is just as I left it: my coat on the rack, mail stacked neatly on the hall table, no difference in the angle of my boots.* She always left items near the door a particular way to give herself warning. Lately her husband seemed to enjoy sneaking back into their flat and hiding as though spying on her.

Walking quietly through the small apartment, she checked the living room and kitchen. Then, relieved, she entered the compact bathroom, locked its door, and started the water. After showering quickly, she toweled herself dry and examined her damaged face with care in the poorly lit medicine cabinet mirror. The facial bruises had begun turning yellow and brown now, the deep blue finally abating somewhat. Her neck had traces of purple, but she could cover that with a high collar. She continued to monitor her healing closely, still terrified by what the doctor had said yesterday during her annual physical.

In order to keep her job at Clarke Shipping—and to keep her status as an employee eligible for insurance through the temp agency—the exam was compulsory.

Blunt object trauma," Dr. Rensfield had said to the nurse, who wrote down his remarks. "Ulnar aspect of forearm."

"Excuse us for a moment," said the doctor to Stacey. He and the nurse left, and after a few minutes the nurse bustled in cheerfully, a camera in her hand. "Just stand right over there in the corner, so we have nice white wall behind you." Stacey shivered in her paper exam gown, feeling even more vulnerable than usual.

With a flash and a whir, the Polaroid spit forth a self-developing sheet. "Now we'll just do one a little closer." The nurse was smooth, never causing any alarm, but never explaining what she was doing. The second shot was a close-up of her face.

"Why do you need to take the photos?" Stacey asked. "Never before have you—"

"We have mandatory reporting in the state of California, Mrs. Chernak. These go right in your file where no one but Doctor can see them. Doctor will explain everything." With a warm smile, the nurse disappeared, leaving Stacey petrified.

Five minutes later Dr. Rensfield returned. "Anything you'd like to tell me today, Mrs. Chernak? About those bruises, for example?"

"Well, I have a problem with my legs," she said.

"Oh, and what's that?"

"Sometimes when I climb the stairs . . . I catch the front of my shoe . . . I do not know, perhaps it is the shoes, but I do not think so."

He seemed to understand her clearly enough despite her accent. "You're saying you stubbed your toe?"

"Ah, *stub*. Yes, that is the word. I think when I get home, I should have broken the big nail, but it was all right. Anyway, that time I fell on the stairs, hit my head."

"Hit your face on the stairs?"

"Ya."

He paused, writing on the chart attached to his clipboard. "The thing is, Mrs. Chernak, this facial wound—while well on the way to healing—is not consistent with contact with a flat object. The object inflicting this damage inside the eye socket bone structure would have to be round."

The memory slapped her, summoned by the doctor's words: Wilhelm rushing her, trying to ram her head into the edge of the stove . . . no, that was the previous time. This time the attack had been so sudden she failed to see the fist coming at her till it was too late. Willing the image away, she said nothing in reply to the doctor's comment.

"Are you safe, Mrs. Chernak? Everyone has a right to be safe in their own home."

"Oh, ya, of course I am safe, Doctor, very safe."

Unbidden, an echo of Wilhelm's words drifted back to her: "I will keep you safe, Liebchen, safe from anyone else knowing our little secret."

"You don't deserve to be hit, Mrs. Chernak," Dr. Rensfield declared.

"What is . . . " Her lip trembled, and she willed it to stop. "What is 'mandatory report'?"

"Mandatory reporting means I must notify the authorities of your attack."

Panic rising like bile in her throat, she reached out for his hands. "You must not! No one must . . . there is no . . . "

"No one will see the photos, Mrs. Chernak, but the abuse will be a matter of record. The police will be notified."

"Police! *Gott im himmel!*" She stood and fumbled for her clothes.

"I'll give you privacy to dress, Mrs. Chernak. Please understand, the law is on your side." He paused, watching her. "Before you leave, I'll give you some information about the local shelter. And if you feel it's not safe to carry it with you, remember there's always 9-1-1."

After he'd quietly closed the exam room door behind him, she dressed. As she passed the physician's desk, he turned to face her. "Here's the information I promised, Mrs. Chernak. Here's a brochure about a local shelter."

Stacey's eyes opened wide in alarm. The last time a well-meaning coworker had given her a business card from the local women's shelter, Wilhelm had found it and nearly killed her.

The doctor continued. "But we also have a small key ring that has nothing but a logo—it looks like a little house—and a phone number. No one would guess what this is. If anyone were to ask you, you could say it's a sewing store or a good will drop off."

Though she took the key ring, she knew she would memorize the simple phone number, then discard the item for her own safety. With a furtive glance around the waiting room, she left as quickly as she could.

Snapping herself back to the present, Stacey had dressed and made out a shopping list. Sundays she went to the market, her one outing of the day. Checking her recipe card file, she chose one for brisket of beef. She'd have a nice supper hot and ready when Wilhelm returned from his trip. Probably she'd have to cover the meat with a broth-soaked cloth to keep it from drying out; usually he was late for her Sunday dinners. Perhaps she'd also go ahead and make a dinner for tomorrow, something easy to save. *Lasagna. Yes. I can make a large baking dish full, and even freeze some for later in the week.*

Finishing her list, she returned to the bathroom and laid out her small pots of makeup; the pale green paste covered red and purple, the yellow diminished the darker grays, and the beige blended to create a smooth, if somewhat caked, complexion. She was expert by now at concealing her problem. But as she opened the last of the small containers, her hands began to shake.

Today is the day. Seldom did she have the advantage of Wilhelm's absence, and she had to make good use of it. If he found out, he'd be so angry it would surely mean another beating. But something was consuming her husband these days, and she had to know what it was. In her heart she knew it was evil, but her better nature hoped against hope that some evidence would prove her wrong.

Carefully checking the angle of her boots at the front door once more, she walked to Wilhelm's desk. An old-fashioned roll-top piece, its work surface was always concealed and locked when not in use. It'd taken her weeks to observe where he stashed the key beneath the felt lining in his wooden cufflink box.

Standing at the desk, key in hand and heart pounding, she looked around the room as though Wilhelm's spirit stood behind her, waiting with a laugh—and a stranglehold. His ominous words came back to her. "When I return from Santa Barbara, *Liebchen*, I vill check very well the house." His accent and syntax still carried the distinctive German tones he couldn't outrun. "Should I discover anything moved, just the slightest change, we will have *das Unterrichten Sitzung*—a teaching session—yes? It will be good for you, and even better for me." Laughing, he'd walked to the entry, shrugged into his jacket and slammed the door behind him.

Trembling, she placed a pad and pencil on the desk chair, wrote down her first action: "get key." She'd be deliberate, meticulous.

"Turn desk key once to right," she wrote. The desk wouldn't yield. *No!* she thought, *I will never have this opportunity again!* "Turn once more," she wrote down, then gave it a try. It seemed to burst open, as though the slatted cover was being forced to hold back too many items.

"Lift desktop." She handled it gingerly by its two carved pulls. But as she began to move the hinged front, papers and envelopes tried to spill in every direction. "*Gott in himmel*," she whispered.

Slowly considering her options—the fingers of her left hand touching the roll-top's edge—she grasped one bunch of envelopes in her right hand and closed the desk with the other. Walking to the kitchen, she studied the ripped envelopes and haphazard tangle of papers in her hand, then placed it all carefully on the dining table. One by one, she examined the contents of each envelope, returning the papers with their original folds, angling the stack exactly as it had been when she lifted it from the desk.

This is bills, nothing but paid bills. There were no extraneous marks on the bills questioning her expenditures. But her scrupulous filing of all their household bills had obviously been undone. Random samples of a gas bill here, a phone bill there . . .

no wonder she'd been unable to find them in her expense file. Bitterly, she considered the beatings she'd taken for "losing" valuable financial records. Apparently unable to fault either her or her filing system, he'd destroyed it, hiding the bills all along.

Suppressing her dismay, she picked up the reassembled stack and placed it on the table, duplicating the precise order of the messy desk papers. Repeating the process, she worked her way through all the remaining items jammed into the front of the desk. Some were letters from adoption agencies, replies to his inquiries about various children. *These should all be kept with the client files,* she thought. *How can we know where we are with an adoption search unless the files are kept up to date?*

But no single name appeared in these documents. Again, they seemed a random sampling, and she could only conclude they'd been removed to torment her—and provide him with a series of excellent excuses for the mistreatment he seemed increasingly to relish inflicting on her, his spouse.

She added to her notes, recording the removal and replacement of each stack of papers. Then another thought occurred to her. *What if Wilhelm left these papers stuffed in the front of his desk intentionally for me to find, should I ever dare go rummaging?* Her hands turned icy at the thought.

These papers contain no actual secrets, so what would be the point of locking the desk? There must be something more. Behind where she'd removed the wads of random papers at the front of the desk were built-in drawers and slots usually concealed.

Stacey checked her watch. *Still early.* Theoretically, he wasn't due home for hours. Walking to the bedroom, she retrieved a large cardboard box from the closet's upper shelf, and emptied its contents onto the bed: hats, scarves, and gloves—the accouterments once needed in the chillier weather of their abandoned home in Switzerland. In case she didn't have time to put the box away, she could always say she was checking for moth damage.

Taking the box with her, she returned to the desk, opened it again, and with utmost care, placed the entire messy collection of papers and envelopes into it, duplicating the precise pattern of the disarray. Now she faced the rows of small drawers and slots built into the desk, and her palms began to sweat.

"Upper right slot," she wrote down on her pad. She pulled out a stack of photos, holding the edges lightly to avoid leaving smudges from her fingers. The first image took her back. Here was a picture of her and Wilhelm at the pier in Morro Bay, the day they'd gone whale-watching. What had happened to those happier times? And there were more pictures, earlier ones.

Stacey had been swept off her feet. Their courtship had been so full of synchronicity, it'd seemed kismet. She'd been returning from Zurich to Geneva when they met, a forty-five-minute business flight. Her two-week holiday in Zurich to visit the aunt who'd raised her had been a whirlwind of social outings. Now she was adjusting to the reality of going back to her secretarial job in Geneva.

University of Geneva was her alma mater, and she'd been excited at being offered the job of research assistant and secretary in the Sociology department. Now here she was, telling her life story to a handsome stranger in the coach section of a plane. She ordered mineral water from the flight attendant, and so did he. He was from Zurich too, worked in Geneva too—so many things in common . . . but always the conversation came back to her.

He listened thoughtfully even to her most trivial replies, seemingly fascinated by the details of her life. His deep, rich voice soothed yet stimulated her.

He was handsome in an unconventional way. Though his nose was a little large, and his deep-set, black eyes burned intensely, they could also sparkle with laughter, and the touch of gray in his hair was dashing.

With his tweed jacket and silk ascot, his sophistication and worldly ways, he seemed everything she wanted in a man, but thought she could never have. Unlike the foolish, immature young men who stopped by her office to tease her when she described the nature of some of her research projects, this stranger seemed to understand before she had to explain. With a sense of daring, she overcame her trepidation and consented to give him her number.

When he called two days later, she agreed to meet him. The day he planned was simple—a tour of the Musee Rath, a walk down the Rade, and a visit to the famous fountain, the Jet d'Eau. He was so well informed, explaining that its construction was started in 1885, when water was pumped for craftsmen's machines. He'd said something about it shooting one hundred forty meters high and two hundred kilometers an hour.

It was a lovely day, but then there was that awkward moment at the cafe. They ordered kaffe mit schlage, but the waiter brought hot schocolate instead. Stacey didn't mind. Wilhelm was furious, berating the poor server and almost punching him—a sudden, irrational burst of temper. As soon as the waiter was gone, Wilhelm apologized to her, explaining how much he'd wanted every detail of their day to be perfect.

Later he also apologized for not spending more lavishly, which only endeared him further. She'd found not a materialistic man, but one of substance.

Even what he did for a living was something wonderful: finding lost children for repentant parents—or lost parents for children desperate to discover their roots. He traveled sometimes for his work, disappearing for up to ten days at a time, returning with stories of exhaustive, rewarding research; tearful confessions; uncanny coincidences; spectacular tales of families reunited.

In two months, they became lovers, his capacity to heighten her excitement—and postpone his own—a source of endless wonder and admiration. Never had she felt so cherished, never so desired. But a lingering dread interfered with their intimacy until she could summon the courage to tell him—with his obvious love of children, she herself wouldn't be able to have a child.

"Liebchen," he murmured, stroking her hair, "I am so glad."

"Wha . . . what?"

"Do you not know, it is not more children in my life that I want. It is you."

Her passion soared that night, and he proposed the next day. Accepting immediately, she called Aunt Jutta, who expressed amazement at the whirlwind romance and concern at ignoring the fifteen-year age difference.

Stacey had planned their wedding to take place in the family church in Zurich. Instead, Wilhelm convinced her to elope to the Geneva courthouse.

Stacey stared down at the honeymoon photograph in her hand. It was still wonderful, despite the age that had slightly altered the original colors, and even with her hat truncated by the camera lens.

The tourist had obliged, she recalled, despite Wilhelm's reluctance to ask. They made a good-looking couple, in their dark suits. Hers was navy wool with velvet trim at collar and cuffs. It hung, now, in plastic in the closet, its matching hat resting on the bed while she borrowed its box.

Yanking herself away from the past, she replaced the entire stack of photos in their original order. Crossing out her previous entry, she wrote on the pad, "second right upper slot." This seemed to be a collection of stamps—some of them unused, but some canceled, and still attached to the torn corners of the envelopes on which they'd been mailed. The postmarks indicated Bern, Neuchatel, Lysin —all Swiss cities, all dated at least two years ago. Again, she could see no special relevance.

Torn between writing down the locations from which all the stamps had been sent, and continuing with the search, she decided to move painstakingly through drawers, slots, and cubbyholes. By the time she glanced at her watch, almost ninety minutes had passed. "*Scheiße*," she said quietly. She should stop this, replace the papers, close the desk, put away her box of hats. But with only a few more compartments to examine, she found the temptation to continue overwhelming.

In the fifth slot from the left, she found something of interest. "Current," the oversized legal folder was labeled. All eleven of their current case files were here—why, she couldn't imagine. Glancing through their contents, she was familiar with all of them. Perhaps Wilhelm was just being cautious, not wanting confidential information to fall into the wrong hands, and for that she admired him.

Opening the "Hugo" file, she glanced over the notes she herself had taken. "Samantha Hugo," she read in her own handwriting, followed by some of the particulars Ms. Hugo had given them. Then she spotted something added to the bottom of the page in Wilhelm's handwriting: "Adoption: Santa Barbara," he'd scrawled, and nothing further.

Glancing up, Stacey considered. *Well, this must explain why he was driving there.* Stacey knew they'd confirmed the Hugo adoption took place in California. She herself had told Ms. Hugo as much. But when had Wilhelm confirmed Santa Barbara as the specific location? *And why not tell me, when I am already familiar with the case?* Slightly hurt, but unworried, she closed the Hugo file to read the last one.

The final file had a heart-stopping label. "Top Secret" was stamped on the aging manila folder, its edges brown and frayed. She knew her husband had once worked for the U.S. government. He'd told her that shortly after they were married. She'd thought it added to his international sophistication and confirmed his inherent goodness. She didn't know whether or not his job had anything to do with espionage. But what else could it mean with such a designation?

Her hands trembling, she opened the file and began to read. "Need to know," the file said, followed by the word "Vermillion." Not grasping all she read, she skipped through the pages.

"Operation Tyro," it said, "utilizing techniques perfected in previous experiments on adults . . . " Skipping down the page, she read " . . . shows the subject susceptible to post-hypnotic suggestion." As she read further, the report seemed to indicate these same techniques would now become a project focused on "children who qualify as candidates only after exhaustive research ensuring no possible connection to natural parents."

Tears pooled in her eyes, and the words seemed to swim on the page. She should read more, she knew, memorize every possible detail, even race to a photocopy store and make copies of every page.

Gasping for breath, Stacey replaced the papers in their file, swiped at a tear with the back of one hand, then returned the file to its original hiding place. Holding back further emotion until each and every paper was back in its place and the desk locked, she wiped the key of fingerprints, put it back in its hiding place, restored her hats and scarves to their box, and the box to the top closet shelf.

Her mind reeling, she stumbled into the bathroom and wept, sobs racking her body and tears cascading down her face. When the sobs subsided, she stared at herself in the mirror.

Dabbing at her wet eyelids, she felt mounting panic. With a sickening sense of dread, she realized she had no idea who her husband really was.

Somehow, she'd have to find a way to continue the marriage with a semblance of normalcy. *If I can discover his secrets and escape alive.* Breathing deeply to slow her pulse, she decided the best approach would be the one that always seemed to work: take this one step at a time.

She looked forward to her long walk to the market. It was coming home she dreaded.

Stacey wasn't surprised to find the Morro Bay Save Mart hopping on Sunday afternoon.

Absorbed in her own conundrum, she progressed from one item to the next on her shopping list, mostly ignoring the other shoppers. But when she pushed her cart down the canned vegetables aisle, she noticed a two-year-old perched precariously in the fold-down metal seat of another grocery cart.

Eager to reach something bright and shiny on a nearby shelf, the child leaned with all his might out over the edge of the cart, in danger of toppling himself, cart and all. Assuming the mother was the woman with her back turned—frowning over two competing brands of stewed tomatoes—and feeling desperately anxious about the child, Stacey was on the verge of calling out to the mother or dashing to catch the boy, when the woman turned around just in time.

"No!" she yelled at the baby, yanking him down to a seating position. "No, no! I told you not to touch that!"

His little face a mask of dismay and hurt, the child puckered up, inhaled a long gasp, and let forth a hearty cry, tears the size of deep-sea pearls sliding down his red cheeks. Longing to lift the child, hold him in her arms and comfort him, Stacey summoned her willpower, turned the corner, and walked away quickly till the child's pitiful sounds were out of range. *If I had ever been blessed with a* Klein-kind *of my own, I would love him, not punish him for being a child who likes to explore his world!*

Steadying herself, she neared the end of the store and saw the bank of phones, considering for the tenth time the wisdom of her plan to call Samantha Hugo. From a public phone, there would be no record of the call for Wilhelm to find, so that much was good. But what exactly would she say?

Her palms turning clammy as fragments of her husband's secret file came back to her. Was it Wilhelm's plan to keep certain children forever separated from their birthparents, so that these experiments could be conducted? But that didn't make sense. He'd reunited scores of families; she'd seen the photos, read the letters of thanks. And besides, that file was decades old.

Could the file possibly have belonged to Wilhelm's father? A moment of relief washed through her body. *Yes! That could be it!* Her father-in-law, long-deceased, had worked for the American government too. Wilhelm had told her as much. So, these could have been his father's papers. *Then why keep them locked in his own desk? Why keep them at all?*

There was another possibility. What if these experiments actually took place all those years ago? Judging by the official appearance of the file, she had to admit it was likely. And what if Wilhelm were somehow trying to trace the subjects of these experiments? *But to what end?* That thought sent fresh waves of fear through her body. Her husband had lately been not just his usual, driven self but had seemed obsessed with finding a particular child, though he would never tell her for which client. Putting that together with his reaction to Ms. Hugo, she realized Wilhelm was always agitated when she called—or failed to call.

It was a leap, Stacey knew, but might her husband have his own agenda for finding Ms. Hugo's missing child?

Looking down, Stacey realized her knuckles were white from clutching the handle of her grocery cart. Releasing her grip, she looked again at the telephone. She had spoken with Samantha Hugo enough times to know the woman was in earnest about finding her son, and that even though she probably agonized as most everyone did in her situation, she was not ambivalent as some clients were. In return, Stacey desired with all her heart to help her.

If only I could convince Wilhelm to let me handle this case! But of course, even the suggestion of such a thing would raise his suspicions. It might work the other way, though, by having the idea come from Ms. Hugo herself. If the client told Wilhelm she would only work with Stacey, Wilhelm would have no choice.

However, she could never be certain when Wilhelm would actually be in the office, and she couldn't ask Samantha to keep calling. *A letter. Yes! If Samantha Hugo would write a letter to the agency requesting that I be assigned to the case!*

Working the case herself, Stacey could protect the client and the client's child. If this were really a secret scheme, Wilhelm would not want to tip his hand. And if all these fears of hers were unfounded, well . . . she could still handle the case, just as she would any other.

This is a dangerous game I propose to play. But then, living with Wilhelm is already dangerous.

So now she was back to the question: what would she say on the phone? How could she suggest to Samantha Hugo that it was in her own best interest to work only with her, Stacey, without Ms. Hugo becoming suspicious? Perhaps she could explain that the office caseload had increased, her husband was terribly busy, and she, Stacey, would be handling the case herself from now on; that Samantha should no longer call at the Chernak Agency, but should call at her other job, her temporary job? No, that did not sound professional. Ms. Hugo should not call at all, but allow Stacey to call, which she would promise to do regularly, each week, without fail, whether or not there was any news regarding her son. Yes, that would be all right. Surely the woman would agree to that, because if there was any news, Stacey would certainly tell her.

Steeling herself, Stacey pushed her grocery cart to the bank of phones, readied her change purse, and looked up the number in the small address book of clients she always carried. Since it was Sunday, no one would be at the EPC office. It was a risk to leave a message, but this was her only chance to place the call.

Glancing around furtively, Stacey dialed the number and left her brief message. "Ms. Hugo, this is Stacey Chernak. We are going to be working out of the office, so we are arranging weekly calls with our clients. I will call you on Monday during the noon hour. Until then, if you do not mind, please wait for my call." Stacey could only hope Samantha Hugo would comply.

Chapter 14

Samantha had made an effort to curb her irritations and settle her thoughts over the weekend. Her session with Deputy Del Friday evening had helped give her a measure of control over the daunting Internet highway. Still, she felt herself on edge.

She'd spent a productive morning in her office, and that'd helped, too. She left Susan alone as much as possible, trusting that she was doing at least some of her assigned tasks. As usual, the young woman's mood seemed surly, and Sam chose not to ask what might be bothering her.

The one odd thing that'd greeted Sam at the office this morning was a somewhat enigmatic message from Mrs. Chernak. It hadn't offered any actual information but had something to do with logistics. In any case, the woman had said she'd call back today at noon, and Samantha found herself glancing at her watch more and more frequently as the hour approached.

Walking out of her private office to approach her assistant's desk. "Susan, I'm expecting a call soon from a Mrs. Chernak. When she calls, would you put her right through please?"

"Is that the yodler-lady?"

"The what?"

"You know, the one who sounds like she's from Europe or something?"

Refusing to react to the ignorance and prejudice embedded in this remark, Sam replied, "I believe she is from Europe, yes. As to her singing abilities, I wouldn't know." Turning on her heel, Sam returned to her office, but then she paused for a moment, and returned to Susan's desk. "I don't mean to sound so high and mighty," she admitted.

Susan looked up in startlement.

Sam continued, "It's just . . . she does have a heavy accent."

"And she does sound kinda funny," Susan muttered.

Sam cracked a smile. "I suppose we'll have to figure out how to remain respectful, though."

Susan nodded. "Yeah, okay. After she calls, I'm heading out, by the way."

"Lunch and then the library, right?"

"Yup."

Sam nodded, and this time when she went back to her own desk, she sighed with relief. *Susan does respond when I treat her more like an equal. I should remember that.*

The phone rang a moment later and Sam waited. Sure enough, she heard Susan call out that it was for her. The array of buttons on the front of her desk phone now had one blinking, so she pressed it and lifted the handset.

"Samantha Hugo," she said.

"Zis is Stacey Chernak, Ms. Hugo. I had said— "

"Yes, I received your message, Mrs. Chernak. You have some news?"

"Oh, I am sorry. It is just zat—" The woman hesitated, then went on. "First, Ms. Hugo, I vould like to explain that we are so busy at the agency now, and I have a particular interest in your case. If you do not object, perhaps if it were only I who—"

"I'd prefer working with you, Mrs. Chernak, if that's what you're trying to say. I found your husband a little short with me on the phone."

"Oh, zat is good. I am sorry, I am hoping my husband did not offend you. He is sometimes so anxious to get good results."

"Yes, well. If I have to call, I'll ask for you," Samantha said.

"Zat is fine. And in fact, if you could write a letter—"

"I'm sorry you want *me* to write you a letter?" Sam asked.

"Yes, please, to confirm you vill be vorking with me."

"Mrs. Chernak, if you'd like to send *me* a letter of confirmation, that's fine."

"I see. And zen, you vould be able to reply to zis?"

"I don't have a problem with that. Now, you said you had news?"

"We have not located your son; I am sorry."

"That much I know!" Samantha snapped. "Why would you call to tell me that?"

"I know this can be very emotional, Ms. Hugo."

"I'm sorry, Mrs. Chernak. I just . . . I was hoping for news."

Sam heard the woman inhale. "Zis is perhaps not much, Ms. Hugo. Ve do have reason to believe your son Gregory was adopted in Santa Barbara."

"*What* did you say?" Samantha shouted. "He's . . . my son was . . . Do you know this for sure?"

"It is not confirmed as yet, but I know you have been vaiting. I vill be happy to call you each week."

Sam tried to steady her breathing. "I see. Well, thank you Mrs. Chernak. I look forward to your next call. Will it be next Monday?"

"It vill, yes."

"Until then. Thank you." Samantha hung up since no further information seemed to be forthcoming. She did, however, decide she'd describe this very odd conversation to Deputy Delmar at the first opportunity.

Delmar Johnson arrived at Clarke Shipping in Morro Bay just as rain began to plink on his windshield. His plan was to visit during the lunch hour, hoping several employees would be out of the office and that a secretary might speak more openly with fewer colleagues to overhear.

Pleased to see only one employee in the spacious office, he noted a middle-aged woman who sat eating at her desk. But she seemed alarmed as he approached, hurriedly wiping her mouth and glancing furtively around the room.

"How d'you do, Ma'am," he said politely. "I'm Deputy Delmar Johnson. I wonder if you might help me?"

Her eyes wide, she seemed too fearful to reply.

"Just trying to get some information," he continued when she didn't answer. "May I ask your name?"

"I am M . . . Mrs. Stacey Chernak," she stammered. "What is zis about?"

"To be honest, Ma'am, we're not sure yet. We think we may have a missing person, and I'm trying to see if I can check out her whereabouts."

Though obviously relieved, she continued to speak haltingly. "P . . . please sit down."

"Thank you, Ma'am." Del looked at her more carefully, noticing now that she was both younger and more attractive than he'd thought, but that she was heavily made up. Not knowing whether his own presence had caused her bad case of jangled nerves—or something else—he sat down, adjusted his belt, keys, and cell phone-pager as they found the back of the office chair. His leather jacket was too warm now that he was inside, but he preferred keeping it on, and reached into the pocket for his notebook.

"Who is zis person you are sinking is missing?" Stacey asked. Her European accent was noticeable but didn't affect the clarity of her English.

"She's a local reporter, probably just on assignment somewhere. It was Mr. Clarke I was interested in talking to, actually. Is he in the office today?"

"Oh, no, Mr. Clarke—he is seldom coming to town, and he has just left. Zis is only one of his offices. He is doing international business." Stacey thought for a moment. "Also, he is sometimes going up the coast from here, because he is building a very large home in Milford-Haven."

That must be the mansion on the bluff, Del thought, *the one Jack Sawyer is building.* "If it's the one I think it is, I hear it's beautiful. Have you seen the house, Ma'am?"

"Oh, no, I only hear because I am sometimes taking phone calls for him."

"I see." Del jotted a few notes, then looked at the woman. She still seemed nervous, yet now she also seemed preoccupied. "So he travels quite a bit. How often would you say he's here?"

"I am not sure . . . once in a month or two, I believe."

"I see no one else is here at the moment. Are you the office manager, Mrs. Chernak?"

"Yes. No." She laughed nervously. "You see, I am still actually temporary, although zis is now a permanent assignment. Zer is a company lunch today, but someone had to stay while the office is open. About Mr. Clarke, I could look up to see when he is coming next time."

Her attempt to be charming and cooperative made her seem fragile. It was when she reached up to the shelf over her head, that he saw the bruises—back side of the forearm, typical of defensive wounds.

His mind leapt forward. *Do her injuries have anything to do with Clarke? Could Chris Christian have been injured as well, and by the same man? Are the cases connected?*

She riffled through pages, then said, "Zis week it says Mr. Clarke would be here, but zer is also a question mark. If he does not come zis week, it vill be one month before he is returning. I did not see him myself. He is usually going straight upstairs to his private office ven he arrives."

Makes sense Clarke would have a private office, Del noted to himself, *and the time frame is about right.* Looking at her desk items, he asked, "Do you mind if I look at your calendar to check some other dates?"

"Yes, of course, you may look. But zis is not the full schedule for Mr. Clarke. He also carries his own calendar." She handed him the spiral binder with "Clarke Shipping" printed at the bottom of each month's page.

Jotting down names and dates of Mr. Clarke's presumed dates in town from the calendar, Del noted "Milford-Haven" scrawled on an upcoming date, along with "Art Show." He looked back two months to see if Chris Christian's name appeared but had no luck finding it.

Returning the calendar and thanking her, Del observed the woman in front of him: *Nervous; defensive wound; uncomfortable talking to me; hiding something.* He tried to be suspicious of her and found mostly she called forth his compassion. He knew from long years of experience how to read subtle shifts in people he interviewed and judged the time might be right to open a door for her.

"You know, Mrs. Chernak, I'm up and down the coast all the time. If you ever need help, I'm easy to reach."

She laughed nervously, but he sensed her decision to trust him. "Zat is very kind. Now that you are saying this, there is a question I would like to ask. It is concerning a friend."

"Shoot."

"I am sorry?"

"No, I apologize. Go ahead, talk to me about your friend."

"She is . . . she and her husband, they have trouble sometimes, and he does not mean . . . but when he is angry— "

"Does he hit her?"

She looked up, nodding.

"You want to know what the police can do?"

"No! No, I am sinking police, if they knew this situation, would make it worse for her."

"Has her abuse ever been reported?"

"Ya . . . her doctor is saying he must— "

"Mandatory reporting," he interrupted.

"Zat is what the doctor is saying to her. Vat is happening next, in a case like this?"

Going along with her apparent deception, Del replied, "Well, as soon as the abuse is reported, officers investigate."

She inhaled sharply, her eyes full of fear. "And . . . and if my friend, if she does not want to—"

The secretary seemed on the verge of hyperventilating and took a sip of water from the tall plastic container on her desk. Del waited for her to continue, but when she didn't, he continued. "There would only be an arrest if your . . . friend decided to press charges. If she does, the batterer would be arrested."

Her breathing slowed and she seemed to calm somewhat.

"Of course," Del continued, "We can't force a victim to press charges. This is how sometimes certain cases slip through the cracks and the suspect gets away, if the victim wants no interference."

"But . . . this is possible? This no interference?"

"If the victim does not press charges."

Stacey nodded.

"I don't recommend this for your friend, because in most cases abuse only gets worse. But perhaps, to buy a little time, until she decides exactly what to do, comes up with a plan—"

"Yes, I see," she interrupted. "Now I can tell her. I sank you very much, Officer."

"It's Deputy, Ma'am. Senior Deputy Del Johnson. Here's my card. You just keep that handy, in case your . . . friend needs it."

"And if you are needing . . . well, I do not know if I can do something for you, but, please . . . I will try."

"Thank you, Mrs. Chernak. You be careful, now." Del stood. "I'll see myself out. But before I go, I'll stop to see Ms. Wilson. She's a friend of mine. Is her office that way?" Del gestured, though he already knew where to find Gladys.

"Yes, zat is the right way."

With a nod, Del sauntered away, keys jangling. *That woman is a hot mess. And she's in danger. It'll be interesting to get Gladys's take.*

Stacey Chernak felt as is her mind were skipping like a small boat on choppy water. She had tried to keep calm with the police officer. Her relief that he wasn't there to investigate her bruises had turned to the realization that, somehow, this might be her only opportunity to talk to the police away from the apartment.

Yet she'd been unable to be completely candid with him, and the chance had slipped away. And now she had a new problem.

Convinced she'd incriminated herself, she feverishly concocted a strategy. In future, she would behave herself. It was the only way. She would give no cause for her husband's abuse. Then, when the police came—and she was sure they would—she'd have no injuries. In a few minutes, she'd be able to convince the officer there'd been some sort of mistake.

Yet now she had to worry about her coworker Gladys, who had already offered once to help. And it seemed Gladys was a friend to this policeman. Either this meant Stacey was in far more trouble than she'd imagined, or it meant she had two allies who might help her escape from her horrible secret life.

Susan Winslow staggered into the Environmental Planning Commission offices, used her rear end to close the door behind her, and dropped a heavy pile of books onto her disorderly desk.

Having heard the noise, Samantha came to the doorway of her private office. "There you are, Susan. I sent you to the library hours ago. What happened?"

Standing with one arm akimbo, Susan thrust her hip to the side and scowled at her boss. Samantha never really listened to her ideas. Yet she yearned for the validation that would come with accepting even one suggestion. "In case you're interested, I just happen to have found some of that coastal information you wanted."

"You mean the information you couldn't find on the Internet?"

"Not *everything* is on the Internet, Samantha."

Samantha made a face as if admitting her assistant was right, for once. "I stand corrected, Susan. What did you find?"

Trying not to look too smug, Susan handed her a Coastal Commission report marked with a sticky-note.

Samantha accepted the document and read aloud. "'Eighty-six percent of California's eleven hundred miles of exposed Pacific shoreline is receding at an average rate of between six inches and two feet a year . . . "Well, we already know that."

At least she's actually listening to me. Undaunted, Susan told her, "The report goes on to explain that when you try to erect a permanent structure on land that is intended to be mobile, you have a serious problem."

Samantha nodded, tracing her finger down the page. "Here's a quotation from the Governor of New Jersey, where he says that if we had known thirty years ago what we know now, New Jersey and much of the rest of the country would be in better shape. Typical. He manages to say nothing, while sounding politically correct."

"Read the part where it says this is happening all over the place: Louisiana, Texas, Long Island, Oregon—it's like happening all over the country."

"It's not *like* happening, Susan. It *is* happening."

"Whatever."

Samantha scowled. "The real problem is the natural process of erosion conflicts completely with our concept of property rights."

Susan harrumphed. "Oh, is that all?"

"Don't be sarcastic, Susan. I don't think we're going to be able to redo our concept of property rights overnight. But this does relate to your Native American heritage, and it might interest you someday in the future."

"Yeah, well, whatever."

"Please don't use that expression, Susan."

Every time I say something, she criticizes me! Susan clenched her jaw to keep from reacting. "You're always trying to snag Mr. Sawyer. I think I found something." Looking down, Susan read, "'Research indicates that houses constructed on top of seaside cliffs create problems the cliffs were never intended to handle: namely, new runoff patterns for rainfall and irrigation, and/or the addition of septic systems, creating drainage, which, in turn, threatens the land.'"

"Jack already knows all that," Sam huffed. She chewed her bottom lip, as if considering a new possibility. "And that's exactly how we might catch him."

"Meaning?"

"Meaning if we could prove Jack's company *knowingly* put up a structure that would damage either the cliff he's building on—or the neighboring beaches—with new erosion patterns, he would face such a protracted lawsuit it wouldn't be worth his while to continue construction."

Grabbing the hair that had fallen over her shoulder, Susan flung it to one side. The effort of trying to get along with Samantha and justify herself to her boss was exhausting. Besides, she was bored to tears being stuck in the office and needed a diversion. *What could be better than hanging around a construction site for a couple of hours? Cute men, all hot and sweaty; I could distract Kevin, watch him get fidgety; and I could even say I was doing my job.* "Well, Samantha, what if I went over there?"

"Where?"

"You know, to the Clarke house."

Frowning, Samantha replied, "No, no, Susan . . . building sites aren't safe, and besides, you won't be able to tell anything just by looking. Jack's too clever for that."

"Then I'll get Kevin to show me around."

Samantha laughed. "Kevin? He'd never make a move without Jack's permission."

"I wouldn't be so sure, Samantha," Susan said with a smirk.

She saw Samantha squint. "Just how well do you *know* Kevin?"

"Wouldn't *you* like to know?"

"You bet I would! If you're on intimate terms with someone from Jack Sawyer's office—"

"Then what?!"

Samantha raised her voice. "Then I'd have something to say about it!"

"You're not my mother!" Susan yelled.

"Thank God!" Samantha retorted.

Susan grabbed her leather jacket and swung it over her shoulder. "I'm going home. I don't feel well."

"You're declaring this a sick day?"

"Whatever it takes to get out of here."

"Good. Then let's close the office early," Sam remarked, looking daggers at her secretary.

Susan spun to face her employer. "You keep saying we're here to save the planet, and that you want my ideas. But when I bring in all this information and come up with suggestions, all you want to do is shut me down!"

Samantha's shoulders sagged. "You have a point, Susan."

"Great. Now that I don't care anymore, I finally get the last word." Susan pounded across the floor and slammed the door behind her.

Chapter 15

Zack Calvin squinted behind his sunglasses against the late morning sun bouncing off the Pacific as he angled his gunmetal gray Mercedes 500 SL north on the 101. He hadn't expected to be driving to Morro Bay this Tuesday but had managed to fit it into his schedule.

He glanced over at his father in the comfortable black leather passenger seat, thinking he still looked younger than his sixty-two years—fit, trim, good looking, and maybe even a little distinguished with his steel gray hair.

The easy relationship between them remained unchanged, despite that news that might've been cataclysmic. Yet it hadn't been. Last Christmas, Zack had found a letter from his late mother, written years earlier. She'd passed on shortly after writing it, and he had only dim memories of her. But his dad had always been there. *Well, stepdad, technically. Yet he's the only father I've known, and he's a great one.*

He'd been a baby when they'd adopted him, Joseph and Joan Calvin. When Joan died unexpectedly, Joseph had carried on with the plan they'd created for their son: a loving home, a solid education, a chance to rise through the ranks at Calvin Oil and take it over one day.

There's even some physical resemblance between us, Zack reflected. Certainly, their sense of style was similar, and friends often remarked on the two being the most eligible bachelors of Santa Barbara—something neither of them took too seriously.

He'd always known himself as Zack Calvin, and that's who he still was. And yet . . . there was more to his identity, the part that didn't quite fit, the renegade part. *Is that the part that got a wild hair and co-produced the Doobies concert?* If so, would he understand himself better if he went looking for his birthparents? *What purpose would that really serve? Whoever they are, they didn't want any part of me.*

Pushing down the uncomfortable thought, he glanced to his left and caught a glimpse of the oil rigs that stood offshore, flashing in the sun. Either he or his dad could have ticked off the names and histories of the rigs, which seemed a suitable reminder of today's errand.

As he and his dad left Santa Barbara behind, he peered into the rearview mirror to confirm there was no lurking California Highway Patrol car ~~lurked~~, and then he stepped a little harder on the gas.

He knew that from his father's perspective, their unanticipated opportunity for a lunch meeting with Russell Clarke had come as a boon—one that Mary, their ever-wise executive assistant, had recognized and implemented.

Zack and Joseph discussed the man they'd be meeting with, surmising that from Russell Clarke's point of view, the offices on the Central Coast were a base of operations, but that he apparently found it necessary to travel almost incessantly. Since he was obviously in town only briefly, he must have thought it wise to place a courtesy call to the Calvin Oil offices and been told that Calvins Senior and Junior would be pleased to meet with him. The Clarke Shipping Line and Calvin Oil were only a year into their contract, and so far, business had been mutually agreeable.

Zack had a counterpart, vice president of the shipping firm, Will Marks. He recalled meeting him for lunch at Dorn's Restaurant in Morro Bay last fall. They'd discussed business but also shared a couple of dating tales, commiserating about the Herculean task of trying to understand women. They still occasionally exchanged emails. He liked the guy, but neither of them seemed to have time to pursue a friendship.

Zack and his father agreed that meeting with Clarke in person might have a practical outcome and was potentially worth giving up a portion of their workday, though Zack mentioned he'd have preferred to stay closer to home, as there was a potential problem on their offshore rig the *Guerdon*.

Zack and his dad chatted for a few more minutes, then Joseph placed a call from the car phone.

While his dad talked shop with Mary, Zack's thoughts wandered into his mounting list of personal concerns. He'd promised Miranda that he and his dad would show up at her art show in Milford-Haven next week. But once again, he'd failed to stay in touch with her. *She must think I'm a flake . . . or worse.*

He couldn't, in all honesty, just pick up the phone and talk to her casually. Why? Because his own feelings were still in conflict. Sometimes he still felt drawn to her—as he had during that sexy, flirty phone conversation with her. *What would have happened if I'd been able to drive up to see her right then?* Other times, she seemed either cool and remote, or tentative and fragile enough to crumble at the slightest thing.

Is that why I've never told her about the family oil business? He'd let her believe he was a professional concert promoter, a field in which he'd dabbled enough to co-create that Doobie Brothers show last winter. As an environmentalist herself, would she understand his actual career? He'd never dared to test those waters but had let the secret ride. Now it'd become a barrier he didn't know how to surmount.

Then, there was Cynthia. Granted, they'd broken up. But that'd happened before. So had the most incredible make-up sex he'd ever experienced. Was that what he had to look forward to with her? Was that really what he wanted? *The women in my life are getting the best of me. Or the worst. I'm not sure which.*

Zack and Joseph were ushered into CSL's private dining room overlooking Morro Bay. He glanced around at the tasteful surroundings, taking in the view and the sense of privilege and exclusivity that permeated the premises in a familiar way.

Their host arrived a moment later and greeted them with a courteous, but superior air, which Joseph matched note for note. *Dad is good at this kind of thing. Polite to a fault, but never letting anyone lord anything over him.*

At the far end of the room hung a wildlife painting of a group of elephant seals. *Could that be Miranda's?* "Nice painting," he complimented their host.

Russell glanced at the piece. "Yes, *Elephant Seals Take the Sun*. In fact, I plan to buy more of the artist's work at her show in a few days."

Zack and Joseph looked at each other, then Joseph spoke. "Well, great minds think alike. We plan to be there as well if we're all talking about Miranda Jones."

"Indeed!"

Zack tried to suppress the tightening in his chest, sensing that—despite his best efforts—his two separate worlds were starting to overlap. Joining the other men at the luncheon table, he sipped water and reached for a lavosh cracker, enjoying the distraction of his own loud crunching.

Their host invited them to look out the window at Clarke's newest prize. In the center of the bay's perfect half-moon of sparkling Pacific floated a shiny new tanker, sleek as a giant whale seeking the shelter of protected waters.

The whale analogy increased Zack's discomfort. *What would Miranda think of this? What would happen to this pristine coastline if the tanker sprang a leak? What if that leak was* Calvin *oil?*

He forced his attention back to business matters. While he and the other men enjoyed excellent Shrimp Louis salads, they discussed the more favorable rates that would be possible with the new tanker in service.

After lunch, Russell offered a tour of the new vessel, and both Calvin men leapt at the chance. She was a beauty. The *Paragon*, Clarke explained, was a VLCC, and despite its designation as a Very Large Crude Carrier, she was considered a moderate-sized tanker of 120,000 dead-weight tons.

"That makes her about eight hundred feet long?" Joseph asked.

"Eight hundred eighty-three, to be exact," Russell replied. "She'll carry 850,000 barrels of oil."

"Must be double-hulled," Zack remarked. *Miranda would approve*, he thought, then corrected himself. *No. Nothing about the oil business would meet with her approval. And Cynthia wouldn't care.*

Joseph darted a look at his son as though wondering if he'd lost his mind. "Naturally, she's double-hulled, Zack. Everything built since that Oil Pollution Act of 1990 has to be."

Russell snorted, seemed to regard Joseph with approval, then offered his own opinion. "Talk about an absurd piece of legislation. Environmental protection is all well and good. But that was nothing more than a knee-jerk reaction to the *Valdez* fiasco. All it does is provide an empty space between the two hulls that can fill with oxygen. Considering our cargo, it's a perfect opportunity for combustion, as far as I'm concerned. We take all the precautions we can, but for my money, this regulation results in a dangerous design flaw."

Zack pondered his remarks while he followed his father and Russell across the main deck, noting how they all seemed to shrink amidships with the tanker's longitudinal sheer, then grow in stature as they approached the stern.

Crew members gave them curt nods in passing, busy with their many responsibilities. As though triggered by seeing a crewman bustle by, Russell remarked, "These new twelve-hour regulations are a nuisance too."

"How so?" Joseph asked, following Russell below decks.

"Each member of the crew spends eight hours on watch, then has to complete a myriad of tasks during the remaining four hours."

"What's the crew complement?" asked Joseph.

"Twenty-four, if you can believe that," Russell replied. "Before we bought her, this ship had no Chief Steward. That's one position I restored immediately. Can't run at peak efficiency if my engineers are struggling to order food and linen."

Joseph nodded approvingly. "Sounds like you have your priorities straight, Russell, putting practicality ahead of profit."

Overhearing their remarks, Zack questioned whether that were really the case, or whether Russell was showing off for his clients.

But the tour ended on a pleasant note, with the Calvins and Russell Clarke shaking hands, affirming their afternoon had been well spent. By the time Zack and his father were back in the car heading south to Santa Barbara, they were enjoying an animated conversation about the fine ship.

The loveliness of the day and the sense of new possibilities led them into wider topics covering everything from the future of oil exploration to the impracticalities of alternative fuels. Zack wondered, though, how long the industry could ignore two essential facts. One, their business was based on fossil fuel, a finite resource. Two, emissions were doing damage that would have to be repaired someday.

There were two ways to define progress. His dad and his generation believed there might be some other element to fuel the planet someday. After all, there'd been a previous energy business based on whale oil. Its demise had been a natural outgrowing of an outdated modality, an inevitable result of a market-driven economy. But in their lifetimes, there was still enough black gold in the ground to handle the needs of the world for the foreseeable future.

Zack had a growing awareness of a different view. He recalled a dinner with Miranda when she passionately described her respect for whales. They were still being hunted even today, and she herself had been part of the movement to stop what she called was needless slaughter, when synthetic oils already existed to replace the spermaceti for which the whales were killed. So getting away from reliance on that fuel had been a protracted battle, rather than a natural evolution. Yet Miranda believed huge change could happen quickly, and Zack couldn't see how it could.

Still, would the need to move away from fossil fuel be the next global battle? And would it happen in his own lifetime, unlike what his father believed? Zack had an inkling that the alternative fuels Joseph and Russell Clarke disrespected and dismissed might actually have financial potential. Should Calvin Oil be positioning itself for an eventual transition? He was VP of the firm and would someday take over as CEO. What kind of leader would he be?

He would have a responsibility to keep the firm afloat, even if it was as unwieldy and power-hungry as a tanker. Neither tankers nor oil companies could change course on a dime. If he were ever to be in a committed relationship with a woman, she'd have to understand that.

Zack glanced over at his dad, realizing each of them seemed lost in their own thoughts. But their silence was companionable, and they'd shared a productive meeting, in itself a promise of progress.

Cynthia Radcliffe had spent most of her time since last Christmas recovering from her breakup with Zackery Calvin.

She'd come up with several ways to fill her time and distract herself from the pain and disappointment. First, she'd joined a new club—someplace where no one knew her. She'd worked out relentlessly, which burned off anger and enhanced her self-image with a toned body.

After careful review, she'd bought one more income property and hired an excellent rental management company to ensure the new condo would pay its own mortgage by having reliable tenants.

For the past several years, the income she derived from investments covered her needs—though no one realized it. *I'm like a seamless bra: no visible means of support.* She allowed herself a moment of delight about her well-kept secret. There were those who believed she'd inherited, which helped to make her a good match for Zackery.

What she'd actually received from her parents was life lessons. She'd learned that when it came to dealing with the big bad world, only two things were important: money and power.

It was her mother who'd taught her about money. Scrupulous about her bookkeeping, her mother kept track of every cent she and her husband earned with their nightclub acts. But she'd quietly gone much further. She'd taught herself how to work the stock market and had invested every cent they didn't need for the bare essentials. Cynthia had been only ten years old when her mother started teaching her. *Thanks Mom,* Cynthia thought. *I owe ya.*

The thing was, in fact, Cynthia owed nothing to anyone. She almost always paid off her credit cards in full, and she kept a close eye on the market, keeping in touch with a good broker she'd come to trust.

Unfortunately, she'd also allowed herself to trust Zackery, and that'd been a mistake. That man would never truly be trustworthy, she now knew. Oh, they'd had a tremendous amount of fun. She'd seen to that. The sex had been off the charts. The social whirl had been exactly her cup of tea. And while she'd been carefully building herself into his life, she'd forgotten to monitor her most important investment of all: her heart.

Well, she wasn't sure she really had a heart anymore. But she did have feelings. That much she knew for sure. She'd soared with happiness as Zack had made her his permanent girlfriend. And she'd experienced both the hottest anger, and the deepest despair of her life when he'd cut her off.

The hurt had been deep enough to cause some authentic self-examination. After she'd thrown her belongings into boxes and vacated his private cottage on the Calma estate, she'd slammed around her own condo for days.

But then she'd gone through the boxes and discovered a little gold key ring that had not belonged to her. Horrified that he might think her a thief, she'd immediately made arrangements to return the little icon.

There'd been something good and pure in returning something that did not belong to her. Had it just been inspired by the sentimentality of the holiday season? No, she'd had an actual epiphany and thought better of herself.

Even that had gradually faded, though, as the weeks wore on. Then she'd begun to recall milder versions of this roller coaster ride that'd happened before, when he'd call off their affair temporarily.

The man was moody, but she knew that and could read the signs. When she saw one of his black moods on the horizon, she'd choose one of her tactics. Sometimes she'd back off, absent herself until he missed her. Other times, she'd lift his spirits with sexual treats. And one memorable time, she'd done both. She'd left town for a couple of weeks, then, when she'd received an almost plaintiff apology, she arrived at his place wearing a full-length coat with nothing under it but erotic sexwear. *Oh, what a night that'd been.*

Things had changed, though, over Christmas. He'd sunk into one of his moods, then never come out of it. No, it'd been more than a mood. Some realization or change of direction had taken over his psyche. And she could only assume it had to be another woman.

That woman, the one up the road in that crappy little town. She was to blame. Cynthia knew in her bones this other woman would never really be able to compete with what she could offer. Zackery would tire of her. And when he did, Cynthia would be there to pick up the pieces.

Until then, it was all the more important to keep her spirits up. Thus, the gym and the wise investments. She would not be financially dependent on Zackery, nor on anyone else. But she had no desire to wind up alone. She'd chosen him, the Calvin name, the reputation of the family, father and son.

She'd also aligned herself with an important and effective ally. Zelda McIntyre was a strong, smart, sexy woman like herself, a mentor who'd already brokered one reconciliation. *After that disastrous moment at the lavish birthday party I threw for Zackery at Calma.*

Her man deserved a birthday bash in his own home. But to ease his conscience, she'd arranged it as a charity event. He also needed a showy, expensive gift, and Cynthia had racked her brain, till she'd figured out the perfect thing.

She'd sniffed around and found out a few tidbits about her wannabe competitor: a painter. What better way to undercut the hold that other woman had on him than by purchasing one of her paintings and presenting it to Zackery? She'd seen it as a double whammy. On the one hand, it was a power play to show him her own reach. On the other hand, it'd been a way to gift him with something he wanted.

And Zelda, who represented the other woman's work, had arranged the sale. Then, when Zackery seemed so stunned and upset by the gift, Zelda had been there to soothe and to advise.

She told me not to be angry, but to be contrite. She saw I was genuinely sad about it and told me to go with my feelings, reveal my inner self, be vulnerable. "Don't even wash your face," she said. And I took her advice. I ended up right back in his bed again, just where I wanted to be.

Did she need Zelda's advice again? Perhaps. But she'd have to play her hand carefully. Zelda respected strength, not weakness. The same could be said of both Calvin men. Cynthia needed to bide her time.

With Zackery, there would always be a crisis. And when the next one came along, she'd be there to fix it for him.

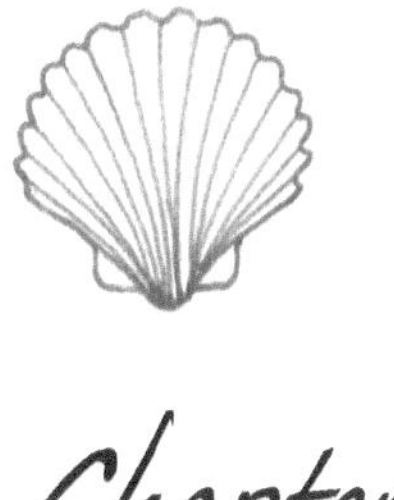

Chapter 16

Sally had been enjoying her time with Mama this week. Since the restaurant back in Milford-Haven was in the capable hands of June, and since Easter was coming up, Sally'd decided to stay in Arkansas through the holiday weekend.

"It's been a month o' Sundays since you took yourself any kinda holiday," Mama had pointed out. But really, it was Mama herself who needed both the help and the company of her daughter.

They'd spent some time in the small attic room that'd once been Sally's, going through boxes and preparing Good Will donations. It'd been the right time of year to take care of that chore, when it wasn't so hot. In summer it'd be unbearable, especially for Mama alone. Then they'd done some weeding in the garden, some sweeping in the Pouting House, and given the living room furniture a good polishing. They hadn't done many visits yet, but there'd be plenty of friends stopping by come the weekend.

Wednesday evening was a perfection of soft air perfumed with spring blossoms, and the crickets were celebrating by moonlight. Unable to rest until her kitchen gleamed, Glenda had applied her usual dose of elbow grease and then retired for the night. A hush settled over the house as Mama's bedroom door closed.

Sally shut off the brighter lights, lifted her cup of warm chamomile tea, and sank into Mama's plush living room chair to sit quietly in the soft glow of an amber glass lamp.

There were any number of things troubling her thoughts these days—the baby, the business, and Jack. Waking and sleeping, her mind churned, first with anger, then with insight; with shock, then understanding; vengeance, then forgiveness.

But like a steady light burning in a distant window, her thoughts of Tony were always there too. *Ever since his trip to Milford-Haven last December.* She admitted to herself that his recent visit had stirred something deep.

Partly, it was their shared history. He'd been her first real love, and she'd lost him when he joined the Marines and was sent off to Vietnam. She'd buried those memories so deep they'd become almost secret even to herself, and she'd been frightened to lift them from their hiding places.

She and Tony now lived in different worlds, and yet when they'd been together for that Doobies concert, the spark rekindled a flame that now burned steadier than she'd acknowledged. She didn't know where it would lead. But she didn't want to snuff it.

Being back in her childhood home was doing her a world of good. The creak of wood floors, the soft movement of sheer blue drapes against pale blue walls, and the ever present smells of home cooking, all fed her soul. Yesterday she'd sat at Mama's dressing table and opened its hinged fabric skirts just to catch the faint aroma of *Cashmere Bouquet* powder that always issued forth. And when she'd first gone into her old room, there on the carved bed with its handmade quilt sat her doll collection—all in a row against the pillows, faces washed, clothes pressed, as though ready for Sunday School.

Though comforted by her time at home, she found she was also astir, as though remnants from her own childhood were coming up for review. The familiarity of Mama's routines hadn't so much steadied her nerves, as given her even more to think about. She'd hoped the trip would give her a mirror, a steady reflection through which she could find herself. Instead, it was more like the surface of a pond constantly disturbed, as though her child-self were tossing memory-stones, each one causing its own series of ripples.

Sally figured Moss Mountain High was like every other school, with its share of cliques and gossips. But Velma Sue had been sworn to secrecy, so at first Sally didn't worry when she noticed the girls clustered around her suddenly hushed.

Cheerleading practice was about to start, so Sally put her books down on the edge of the gymnasium floor and changed into her tennis shoes. Just then Principal Pringle came in and dismissed the girls to go practice on the field—all but Sally O'Mally.

She'd have to skip a year, he explained. She'd get full credit for this year because her course work was finished, and her grades put her on the honor roll. But she couldn't come back in the fall with the rest of the class. Not in her condition.

Racing out of the school, she hardly knew where to go—anywhere but home. She walked and walked, till asphalt turned to dirt, and she found herself at Fellows Pond, where she sat on her school jacket, sulking till the tears came.

At first, she thought the circles on the water were fish surfacing, looking for tidbits. Then she realized someone was throwing pebbles. Looking behind her she saw Tony, standing quietly by a tree.

She'd had such dreams about the two of them. Though he didn't match her Southern upbringing, his soul fit to hers in a way she couldn't explain. She should tell him now—tell him about his child growing in her belly. But there didn't seem to be a way to find the words—not when he was about to put himself in harm's way. She knew he'd read her crying as devastation in response to his leaving. She decided to let him believe there was nothing more to her heartache.

"I'm gonna be okay, Sal. I promise."

Walking to her, he took both her hands, lifting her to her feet. Then he held her, sobs racking her small shoulders, her body enveloped in his large embrace.

In the morning, he left for Vietnam.

Sally hadn't told him her news that day, nor had she ever told him her decision not to have the baby. He'd written, his return address a strange string of numbers and letters that gave no indication what country he was in. By the time she'd gotten his first letter, the baby was gone.

Terrifying and difficult as it had been, she'd known it was the right thing for her at the time. But what she hadn't expected was how hard it hit her after the fact. She felt haunted by the ghost of someone she'd never known, so the child that was never born was a presence not of joy, but of guilt. With Tony away at war, she felt the burden was hers alone, and she held herself away from him—the love of her life—knowing that connecting with him would only attach the burden to him as well, making it more than she could bear.

She only wrote him once, giving a complex explanation for ending their relationship: she was still in high school; her parents thought she was too young; she was expected to graduate before making any relationship commitments. His letters had questioned, then implored.

Once, she almost relented. Twisted in knots, she'd decided to take Mama into her confidence. But then Papa was killed. Though busy as always with his farm work, he'd answered the call that day. Being a volunteer fireman meant a lot to him because he saw his neighbor's need as his own. The Pulaskis' old barn had looked stable enough, and the flames hadn't engulfed the whole structure. No one could have predicted the collapse, nor its deadly consequence.

With Papa's sudden death, Mama'd had no ear left for listening. Sally had gone numb, unable to feel her own pain, let alone Tony's.

Weeks after her father's death, she and Mama had gone through Papa's things. It was then she'd finally let herself cry, and while her mother comforted, the truth about her baby tumbled out between sobs. Glenda had only nodded quietly. "Back then I had a dream. I suspicioned there was a baby, Sally girl. I'm so glad you told me."

Since seeing Tony again last autumn, guilt surfaced when she thought about him. Somehow his lost mobility and their lost child all seemed tangled in one morass. She played through the events of the past again, unable to stop the internal images that played like an old-fashioned home movie. By the time she'd known she was pregnant, he'd already enlisted in the Marines. Remembering how strongly he'd felt about serving his country, she saw nothing would have stopped him. *If I'd told him about the baby, he might have proposed. If we'd married, he might not have been assigned to combat, might still be walking. No! . . . don't go there.*

Even way back then, he'd been such a strong guy, a natural leader, a basketball legend at their high school. He'd never been accepted as a hometown boy, not with that faint Brooklyn accent. While his mother remained in New York recovering from an illness, he'd come to stay with his aunt and uncle in Moss Mountain, Arkansas, for his last two years of high school. In spite of that tough transition, he'd been captain of the team his senior year.

Four grades below him, she'd noticed him right away. But of course, so had every other girl. "Tall, dark, and handsome," they'd chant, giggling by their lockers. The giggling had stopped when Tony started dating her—a mere freshman—and the jealousy had begun.

She used to know so much about him. What she needed to do was find out who he was *now*. They'd had so little time to visit last December. And she'd told him she was seeing someone else, which he accepted graciously. *But I sure ain't seein' Jack now! Nor do I ever want to.*

Checking her watch, Sally calculated the time difference to New York. *Oh,* she thought, *only an hour later from here. He'll still be up.* Before she could stop herself, she dialed Tony's number.

"Fiorentino," he answered, shouting to hear himself over the noise of what sounded like a ball game.

"Tony?"

"Yeah. Hold on!"

"Oh, fiddle," Sally muttered to herself. She hated to come between a man and his basketball.

"Yeah, Fiorentino here."

"Tony, it's um, it's—"

"Sally? Hey, Sally!"

His exuberance was more welcoming than anything she'd heard since the creaking of Mama's screen door.

"Yes . . . Tony, it's me."

"You get off early? I thought you usually cleaned up that restaurant of yours till all hours."

"Oh . . . well, yes I do, but uh, I'm not there tonight."

"Good! Glad you're off your feet."

"Well, how d'you know—"

"You sound relaxed, but not exhausted."

"You know too much, Tony Fiorentino."

"Mmm. So how's Milford-Haven?"

"It's fine, I guess. I had to get away, though. I . . . I broke things off with that fella I mentioned. And anyway, wa-yil, right. That's what I did."

"Where are you?"

"Decided to visit Mama."

"You're home in Arkansas? Sally, that's great! Oh, boy, I can just about taste one of those pies your mother makes."

Sally laughed softly. "They're awful good."

"You spend so much time feeding other people. About time you let someone feed *you*."

"Oh . . . well, yes. It's not like I usually starve myself, though."

"I don't know about that."

"But Tony, I don't!"

"I'm not talking about food."

"Oh." She paused. "Oh." Sometimes that was all she could think of to say to him. "Like I said, Tony, you know too much."

He grunted, the sound reduced in amplitude by the phone lines, but the meaning clear.

While static filled a long pause, she wondered what they could talk about next. There was the past. There was the future. But maybe most importantly there was the present—the current reality for Tony, the fact of being in a wheelchair. It was the proverbial elephant in the room they both had so far avoided. If she got really honest with herself, she'd have to acknowledge Tony wasn't avoiding the subject—*she* was.

She thought about how little she knew of veterans. They were a category, rather than being real people; they were a "they."

Maybe they had certain things they'd just as soon never talk about. Or maybe that was one of those myths that everyone believes is true but really isn't.

"So, Tony, I . . . I never really asked you anything about the war. Do you . . . is it okay if . . . can you tell me about it?"

She heard Tony blow out a breath of air then say, "Holy shit, girl. Talk about not pulling any punches."

"Well, I never did ask. And I do want to know. But you don't have to talk about it if you don't want." Sally heard him breathe, and imagined he stroked his beard, as she'd seen him do not long ago.

"What, Sal? What do you want to know?"

"Well . . . I s'pose . . . what I'd really like to know is, how you survived it all."

"Mmm. I like that question." He thought in silence for a moment. "I think it's the child."

Alone in her mother's living room, Sally sat in stunned silence, then sputtered, "Wh . . . what? I *did* ask you about *that*. I thought you said you didn't have children? I'm sorry, I—"

"No, no, what I mean is, the child in *me*."

Her heart pounding, Sally tried to switch gears fast enough to keep up with him. "Oh . . . I see. The child in you—"

"The child qualities."

"You're talkin' backwards again, Tony. I can only think that war would kill the child inside everyone who ends up in battle."

"There's a lot more to war than battle, Sally."

"Like what?"

Sally listened as he took a breath, then let it out. "Like keeping clear, remembering where your loyalties are, having the smarts to outdo the enemy."

"I thought you mostly had to just follow orders," she remarked.

"Oh, you do. But you have to do more than what your commanding officer wants you to do. You have to do what the enemy *doesn't* want you to do. If he wants you upset, you stay calm; if he wants you hungry, you convince yourself you just ate at a banquet; if he wants you to go left, you go right."

"Like an ornery little kid."

"Yes! Exactly. Exactly! I probably did better in the war because as a kid I was such a brat."

Sally chuckled. "Were you, Tony?"

"Oh, yeah."

"I didn't know the war was like that. Makes sense, though, now that you've explained it to me."

They were each silent again for a moment. She wanted to ask him how it'd happened, how he'd lost the use of his legs, but couldn't figure out how to broach that subject. Maybe this wasn't the time—not yet.

Tony Fiorentino sat alone in a city of millions, looking out the window of his Manhattan apartment. Across West 157th Street, neighbors' open blinds revealed the occasional movement from room to room. Holding the phone with one hand, with the other he gently pushed back and forth on the right tire of his wheelchair, rocking himself. "I was talking with my friend Wade," Tony said. "He was a POW."

"Oh, my word. For how long?"

Sally's voice was quiet but clear, and he thought he could hear crickets in the background. "Seven years." Through the phone's tiny speakers, he heard Sally inhale sharply. "He talked about the high jinks he and his buddies used to keep sane."

"Uh . . . I don't understand." Sally said. "While they were prisoners, you mean? How'd they do that?"

"You wouldn't believe what all they managed to pull off. They made a deck of cards from pieces of toilet paper stuck together with glue they made from their rice gruel suppers. A couple of guys knew how to play bridge, and they taught the others."

"Takes a lot of gumption to play a game in that kinda situation."

"It took more than that before they were finished."

"Oh, no. You mean they got caught?"

"Oh, yeah, they were caught, and the cards were confiscated."

"That musta made their spirits sink," she offered.

Leaning forward in his wheelchair, Tony continued, "Yeah, but they continued to play *without* cards."

"How in the world?"

"There were nine men. One became the dealer—"

"But I thought you said they didn't *have* cards," Sally interrupted.

"Right, the *mental* dealer. Then four guys became the players. And they each had a partner—a memory bank partner who helped them to remember each card that had been played."

Silence fell over the conversation as Tony reflected on the torment and the bravery of his friends and allowed her to do the same.

Sounding awestruck, she almost whispered, "Wa-yil, I'll be a mashed potato pie!"

Laughing in spite of himself, Tony fired back, "Haven't heard that expression in decades!" *Funny how comforting her homey Arkansas talk can be.* Then they both began talking at once. "I like for you—"

"It helps—"

"Sorry," said Tony, "you first."

"I . . . it's good to hear your stories, Tony. It helps me."

"Helps you . . . what?"

"Just . . . helps me . . . get through the day."

"That's funny."

"Whatta ya mean?"

"It's *me* it helps. Helps me get through the night." Feeling suddenly vulnerable sharing that much information with her, he paused a moment, then plunged ahead. "I don't share these stories much. It feels good to tell them." Tony rubbed his hand across his beard and stared at his blank wall as though it were a screen on which he could see a projected image of Sally. "Are you trying to figure me out, Sally O?"

Sally giggled. "Noooo!" Static hung in the air, louder than the city streets outside Tony's window. At last, she admitted, "Well, maybe I am."

"Good," he said. "It's a dirty job, but someone has to do it."

Sally laughed, then stuttered, "Oh, T-Tony. " Tony listened as she laughed some more, recognizing the release of the nervous tension that always built up around the touchy issues of disability.

But in spite of recognizing the source as tension rather than true humor, the laughter was infectious, peels singing down the wire, changing him, and, as though he were being tickled mercilessly, he chuckled, he belly-laughed, he roared.

The more he laughed, the more Sally did, until, gasping for air, she sputtered, "Don't . . . I can't breathe . . . I don't want to wake Mama . . . oh . . . oh!"

Gradually recovering, wiping wet cheeks, and sighing into receivers, they quieted themselves until Tony could hear the traffic outside his windows.

"You always could make me laugh, Tony."

"Yeah," he said, his voice hoarse through the phone line. *She said she's not seeing that guy anymore. That makes it easier. And harder, too.* He blurted out, "God, I've missed you, Sal."

"I've missed you, too." She paused. "I'm headin' back day after tomorrow."

"Good. I'll see you soon."

"You will?"

He liked hearing her surprise and delight. "Yeah . . . I'm . . . I'll be coming to Milford-Haven soon."

"Oh. That's nice . . . why—"

"I don't want too many weeks to go by this time, Sally."

"Well, I—"

"It's a great little town." Suddenly, he wanted to get off the phone. Knowing he'd be seeing her in person, it was no longer enough to have only her voice. "I'll call you when I know my plans."

Sally answered simply, "Okay, Tony."

"Thanks, Sal. Thanks for the call. Good night."

"'Night."

Quietly, he placed the receiver back in its cradle. *She called me!* His heart beat a little faster. *I'll be seeing her in a few days. I'll be her neighbor at work. Need to take it slow, though.* But as he thought about his upcoming plans, taking it slow would be the hardest thing he'd done.

Chapter 17

M iranda had spent Thursday morning preparing for her collaborative project in Lompoc.

She'd gathered the special painting supplies used recently for the two mural projects she'd completed in Santa Barbara last month. Larger brushes, paint that stood up to weather, portable stepladders were among the items specified by Lompoc's "Mural in a Day" program. She'd added a sun hat, sunscreen, and a fleece. She was sure it would be hot during the long day of painting she'd share with new colleagues. But if they were still at work as the sun went down, it might also get breezy and cool.

Once everything was in her Mustang, she checked to make sure she had a thermos of water and another of hot tea. Then she headed south on Highway 1. She hadn't packed anything for lunch, but she imagined there'd be restaurants near the mural site. Not having shopped for food since her return from Oregon, she didn't have the fixings for a sandwich and didn't want to take time for a to-go stop before getting some miles behind her.

As she transitioned to the 101, she opened her green thermos for a sip of tea and pushed the Metheny cassette into the Play position. Morning fog still clung to the coast at home, but as she drove, the skies cleared and it promised to be a lovely day.

This project would be different from all her previous ones. She was used to being her own boss, as it were, but she wouldn't be the master artist, so she'd be painting the section she was assigned. Still, she was delighted to be included, and continued to enjoy her growing specialty of creating these oversized exterior projects.

Interestingly, the adjacent building to the one where the city project was happening had petitioned to have a mural of their own. It wouldn't compete or interfere, they'd written in their proposal. It faced in the direction ninety degrees away, and, they suggested, would guide visitors to the larger work. The owners had been granted permission, then contacted her to be the artist. Evidently, they'd seen the mural she'd painted for the Environmental Planning Commission, the very first job when she'd moved to Milford-Haven.

Miranda had asked both these owners and the larger mural master artists whether she might also paint Point Conception, but from a different perspective. The master artists had liked the idea and said yes immediately. After all, the large mural they'd planned already included three views of the iconic lighthouse, so Miranda's smaller piece would be an extension of the core idea.

That's what I call synchronicity, she thought, smiling as her car sped down the highway.

Accordingly, she'd created her own sketch and even done those miniature watercolors she'd made into the postcards for Cornelius and her sister. The image included the short lighthouse, the rectangular building out of which it protruded, and the hillside covered with pink blooms cascading down toward the ocean. Her view also encompassed the adjacent beach, which the other view did not. So a future visitor seeing the murals could pretend to be hovering over the dramatic point of land in, say, a hot air balloon, seeing a series of still shots from each perspective.

After passing Santa Maria, she took exit 166 onto Union Valley Parkway, then south on the Orcutt Expressway—both of which sounded like bigger roads than they were. Eventually, her route narrowed down to Highway 1, which locals knew as PCH, or Pacific Coast Highway, an iconic road that wended its way the full length of California. In this community, it reached the edge of Vandenberg Air Force Base, then turned left until it fed into the town of Lompoc.

At a deserted stretch of road, she pulled over to consult her map. Then keeping one finger on the designated destination, she continued to the corner of South H Street and West Ocean Avenue and found a place to park.

She found the other artists already gathering and introduced herself before setting up her ladder and supplies. By thirty minutes later, she'd already lost track of time, absorbed in filling in the details of her section, watching as the image began to appear.

Cornelius had spent the previous day faithfully carting the spring silk flowers into his parents' living room, then hauling the boxes filled with winter blooms back to the shelf unit his father had erected in their garage.

Not that he had any idea what the difference might be between winter and spring flowers of the silk variety. They all looked much the same to him, though he could identify the bright pinks and yellows as his mother began placing them in various rooms.

Neither he nor his father had been in favor of letting her continue to climb up and down the small kitchen ladder. Though she protested that she was perfectly fine and as strong as ever, she eventually relented, as her compliance was the price she had to pay for their help. Of course, she'd rewarded them with her spectacular chicken and dumplings dinner, so at the end of the day, no one was complaining.

Though he had work of his own to do afterwards, he'd opted for going to bed earlier than usual, because today he had plans. Having made a few phone calls, he'd discovered when and where Miranda would be working with the group of muralists in Lompoc, and he planned to surprise her with a picnic lunch. After all, she'd written in her postcard that she hoped he'd see the mural one day. Well, he'd be seeing it sooner than anyone expected.

He'd also found out that Sally was a friend of hers, so he figured Sally or someone who worked at her restaurant would know a couple of Miranda's favorites.

"Is Sally here?" He asked after walking into the diner.

"Sorry, no," said a slightly older woman. "Help youse with something?"

Everyone who works here has her own accent, I guess, he observed. *This woman sounds like she's from Brooklyn.* "Well, you know Miranda the painter, right?"

"Sho-wa," she said.

That must mean "sure." "She's working on location today and I wanted to take her a picnic lunch," he explained.

The woman's face opened into a wide grin. "Swell!"she said. "Roasted veggie sandwich, baked chips, pickle, piece o' poppyseed cake. That's what she ordered when she went up to Piedras to paint last time."

"Perfect! Can you make it two of everything?"

"You betcha. Got somethin' youse can do for twenty minutes?"

"Yes, I'll go next door and talk to Mr. Hargraves."

"Good deal. I'm June, by the way. I'll have it ready for youse."

Cornelius asked for a coffee to go when he picked up the order. The food was beautifully packed in an actual basket, which he found charming. He'd be sure to return it, and maybe add a note of thanks for June and Sally.

He'd have preferred driving the EV to Lompoc, but it was too far to go without a charging station there, so he drove the Durango and enjoyed listening to a taped lecture en route.

He found the location easily, then stood beside his parked car, watching for a while as the artists each worked at their sections, marveling at how the separate pieces were already coalescing into a delightful whole.

As pretty as the new work of art was shaping up to be, it was one artist in particular whose . . . shape he couldn't seem to stop appreciating. *Fetching in that hat, and those tight jeans. And so intent on her work that she has no idea how good she looks.*

He saw the moment Miranda noticed him, squinting for a moment as if trying to confirm it was him, then offering a broad smile. He couldn't help but return the grin. Then he waited while she cleaned her brush, closed her paint containers, and chatted with the others for a moment.

Finally, she headed in his direction. "This is a nice surprise!" she exclaimed. Looking back over her shoulder, she added, "Beautiful, isn't it? Vicki and Linda's design is marvelous. I think we're gonna get a crowd this afternoon. Apparently, the local news crew is coming to get some video."

"Makes sense," he commented.

"Listen, I'm starving. Can you join us for lunch?" But when she turned to look, she saw that the others had wandered off somewhere. "Oh. Well, we can find a restaurant ourselves, unless you have to get going."

"Actually," he started, "I, uh, brought something."

"Oh, good. I didn't, so do you mind if we—"

"What I mean is, I brought something for both of us. All we need is a picnic table. Or we can eat in my car if you'd rather."

"You . . . you brought lunch for me? For us?" She gave him that smile again. "Oh, picnic table for sure. There's a little park I saw not far from here."

She climbed into the passenger side of the Durango and directed him to a sweet urban park with a couple of shaded rough-hewn tables. She chose one, and he pulled the basket and a blanket from the back of the vehicle.

"You stopped at Sally's," she exclaimed when she saw the basket.

"Guilty," he admitted.

He spread the thin blanket over the table, and she dug into the basket of treats, placing the offerings.

"Oh, this looks fabulous," she said, the last word partially lost as she sank her teeth into her sandwich.

He chuckled as he watched her eating with such gusto, then dug in himself, enjoying the vegetarian concoction more than he'd expected. But more than anything, he was enjoying her.

Miranda had been startled, then pleasantly surprised, then utterly charmed by her picnic lunch with Cornelius.

His looks dazzled her: tall, long-muscled and broad-shouldered, he had that classic male build, yet seemed so unaware of it. She wanted to run her fingers through his thick black hair, worn just long enough to edge over his collar. And the look that came into his indigo-blue eyes drew her.

But he was much more than a handsome guy. No man had paid her that kind of attention in months, or maybe years. It'd seemed strangely natural for him to join her. Normally she kept her work separate from anyone except a client, or a student. Why, she wasn't sure. Of course, it had to do with avoiding distraction.

And she did have that negative experience with a fellow artist in a shared studio in San Francisco a few years earlier. But it was something more, some sense that if she let others into her workspace—whatever it happened to be for any given project—the Muse might feel jealous and desert her.

What a ridiculous notion! She chided herself. Still, she always chose to honor the sense of inspiration and do nothing to interfere with the flow of ideas once they started. That was a core value in her practice of art.

The interesting thing about today was that Cornelius' energy did not interfere with her own. She felt his presence as complementary rather than competitive. That in itself was a gift.

When she explained the schedule for the rest of the day, and that she'd be staying at a local motel, then painting her own mural tomorrow, he'd offered to come back with dinner the following night.

"Drive all the way back here tomorrow evening? Oh, I couldn't ask you to do that!" She'd begged off, saying it was too long a drive, he'd already done so much, and she'd be fine.

Somehow that hadn't mattered to him. "I have an important errand nearby tomorrow," he'd explained. "And I have an idea." He paused as he looked into her eyes. "Is there any chance you enjoy camping?"

"Of course I do," she'd said, more defensively than she'd intended. "I was just camping in Oregon so I could photograph the meadowlark."

He nodded. "Okay. That's great. So how about this. There's a gorgeous place near here called Jalama Beach. I'll come back to Lompoc at about 5:30 p.m. tomorrow. Civil twilight ends at 20:36," he said.

She stared up at him.

"Sorry, dusk happens at about 8:30 tomorrow night. If we leave here at, say, 6:00 p.m., we should have time for dinner and a beautiful sunset."

"That does sound lovely," she'd answered.

"There's nice camping there, if we're so inclined."

"But I don't have my stuff."

"I've got plenty. No pressure, but it could be fun. And I can tell you about the stars."

After a moment, she said, "Who could resist that?"

Miranda had worked hard and fast alongside her colleagues all afternoon.

When the group mural was complete, she and the other artists high-fived each other, then joined in the lovely ritual of signing their names onto a painted plaque at the bottom edge of their mural. In perpetuity, everyone would be able to see who did the work today, and each of them was pleased and proud.

As her new colleagues prepared to go home, Miranda packed up her supplies and drove the short distance to her motel. Next door, she'd found a diner and ordered a big bowl of vegetable soup to go. That'd be all she needed before dropping into bed after an exhausting, but satisfying, day.

Meredith Jones wanted to see her boss briefly before leaving for the weekend.

Technically, he wasn't her boss any more. She now ran her own financial consultancy and leased a private space on the same floor where she'd previously worked. But Ron Mansfield had been, and still was, a mentor and friend.

Grabbing her purse and briefcase, she locked her door behind her and walked the short distance across the lobby of the twentieth floor. Smiling at the receptionist, who smiled back and waved her in, Meredith glanced around before heading down the long corridor to Ron's corner office.

Hope Rothman has already left. Last thing I need is to run into him. Albert Rothman had been a jealous, resentful colleague who'd done everything he could to undermine her—and every other woman—at this firm. Even now, he gloated that he'd "won" their imagined competition because she had left. She couldn't take the pressure, according to him. He was evidently still working on a plausible story to explain why she'd taken a few of his key clients with her when she'd opened her own small firm.

No longer my concern! She thought, slamming her mental door on the man and his schemes and insecurities.

Arriving at Ron's private office, she tapped on the door and pushed it open. "Mer!" He called out warmly. "Come in and take a load off."

Smiling, she slid into the chair facing his desk and sighed.

"You look beat. Care for a snort?" He leaned over to reach for the bottle of Cutty Sark he always kept in the bottom right drawer.

"Not this time, but thanks."

"Mind if I do?"

"Of course not," she said.

"Seeing your folks over the holiday weekend?"

"Yes. I plan to drive to Belvedere tonight, after the traffic dies down. They're dragging me to the club Friday and a party Saturday night, but Sunday will be Mother's Easter brunch, and it'll just be me and my folks."

"Nice. No sister?"

"Nope. She says she's too busy getting ready for her big art show the following weekend."

"Down the coast? You going?"

"Yes, and yes. I'm not allowed to miss this one."

Ron gave a knowing nod. "Good. You two seem to be doing better since she moved. Someday it'll be just the two of you, you know. Best to keep things friendly."

"Wise words from my favorite wise man," Meredith offered. He guffawed, but she saw the warmth of appreciation in his eyes. "So, what about you? Marjorie have a slew of plans for the family?"

"New grandson is coming with his entourage," Ron said, beaming. "I mean, it'll be good to see the kids, of course."

"If you can see past the blinding light emanating from your grandson's face, that is," Meredith added, returning the smile.

"Itching to get my hands on him," he admitted. "When the little tyke gives me that toothless grin, I'm done for."

"Aww, I always knew you were a softy."

He squinted and gave her a fierce stare.

She burst into a fit of laughter.

"Hey!" He demanded. "I have a reputation to protect."

Subsiding, she promised, "Your secret is safe with me."

"And yours are safe with me, Mer."

She inhaled sharply, but when she looked into his eyes, she saw only reassurance. She'd put that private indiscretion behind her more than a year earlier. She knew that if Peter Sylvester, with whom she'd had a one-night stand—or the wife she hadn't known about—threatened the firm, or her, Ron would have her back.

"So, how did it go with Ferguson?"

"Great. And thank you again. You're right, he's going to be a good client. I appreciate the referral." Meredith stood. "Have a great time with young Master Ronnie," she said.

"I certainly will," he replied, a goofy grin changing his appearance from sophisticated CEO to eager grandpa. "You too, Mer. Let's have lunch next week and we can swap stories."

"And photos," she added as she left his office.

Chapter 18

Miranda awoke in her motel room Friday morning, realizing today was the start of Easter weekend.

It'd be odd not to be with her family this year. Her mother loved the holiday, not for religious reasons, but because she always managed to turn it into a time of sweet family traditions: colored eggs and a delicious brunch menu, gorgeous flowers and lovely spring outfits, showing off her girls to friends, then relaxing together at home.

Miranda knew she'd disappointed her mother. But she also knew that a visit to the Belvedere homestead just wasn't possible this month. *First Oregon. Now Lompoc. And next week, my art show.*

It was odd to be thinking about this in a motel room. Is this where she wanted to be? Did she feel sad at missing out on another lovely family holiday? Did she feel guilty about not going?

Yes, a little, she admitted. And she did look forward to her next visit with her parents, whenever that might be. But she also recognized that she'd managed, for once, to give herself space both to do the work she loved and to respond to the possibilities that arose organically as she did. *I'd have missed out on this mural project. And I'd have missed Cornelius.*

She would, however, call her folks over the weekend after she got home. Now it was time to get her day started. She returned to the same diner where she'd bought soup the night before and sat down to some pancakes and hot tea. After checking out of the motel, she headed back to yesterday's location, parked, and carried her supplies around the corner to begin work on her own separate mural.

Fortunately, she'd used chalk to sketch in the image during a previous visit, to make sure the building owners approved. Now, she just had to fill in the colors. Still, she'd had a big job to complete in a short time.

Between holding her arm overhead and climbing up and down her small ladder all day yesterday, she'd already gotten a heavy workout. Today would be another one. *Good thing Tai Chi and biking keep me strong.*

While she worked, she kept thinking about Cornelius. *What am I doing? Why did I agree to go camping with the man?*

Well, it'd sure seemed like a great idea at the time, what with watching the sun sink into the ocean at a beautiful beach with a beautiful man. But now she wasn't so sure. She could always go watch the sunset with him, then say she really needed to get home. She did have her own car, so she wouldn't be stuck without transportation. *I should've said let's play the camping thing by ear, then see how we feel after dinner.* But she hadn't.

That smile. That twinkle in his eyes. That jaw line with just a hint of whiskers. Those hands . . . the ones that are healed, now. Her heart did a little dance as she thought about him, and a drip of paint escaped her brush to land on her jeans.

Focus, kee-do, as Monsieur Gilroy would say. Cornelius will be here soon enough.

Miranda walked across the street to see how the new mural looked from a slight distance. *If I'm honest with myself . . . I love it!* There was something cozy about it, despite the rather forbidding plunge of the hillside into treacherous currents. The blooming flowers made it cheerful, and the sandcastle in the foreground brought along with it a childlike energy she thought viewers would enjoy.

As she closed up her paint supplies and loaded them in her car, she glanced at her watch. *Almost 5:30.* Time had flown by while she'd worked. She'd taken a quick lunch break, but then gotten right back into the project. *Flow. That book Samantha and I talked about, about optimal experience. That's what happened today. I got myself out of the way. That's when the work just seems to take care of itself.*

She slammed the trunk and opened the car's windows to let some breeze cool the interior, then she sat for a moment behind the steering wheel. *Wish I could take a shower and fix up a little. But . . . I don't have the motel room anymore. At least I have that little vial of tuberose oil. Maybe that'll help.*

"Wow."

The word startled her, and she looked up into Cornelius' face where she saw twinkling dark blue eyes and a smile.

"It's great. Really great! Wish I could pack it in the back of my SUV and take it home!"

Miranda laughed. "Thanks!"

"Fortunately, the artist did give me the small version."

She smiled, feeling her face get even warmer than it already was.

"So. Still up for dinner and a sunset?"

"Absolutely!"

"I brought corn on the cob, eggplant, soy burgers and a few other things. Also, here's a smoothie to tide you over. You can drink it on the way. It'll take us about forty-five minutes to get out there, and then we have to get set up."

Miranda shook her head. "You've thought of everything!"

"We'll see about that. Okay, follow me. I won't go too fast, and we'll be on sort of a windy, country road."

"Got it."

I love roads like this, she thought, as they got underway. *This is turning out to be a* very *Good Friday.*

Cornelius pulled away from the curb and headed east on Ocean Avenue, checking his rearview mirror to be sure Miranda followed.

They continued for a few blocks, then turned right on Cabrillo Highway, better known as California 1. The small town was left behind gradually as spacing between streets widened until the road threaded its way past broad moors, rolling hills, and some rocky escarpments. Ranchos, wineries, and various private estates made up this part of the county, with fields alternating between wild grasses, pastures with grazing cattle, and cultivated rows.

He glanced in his mirror again. *Not a tailgater. Not a dawdler.* The dark green Mustang followed at just the right distance, and he began to wonder what this landscape looked like from her perspective. Just thinking about it for a moment, he noticed the different shades of green: vibrant and bright by the edge of the road; emerald on the hillsides.

But it was the spring blooms that he imagined she'd find hard to ignore. To his right a pocket of California poppies seemed to bob their heads as they passed, and he pointed at them, noticing that she nodded her head in acknowledgment.

After twists and turns through the colorful countryside, a view of the ocean broke across his windshield. He took a sharp breath and felt himself smiling with anticipation. He pulled into the lot by the Jalama cabins and parked, glad that Miranda pulled in right beside him.

"Oh, those flowers! The poppies, the yellow coreopsis blooms!" she exclaimed as she exited her car.

Cornelius stood there grinning at her.

She looked around and added, "I didn't know there were actual places to stay. I thought we were going to the beach."

"We could do that. But these little cabins have kitchens, showers—all the conveniences, even if they are tiny. I reserved one for us, just in case. We don't have to use it."

"Are you kidding? This is perfect! I was longing for a shower after working in the sun all day."

"Good. Then if we do decide to stay, there's a queen bed, bunk beds, and a pull-out. Plenty of options."

He stood opposite her, nearly eye to eye. *She must be what, five-nine to my six-one? God, she looks good.*

"Sorry, I know I look a mess. Maybe I could clean up before we have dinner?" she asked.

"Of course," he offered. "Let's get our stuff inside. Then I'll fire up the grill while you do your thing."

A few minutes later, as he headed out to the small porch overlooking the beach below, he called back, "You don't look a mess, by the way!"

"Thanks!" she called back. "Liar!"

He chuckled while he laid out the vegetables and turned on the gas. *This all feels so domestic,* he thought, *cooking with the hiss of the water running in the background. I brought the food but should have brought flowers. Or maybe that would have been too much?*

When she emerged, she joined him on the little balcony "Wow, the color's coming into the sky. The view is beautiful!"

"It is," he confirmed, looking not at the sky, but at her. *She looks radiant after her shower*, he thought, but all he said was, "Better?"

"Much. Thanks again. Had to put back on the same clothes," looking down at her pants disdainfully. After a moment, she said, "Come to think of it, I do have my emergency go bag."

"Seriously?"

"Always," she affirmed. "Earthquakes, fires, floods . . . If you live in California, you pretty much have to expect the unexpected."

"Couldn't agree more," he said approvingly. "In addition to my go bag, I've got an avalanche blanket, tire rugs—"

"What?" she asked.

"You know, to slide under a tire in case of snow, ice, whatever."

"Oh! Good idea. Um, I want to grab the backpack from my trunk. I've actually got jeans that don't have paint on them. I'll be right back."

"Okay. Don't be long. Everything's just about ready. They've got plates and things in the kitchenette. Can you?"

"Got it," she said, walking inside.

He flipped the burgers and the slices of eggplant a couple more times, making sure their food was done, but not burned. He wrapped the hot food in the foil he'd brought and closed the grill, then walked inside to see the small table set with plates and flatware. She'd even stuck some wildflowers in one of the extra glasses.

They sat and looked at one another for a moment. Then they both started to laugh.

"Okay, you first. What's funny?" he asked.

She hesitated. "Well, this is wonderful. And I just . . . this is sort of embarrassing."

"Did I do something—"

"No!" she cut him off. "It's just, I have this thing, that a man should know . . . that he should be prepared—"

"—for any emergency?" he offered.

She nodded.

He looked down at his hands for a moment, then looked into her eyes again. "Thing is, I have the same expectation. It just makes sense to me, but it never even occurs to a lot of folks."

"Right. My sister would be a case in point. Her expectation is that there will always be a rescuer, so why worry?"

He shook his head. "What about your folks? Your dad the rugged outdoor type?" he asked, unwrapping his corn.

Miranda burst out laughing. "Not even remotely! Unless golf is involved." She put the paper napkin in her lap and reached for her knife and fork.

Cornelius asked, "Your mother?"

Still laughing, she said, "Perish the thought."

"Okay . . . so why you?"

She took a bite of eggplant, then said, "Delish. Um, I suppose it's connected to my work. I mean, I paint wildlife. I have to go where *they* go, at least to some extent. But I think the desire, the need, to be independent was always there, even when I was little."

"To be independent and safe and prepared," he amended.

"Yes, all of that," she agreed. She lifted the bun off her burger. "Hey, you even brought ketchup," she said, adding some, then taking a bite.

"What's a burger without ketchup?" he asked.

"Mmm, this is great!"

"Glad you like it," he said.

They ate in silence for a few minutes, except for a few more pleased exclamations from Miranda.

Then she asked, "So, what about you? I picture these banks of high-tech equipment at NASA, like Mission Control in Houston. Is it actually like that when you study the stars? Or do you camp out and look at the sky?"

"Yes," he answered, which made her laugh. "All of that. Mission Control, not so much. But, of course, we do all work on computers. And the way things are going, I predict our world, and everyone's world, will become more and more digital."

"Not sure that'll happen in the arts," she observed.

He thought for a moment as he worked his way down a row of corn. "I agree, there will always be a handmade element to painting, sculpting, all the visual arts, because I'm sure artists will insist upon it. But eventually, we'll probably have a sophisticated stylus that'll work on a computer screen. And look what's happened with music! Already there are synthesizers that mimic instruments, but they also create new sounds."

Miranda nodded. "One of my favorite musicians is Pat Metheny. He's a guitarist, but he gets all kinds of new sounds with synthesizers. Anyway, okay, so sometimes you work in a computerized environment. And other times, you look at the sky. But . . . really? You just lie on the ground and observe with the naked eye?"

"Every chance I get," he confirmed, wiping his mouth with his napkin.

They ate some more, finishing their dinners as though they'd been starving.

"So, work requires both of us to be proficient campers," she said, wiping her mouth. "But we kinda love it too, right?"

"Love it and would do it anyway. And speaking of being outside . . . we oughtta catch the sunset. Want to watch from here? Or down on the beach?"

She thought for a moment. "Got a beach mat?"

"Yup."

"Me too. Let's grab them and head down."

After navigating the rough-hewn stairs down slope, they walked several paces and looked northward at the arc of the long, wide beach. In the middle distance, stood the remains of a sandcastle.

"Oh!" she said.

"Wow, that was a good one," he agreed. "Fancy round keep tower, battlements, turrets, and a good-sized moat."

"Sounds like you know your castles."

"Part of the job description."

She laughed. "For astronomers?"

"For knights," he corrected.

"Of the shining armor variety?" she asked.

"Is there any other kind?"

She smiled, and he watched as her gaze toward the sand-castle softened. "I put one in my mural."

"And in your postcard."

"My dad used to make those with me when I was little," she shared. "When it was nearly finished, he'd scoop up some very wet sand and let it drip onto the turrets, making these artistic decorations."

"When they dried, they must've looked as if they were carved in stone," he observed. Though it was a sentimental moment, she also seemed sad at the remembrance. "Glad you had those times together."

"Yes, me too."

They walked back to a spot below their cabin. The sand was cool to the touch by the time they unrolled their grass mats. The tide was still out, and he figured they had just enough time to enjoy the sinking of the sun into the ocean.

She stood for a moment, gazing to her left. "We can't see it from here, but around that promontory, that's where the Point Conception light is, right?"

"Right. Private property now. And apparently the owners are very nasty about trespassing," he added.

"That's what I found out when I tried to visit. But the reason I'm asking . . . basically, we're standing right—"

"—in the middle of your mural!" he said, finishing her sentence.

"If we imagined this beach were closer," she began.

"All we'd need to do is build the sandcastle."

She turned to face him, appreciation and maybe even wonder in her eyes. "You *see* it," she said.

"Of course. That's what you do with your art, give the rest of us windows."

She sighed as though with a sense of relief.

He stood there watching her for another moment. Breeze riffled through her long hair, and the sun was still just bright enough to show the green of her eyes, shining like jade. *She sees beauty. She is beauty*, he thought, then said, pointing to the mats, "This okay?"

"Absolutely." Once they were settled, reclining side by side so they could see both the water and the coming light show, she said, "It's kind of nice just to watch and not worry about painting it."

"Hmm. It's kinda nice to watch and not worry about calculating star rise."

They both chuckled.

"Are we workaholics or something?"

"Or something," he agreed.

After a moment, she asked, "We talked about being prepared, but why do you have *two* sets of camping gear? The extra sleeping bag belong to an ex-wife or someone?"

"No, no, nothing like that. I . . . I don't know. I think maybe it's because I'm an only child."

"Sorry, I don't quite understand."

"Well, my parents always worked hard to make sure I had friends to play with. So they bought two of everything like bicycles and boogie boards. I guess I picked up the habit."

"That's sweet. And it works out. I mean, in case you happen to have a friend show up who wants to have a sleepover."

He turned to glance at her, noting the teasing smile. He was going to say something, but noticed her shaking. "Cold?" he asked.

"A bit."

"Here," he said, scooting himself closer and opening his arm. She snuggled in, and he wrapped the arm around her. *She fits*, he thought.

"The sun's sizzling down into the water," she commented.

He chuckled. "An unscientific observation."

"A metaphorical one," she countered.

"Wonder if we'll see the green flash." And then, they did.

Cornelius had made quick work of rolling up their mats and heading them both inside when he noticed Miranda shivering, then yawning.

"You don't want to do the drive tonight, do you?"

"Not a chance."

He nodded. "They don't provide linens, but I've got the two sleeping bags. I can take one of the bunks."

"But," she hesitated. "I don't want you to."

He stopped rustling around and looked at her, his heart hammering. "Meaning?"

"Meaning . . . can we share the queen?"

"If that's what you want."

"I'm not . . . ready for—"

He stepped to her, cupped her face in his hands. "I would just love to hold you. Will that work?"

"Oh yes, please," she said quietly.

He nodded again, then moved his hands down to her shoulders. "So we have a couple of options. With the bags, I mean. They're the kind that lay flat, and they can be used separately, or they can be zipped together, so they're more like a bed. You know, kind of like a bottom sheet and a quilt."

"That sounds good," she said.

They took turns in the small bathroom. While she used it, he changed into sweatpants and a T-shirt. When she emerged, he said, "I put an extra sweatshirt over the chair in case you'd rather not sleep in your clothes. But do whatever makes you comfortable."

"Perfect," she said, grabbing it and disappearing again into the bathroom. She turned out the light when she left it this time, plunging their small abode into the dark blue of twilight. He felt her touch the edge of the bed.

"That zipper's the bag opening. Just slide in."

When she did, he held her as he had on the beach, feeling her breath on his neck, her soft hair against his skin. *That aroma . . . floral? Almost tropical.* The delicate scent of her filled his nostrils, and he worried that his hammering heart must be a percussive pounding in her ear.

"Thanks for tonight," she said quietly. "I loved it."

"Me too. Hope you sleep well."

He'd wanted to stay on the beach with her while the sky darkened and the stars began to pop into visibility. If the cabin had a skylight, or if they were sleeping in his tent with the sky view unzipped, even without his ephemeris, he could point out a few constellations before cloud cover.

In Santa Barbara, we'd be facing south, but here at Jalama, we're facing southwest. Mars would be pretty bright overhead, Ursa Major just to the right. Up and farther right, she might recognize Cassiopeia, and over to the left, Virgo.

He lay there holding her, feeling like a man who'd found the legendary pearl of great price. He wanted to thank her again or recite her a poem. But when he listened closely, he realized that her breathing had slowed and she had already drifted off.

She feels peaceful and safe enough to sleep. It's a good time to count my lucky stars.

Chapter 19

Veri Jones tightened the belt of her peach silk dressing gown and poured coffee from the silver pot on the kitchen sideboard into her Limoges china cup.

It was Saturday, so her husband Charles had left their Belvedere home at five-thirty for a regular golf date at the Sea Greens Club.

Meredith had arrived late-ish the previous night and had announced she planned to sleep in. Miranda had said she wouldn't be coming home for Easter this year. *I'm disappointed. I'll miss my Mandy. And it means we won't have her watercolor eggs this year. But I understand. She wants to be ready for her big art show.*

Veri, having slept in till seven-thirty, decided she'd enjoy using the rest of the morning to complete her letters. In a few minutes, she'd change into house-chore clothes, for she and Pilar had much prep work for Easter brunch.

I could ask Meri to help, but that never works out, unless Mandy's here too. Never mind. Meri needs her rest.

Veri shook her head, swirling cream into her cup. Her feather-trimmed mules clacking as she crossed the parquet foyer, she carried her coffee up the sweeping stairway into her study. As she opened the door, a puff of wind from the Bay Area's latest spring storm billowed the sheer vanilla curtains, and she stepped over to close the window.

The gust had also riffled papers on her small antique writing desk. Purchased during one of their trips to London twenty years earlier, the desk was a favorite—one of the treasures of their household. Though it was her husband's when it first arrived, Veri had negotiated for it and long since considered it hers.

Though small, it wasn't feminine. Indeed, provenance proved the desk had belonged to Charles Dickens in 1827, when he worked as a solicitor's clerk at the law firm of Ellis and Blackmore. Her own Charles had called it his namesake desk and put up quite an argument on its behalf. But in the end, Veri had purchased him something grander and come away with her prize. With its sloping green-leather top adjoining a flat galleried shelf, it had storage space for papers and notebooks. And with its solid mahogany construction and fine-turned legs, it had both elegance and quality.

The desk stood slightly higher than most, and they'd found a chair made in the 1800s to coordinate both in style and utility. Ever careful not to mar the leather, Veri placed her saucer along the desk's top edge and opened the drawer to retrieve some of her monogrammed stationery.

Veronica Merit Jones was embossed in silver on the smooth, cream-colored sheets, notecards, and envelopes. Though a new box had arrived, she wanted first to use up the old, and pulled the final card from the bottom of the stack. *What's this?* Surprised, she found an old, yellowed envelope stuck to the underside of the card. It was addressed to Mr. Charles Jones. The return address was Joseph Calvin's in Santa Barbara. *They haven't been in touch for years,* Veri considered, *not since shortly after Joan's death.*

Veri took a sip of her coffee, her gaze lifting to the window. The Calvins were their friends all those years ago, two couples with exceptionally good fortune and wildly ambitious plans. But soon they were all busy parents. And when Joan had become ill and died, Joseph withdrew completely.

Veri looked down at the slit envelope and hesitated. *Why is this here? Charles must have left it in the drawer years ago. It's his letter. I shouldn't read it, but after all this time, would it matter?*

Unable to resist the temptation, Veri slid the letter out and looked at the handwritten note. *No date. Frustrating!* Perhaps some reference in the text would clarify when it had been written. Tentatively, Veri began to read.

> Dear Charles,
>
> Apologies that it's been so long since I was in touch. Business demands most of my time, as I imagine it does for you. And whatever time I have left is devoted to Joan and our boy.
>
> Zack has just turned five, and he's a precocious tyke—the light of Joan's life and the hope of mine. Sounds like you and Veri have your hands full with two girls!
>
> Say, I think your idea about our progeny marrying is a fine one. Which of the two daughters would it be? I imagine if they're as beautiful as your lovely wife, Zack would be a lucky man in either case. Certainly, it would secure the family fortunes for all.
>
> Hope we can manage a visit one of these days.
>
> Kind regards to both of you,
>
> from both of us,
>
> Joseph

Veri had no recollection of a discussion between herself and her husband regarding a possible marriage between the Calvins' son and one of her own daughters. The notion seemed as dated as her antique desk. She was inclined to dismiss the mention as a joke between two pals.

Not the kind of thing women would joke about, she mused. She looked forward to showing the letter to Charles when he got home and wondered if he'd remember it.

She tried to return to her note-writing task but found the unexpected letter distracted her. The more she thought about it, the more irritated she was that Charles had never mentioned this idea he and his friend had concocted. Nor did she believe Joan had ever been consulted.

The notion of an arranged marriage was preposterous! On the other hand, the practice did continue, disguised as the kind of "fortune" or "serendipity" that arose as a result of carefully planned social events.

If either of her daughters heard about this, they'd either be outraged or consider it a wildly inappropriate joke. Certain she herself would have plenty to say on the subject, it would assuredly not *all* be in the hands of their father.

Could Charles and Joseph have been serious?

If she confronted Charles, he'd no doubt laugh it off and deny that the idea had any substance. The only contact with Joseph these days was a brief annual Christmas card, so it seemed highly unlikely anything further would come of it. Perhaps then, she'd leave the note out on her desk. That would be as passive-aggressive as his secret letter to Joseph. Still, she knew her curiosity would get the better of her, one way or another. *I do wonder what Charles might have to say about it!*

Family secrets. They had a way of surfacing unexpectedly. Even as the realization struck her, she thought of that larger, even earlier one. It'd been huge at the time, and now had receded so far into the background as to have virtually disappeared.

She thought back to the early days, seeing it from Charles' perspective. Married two years and blissfully happy. His inherited import export business already a success, thriving beyond expectations through his own efforts.

She'd joined him on some of his many trips, but also loved that she could now devote more time to her beloved ballet, fundraising when she planned the big events, friend-raising at the smaller ones, and thrilled to have been invited to serve on the board.

During those two years, they were the happiest couple. She missed him madly when he was away. But then there were those homecomings, romantic and spiced with the surprises he always like to plan: a dinner in the city, a weekend getaway to the mountains, some fabulous new gem. He had never really stopped wooing her. Even now, he relished his roles as mogul and lover in equal measure.

Then it'd been time to start their family. A subtle shift began, as he established preliminary educational funds, while she made sketches, thinking of ways to transform their extra guest rooms. Two children, they'd agreed, would be right for them. Almost as though the universe had overheard their plans, but on a far faster timeline than they could've imagined, they received a startling letter.

She thought back again to that first crisis. *Charles, happily married, gets the shocking news. The woman he'd loved in Japan had died, leaving behind the infant he knew nothing about.*

Where such a circumstance might have torn apart some couples, for them it strengthened their bond. They'd flown to Tokyo, met with the grandparents who had no capacity to raise their late daughter's offspring—a "half" or "ha-fu" as they'd called the mixed-race child.

For Veri, meeting that baby had been love at first sight, and she'd welcomed the infant into her heart. En route home, they talked about names, then did some research the moment they returned home. The mother's had been Mariko, her nickname Mari. Depending on the kanji character used, it meant either truth or reason. Charles' own heritage being Welsh, they settled on Meredith, meaning ruler. *She certainly ruled our house from day one!* What made it work so well, was that her nickname "Meri" held the echo of her birth-mother's, while at the same time paralleling Veri's.

All signs of the rightness that she would be their first daughter. As they adjusted to their new parenting roles, Veri watched Charles expand into an even deeper love not only for his little daughter, but for his wife.

Their second child had arrived in the more usual way, a couple of years later, the timing perfect. They'd named her Miranda, a name Veri had secretly held dear since years before. "To be wondered at, worthy of admiration," it meant. And had always filled Veri's heart with wonder.

Charles loved being a father. He had from the very beginning. *He just has a easier time of it with daughter number one, because she's so much like him.* Competitive, whip smart, strategic, with a heart for business and a mind for money. Meredith had even helped him with some of his recent investments, to their mutual delight.

Bless him, he wrestled with Miranda's way of thinking. For him, the arts were decorative but not essential, and certainly not lucrative. As a temporary pass-time before marriage, he allowed it was acceptable. But then what? A daughter couldn't be supported by parents all her life. She'd either have to marry or get a real job.

Veri admitted to suffering the occasional pang when her husband seemed to prefer the child he'd had by another woman to the one she'd born him herself. Yet she knew this wasn't true. She remembered his intense joy and deep satisfaction when their Mandy came along. That second daughter was the arrival of fulfillment, confirmation that their family was now complete. Two daughters, as different as the two continents from which they sprang, yet a matched set nonetheless integral pieces of the familial whole.

The morning was slipping by quickly, and Veri needed to choose her wardrobe for this evening's party. Even though it was labeled a "casual" get together hosted by another family in the neighborhood, she scarcely knew how to respond to that word.

What did it actually mean? Were she and her family supposed to show up in velour running suits? Heaven forbid. In jeans? She only used hers for gardening.

Mandy would likely say "casual" meant hiking clothes; Meri would pronounce the category as anything made of cotton. Charles would take it to mean a golf outfit.

Veri sighed and stepped into her long walk-in closet. She poked through the "informal" area until she came across a pair of navy linen slacks, and a matching cashmere sweater set. "Perfect," she said aloud. *And if I add the simple gold earrings, they won't overwhelm the ensemble.*

After removing the chosen clothes from their hanging bar, she placed them on a special hook she used for staging, then she sat down at her dressing table.

Switching on the bright lights surrounding her mirror, she gave her unadorned face a close inspection. *Those tiny lines aren't quite so tiny any more,* she thought ruefully. *Still, Charles says he likes them.* Her husband might be a clever diplomat, but she loved him for it. The mirror wasn't as kind and forgiving as it had once been. But if she were honest with herself, she felt a certain pride about earning those not-so-tiny lines.

Susan disliked her rented cottage in Milford-Haven just as much as she hated the rest of the town. She stood at her dingy mirror and carefully surveyed the results of a twenty-minute effort to make herself up for a Saturday night on the town.

Deciding the competition around here was pathetic, she figured to conquer it easily, confirming this as she stood back and flung one hip to the side. The little black T-shirt clung nicely; the perennial black skirt seemed short enough, but a little loose; the black fishnet stockings were a nice touch—they'd be subtle in the low lights; the heavy shoes made it clear she could out-stomp the competition. Looking down at the edge of the shirt, she pulled at a thread, annoyed to find it still attached. She yanked and it refused to break. Pulling harder, she succeeded only in lengthening the string, which she wrapped angrily around her hand, not realizing until too late that she'd unraveled the entire hem.

A surge of self-loathing welled up, and she fought it down with defiance. *I meant to do that*, she decided. The shirt had been too perfect before, too ordinary. Now it looked battle-fatigued. Switching off the light, she grabbed her leather jacket, and beat a path to Milford-Haven's only night spot, ready for combat.

Susan decided the night was a bust by the time she'd consumed her second beer.

Wing Ding's had nothing new to offer in drinking buddies, pool partners, or possible bed mates. Despite the crowded room and loud music, pesky thoughts of Kevin Ransom kept interrupting her trolling, and even the beer wasn't doing much to numb her conscience.

So what if she'd punched him in the face after that concert? That was weeks ago. And anyway, he'd been out of line, putting his arm around her. Of course, they *had* been on a date—sort of. He'd picked her up and driven her all the way to the Central Coast Bowl, and then waited a good hour and a half after the Doobies concert while she interviewed Keith Knudsen for the *Milford-Haven News.*

Now, there's a neat guy, she thought. *Old enough to be my father, but so cool! A rock-and-roll drummer, no less.* And when she'd requested the interview, he'd said *yes.* When Knudsen looked at her, she didn't feel she was disappearing, as she usually did when she wanted something from a white man. Keith had looked at her like a human being. *Why couldn't I have had a father like that?* After taking another long pull on her Dos Equis, she slammed the bottle down harder than she'd intended. It brought a sharp look from the bartender, but she stared him down.

Shifting her eyes to the big mirror behind the bar, Susan caught sight of a familiar face over her shoulder. *It's that guy from backstage*, she noted, her heart racing. The opening band had been led by a guitarist, a Native guy who played like the gods were with him but who'd refused to talk to her backstage. He'd looked at her, though, looked *into* her, reaching her in a way she didn't understand. She'd worked hard to get rid of thoughts about him, and now here he was! Trying to be cool, she spun on her barstool and looked up into Kevin Ransom's face.

"Hi, Su . . . Su . . . Susan," he stammered, shouting over the song being played by the in-house disc jockey.

Susan was silent, confused. Looking past Kevin, she tried to find the mysterious man she'd nicknamed "Notes," but he was nowhere to be seen. Leaping down off the barstool, she hammered across the wooden floor toward the back pool tables, but no one meeting the description was in the place. Returning to her perch, she jumped up, and Kevin's large hands involuntarily reached out to help her. She slapped his hand away.

"No free skin, Kevin."

She watched as he checked her expression, registering his relief at seeing more humor than anger. His huge body visibly relaxed.

Sucking on her beer, she looked up at her tall friend. "What are you doing here, Kevvy? I thought it was past your bedtime."

"Well, I . . . it's . . . I couldn't sleep, and I don't know, I just had this . . . I wanted to talk to you."

"Talk? This isn't really the place for that, you know." She looked up into Kevin's warm hazel eyes, and he stared down at her, obviously at a loss. "Wanna dance?"

Before he could answer, she grabbed his hand and dragged Kevin to the dance floor. Delighted to have captured a victim, Susan chose a dark corner away from the bar, and he followed her lead, gyrating as best he could to the pounding, country and western tune.

But in a world of her own, Susan paid little attention to the undulating pillar of Kevin next to her and wiggled rhythmically, bumping and grinding as an independent expertise.

When the song ended, they hung suspended in their dark corner for a moment, until a slow song started to play. "And now here's Garth Brooks with 'Friends in Low Places,'" the DJ announced.

Kevin Ransom hesitated, not knowing what to do. But Susan pushed herself into his abdomen and reached around his waist, grabbing his belt with her left hand. Feeling pinned like a human by a cat, Kevin's arms flailed, until his left hand was safely captured by hers, and his right came down gingerly on her shoulder. Seeking safe purchase for his feet, he worried his size fifteen work boots would flatten her size sixes, somewhat relieved to find what appeared to be her steel-toed protection.

Towering two heads above her, he struggled to know how far to bend over, till he felt her cheek press into his chest, and a wave of warmth swept over him. His eyes casting helplessly around the room, he finally closed them, trusting intuition more than logic in this precarious situation. Losing himself in music and the heat of her body, he took tiny steps and shallow breaths, scarcely allowing his chest to rise against her delicate face.

Unaware of the magic transpiring in the corner, an adjacent couple were more grandiose in their movements. Bending his partner backwards over his arm, the slightly inebriated dancer careened into Susan, stepped sideways, and swept Susan's feet out from under her. Clutching at Kevin to avoid hitting the floor, Susan yelped. Startled out of his reverie, Kevin grabbed Susan, and as quickly as she'd lost her footing, she'd found it again with his strong arms and sure hands.

Laughing their apologies, the other couple wheeled away, leaving Kevin and Susan to recover. "You okay?" Kevin asked over the music.

Susan snarled at him, fury in her dark eyes. This time he should have seen it coming, but the punch took him upward on the chin. He didn't turn to watch her as she left Wing Ding's. Instead, he reviewed the near-fall, seeking a kinetic memory that might yield what logic hadn't disclosed. It was then he realized how he'd caught her—recognizing that the softness he'd grabbed had been her breast.

Kevin always understood animals better than humans, and it helped him now. Like a cat, she had her boundaries. Without warning she'd flailed out with her claws. In a flash of sudden understanding, he saw Susan was a feral thing and,like any wild animal, she had no choice but to defend herself.

Turning to leave the dance floor, Kevin slipped through the crowd and departed unnoticed from the bar, curiously undisturbed by Susan's second attack. Not even her dangerous claws and bared teeth could prevent him from savoring his brush with intimacy.

Chapter 20

Joseph Calvin looked forward to a delightful Easter Sunday at home. Already, it'd started well. He sat on his terrace in the comfort of shade provided by a jasmine-laden trellis. The delicate scent of blooming orange blossoms mixed with the jasmine, and a light breeze ruffled the tall eucalyptus.

He paused in his reading of the *New York Times* Business Section and looked up, noticing the Channel Islands were visible across a sparkling blue strip of Pacific.

Glancing up, he watched as James appeared, wheeling a cart onto the terrace from the kitchen. Santa Fe Nambe pottery serving dishes gleamed like polished silver in the morning sun. Adding them to the wrought-iron-and-glass sideboard already laden with Mexican pottery, heavy and brightly colored, James seemed slightly puffed with pride at his own handiwork. He pulled on a bright yellow oven mitt, lifted the Nambe lids, sending forth enticing aromas to mingle with breeze and blossom.

Folding his paper, Joseph pushed back his chair. "Can't resist those smells, James." Walking to the serving table, he leaned over to inspect the array of breakfast delicacies. "Smoked salmon!" he exclaimed with delight. Helping himself, he listened as James announced the rest of his morning menu.

"Omelette of chives and Boursin cheese, tomatoes seasoned and lightly broiled, toasted onion bagels, fresh mango."

"Excellent," said Joseph, looking up just in time to see Zack walk through the patio door. "Perfect timing, Zack," he called. "James has worked his magic again." As no reply was forthcoming, Joseph added. "Everything all right?"

"Yes, actually. All right."

Joseph took in the sight of his son, freshly showered and seeming to enjoy the comforts of home—including the anticipation of James' cooking. "Good. Grab some vittles."

"Don't mind if I do."

"The real coffee is in the cylindrical pot, Mr. Zackery," said James. "The decaf is in the round."

"Great." Zack stuck a serving fork into an enormous, juicy half of a beefsteak tomato. Peeling off some slices of smoked salmon, he slathered two bagel halves with whipped cream cheese. When he'd added one of the delicately turned omelettes, he carried his plate to the table.

Father and son ate in silence for the first several bites, and James disappeared into the cool, dark house. They were silent for another moment, enjoying their food.

"Got plans today?" Joseph inquired.

"Nothing much. Thought I'd watch the Knicks and the Magic later."

"Mm-hum," Joseph said, munching food. After swallowing, he added, "Think I might watch some of the PGA Championship."

"Figured you would."

"I notice you haven't had any dates lately."

"I could say the same about you," Zack quipped, spearing a chunk of mango.

"Something wrong, Zack? You seem a little testy."

"Sorry. No, everything's okay. I mean, work is fine. Great, in fact. Though Ron mentioned he's keeping an eye on the *Guerdon*."

The *Guerdon*, their only offshore rig, shone in the distance, a bright spot in the dark sea. Joseph glanced in its direction, frowned, and asked "What do you mean?"

"You know him. His OCD kicks in now and again."

"Right. He's a good man. But he has been known to be over cautious. You looking forward to next weekend?"

Zack Calvin took another bite and chewed for a moment. His father's question sparked an immediate recollection of a confusing conversation he'd had with Miranda. When it came right down to it, he'd only taken her out on one date, a rather sedate dinner during which she'd seemed painfully shy.

But when he'd called one day, she'd shown a completely different side, almost as if she had an entire personality she'd been keeping under wraps. *Vibrant, teasing, and sexy as hell.* Yet since then, during their few long-distance contacts, she'd seemed distant.

To be fair, it's not just her. It's me. I love Dad as I always have. But how well do I really know myself? I've been all over the map with Cynthia, and absolutely nowhere with Miranda. Is the adoption why I've been holding back?

"Yes," he finally said.

"Well, that didn't sound too enthusiastic," Joseph remarked.

Zack took a sip of coffee and looked out at the ocean, trying to decide just how much he wanted to reveal. *Not much. Not till I figure it out myself.* Then he offered, "I think it'll be good. I mean, her work is beautiful, and I know we'll both enjoy seeing more of it at the art show. And I think things will be clearer when I get to see Miranda in person."

Meredith had enjoyed her weekend at her parents' home more than she'd expected.

On Saturday, when she'd finally rolled out of bed in her old —but beautifully refurbished—room, it'd been to the sounds of laughter coming from her father. He'd "beaten the pants off" his archrival at golf, and that'd put him in a good mood that lasted through her entire visit.

Dinner at her parents' club had given her a chance to catch them up on work—her new consultancy, new clients, and steady support from her former boss. The party at their friends' home Saturday had been fun. Though they could've walked there, instead they arrived in dad's trusty Mercedes E-Class wagon. He called it the "family" car, while Mother called it the "golf-mobile." At the party, Mer settled right in to chatting with the neighbor family. While the respective parents visited, Mer caught up with the three kids she'd known all the way through school.

Sunday's Easter brunch had been spectacular. As always, both Mother and Pilar had outdone themselves. Mother had done her Goldenrod eggs, a family favorite. Hard-boiled eggs were delicately broken into bite-sized pieces, arranged on crisp English muffins, then smothered with Mother's bechamel sauce. As always, Dad had asked what her secret ingredient was, the one that made her dish so distinctive. As always, Mother had replied that if she divulged the answer, it would no longer be a secret. Then she'd lifted her napkin, and behind it, grinned at Meredith and mouthed "nutmeg."

These familiar rituals were a comfort. *They're more fun when Mandy's here and we can share them,* she admitted to herself grudgingly.

And thinking of Mandy brought to mind the idea she'd wanted to run by her parents in private.

Pilar cleared their plates, then brought in some small chocolate egg confections, which were passed around the table. After she left, Mer took another sip of coffee and said, "As I explained, things are going well with my consulting work."

"Yes. And we're proud of you," her father said.

"Thanks, Dad. So, um, I've decided to look for an investment property. I mean, I'm always telling my clients it's smart to diversify. Most of my own money is in the market, except for the house in the city."

"Your mother picked wisely, didn't she?" Charles beamed down the table at his wife, and Veri smiled at the compliment.

"She did. Good job, Mom," she added, looking at her mother. "I had my doubts about it, especially with you having to pay Miranda's share of the purchase."

"Well, it was a way of keeping you both safe, living in a much better neighborhood than either of you lived in previously. She couldn't make the investment at the time, but it was easy for us," her mother said, needlessly explaining what all of them already knew.

"And then I bought her out," Meredith added. "Well, I bought *you* out when she moved. And I love the house. On Mandy's old floor I've got a beautiful guest suite now. And I could even rent it out if I want to. It all worked out."

"It did, yes," Veri confirmed. "Although now Mandy's back to renting again. But from what I hear, it's a cute town, and very safe."

"Speaking of her town, if it's as up-and-coming as she claims, I think I should look there."

"What do you mean, look there, Meri dear?" her mother asked.

"Look for an investment property. I mean, it's coastal, so it'll only appreciate in value."

"Sounds smart to me," her father put in.

"So, I figured, since I'll be there next weekend for her art show, I could look around a bit."

"Oh, that sounds like fun! I wish Mandy's show didn't conflict with my ballet fund raiser! I'd have loved to go with you," Veri complained.

"She understands, Mom."

"She'll have other art shows," her father added.

Veri gave Mer a rueful smile. "I'm so glad you'll be there, dear."

"Yes, you'll have to represent the whole family," Charles said, sounding a bit relieved to be off the hook.

"Who else will be coming? Anyone we know?" Veri asked.

"She said the guy who invited her to the Doobie Brothers concert will be coming, and that he planned to bring his father."

The moment the words were out of her mouth, Mer felt heat rise in her face. All she could think of was that call. The phone had rung in Mandy's house while Mer had been waiting for her. For some reason, she'd answered it. She'd replayed that conversation time and again over the past couple of months.

A man's rich, deep voice had said, with a sense of surprise. "Caught you in."

Instead of immediately explaining that she wasn't Miranda, she'd answered with a teasing, "Caught me in what?"

"In the mood, I hope."

That'd been the moment she'd felt that irresistible tug. It'd started in her solar plexus and taken over her brain. She'd flirted mercilessly, enjoying every minute. *How had it escalated so fast? Good Lord, he was about to get in his car and race up the coast from Santa Barbara!*

But that was also the moment she'd realized he thought he was talking with someone else . . . with her *sister,* not with *her.* Then he'd had an unexpected meeting and had to go. And she'd been left trying to disconnect from what'd seemed so real.

"Meri dear. Did you hear what I asked?"

Mer coughed into her napkin, then said, "No, sorry. I thought I was choking."

"Take a sip of water, dear. What I said was, it'll be nice to meet Mandy's beau, though I haven't heard anything about him from her."

"Honestly, I'm not sure she's seeing him anymore."

"But if he's driving all the way to Milford-Haven for her show, that must mean something," Charles put in.

"Well, I guess we'll find out."

"Really, I don't know why she has to keep it a secret," Veri complained.

"What's the last name?" her father asked.

"I think it's Calvin."

"Funny," Charles added. "We used to have good friends by that name in Santa Barbara. But they were in oil, not entertainment."

Veri Jones twisted the napkin in her lap. *Charles knows perfectly well it has to be the same family. We just talked about it this morning.*

She peered down the table meaningfully, trying to read her husband. But his expression remained inscrutable.

Why is he being so cagey? He said this morning it had all been a joke. He must be worried about what would happen if that secret pact of his and Joseph's were ever revealed.

Sally dried her hands on Mama's clean towel and glanced around the kitchen. Everything was in order. She took off her apron, hung it on its hook and felt the goodness of the place.

When she opened it, the back screen door sounded the same familiar screech that matched the screen door at the front of the house. She knew she'd never oiled her own screen door at the restaurant so she could hear a sound that reminded her of home.

Standing in golden light on the back porch, she inhaled deeply the rich fragrance of freshly watered ground after the rain. She went to plump the pillow in one of the wooden rocking chairs and then relaxed into the familiar seat. The screen door screeched again.

"You don't never get tired of sittin' out here, do you?"

"I reckon not, Mama." Sally answered quickly, afraid that with the bright afternoon sun low in the sky her mother might not see the step clearly. She knew it was a foolish worry. Mama knew that first step like she knew the back of her hand.

"Well, I guess I could set a spell with you."

"Good, Mama. You don't sit nearly enough, you know, standin' in that kitchen practic'ly all day."

"Well, look who's talkin', girl. You're the one who cooks all day for a livin'."

They defended each other like the two allies they had become. In a world of changing values, theirs had remained constant at the core.

"Well, it's one thing I *can* do. You saw to that." Sally knew her mother didn't care for compliments when the simple truth would do. She took a deep breath. "Listen Mama, it's time I was gettin' back to it."

Sally knew Mama hated the thought of her girl leaving again so soon. "I never did like the idea of you bein' out there where they have earthquakes, and fires, and floods, and rattlesnakes, and the good Lord knows what all! I just never have seen what they got out there that you can't find right here in Arkansas."

They'd had this conversation many times before. It seemed to carry more weight as time marched on. "Oh, I don't know, Mama. I think I just had to try my wings. And now I got used to flyin'. Can't get back into the old cage now. Couldn't ever get used to it."

"Well, I know there's never been any use in my tryin' to talk sense into your head once you made up your mind."

"Like Mother, like daughter," Sally said gently. The two women laughed in a moment of good-natured self-knowledge. Glenda took the second porch rocker and sighed as she sat down. For a while there was no sound but those that nature made, blending with the steady creaks of one rocker, then the other.

Sally was the first to speak. "It has been so good to be home. I can't even tell you how good. Nights on the porch . . . these visits with you . . . "

"Now don't go all sentimental on me, girl," Glenda said breezily. "You know there's nothin' I like better than to see you've put a little meat on those skinny little bones."

Sally chuckled softly. As long as she could remember, Mama had been telling her she was skinny, though both of them were slender—always had been, most likely always would. *But I won't be skinny for long.*

She looked at her mother's face—the soft wrinkles that lined her cheeks now, yet could do nothing to diminish the strong simple beauty that had always been hers. She looked at Mama's hands, which had never known a day without toil, and at her shoulders, rounded now just a little more than last year.

Sally leaned back in her chair and looked up at the familiar canopy of the oak tree. "Well, I just hope somebody wants to come home to me one day just as much as I wanted to come home to you." Sally felt a serenity settling over her like calm on a lake.

"So, you've come along about four months now?" Mama said quietly.

"I never could hide anything from you." Sally paused and turned her head. "Yes, Mama, about four-and-a-half."

"You're *sure* about this, now. There's no changin' your mind on this kind of thing, you know." Glenda said the words it befitted a mother to say. But both women understood what was being said with a knowing that was basic and hallowed. They each continued rocking, the sounds of their chairs blending with the gentle rhythms of the evening birds.

"That's right," said Sally. A wonderful calm washed over her. "I'm sure, Mama. I'm gonna raise me a child." It felt good to speak the words out loud. "And for now, it'll be our little secret."

Sally took another moment to glance around her room. Long shafts of reddening light cast the Venetian blinds' pattern across the maple wood bed and dresser, which shone with many years of polishing. Lace doilies adorned the dresser top. The hand-made quilt was tucked neatly alongside the footboard, and the dolls huddled together in the well-worn chair, waiting for some-one to read them a story. They seemed a little sulky, as though they were holding their breath, hoping they could change her mind about leaving again. Reluctant to leave the room till she'd rememorized every detail, she realized how much she wanted to create this warmth and comfort for her own child.

Putting on her jacket, Sally noticed she could no longer fasten the button in front and smiled to herself as she carried her bag down the hall, through the kitchen and out the front door.

Following her, Mama held out a large paper shopping bag.

"What's this?" Sally asked.

"Just a few things to take back to California."

"Oh, Mama." Looking into the bag, Sally saw several packages carefully sealed in plastic wrap and cushioned with newspaper.

"I put the cornbread in an aluminum pie pan, and that way it'll stay all-of-a-piece till you cut into it," she said, all efficiency.

"Then there's a jar o' beans, a jar o' 'fridgerator jelly, and then in the tin foil on top, that's a hot biscuit with country ham, so you have somethin' for the airport."

As her mother rattled on, Sally took in every detail, memorizing her too: gray hair held in place with beautiful wide combs, small antique gold earrings dancing as she talked, faded lavender cardigan over a round-collared white cotton blouse, small waist cinched in apron strings, sensible tan shoes.

"You could come and visit me sometime," Sally said.

"Oh, land sakes, what'd I ever do in California?" Glenda asked, pulling a stray hair from Sally's jacket.

"Well, I do run a rest'r'nt." Sally chuckled, then held her mother in a fierce hug, stifling sudden tears.

Still in the embrace, Glenda said, "You know those dreams are just as normal as can be at a time like this."

"What dreams?" Sally asked, releasing the hug.

"Kind you mentioned th'other night."

Shaking her head, Sally said, "So . . . you knew back then, didn't you?"

"I suspicioned it." She pressed on with her point. "Actually, it's a good thing, 'cause it helps us to free our minds from the old life."

Sally looked at her mother carefully. "I'm not sure what you're saying, Mama."

"We get set in our ways, have certain ideas about how things go. Then a new baby comes along, and the whole world changes. These strange dreams—they help to get us ready for all that."

In her homespun way, Mama'd put her finger right on the pulse of life itself. She had a knack for it, and Sally's pregnancy seemed to be bringing it all to the surface.

"Go on, get on your way now. You don't want that airplane goin' to California without ya." A stoic smile was now fixed across Mama's face.

Delivering one more quick kiss to her mother's cheek, Sally opened the driver's side and climbed into the rental car, slammed the door, and lowered the manual window.

"Get that seat belt around yourself, now."

"Oh, Mama, I'm doin' it!" Sally took a long breath. "Love you, Mama. Come see me sometime."

Touching the car door, Glenda leaned over and looked deep into her daughter's eyes "If ya need me, Sally girl, I'll be there in two shakes."

"I know, Mama. I know."

Putting the car in reverse, Sally touched her foot to the gas just as Mama stepped to the car again, as if to share one final thought. *She always does like to have the last word.*

Sally listened. Then, backing down the long driveway, she turned the car and waved as she started down the country highway. Sally knew Mama would stand waving until the car was out of sight.

As she drove the long miles to the Little Rock airport, it was those final words Sally heard again and again. "Just remember," Mama'd said. "Babies come to change the world."

Chapter 21

M iranda felt she could oh-so easily be a fool for love. In fact, maybe she already was. *That's perfect*, she thought. *It's April Fool's Day.*

Since returning home from that night with Cornelius at Jalama Beach, she'd managed to get through some of her to-do list. Certainly, she had plenty of work to keep herself fully occupied. But every time she looked up from her desk, she found herself gazing out the window daydreaming again.

She'd had several long conversations about this with her cat, who seemed suitably sympathetic most of the time. She hadn't said a word to Samantha, who seemed preoccupied with her own issues these days. And she hadn't seen Sally since she got back from Arkansas. *I could call Mer. But I know she's busy. And she'll be here over the weekend.*

The two lions stared out at her from the canvas that still rested on her studio easel. Though their pose was dignified, she thought she saw the slightest smirk on their faces.

"What?" she asked aloud. "Don't look so smug!"

Oh, great. Now I'm talking to my paintings. Get a grip!

But really, how could she? The man was handsome. He was brilliant. He was funny. He was tender. *Oh, so tender.*

Most importantly, he liked her. *He likes me!*

A postcard from him had arrived this morning, mailed from Lompoc. *That means he wrote it Monday morning and dropped it in the mail right after we left Jalama in our two cars.*

Here it was Tuesday morning, and the card had already arrived. That likely meant that today he'd be receiving the post-card she'd sent to him yesterday.

"Loved it. Cornelius." That's what he'd written on his postcard.

Love cards. Are we sending each other love cards? Oh my God, a man who writes me cards. How can I resist?

And why should she? Resist, that is. Well, because it's what she always did. With startlement, she realized that was indeed her pattern. She ran at the first sign of . . . what? Real connection? Genuine interest? Is that what she'd done with Zack?

Then she thought back to her conversation with Kuyama, about finding her voice, trusting her instincts. What did her instinct tell her now? *That he's good. That he's right.*

Whew. The feelings swirled through her chest, dropped into her center, zinged down her legs, and made her weak in the thighs—and then, they made her heart sing.

She was gazing out the window again. It was time to get back to work. Thank goodness she had so much of it to do.

Sally felt good to be home in Milford-Haven.

Even saying that to herself felt right. Wonderful as every moment of her week with Mama in Arkansas had been, she knew the life she'd made for herself here was a good one.

This is where she'd founded her very own business, and it was a going concern. This is where she'd established herself as an independent woman. And this is where she would rear her very own child.

A thrill ran through her—part fear, part excitement. And she figured every mother-to-be had those same feelings at one time or another. *This sure ain't gonna be easy. But what good thing ever is?*

She'd called June from the airport to let her know she'd be back Monday but would come into work Tuesday, giving herself a day to unpack, clean house, and sort her mail.

And in the mail she'd found a note from Tony, telling her he'd be arriving soon and would like to catch her up on his plans. *He must o' sent this before we talked on the phone.* These undisclosed plans sounded just a little bit mysterious, but in a way that made her smile. After all, she had a pretty big secret to tell him, too. She'd rather he heard it directly from her and heard it before a lot of other folks figured it out.

When she got to her restaurant at 6 a.m. Tuesday morning, she flipped on the lights, started the coffee, and carried a new addition out to the dining area.

Each season, she placed a life-sized doll on the first stool at her counter. During Christmas, of course it was a Santa. During autumn, there was her straw man with his corncob pipe, except for Halloween, when she'd invite one of the local scarecrow festival participants to place a character on her stool. The new doll was a Raggedy Ann she'd found at the local fair she'd visited with Mama. This was no ordinary Annie-doll; she was full-sized, and she'd caused a lot of comments as she was being carried through the airports.

Annie, as Sally called her, fit right in with the decor. She'd fit even better when Miranda finished the mural she had planned. And if anyone did figure out that having a Raggedy Ann meant a child was coming, well that was bound to happen anyway, sooner or later anyhow. For now, though, Annie would keep Sally's secret.

Samantha stood staring out her living room window as the sun plunged into the Pacific, barely able to see her view of pine trees and ocean in the twilight.

Since yesterday, she'd been replaying the words Stacey Chernak had spoken, "This is not much, Ms. Hugo."

Not much! It might be everything in the world. The thought of her son being so close was both exhilarating and claustro-phobic. *Santa Barbara is only two-and-a-half hours south. Is it possible he still lives there?* Both thrilling and terrifying, it was too much to hope for and not enough to go on.

Not knowing what to do with herself, she walked back to the front door to retrieve something from her bag, but by the time she got there, she'd forgotten what it was. Then she headed to the kitchen to make coffee. Thinking better of it, she lifted one of the wine glasses hanging from its rack, uncorked a partially consumed bottle of Merlot, and poured.

Moving back to the living room, she placed the glass on the coffee table, then stared at a drawer in her wall unit that contained old home movies. She'd never had them converted to video. To view them, she'd have to find her old projector, set up her screen. Instead, she ran her hand along the bookshelf lined with photo albums, their spines date-embossed. She continued backward till she found the one she was looking for: 1960. Careful not to damage the edges, she pulled it out, plunked her-self down on the sofa and placed the heavy book across her lap.

After taking a sip of her wine, she opened the cover, heard the crackle of the binding, and inhaled the scent of old leather. Touching the plastic-covered sheet, her long finger traced the lock of Gregory's baby hair captured on the page, the blond curl pressed above a picture of the Santa Carlita Cove—a second print of the same picture she'd placed among his things the day she'd left him with the Northern California Orphanage Association.

Terrified at the strength of the images to which she was about to subject herself, she was nonetheless unable to resist the temptation to continue and took another long swallow of the Merlot.

There they were on their day at the beach, the day she'd written about in her journal not long ago. Suddenly tasting a faint trace of salt, she brushed hair from her face as if a breeze had moved it out of place. Squinting, she adjusted the standing brass lamp next to the couch and bent over the book to look more closely. Here was another shot—the pier overlooking the curve of the Cove where it swept north and upwards to the woods high on the peninsula. The Enchanted Forest, the locals called it, and she'd always believed it *was*.

Turning page after page, it was as if, magically, she were turning back the pages of time. The longer she looked at her photo album, the more vivid the pictures seemed to become, rekindling the original images buried deep in her memory. Almost . . . she felt if she closed her eyes, she might again be playing, hearing the squeals of her baby boy, as though awakening from a long, fitful sleep on her beach blanket.

Peek-a-boo, where are you?" she called out, her hands over her eyes.

She heard a gurgle, something like a chuckle. Already, he knew this game so well.

"There you are!" she said, removing her hands. Now it was his turn. Placing his tiny hands over his own eyes, he waited for her words.

"Where's Mommy?"

Down came his hands.

"There she is!"

Delighted giggle eruptions issued forth, and eagerly, he awaited the next Mommy Game. Placing a linen napkin over his head, she hid his face. "Where's the baby?"

A genuine chortle could be heard from under the napkin. Now she removed it.

"There's the baby!"

A high-pitched squeal of delight.

Taking a pull on her wine, Sam regarded her glass ruefully and slammed the heavy album shut.

I must rid my mind of these far-gone images, she told herself. They were no longer true. That little boy no longer existed, nor did his half-brained, cowardly mother. Now in their place were two people: one in the full stride of his young manhood and the other, a fading environmentalist slipping rapidly over the hill.

She laughed bitterly at her sorry state and stood to put the album away before she damaged it, staggering a little, whether from the wine or from a deadened leg, she couldn't tell. Either way, she liked the idea of deadening herself further.

More than anything else, what she longed for now was numbness.

Sam awoke with a headache and a heartache. Which was worse, she couldn't determine.

The cure for the first was simple, so she pushed out of bed to go in search of a bottle of painkillers.

The second ache had been with her so long, she was surprised to find it sharp rather than dull. *That's what I get for looking at those photos*, she scolded herself. *Yet how could she have resisted?*

She knew of only two cures for heartache. One was her journal writing, the other was work. Quickly, she checked her calendar. It was only Wednesday, and the week would be full of meetings, reports, follow-ups, and research sessions. She couldn't skip out on a workday, so she flipped ahead to the weekend, remembering that Miranda's art show would be held Friday night.

Whatever might be going on in her own world, Miranda's first public show since moving to Milford-Haven would be very important for her young friend, and Sam would be there with bells on.

She also knew she should call Miranda to touch base before the show. Who would be coming? No doubt her representative would. What about Zack? Were they still in touch? How nervous did she feel about the show itself? Sam jotted a note to call her, even try to get together before the big event.

Then Sam looked further into her day planner. The week following, all manner of reports would be due, as would the slides for an upcoming presentation she'd be giving for a state-wide eco conference in Sacramento.

So, any time off would have to wait till about ten days from now. *I'll go to one of my writing spots*, she thought. *If I don't get my head screwed on straight, I won't be much good to anyone.*

She couldn't afford to just let this drift but needed to actually schedule a date with herself. She'd take a mental health day, book a room at a hotel up the coast a bit . . . San Simeon, or maybe even Ragged Point.

Looking to the week beginning April 14, she glanced at the pre-printed notation on that page. "National Ex-Spouse Day," it read.

Sam burst out laughing. *If that isn't the perfect day to spend collecting my thoughts and journaling, I don't know what is!*

Chapter 22

Kevin Ransom unlocked the door of Sawyer Construction, stepped inside, and quietly let the door lock behind him. He loved coming to the office alone. With Mr. Sawyer gone to visit clients in Cayucos and Morro Bay for the day, the quiet was blissful, and he could complete some of his tasks without constant interruption.

Primary on his list was the photocopying, and he turned on the oversized machine to warm it up. From the top of his stack, he pulled the first architectural drawing and walked back to the machine. Handling the drawing with care, he allowed it to float perfectly into place against the newly cleaned glass, checked the registration marks to make sure it was aligned, then pressed Nine, then Copy.

The efficient whirring of the machine was like a good back-beat on a tune by the Eagles, and Kevin found himself humming along with the big copier, as usual, as much at home with machines as he was with animals.

Things mechanical and electrical revealed themselves to Kevin, as though they had no choice. When something malfunctioned—or often just before—Kevin tuned in to it as though receiving code on an arcane radio bandwidth. Then, with a focus reserved for geniuses and savants—though he was neither—his mind would penetrate the device, be it automobile or cassette recorder, saber saw, or copy machine. As though in a trance, he'd mentally follow the schematic, reasoning his way along the wires and circuits, until he burst out with a simple, "Oh!" Next, he'd open the machine, go to the source of the problem, and repair it, as though all this were a kindergarten puzzle and anyone could do it, all the while saying out loud, "I knew there had to be a reason."

The copy machine in front of him hummed perfectly now, and he returned to his desk, checking through the next stack. Moving to the oversized worktable against the wall, he collated the sheets already copied. By the time these duties were performed, the machine had quieted and was ready for the next task.

Lifting the original from the glass, he placed it upside down in sequence, retrieved the next original from his desk, and the series of movements repeated, as though Kevin himself had become a cog in the proverbial well-oiled machine.

It was sequencing he loved, moving in a regular pattern from one task to the next, all the while keeping the details of the job running smoothly at the forefront of his thinking. All this freed the rest of his mind to think deeper thoughts, and they turned now to Susan.

He'd had no contact with her since she'd hit him— again— at Wing Ding's, and he wondered if this battering was now a permanent part of their relationship. *I understand it, kind of,* he acknowledged to himself. When she was unable to talk about something, she did something physical. He could think of physical things he'd prefer to being hit.

For his own part, he couldn't imagine hitting. Unable to spank a dog's backside—or even swat a fly—he was incapable of using his large hands in any way except to help others. It was encoded in his personal schematic, and he accepted his own nature unquestioningly, just as he accepted the natures of others so unlike himself, be they mechanical, animal, or human.

Still, Susan was a puzzle he wanted to figure out. His logical mind occupied with a perfect series of repeating tasks, his intuitive mind began to spin into life like a hard drive coming out of Pause.

"Oh!" he said out loud. *She's been hurt before! She's been hit.* He saw that now, or rather, felt it. It was the first thing that'd made sense about Susan in several weeks, and he listened quietly for his inner guidance to tell him more.

Into this peaceful hum of activity stormed Jack Sawyer, key chain jangling, work boots hammering—disruptive before he opened his mouth.

"Jack . . . I thought you said you'd be with clients all day."

As though Kevin hadn't spoken at all, Jack said, "Oh, good, Kevin, you're here. And you're not doing anything."

Yanking himself from his meditative state, Kevin blinked, confused.

"I can talk to you now, instead of tomorrow," Jack said, barreling past him toward his private office.

"Well, I . . . I'm copying the plans for your Monday meeting now," Kevin managed to say.

"What plans?" yelled Jack from his desk.

"The Smithers house!" called Kevin.

"Oh, forget that, for now. I don't need those till later."

Kevin looked down, miserable at the interruption. He'd lost track now of the numbering and couldn't figure out which sheets had been collated, and which still had to be copied. He'd have to start over with the count. He hated that.

"In my office, Kevin. Now!" yelled Jack from the next room.

"Sure, Boss," Kevin replied, turning his back on thoughts both inner and outer, preparing for the next barrage from his employer.

Entering Jack's private office, Kevin let his eyes sweep the room for free desk space, free windowsill space, even free floor space, and found virtually none. Papers, manuals, plans were strewn everywhere, held in place by dirty coffee mugs.

Sitting at his desk, Jack looked up and seemed annoyed to discover Kevin towering over him. "Sit down, Kevin."

Sure, there were two chairs against the wall, but they were burdened with phone books and paper bags full of nuts and bolts.

"Move that stuff. Just put it on the floor."

Obediently, Kevin placed the stacks of phone books on the floor adjacent to the chair, then sat.

"Oh, for heaven's sake, Kevin, move the chair over here!"

Leaping up suddenly as though he'd sat on a spring, Kevin levitated, moved the chair opposite Jack's desk, and sat again, his long legs and tall torso dwarfing the simple wooden seat. He regarded his employer with patience, an old soul tolerant of immaturity.

"By the way," Jack began. "You looked over the wiring schematic for the Clarke house carefully?"

Kevin thought for a moment. "Yeah, most of it. That's gonna be a pretty fancy screening room."

"Damn place is going to be a fortress, if we build it to code."

Kevin looked at his boss quizzically, formulating a question.

"Don't quote chapter and verse to me, Kevin," Jack said, holding up a hand. "Anyway, that's not why I asked you to come in here." Jack chewed the edge of his mustache. "I've been thinking lately about the fact that you've been doing quite well since you came to work for me, and I think maybe it's time we adjusted your salary a little."

Had Kevin not been sitting, he'd have fallen down.

A wicked gleam came into Jack's eye. "Caught you off guard, did I? Good! Now, I'm not talking about a great deal of money, but something that we should consider a merit raise."

"Like in the Boy Scouts." It was all Kevin could think of saying.

Jack snorted, "No, I'm not going to be giving out badges. Just money."

"Even better," said Kevin brightly.

"Yes, I've always thought so."

Kevin listened for additional duties, but hearing nothing further, he stood to leave. "Well, thanks, Boss."

"Just a minute, Kevin," Jack interjected quickly. "There's something else."

Sitting again, Kevin waited in silence.

"I don't know what you overheard the other day at Sally's."

Kevin gave no reply.

"Whether you know this already or not, I want you to hear it from me: Samantha says she had a child by me after we divorced, and kept it secret from me all these years."

Kevin registered no surprise.

"Samantha's working on tracking down this son she says is mine—not that I necessarily believe her after all these years."

Kevin's remained impassive.

"In any case, I want an eye kept on her."

Kevin raised his eyebrows in question. "On Samantha?"

"No!" Jack contracted, "On Susan. You've already got a line on that girl, the one who works for her. While you're at it, get her to tell you what's going on with tracking down the kid. Do whatever you have to do, but I want to know every lead she comes up with, understand?"

Kevin didn't want to understand but was afraid he did. "You mean . . . if Samantha finds her son, you want to know." He paused. "But wouldn't she tell you anyway?"

"She might." Jack looked out his window and pulled at his mustache. "And she might not."

"She might not be able to find him, Mr. Sawyer," Kevin said quietly.

"I wouldn't be so sure. When Samantha goes after something, she generally makes pretty good headway, and I want to know what she finds out." Giving his employee another stern, steady gaze, he continued. "Get close to Susan and report back to me on Samantha. Your job depends on it."

Recognizing Jack's dismissive tone, Kevin stood and left his boss's office.

Kevin got home just as golden afternoon light poured through the trees. The air was fresh with promise. Too bad the only promise he could think of was his own to Mr. Sawyer, a promise he didn't want to keep.

He made a habit of carrying his tools wherever he went, and, as always, he placed his heavy carpenter's apron on its sturdy hook by the front door. He took off his cap, poured himself a glass of spring water from the cooler, and slid open his back door. Stepping out onto his balcony, he was grateful again to Jack for helping him build this place. Overlooking state land that would never be developed, it was a two-story built on poles, which put the second level three stories above the ground—his idea of heaven. It had come at a price: loyalty to Jack. Usually that didn't bother him. But today's "request" had generated conflict —the thing Kevin dreaded most.

He peered into the tree, trying to detect his friend the opossum. The water Kevin had left in the bowl after the last encounter had been consumed. But it was likely the creature had climbed into his favorite tree again.

Kevin stood still and took a quieting breath, waiting as his peripheral vision tracked a small movement. "There you are, fella," he said softly. "I've got a carrot for you."

He headed downstairs, grabbed two carrots from his fridge, and hefted half a watermelon, all of which he carried to the base of the tree. The opossum appeared, already about halfway down the tree, clinging upside down to its bark.

"Bet you want me to get out of the way, don't you?"

The opossum made a ratchety sound—probably the scariest he could muster—and Kevin obliged by returning inside, realizing he was hungry himself.

As always, his wildlife encounter had cleared his mind. Chuckling several times over the opossum, he fixed a vegetarian burger, slathered it with organic ketchup, and consumed it on the deck, watching as the critter munched his own snacks.

In the fading light and rising breeze, he leaned back in his solitary deck chair, stretched out his long legs and considered Jack's ultimatum from the point of view of his own ethics.

On the one hand, Jack had asked that he invade someone's privacy and told him his own job was at risk if he didn't comply. *Would he really fire me?* On the other hand, he already knew Susan was curious about her own employer's private affairs—too curious to please Samantha, who nonetheless let Susan keep her job at the Environmental Planning Commission.

He wasn't sure why, but he felt protective of Susan. Perhaps it was because of his recent insight into her defense mechanisms—that she'd been hurt sometime in the past, probably more than once. Though he knew none of the details, he could picture her as a child, could feel both her urge to cower and the raw courage she summoned in the face of danger.

It brought to mind a documentary about "instinct injury" he'd seen. In a horrifying segment, a caged dog had been given so many electric shocks it had finally had no response at all. Yet when the dog was later released, it cowered at the approach of anyone, unable to distinguish friend from foe. Dogs in their natural state were almost always companionable.

His own feelings toward animals were simple and unencumbered. But his feelings toward Susan seemed to have multiple levels. At the very least he knew he wanted friendship. He also felt himself responding to her almost audible call for help. He could and would protect her, enjoying a sense of chivalry he'd never expressed to anyone else. Beyond that, he knew there was a mutual attraction. She fought it. He suppressed it, unwilling to scare her off.

With all these feelings churning in my gut, how can I do what Mr. Sawyer asked?

If Susan confronted him, he could just tell her the truth. But that would likely destroy whatever trust she had in him. There might be another option. His opossum friend had taught him a lesson the other day in how to fool one's captor. If he were ever caught, he supposed he could do the same.

Tony Fiorentino's realtor had been even more efficient than she'd promised. He'd be signing papers at his closing when he rolled into town on Friday. His plan had been to take the week driving cross-country, enjoying both the ongoing change of scenery as well as his new fully equipped van.

The moving truck would arrive in a few days, and the crew would not only unload but help him place the incoming furniture pieces. Meanwhile, he'd stay at the Belhaven Inn, where he'd reserved an accessible room.

Tony felt excited in ways he hadn't since . . . well, since never. He'd had momentary bright spots in this life. And he'd had a surge of excitement when he'd become a Marine. That was something he'd never forget and never lose.

But this was different. This was him taking charge of his life, creating a new chapter from scratch, taking a chance.

The years since his injury had been tough but eventually had stood him in good stead, as it turned out. Adapting to the chair had involved tremendous athleticism—something known mostly to other paraplegics and to physical therapists. Balance was different, upper-bod strength was accelerated, and the all-important stretching was accomplished mostly during his daily use of a devise called a standing frame. When he added wheelchair basketball to his life, along with it had come those familiar things he thought he'd lost: competitive spirit, strategic moves, and joy.

He'd bring all this with him: the physical things like special equipment and furniture; the mental qualities like persistence and patience; and as for joy . . . well, he had the feeling he'd find more of that than he'd bring along.

But he wanted to make this move all the way across the country with what might be an unusual balance in his attitude. He's learned, over the years, to have few expectations. On the other hand, he'd also learned to relish every good thing that came along, no matter how small.

It'd been a long day. He'd spent seven hours in the saddle and made it from Grand Junction, Colorado, to Las Vegas, Nevada. He driven down the iconic Las Vegas Strip, ogling the lights along with all the other tourists. Then he pulled into a gas station at the outskirts of town, near the motel where he'd stay the night.

After turning off the ignition, he worked the mechanism to release the driver's seat and allow it to rotate. From there, he transferred to his wheelchair and let the mechanical lift lower him to ground level. When he'd filled the tank, he reversed the process and settled himself in the driver's seat.

He leaned toward the passenger seat and drew a finger across the map he'd marked for the trip. By the time he arrived in Milford-Haven, he'd have driven 2,986 miles, according to his calculations. All told, he'd travel across eleven states: New York, Pennsylvania, Ohio, Indiana, Illinois, Missouri, Kansas, Colorado, Utah, and the bottom corner of Nevada, before entering the great state of California.

Tomorrow he'd travel the final 400 miles by continuing on I-15 till he'd transfer to CA-46. He was itching to arrive, now. He had so much to do.

Mr. Hargraves looked forward to his arrival; that much he knew. And based on that recent phone call from Sally, she'd be happy to see him too. Would she feel the same when she found out their businesses would be side by side? Could they navigate the tricky waters of being former lovers, recent friends, new neighbors? As for considering more than that, he dared not venture yet into those depths.

Years ago, he'd rushed off to war. Now, he wanted to take it slow as he began this new adventure. He reminded himself of the old adage: *Slow and steady wins the race.*

Chapter 23

Samantha picked up the phone first thing Thursday morning. When Miranda answered her call, Sam said, "Apologies!"

She heard her friend chuckle, and ask, "What for?"

"For being silent and absent. I've been up to 'here' at work and dealing with a few sticky situations."

"Hold on a sec," Miranda said. "I'm gonna grab my tea and sit in the living room."

She's such a dear. Should I talk to her about the adoption news from Stacey Chernak? Maybe not yet.

"Okay, I'm back. What sticky situations?"

Sam sighed and said, "Well, one of them is Susan. One minute she's doing a great job. The next, she's slamming out the door with a chip on her shoulder."

"She can be a puzzle," Miranda commented. "But nothing new about that, right?"

"No, not really," Sam agreed. "Then there's Jack."

"Ah, the ever-popular Mr. Sawyer," Miranda said, a slight edge to her voice.

"He gotten on your bad side too?" Sam asked.

"No. I mean, I don't really know the man very well. It just seems like he's hard on Kevin, who is about the sweetest guy I've ever known. He's nasty to Sally. And he's always running afoul of you as well."

Sam let out a sound that was somewhere between a growl and a groan. "The never-ending battle. And I can't tell whether it's personal or professional with him. It's as if he enjoys breaking the environmental rules to which he's already agreed."

"Maybe it's because he knows you're too understaffed to enforce the regulations, which is really something the state should be doing."

"If I report him often enough, the state will certainly come down on him. But my worry is that it could impact so many other people. I don't want anyone losing their jobs because of me."

"Your own job is one of the toughest," Miranda noted. "And you do it so well."

"Enough about me. How are you? How was Oregon? Are you ready for your art show? Who all will be there?"

Miranda burst out laughing. "Uh . . . which question should I answer first?"

"Sorry," Sam said. "I guess we really ought to meet for lunch and catch up properly. If you have time, that is."

"You know I'd love it, Sam. Um, I have lunch plans today. But how about breakfast tomorrow? I expect my sister to arrive at some point, and Zelda. Before they get here, I'd really like to catch you up and run a couple of things by you."

"Perfect! Want to say 8:00 at Sally's?"

"Great. See you then, Sam."

Samantha hung up the phone feeling better and also wondering what it was that Miranda was keeping secret until they met in the morning.

Miranda looked forward to getting together with Sam. She hadn't mentioned a word about Cornelius. She didn't plan to divulge much about their relationship yet. *Is it a relationship? It already feels like it is.*

It'd been nearly a week since their night at Jalama. He'd called regularly since then—brief, but wonderful check-in conversations. If he weren't calling her, she worried that their special evening would have begun to fade and drift away like a lovely dream that had no real substance. His calls made the connection real.

She'd invited him over for lunch today. She'd straightened the living room and studio, piled the mail in a basket on the breakfast bar. *That letter from Alaska . . . fantastic! Have to reply to that.* She'd fed Shadow, who seemed to be wondering what all the clean-up was about.

She did want to make dinner for Cornelius, but he had plans with his parents tonight, and she had a house guest tomorrow. She wanted to see him before the art show. Things might get complicated, considering the Calvins were planning to attend.

She'd think about all that later. For now, she felt nervous and excited to see him. *It feels like forever since last week!*

She'd made a batch of fresh, chunky gazpacho and bought a boule of French bread. For dessert, she'd made a quick custard. Dividing the recipe into the small cut-glass pedestal cups her mother'd given her, she'd added a few fresh berries to the tops and placed them in the fridge. *Nothing too fancy, but mostly homemade.*

When she heard the rumble of his SUV outside the kitchen window, she smoothed her hair, took a deep breath, and opened her front door.

He climbed out of the driver's side and stood there looking at her, while she gazed back, feeling her heart kick against the wall of her chest. *Those eyes . . . his long arms and legs . . . I want those beautiful strong hands on me.* She wanted to smile, but all she could do was absorb his presence across the length of the driveway.

"Hey, you," he said, walking toward her.

"Hey, you," she echoed.

Then they both did smile, right before they embraced. She inhaled his scent, felt his warmth. Since they were still outside, she pulled away and grabbed his hand. "Come in," she said.

He took a moment to look up and around, apparently liking what he saw of the high redwood beams and walls, the light spilling in from the tall windows. "I love what you've done with the place," he said, the twinkle in his eyes hinting at the tease she heard in his voice.

She laughed. "It's a rental. But I do love it. Can I show you my studio before we have lunch?"

"I thought you'd never ask."

Grabbing his hand again, she led him through the living room and into the studio, where the row of windows continued and a set of double doors led out to a wide deck. He wasn't looking at the view, however. His eyes fixed on the two lions' portrait, then on the miniatures standing on her desk and leaning against the wall, and then on the day bed in the corner. "Beautiful," he said softly. "A living, breathing workspace."

Miranda nodded and said, "Hungry?"

He turned to look at her then, giving her the hungriest look she'd ever seen. In one long stride, he reached her, held her tight enough to lift her nearly off her feet while his lips met hers. She opened to his kiss, lost herself in the silky, breathless sensation, then felt his hands sliding down her back and grabbing her hips.

When the kiss ended, he leaned his forehead against hers and they stood there waiting while breathing steadied. "Yes," he said.

She laughed out loud. "Good. Okay. Right this way."

He sat on the last bar stool while she dished up the meal. "Oh, wow," he said.

She looked over at him. 'What, you like soup?"

"No. Yes! I love soup! But . . . sorry, I didn't mean to snoop, but I see you got a letter from University of Alaska, Fairbanks."

"Yes! I was going to tell you. I've been invited up there."

"Really. What will you be doing?"

"Teaching at their Summer Fine Arts Camp. Super exciting."

"This coming June?"

"Yes. For a month." She put on an oven mitt and pulled out the round of warmed bread.

"Interesting. That's when I'll be there."

"What?" She nearly dropped the bread on the floor.

"I'll be working with the Chair of Arctic Studies."

She smiled at him, shaking her head.

He laughed, then asked, "How do you feel about camping in Alaska?"

"Uh, I feel fine, so long as the grizzlies aren't invited."

"I'll speak to the wildlife manager about that."

They sat at one end of her dining table, enjoying the cold soup and hot bread.

"This is great," he said between bites. "You made this?"

"The gazpacho, yes. The bread, no. That's above my pay grade."

He chuckled. "Listen, I know you're focused on your show now. And I have to travel next week. But when I get back, there's something I want to show you. It's a local project, at a really special location. And, you know, if you feel like it, we could camp out and actually see some stars."

She beamed at him. "I'd love that!"

"So tell me about your show."

She took a breath. "It was Zelda's idea to put 'Secrets' in the title of the show, but it was Nicole who first noticed it as a theme."

"Seems like a great idea. Very catchy," he noted, taking a first bite of her custard dessert. "Mmm, this is delicious."

Cornelius looked at her after another bite, watching as nerves seemed to jitter down her arms to her fingers, which began playing with the edge of her placemat.

"Glad you like it. Um . . . it might be . . . I'll probably be . . ."

"Busy? Distracted? Of course, you will. You're the star of the event. Everyone will want to be with you, talk to you."

"I really want you to be there. It's just that . . . well, I apologize in advance if I don't pay much attention to you." Her nervous patter continued. "Honestly, I'm not that great in a crowd. The more the focus is on me, the more uncomfortable I get. But if I can introduce people to each other, then I do better. Okay if I introduce you?"

He looked into those beautiful green eyes, so full of earnest intent. *Could I ever deny her anything?* "Of course, it's okay." He broke off another piece of bread. "Besides, magical things happen in that gallery. I've experienced it myself."

Now he saw joy come into her expression and watched as her cheeks tinted. "But I . . . it wasn't me. I didn't . . . I don't. . . ."

He reached a hand out and covered one of hers. He knew she still felt uncomfortable about taking credit for his rescue. Last winter, on a beautiful sunny day so typical of southern California, he'd climbed a mountain in the Angeles Crest near L.A. But a sudden storm had trapped him on a steep escarpment until he'd followed a persistent—but nonsensical—intuition to reach around the edge of the ledge on which he stood precariously. He'd found a rope and been able to let himself down.

The next day, visiting his parents in Milford-Haven and searching for a Christmas gift for them, he'd come to the gallery where Miranda's work was on display. They'd bumped into each other, literally, and she'd discovered the welts on his palms. That'd sent her to the back room to retrieve a small painting she'd done the previous day: a rope hanging down a steep, rocky mountainside. They'd spoken about that experience a bit, enough for him to recognize the signs of wonder, something else they shared.

"In quantum physics, we call it entanglement."

"Really? What does that mean?"

"Well, Einstein called it 'spooky action at a distance.'"

She laughed. "Okay," she said, but he could see curiosity illuminate her expression.

"It's about things being in touch instantaneously, faster than light could have sent a message. You do something over here," he said, extending one arm to his right, then continuing. "And whatever is entangled with it," he said, holding out his other arm in the opposite direction, "reacts instantaneously. So, there's this underlying connectedness that's called entanglement."

"Underlying connectedness," she repeated. "That's what I feel when I photograph wildlife."

"Yes. I can see it in your work." *And I can see it in your eyes,* he thought, but didn't say.

"We have to talk more about that," she declared.

"We will."

When lunch was finished, they rose from the table. This time he took her hand and led her to her front door, where they stood for a moment. He could feel himself begin to smolder. "Listen, I better go now, or I might have to stay."

He heard the hitch in her breath, held her shoulders, and looked into that beautiful upturned face. *If I capture that mouth the way I want to, I won't be able to leave.* Instead, fighting to maintain control, he pressed his closed mouth to her soft lips, offering a chaste kiss. "Soon," he said. Then he walked out the door.

Delmar had picked up an order of fish-and-chips and taken it back to his office Thursday evening.

The crisp, satisfying meal, complete with tartar sauce, ketchup, and fries, had given him a second wind, and he sipped a cup of coffee he'd brewed fresh in the office pot.

He'd been so busy with his regular case load over the past several days that he hadn't been able to get back to any of the "back burner" work. Those projects—not officially on his roster, but of great personal interest—now included Samantha Hugo and her adoption investigation; Stacey Chernak and her abuse situation; and, of course, the still missing Chris Christian.

He could have knocked off work for the day, driven home to Milford-Haven, and come back early tomorrow. But one glance at the large envelope of notebooks and memos next to his monitor, and he felt good about the decision to put in a couple more hours tonight.

He'd found the notebooks at her condo when he and Joseph Calvin had visited there weeks earlier. Del had gone through them once. *I should go through them again more carefully.*

According to her employer, Satellite TV news in San Luis Obispo, the story she'd been working on most recently was about earthquakes. They confirmed she'd given them an itinerary that included Turkey and Japan. But the information she'd provided contained no details, which was usually the case, since she worked freelance and on her own schedule. So neither they nor Del had been able to confirm her arrival in either country, nor even the location of her car, which he'd have expected to be parked either at her condo or at the Santa Maria airport.

He remembered glancing through a section of her notebook labeled "Seismic," and he found it again now. The passages were a curious combination of narrative journaling and cryptic research notes. *Maybe she was planning to write her memoirs later. She did enjoy mentoring young writers. I read something about her teaching a course at Alan Hancock in Santa Maria.*

The first section he found caught his eye because she mentioned Joseph Calvin.

> I know Joseph wants me to spend more time in Santa Barbara, and it is beautiful there. But I love my place in Santa Maria. Much more my style. Smaller, simpler, but clean and bright, views of the hills, blooming jacaranda everywhere. And so near the airport it makes my story-trips easy. He seems to like it here when he visits, but he probably just feels like he's slumming. With an estate overlooking the Pacific, why would he want to spend time anywhere else?

> Funny, that I actually like it here now, rather than the big city. I was itching to get out of tiny-town when I was a teenager. That first job for the local paper gave me the initial inkling I might actually make it out. Then the regional paper in Riverside County; then the thrill and challenge of New York; then all that freelancing in L.A. When the audition for Satellite TV news in SLO came up, that was it for me. The conflict between beauty and brains was over: as a TV journalist, I could be both. Ha!

Del reflected for a moment on this woman who had keen self-awareness but could also look at herself objectively. The next segment provided some background as to why she'd chosen to create one of her special broadcasts on tectonic plate movement.

The L.A. earthquake in '71 . . . that started my fascination with all things seismic, even though I was in New York at the time. That's what took me to Tokyo, Bangkok. Did those special reports for NBC. The graft and greed that meant Phuket got funded as a top international resort, but that there was still no early warning system in place for tsunamis . . . That got me interested in all things financial. And then I happened to be in LA in 1994 for the Northridge quake . . . firsthand experience at last.

The more I researched that earthquake and the San Andreas, the farther north I traced it, the closer to home I was getting. Something about this cusp between land and sea, something about facing the orient from the occident. Maybe that's what my next bunch of writing will be about. Yes, take the issue-driven writing I've been doing and using the perspective of the Pacific Rim. I like that.

Maybe that reporter for the Milford-Haven News will write about me one day when I'm old and retired. Emily Wilkins, that's her name. She'll write "Local girl ran away, made good covering issues in foreign lands, came back to Central Coast for final chapter."

Again, he was struck by her ability to stand back and see her own life from the overview of past and future, as though she had a personal satellite capturing images from far overhead, or a time machine she could use to review or to forecast the events of her life. *It's a unique ability. Something writers have, that the rest of us don't.*

Del took a moment to put the journals in chronological order as much as possible. The 1997 journal was missing, which made sense, as she would likely have it with her.

The 1996 journal had a notation about an August '96 quake in Northeast Japan she apparently hoped to investigate at a future date.

Methodical. Meticulous. Talented. As always, he felt a tug of sadness about the journalist he had never met. Yet so often, he felt he had, felt she was an acquaintance, a friend. Someone who shared his passion for investigation, his predilection for curiosity.

He stacked the journals carefully in their order and tucked them away in a private file drawer. He didn't need anyone rifling through them. Then he thought about his own calendar.

The weekend would be busy in Milford-Haven, partly because of a big art show at Finders' Gallery. According to its manager Nicole, Miranda Jones had become enough of a draw that people would be driving in from both north and south.

If they're art lovers, they likely have money to spend not only on paintings but at local eateries and shops. That'll please the merchants. He didn't expect any trouble, but he planned to drive down Main Street, park at one end and then the other, just to make sure his presence was noticed. The last thing anyone needed was a theft of any kind.

Del yawned, feeling the effects of a dinner, a long day, and a long week. His only worry about heading home was that the recurring nightmare about Chris Christian would once again confuse and confound his sleep.

Part III

Revelations

"The highest revelation is
that God is in every man."

—Ralph Waldo Emerson

Chapter 24

Miranda parked her bike outside on the front patio of Sally's Restaurant, then went inside to claim the table where she and her friend usually sat. A moment later, Sam walked in, and the two friends embraced.

They both glanced up as the owner approached.

"Hey, Sally, welcome home!" Miranda said.

Sam offered a cool nod of her head.

Wish I could get these two dear friends of mine to like each other! Oh well. I love them both, Miranda thought.

"How was your trip?" she continued.

"Grand. Nothin' like spendin' time with Mama. And by the way, all the fixin's for your big art show are gonna be ready a little early tomorrow."

"Thanks *so* much, Sally! I really appreciate it!"

"O' course! Glad to do it for you. So, what can I git you ladies?"

Miranda would have liked to discuss the hors d'oeuvres to be served at the gallery further but didn't want to irritate Sam nor interfere with Sally's busy restaurant trade. "Two soft boiled eggs and a bran muffin for me," she said.

"You got it," Sally confirmed, scribbling on her pad. "With tea, o' course, right?"

"Right."

"And you, Samantha?"

"Uh, I'll take scrambled eggs and whole wheat toast. And coffee."

"Comin' right up!" Sally marched away in her sensible shoes.

"Okay, Miranda, you mentioned you wanted to run something by me. Is this about your show?" Sam asked.

"Yes. You know the Calvins are planning to be here, Zack and his father." Miranda bit her lip. "Honestly, I'm not sure why. We haven't spoken, so I haven't asked. I have a feeling Zack feels he owes it to me, for some reason."

"If that's how he feels, he's not wrong," Sam observed. "He did leave you in the lurch more than once. First, he never followed through with the commissioned painting. Then, he sort of dismissed you after the concert, if I remember correctly."

Miranda nodded, taking a sip of her tea, which had arrived. "True. But I don't . . . I'm not sure what to do. I mean, if I were still dating Zack—as if I ever really did—I'd prepare a meal at my place, I'd take them sightseeing, I'd go out of my way to make sure they felt welcome."

"Of course, you would," Sam agreed.

"But now what? Do I just see them at the art show, then say goodbye?"

"Hmm, interesting question," Sam said. "Didn't you say your representative is coming, too?"

"Zelda. Yes. She'll arrive today or tonight sometime. She wants to make sure everything is 'just so' at the gallery."

"That's good. She's working hard for you, just as it should be."

"And there's more. Apparently, she's been dating Mr. Calvin."

"Oh, really?"

"I saw them together at the Doobie Brothers concert that Zack invited me to. And I thought it was just, well, I don't know, a friendship. But she's mentioned him a couple more times and dropped several hints," Miranda elaborated.

Sam considered for a moment

While she did, June brought their breakfast plates to the table. "More cawfee?" she offered.

"Please," Sam replied. After June left, Sam asked, "Everyone's planning to stay overnight in Milford-Haven, right? They wouldn't want to drive a couple of hours back to Santa Barbara."

"That's right, they're staying at the Belhaven. And my sister will be arriving, though I assume she'll stay with me."

"So . . . what about making plans to meet for brunch Sunday morning? You could make a reservation at Michael's Lighthouse Tavern. It's beautiful there, right on the water."

Miranda thought back to the one dinner date she'd had with Zack at that very restaurant. *But why not reclaim it? Make a different memory there?* "That's a great idea," she agreed. "That's what I'll do."

They'd finished eating, and now each of them sipped from their mugs. "There's one other thing."

Sam smiled. "Do tell."

"I . . . it's not official or anything, but I sort of started seeing someone else."

"Wonderful!" Sam said, a little too loudly.

Quietly, Miranda said, "We're just taking our first steps, and we're not ready to share it yet. So . . . just keep it under your hat for now."

Sam nodded. "Of course. And . . . will *he* be at the art show too?"

"He will."

"I **see** what you're worried about. And yet, really there is nothing at all to concern you, is there?"

"He knows I was sort of seeing Zack and knows the Calvins will be here. I don't think it's an issue for him. But I'll want to introduce him around, you know. And then . . . I don't know, it's too public, too soon. But I don't want him left out."

Sam took another sip of her coffee. "He's a grown man, right?"

"Oh, yes, absolutely." Miranda felt a blush overtaking her face.

"And, evidently, you like him," Sam said with a big smile.

"I certainly do."

"Well, just be your kind, considerate self and let the chips fall where they should. Not where they may . . . but where they *should*."

"Guess I'm overthinking it a bit," Miranda said ruefully. "Maybe I'm just nervous. And excited. And I better pedal back up the hill so I can finish getting my house ready for my sister."

"It's all going to be wonderful, Miranda. Really. Your art will speak for itself, and all you have to do is smile at all your admirers."

"Thanks, Sam."

"I'll be there with bells on. And if there's anything I can do to help, just let me know."

Zelda McIntyre regarded the outfits she'd laid out on her bed.

Though she still considered Milford-Haven to be a podunk town, she did have to dress carefully for three reasons. First, this was a professional event and she'd invited the press. She had to make sure she—and her client Miranda—were camera-ready. Second, Joseph would be there, and she had a certain image to maintain now that they were rapidly becoming an "item." Third, she loved an excuse to wear a bit of finery.

Of course, she'd have to play it down just a little. This would not be a gala where she'd wear a gown. *Do they even have galas in Milford-Haven? Not that I've ever read about.*

But neither would a plain business suit be appropriate. No, this would require one of her colorful—one of her artistic—

scarves. She had plenty to choose from in her Hermes collection. The question was which to wear with what outfit and for what event. There would be the art show. Then there would be Sunday brunch with Joseph. Possibly with Zackery. Or even with Miranda and her sister. One had to be prepared for any and all eventualities.

The soft purple wool dress kept catching her eye. Across it, she draped her yellow and purple silk scarf. With its wide purple border, a background of bright yellow, the scarf showed flashes of slender ribbons trailing across the field, and some brightly hued medallions. *Lovely spring colors. Just right for the season.* So that would work for the gallery.

For brunch, she pulled out a smaller, less vibrant scarf with a pink border and a yellow center. To coordinate with this, she chose her pale pink pantsuit. *Casual, but still elegant.*

Satisfied she'd easily fit both outfits into her hanging bag, she put all but some navy blue slacks and a matching sweater back into her closet. *I can wear that today when I drive up.* She'd have liked to make the drive with Joseph, but she had to get there early, and she knew Joseph planned to ride with Zackery.

She walked to her desk, where she sat down, opened her Filofax planner, and flipped to the Project tab, currently in use for Miranda's art show. On the "Press" page, she noted with satisfaction that *Montecito Magazine* had indeed agreed to publish a feature about the show. Of course, the price for their agreement had been Zelda's commitment to run a print ad. But this she considered to be very worthwhile, particularly as Nicole had agreed to share the cost. After all, it would benefit Finder's Gallery as well as the up-and-coming artist Miranda Jones. Their photographer had agreed to meet her at the gallery before the doors were opened to the public. And the journalist would be there early as well.

Zelda sighed, still trying to let go of the last vestige of resentment about Miranda's move away from San Francisco. *Just when I'd gotten her name established and rescued her from that plagiarism accusation, she had to go and move! Still, she does seem to be thriving in Milford-Haven. Perhaps it's a good thing to be a big fish in a small pond.*

Meredith had her BMW Coupe packed and ready for the trip to Milford-Haven. She'd decided to work till mid-morning, eat a quick, early lunch at home and hit the road before Friday afternoon traffic clogged the route out of the city and onto the 101 south.

She had strict orders from Mother to bring roses "from the family" and to deliver them in person at the art show. That would be the fun part. And of course, it'd be fun to stay with her sister and have their own private pajama party. Now that they were no longer roommates, these brief visits were delightful again. They each had their own lives and could enjoy catching up.

But there was one thing that might not be fun at all. And that was coming face to face with Zack Calvin. Was he her sister's boyfriend? Was he her ex? These questions didn't seem as important now, because Miranda had made it pretty clear they weren't actually dating.

But what Meredith would have to reckon with was her own deception. She'd knowingly let Zack believe he was talking to Miranda, and she'd enjoyed every second of it.

When they did meet in person at last, how would it be between them? Would he be the dull, uptight, stuck-up, haughty entitled son and heir to the Calvin Oil fortune? If so, she could step away both mentally and emotionally, maybe even physically. She could be polite and dutiful, attending the event purely to support her darling sister.

But what if, when they met, the same kind of fireworks that'd sizzled over the phone, happened in person? How long would it take Zack to figure out it'd been wise-cracking Meredith and not quiet Miranda who'd entertained him during that phone call?

She had absolutely no idea how she'd be able to hide her embarrassment, cover her shame, nor conceal the raw attraction she'd felt for the man that day.

She could pretend she hoped for the former. But in her heart, she hoped for the latter. Whatever havoc it might wreck, she thought it might be well worth it.

Zack pressed the accelerator as traffic thinned on the 101 North.

"It's deja vu all over again, isn't it, Zack?" Joseph remarked.

Zack chuckled. "Yeah. Same route we drove to Morro Bay. Just a little farther this time."

"Sorry I couldn't get away earlier," his father said.

"That's okay. Worst of the Friday traffic is behind us now. Besides, most of it's heading south."

They'd passed Isla Vista, site of the U.C.S.B. campus and the Santa Barbara Shores City Park. At this point the highway drew close to the edge of the Pacific.

"Never get tired of that view," Joseph remarked.

Zack wasn't sure whether his dad meant the natural beauty of the winding coastline or the view of the Guerdon offshore oil rig marching along with the others in the water.

Both men squinted against the sun as the car proceeded up the highway. Again, Joseph was the first to break the silence. "When did we take that fishing trip to Colorado? It has to be, what, two years ago?"

Zack smiled at the memory. "Devil's Thumb Ranch. Gorgeous country."

"Nice catches, too."

"That guide knew what he was doing."

"More than I can say for . . . what was her name?" Joseph paused a moment.

"You mean Darlene." Zack glanced over at his father and both men burst into laughter.

"When she first came outside in those rented hip boots, I thought our guide was going to faint."

"I don't think he'd ever imagined that lace . . . whatever it was, as appropriate outer wear."

Still laughing, Joseph wiped a tear from the corner of his eye. "And then when she tried to cast and got her line caught in yours," Joseph continued with difficulty, "Oh . . . I wish I had a picture of your face at that moment!"

Clutching the steering wheel, Zack had another fit of laughter.

"I'm surprised she lasted as long as she did," Joseph gasped between laughs. "I thought she was going to lose her waders when she stamped her boot and insisted on a ride to the Denver airport."

When the laughter began to trail off, Zack sighed. "To tell you the truth, Dad, I had more fun after Darlene left."

Zack glanced over in time to see that Joseph had raised his eyebrow, seeming to bask in the implied compliment.

"I did too, son. Not to cast aspersions on your young lady."

At the unintentional pun they both broke into another round of laughter. Then they rode in a warm silence for a few miles, Joseph reclining his seat to a more comfortable angle, Zack hitting the cruise control button and settling in for the two-plus hour ride.

"While we're on the subject of women we used to date," Zack said, "what ever happened to Chris Christian?" Glancing to his right, Zack noticed his father press his lips together. "Sorry if it's a touchy subject. You still haven't heard from her?"

"The Sheriff's department can't officially list her, but their deputy has started looking into it."

Zack glanced over to see a deep furrow had appeared between his father's eyebrows. "To some extent, I blame myself," Joseph said.

"Why do you say that?"

"Well, when she didn't show up I was disappointed, then I was annoyed. I dismissed my worries. Should have reported them. At the time the concern felt . . . foolish."

"Whatever happened to her, Dad, it's not your doing."

"No. No, it's not."

A sad, awkward silence fell. Zack noticed his father looking past him to the ocean off the coast of Avila Beach, sensing his father's concern about his long-missing friend. Zack wished he could think of something reassuring to say.

"This road takes me back," Joseph said quietly. "Your mother and I used to drive up the coast."

"I didn't know that," Zack said.

"When you were old enough to travel, we'd put you in the back seat and make a family outing of it."

"Really? How far north did we go?"

"Oh, sometimes to Morro Bay, sometimes to Cayucos, or Cambria. We took you to the Hearst Castle one trip."

"Wish I could remember."

"Well, you were very young, too young to recall the details, but we thought you'd like the sights, the sounds, the stimulation. You certainly seemed to enjoy yourself."

Zack paused a moment. "Dad, did we . . . did we ever go to Milford-Haven?"

"I'm not sure. We might have stopped there once." Joseph looked over at him. "Actually, I do remember a time at the beach just north of Milford-Haven. It was a preserve across from the Hearst Castle. You saw that beach and took off running with a giggle. It was all your mother could do to keep up with you. She was terrified you'd fall over a piece of driftwood or cut your toe on some glass."

Zack was catching every word, fitting pieces of a puzzle. "This place you're talking about—it wouldn't be the Santa Carlita Cove, would it?"

"Why, yes, that does sound right."

"Now it's all starting to make sense." Zack pursed his lips. "When I visited Miranda she took me to that cove. It looked so familiar it was absolutely uncanny. I swear I did have a deja vu. But I thought I'd never seen the place before."

"Interesting she'd take you there."

"It was because I liked one of her paintings and was considering commissioning her to do something similar."

They rode in silence for a moment, then Joseph asked, "That painting Cynthia gave you—it was a beach scene, wasn't it?"

"Yeah," Zack said simply. "It is."

"So let me get this straight. Miranda takes you to this cove, you discuss a commission. Next thing you know, Miranda's own painting of the Cove shows up as your birthday gift from Cynthia." He paused. "No wonder you had such a strong reaction at the party."

Zack flashed back to that awful moment during the huge charity event—held at the family estate—for which his birthday had been the excuse. When Cynthia had unveiled her gift publicly, Zack had frozen, caught somewhere between fury and shock, serendipity and betrayal.

Sighing, he told his dad, "How it all started was that I saw that painting, tried to buy it, and the gallery said it was on loan from the artist, so I decided to go to her studio to ask her directly."

"And that's when you first met Miranda."

Zack nodded. "The weird thing was that later, somehow Cynthia met Zelda."

"And Zelda arranged the sale of Miranda's painting to her." Joseph pressed back into his seat. "Wonder how much Zelda knew at the time?"

"No idea," answered Zack. "At first I thought it was Cynthia's doing. It *does* fit her style to knock another woman out of the way."

"Yes, but she was too taken aback that night."

Zack thought again of Cynthia's tears and misery at the failure of her gift. But he thought, too, of their steamy reconciliation later, squirming at the memory.

Joseph drummed his fingers on the dashboard. "Zelda's quite an operator. She'd never let herself miss a business opportunity."

"Maybe that was Zelda's motive all along—snag a nice gift for me to ingratiate herself with you."

Joseph chortled. "Maybe so. Kind of flattering to think so."

Zack glanced over and noticed his dad was smiling to himself. "She is a dynamic woman," he commented.

"And then some," Joseph agreed. As the sun continued to slant through the windows of the Mercedes, Joseph added, "I've been wondering, if you're not really seeing Miranda these days, why are you going to her show?" Joseph asked.

"I've thought about it a lot, and I think it's to answer a question," Zack said.

"Which is?"

"Well, to be frank, Miranda and I never really hit it off. She's beautiful, talented, kind. But there's been . . ."

"No spark?"

"Exactly. Except once. I called her, and we had this, I don't know, quick exchange that was so . . . exciting, for lack of a better word, that I began to think I was wrong. So since then, I've wondered whether it was circumstances that made her shy, or we didn't know each other well enough yet, or something. I figured making the effort to see her when it's *her* home ground, I might be able to figure it out."

Joseph nodded. "Makes sense. But Zack, I doubt you'll be able to find in her what you had with Cynthia."

Zack pressed his lips together and kept looking at the road ahead. "Yeah. Well, Cynthia *is* exciting. But . . . there has to be more to it. Cynthia wants what I *have*, not what I *am*."

"Wise words. And that's one of the trickiest things about having money. It offers great freedom, but also significant traps. Books have been on the subject. Plays. Epic poems," Joseph observed. He glanced at his son. "That doesn't mean you won't figure it out, though. And maybe during this trip some of the puzzle pieces will fall into place."

Zack nodded his head "That's what I'm hoping."

Chapter 25

M iranda had spent the two hours following her breakfast with Sam cleaning her house.

Her sister would be arriving at some point and would stay the night, so the daybed in the studio had been fitted with a lovely set of sheets, along with the guest comforter and shams she kept tucked in the cupboard. The kitchen and bathrooms shone, the dining table gleamed, and even Shadow seemed to approve.

Just then her doorbell rang, shooting a jolt of panic through her. But when she opened the door, she was charmed to see flowers being delivered. After dashing to her purse to grab a dollar tip for the delivery man, Miranda read the card. "For the blooming artist," it read, "Good luck tonight! Love, Sam."

Samantha is always so thoughtful! She didn't even hint about this at breakfast! Stripping away the plain brown wrapping, she grinned to see bright yellow freesias and paused to inhale the delightful scent. Finding a pottery vase that contained a swirl of the same bright hue, she trimmed the stems, placed them in water, then carried the filled vase to her studio, where the flowers seemed to illuminate the room like collected rays of sunlight.

As though expressing her own opinion about the gift, Shadow appeared at the edge of the room and gave a long, considered, multi-toned *meow*.

"Is that so?" replied Miranda. Then, sweeping the kitty into her arms, she draped her over one shoulder. Shadow seemed sublimely pleased with her new perch and gave a smug glance toward her human.

Miranda glanced at her wall clock. In honor of her event, she'd booked an appointment to have her hair washed and blow-dried. "It's time to go, Pooder," she explained to her cat.

With a curt reply, Shadow leapt down.

Miranda grabbed her keys, and the note for Mer, which she hung from the front doorknob. *In case she arrives while I'm out.*

But as she was about to close the door, she was surprised to see the same delivery man coming up her walk. This time he handed her an even larger floral package. "Your birthday, or something?" he asked with a grin.

"Or something," she replied, pulling another dollar from her purse. "Thanks!"

Meredith arrived in Milford-Haven in mid-afternoon.

Her plan was to stop by her sister's place first to drop off the yellow and pink roses she'd bought and get them into a vase. She could say hello, freshen up a bit, then reconnect later at the art show.

As she walked up to Miranda's door, she saw a familiar note hung by an elastic band that read, "Hi, Mer! Come on in. Back soon." *This looks like the same note she left me last winter. I bet she still hasn't learned to lock up.*

Sure enough, the door opened easily. Meredith stepped into the room and glanced around more carefully than she had during her last visit. *Too much wood, but nice open space and rustic charm. Yes, this would do nicely as a rental.*

She couldn't help it if she had a good eye for investment. The building Miranda currently occupied was located in a prime location for someone who wanted privacy, quiet, and an ocean view. Well, the view could be improved if a few trees were removed, but that could happen later.

The building had good bones and was already divided into two dwellings. The new owner could live in one side and rent out the other. The rental income would pay the mortgage—an ideal situation that frankly didn't come on the market all that often, which was one reason it'd caught her eye. And when Meredith had made a preliminary call, just to investigate the possibility of purchasing something in Milford-Haven, sure enough, the current owner had expressed interest in selling.

Miranda can't see past her own nose when it comes to money. Actually, it's her painting she can't see past. Evidently, that was all that mattered to her these days. Ever since she'd moved to this little town. And that was fine, as it seemed to make her happy.

But eventually, Miranda would have to move again. There was really no future for her here. It was a town for retirees and for those with enough cash to own a vacation home. That was where Meredith came in. She had enough funds to invest in something other than stocks, and this building fit the bill perfectly.

Of course, Miranda would have no idea the new owner was her own sister. For now, Meredith planned to keep that a secret. She'd be happy for her sister to continue living here for another couple of years. The building would only appreciate in value, and Mer could afford to wait. She'd just have to be careful not to spill the beans.

Meredith remembered there'd been several vases on a high kitchen shelf last time she visited, and stepped farther into the room to find one. But what she saw was another bunch of flowers already displayed.

On the dining table stood a majestic arrangement of lilies that shot up from an oversized vessel. Drawn involuntarily to her favorites, she inhaled, careful to avoid touching her nose to the pollen-rich stamens. It seemed an extravagant expense. *Unless Miranda's doing better than I thought. Or maybe she's trying to butter me up.*

Then she noticed a card stuck in amongst the flowers on a transparent plastic holder. Reaching for it to find out who'd sent these, she pulled the card out of its tiny envelop. "Good luck tonight, Zack," it read.

Miranda doesn't even care for lilies, she thought. *But they happen to be my favorites.* Meredith sighed while she carefully replaced the card in the envelop and the envelop in its holder. *As if this weren't already complicated enough!*

She stepped away from the table and glanced around the living room. She felt a brief pang of conscience when she noticed the quilt draped on the back of the comfortable-looking sofa. *Mandy's actually using it.* Mer had ordered it for her sister, photographs of her paintings printed onto fabric, then stitched together—her watercolor landscapes all forming a patchwork in blues and greens, yellows and reds.

Rather than succumb to the sentimental moment, Mer glanced at her watch and realized it was time to meet with the realtor with whom she'd spoken on the phone. The woman had promised to show Meredith a few properties and, at least for the sake of appearances, she'd agreed. She'd learn more about the town, its home valuations, growth prospects, and other pertinent facts.

By the time she arrived at her sister's art show this evening, she'd know a lot more than she knew now. If she did make an offer today, she'd tell the agent not to let the tenant know. And that would make two secrets she'd be keeping from Miranda.

Tony pulled into the one accessible parking space behind the gallery at 5:00 p.m., and shut off the engine. He looked over at Sally in his passenger seat, fresh and pretty as a bunch of daisies.

Because Sally had prepared the fancy tidbits that'd be served during the event, they'd come early. The food trays were carefully slid into a rack that she could wheel to the lift inside his van, once he used it himself to exit. The delicate aromas of cheeses and various savories infused the vehicle but not enough to overcome the light floral fragrance Sally wore.

"You ready to do this?"

"You're doin' riddle speak again, Tony. Do what?

As if she don't know. "Be seen out in public with the likes of me."

"I jest happen to be proud and honored to be seen out with the likes o' you. And you know it perfectly well since we bin out before."

"We have. But not since you stopped seein' what's his name. And not in your hometown."

"Well then, seems to me it's high time." And then she gave him that impish smile he'd fallen for in the way-back time.

She's a marvel. Didn't even blink when I told her I bought the hardware store right next to her restaurant. She'd finally admitted that she'd wheedled it out of Mr. Hargraves, who, after all, had been her friend and neighbor ever since she opened her place, and who felt he couldn't continue to keep such a big secret from her.

She'd come right over to the Belhaven when she found out that's where he was staying till his house was ready. And she'd invited him over for dinner. A genuine O'Mally home-cooked dinner, no less. She'd been so thoughtful . . . removing one dining chair away from the table so he could fit his wheelchair there; remembering his favorite peach pie and making it for him; fixing him a good, strong cup of coffee, though she didn't drink any herself.

After dinner, she'd folded her napkin two or three times, finally put it down, and begun with, "Long as we're tellin' secrets, I got one for you, Tony."

During the pause that followed, he'd tried and failed at filling in the gap with his own imaginings. *She married that guy she was seeing and was afraid to tell me. She has a fatal disease and only three months to live. Her mama is ill, and she has to move back to Arkansas.*

"I'm," she started.

And for some strange reason, in that next second he knew what she was going to say.

"I'm gonna have a—"

"—baby," he completed her sentence.

They'd sat at her table staring at one another for a long moment. Then he felt a foolish grin spreading across his face.

"You're... not mad? Upset? Disappointed?"

He couldn't explain all of it right then. There hadn't yet been enough time to reach that part in the many conversations he hoped they'd have. That he'd always wanted a family with her. That he wasn't sure he could father a child at this point.

But he did know that, after all the years of separation, life had finally brought them together again. And that nothing would make him happier than to share a new life with her.

When he could finally summon words, he'd said, "Happy for you, Sal. And happy for me, too, if you'll let me help."

Tears ran down her face, and he reached a long arm to gentle them away with his thumb.

"I'd like that, Tony."

They had a long way to go, but here they were tonight, ready to go see her friend's art show and *be* seen in public. Would her customers and friends make assumptions? They might. But since that was okay with Sal, it was certainly okay with him.

He glanced around the still-empty parking lot, wondering what the evening would bring, surer of himself than he could have imagined.

Cornelius knew he was arriving a little early at the art show, but he wanted to see whether he could help in any way. If Miranda herself were too distracted even to reply, he could just ask the manager—Nicole was her name, if he remembered right.

He'd brought flowers for Miranda. He'd actually done some research, with his mother's help, even though it meant he'd divulged a little more information than he'd intended. When he'd described the scent she'd worn at Jalama as "floral, maybe tropical," Mom had suggested it could be jasmine, pikake, or tuberose. Armed with these names, he'd driven to SLO where he'd found a perfume shop. He'd recognized the tuberose immediately, and then gone hunting for the flowers themselves. They did emit a heady scent, but the stems were long and unwieldy, so he'd bought a vase for them too.

He glanced toward the center of the room, where a spectacular arrangement already stood—including tuberoses. *I should have known!* Well, maybe Nicole can tuck these away somewhere. He headed for the back room, which he remembered from that Christmastime event. "Got a place for these?" he asked. "Sorry, you probably don't need any more flowers."

"Oh, these are beauuu-tifool!" she exclaimed. "And you have brought a vase? Parfait! We 'ave nothing at the front! I know the ideal place. So nice of you!"

Just the then the phone rang and Nicole answered. Cornelius was surprised when Nicole told him the call was for him. *Now? At the gallery?* He stepped behind the desk and picked up the handset.

"So sorry to bother you, son. I, uh, we . . . well, your mom and I are stuck. Any chance you can pick up us? Then you can head right back to the gallery for Miranda's art show."

Cornelius saw people entering and turned his back to preserve what privacy he could. "Sorry, Dad, you and Mom are stuck where?"

"Thing is, we drove the EV but I had forgotten to get it fully charged last night. We made it as far as a gas station in Cambria, but—"

"Got it," Cornelius interrupted. "You're at Art's?"

"Right."

"Okay, take Mom to the bakery across the street, you can sit at one of their little tables. They're closed, but they keep their tables outside. I'll be there as soon as I can."

"Thanks a million," his father said. "I feel like an idiot."

"Could happen to anyone, myself included. Sit tight, see you soon."

Cornelius turned around in time to catch Nicole. "Tell Miranda I'll be back as soon as I can." And with that, he dashed out the door.

Chapter 26

Miranda arrived at the Finders Gallery lot and pulled into the space reserved for employees, as Nicole had suggested.

It was all she could do not to jump out of the car. Instead, she disciplined herself to take a moment to breathe. Striding into the gallery's entrance, her artist's eye appraised the room, which brought a moment of calm reassurance.

In a tall vase-sculpture made by one of the gallery's glass artists stood a stunning arrangement of multi-colored gladiolas and white tuberoses, their distinctive fragrance already perfuming the air. The classic Stan Getz album *Cool Sounds* was playing just loudly enough, and her paintings hung perfectly illuminated like silent windows into nature.

Nicole Champagne approached and greeted her warmly, then took her by the arm. "I must borrow you just a few moment," she apologized in her distinctive Montreal accent.

"Your friend Sally, she 'as delivered the food. I just wanted to show you."

"Oh, great!"

They headed toward a galley kitchen along the back wall of a second room, where Tony, Sally, and June were gathered next to a large rolling rack of hors d'oeuvres.

"Wow!" Miranda commented. "All of this looks amazing!" She hugged her friend, then shook hands with Tony, as she added, "So good to see you again. Thank you for being here!"

"Look," Nicole gushed. They 'have brought *les petites canapes!*"

"Sally, you must have brought three hundred! They are tiny cheese cookies like little coins—my mother's recipe." Miranda squeezed her eyes shut for a moment. "Did you and my mother conspired to create these? You know I love them."

"Voila. And also, I 'ave for you the *real* champagne and also some bottles without alcohol, as you like," Nicole said. "It is 'ere in the mini-fridge."

"Champagne from Ms. Champagne." Miranda smiled, appreciating the thoughtfulness.

And then, before she could say another word, Zelda swept in, list in hand. With a nod, Nicole disappeared to resume her duties out front.

"Hi, Zelda," Miranda said, leaning in for a gentle hug. "So good to see you. And thank you for being here."

"Of course, I'm here!" her representative exclaimed, after providing an air kiss. She held her young client by the chin for a moment. "You look quite beautiful and quite professional," Zelda said approvingly before glancing at her watch. "We have about an hour before your guests begin to arrive. But you never know, some could get here early."

"True. You look beautiful too, by the way. Stunning outfit, as always."

Zelda McIntyre took a brief moment to enjoy the compliment. "Thank you, Dear. Now, I just need to explain a couple of things to you. Do let me do all the introducing. Sometimes these are delicate matters, you know, and that's what you have me here for." She peered up intently at her client. Though she drew herself up to her full height, the top of her head didn't clear Miranda's shoulder.

For three years, she'd been Miranda's sole representative. The investment had begun to pay off when they were both in San Francisco. And, if Zelda were honest with herself, the girl's reputation, work, and income had improved since her move to this little town. *Mostly due to my efforts. But then again, I've been able to play off the artist being "unavailable" and "entirely dedicated to her art."*

She sometimes imagined Miranda as her own creation, as though she'd been a street urchin, a discovery whom she, Zelda, had groomed and improved beyond recognition, someone with a mysterious past and dazzling talent, her own little Pygmalion. She was instead, however, a young woman of tremendous pedigree—if only she'd allow Zelda to use it as part of her PR.

Miranda stared off into space. "Are you getting all this?" Zelda asked.

"What? Oh . . . yes, of course. You do the intros."

"Also, you need to remember that not everyone is as fond of environmental issues as you are, and you're not to engage in any sort of diatribe with your audience this evening. This is neither the time nor the place. Understood?"

Clasping and unclasping her hands, Miranda stood with a dazed expression, as if her nerves were sending electrical jolts through her system. "I suppose," she answered.

"I still think it was a mistake to include that oil spill painting of yours, but it's too late to take it out now. You wouldn't relent, would you? I truly think it's a social blunder."

A nervous laugh escaped Miranda.

Zelda sighed and returned to her checklist. "Oh, yes, the president of Associated Coastal Artists is going to be here—

we're trying to get you a spread in their magazine. Of course, we invited Dennis Curry from Cambria, and he's such a well-known wildlife artist, it'll be great PR for you."

"Oh, I'm glad he's coming! It'll be so good to see him again."

"And uh . . . let's see. Oh, yes, we need to get our signals straight."

"Signals?"

"Yes, dear. If I nod toward you, you know that means you're to walk in my direction *immediately* no matter who you're talking to, because I've got a hot prospect who wants to meet the artist. Is that clear?"

"Yeah, okay, I guess. I'll try, anyway."

Miranda seemed to grow edgier by the minute, and she glanced past Zelda to the main room where the first early guests were beginning to arrive.

"Here they come," Zelda said. "Ready?"

Zelda caught sight of Joseph Calvin as he peered in through the gallery's plate glass window. Then, as he stood for a moment framed in the open doorway, she couldn't help but note the steel gray hair perfectly barbered, the seamed-but-sculpted face, the sharp crease running down the gray slacks, and the high polish on the shoes. *No wonder every available woman in Santa Barbara has set her cap for the man*, she mused.

"Joseph!" she called out. "Do come and meet the artist."

With a smile, he walked in her direction. Zelda reached out to grab his left hand and, as she held it, stood on tiptoe to plant a kiss low on his cheek. Then she said, "Allow me to present Miranda Jones, my foremost painter, as you already know. Miranda, dear, this is Joseph Calvin, from Santa Barbara."

Smiling, Joseph took Miranda's hand firmly. "I'm delighted."

"How do you do, sir. I've been looking forward to meeting you," Miranda offered, a grin brightening her nervous face.

"I'm already an admirer of your work."

"Oh, well, thank you. I—"

Before she could continue, Zack interrupted. "Hi, Miranda."

Zelda watched carefully to see what sort of interplay was at work between them. *She's shy, hesitant, as usual. He seems ... hesitant too, as though he's holding himself back.* Calvin Junior appeared youthful, handsome, in a classic blue blazer over khaki chinos.

A waiter walked toward them, slender flutes of champagne balanced on his tray. Everyone but Miranda chose one.

Zack put in, "I see you've met Dad. I'd have preferred to do the honors myself, but apparently, you have to be quick when Zelda is around."

Zelda watched Joseph lift his glass in her direction as he added, "Yes, you do."

"I'll take that as a compliment." Zelda smiled up at him, clinking her glass to his. His eyes fell involuntarily to her cleavage, not quite concealed by the scarf. Allowing him to take full advantage of the view, she gave him another dazzling smile. "Enjoy yourselves. I must see to the other guests for a little while."

Miranda watched Zelda walk away, leaving her standing in a small, tight circle with Zack and Joseph, the crowd beginning to swirl around them. Fragments of conversation floated past, which she tried to ignore but longed to overhear: "Not sure I like the bird painting as much as . . . Could you have a lion staring at your dining table? Loved that one . . . I've heard about Miranda's . . ."

Realizing she was saying nothing to the Calvins—who'd driven all this way on her behalf—she offered, "Mr. Calvin, I'm really so pleased you were able to come. I do hope you'll forgive my being distracted at our first meeting."

"Of course! This is your big night. Don't let us monopolize you."

Miranda had taken the opportunity to escape the awkward moment with Zack and his father, hoping she hadn't made her discomfort too obvious. *He looked handsome as always and vaguely ... angry? I don't know. And where's Cornelius? He promised he'd be here..*

Looking up, Miranda caught sight of Samantha just arriving and smiled at her friend.

"Here you are!" Sam said exuberantly. "Miranda, it's thrilling to see the turnout, isn't it?"

Grateful to feel her friend's support, she said, "I guess it is pretty good, isn't it?"

"I don't know when I've seen such a turnout at the gallery. You're a 'draw' my dear, if you'll excuse the pun."

Miranda laughed. "That made my night, Sam. A bit of humor is just what I needed." Over Sam's shoulder, she noticed Zack and Mr. Calvin eyeing her beautiful friend. Of course, her statuesque beauty and vivid red hair would catch any man's eye, particularly set off to perfection by a simple mocha wool wrap and her favorite amber jewelry. "Mr. Calvin," Miranda called out, gesturing, "let me introduce you."

The Calvins walked toward them. "Sam, I'd like you to meet Zack Calvin. Zack, this is my dear friend Samantha Hugo." Sam extended her hand toward Zack, who met it with his own. Miranda's artist-eye noted the pairs of long fingers and graceful movements, the two hands like a matched set, fitting together with uncanny symmetry.

"And this is his father," Miranda continued, "Mr. Joseph Calvin. Mr. Calvin, this is Samantha Hugo."

Now Sam released Zack's hand and reached for Joseph's. "Mr. Calvin," she said.

"Please call me Joseph." They stood almost eye to eye.

"All right, Joseph. I understand you've come up from Santa Barbara?"

"Yes, for the first time in many years."

"Oh, did you used to visit Milford-Haven?"

"When Zack was very young, we did."

"How nice. And is your wife here?"

Admiring Samantha's smooth way of asking the question, Miranda glanced at Joseph.

"Oh, no, she's ah . . . she passed away several years ago."

"I'm sorry." Her clear brown eyes exuded warmth. "How nice you can be here with Zack again."

"Milford-Haven does seem to be a charming town, and if I remember correctly, it's grown quite a bit over the years."

"It has, yes," Sam confirmed. "But we try to keep things in balance, so we don't lose its natural beauty."

Zelda McIntyre felt a charge in the air as though she were picking up radio signals. When she glanced toward Joseph and saw him with the tall redhead, she made a beeline for the group and slipped her arm through Joseph's. "You've met another one of the locals I see, Joseph. Hello, Mrs. Hugo, wasn't it?

"It's *Ms.* Good evening, Zelda." The chill in the air seemed palpable to Miranda. Sam seemed to eye Zelda suspiciously but kept a smile frozen in place.

"We're just getting acquainted," Joseph said warmly, "and she was talking about the town."

"Really?" Determined not to let her fury show, Zelda made a failed attempt at keeping sarcasm out of her tone. "I'm sure Ms. Hugo knows every inch of it." Refraining from adding, *With a town the size of a thimble, that isn't saying much,* instead she thought of another tactic and turned to Samantha. "You'll have to get Joseph to tell you all about his oil company."

An environmentalist and an oil man? Ha! Just one glimpse of Joseph's business card and Samantha will start lecturing him before they've finished their champagne. Then Joseph will realize his need for a business-savvy woman, not some bleeding heart on a constant rampage to save inchworms.

"I'm so sorry I won't be able to linger," Zelda continued. "We have so many guests. Do excuse me. I'll see you later, Joseph," she promised, reaching up to deliver one more peck on his cheek. As she walked away, she wondered, *Is he watching me?* She resisted the temptation to look back.

Samantha found herself fascinated by the two Calvin men. Joseph seemed personable and polished—the polar opposite of Jack Sawyer, for example, with whom Sam had almost daily contretemps and with whom she'd once shared so much.

Yet, if what Zelda had just said was true—that he worked for an oil company—she doubted they'd have anything more than polite manners in common, and these could wear thin quickly.

Then there was Zack, about whom she'd heard so much from Miranda. Obviously, father and son didn't work together, as Zack was a music promoter, according to her friend.

She felt a moment of sadness for these two young people who'd tried, and apparently failed, to launch a relationship. Knowing Miranda had, in fact, already moved on, she felt for Zack, who perhaps didn't yet know he'd lost the affections of a special woman.

Why am I feeling for this young man I've only just met? She had no answer for this, except for the fleeting thought that he'd be about the same age as her son. And since she'd been told her son had lived in Santa Barbara at some point, perhaps they'd even met, gone to the same school. . . . *All that is pure fantasy. No point indulging such ideas.*

Sam reached for a flute of champagne, as Nicole passed around the tray, and headed toward a wall of Miranda's paintings.

Miranda felt the need for a brief retreat from the swirling cacophony and headed for the back room.

Nicole will know where to find me if I'm needed. I bet Cornelius would figure out where I am . . . if he ever gets here. She pulled open a folding chair and sat down, taking a deep breath. Idly, she wondered whether any of her paintings had yet sold. Certainly, if Zelda had anything to say about it, she'd sell several tonight.

Just as guilt was about to force her to return to her guests, Zack loomed up in the entrance to the small room. "There you are," he said, almost as accusingly as Zelda might have.

"Sorry, I . . . I just needed to get off my feet for a moment."

"Glad I caught you alone, actually." He pushed a hand through his hair. "Listen, uh, hey your work is beautiful. I mean, I've always thought so, as you know. It's . . . it's a great show."

"Thank you, Zack," Miranda said quietly.

"I should have called. I'm sorry."

"No need to apologize. I think—"

"I've been—"

"You were very kind to invite me to the Doobies concert."

"Yeah, well, no big deal."

"It was to me."

"I didn't mean it that way. What I mean is . . . we didn't seem to—"

"We didn't really connect, did we Zack? We tried. But it's good to be friends. Don't you think?" *Wow, I think I really have found my voice*, she thought, surprised she could suddenly speak her mind.

He seemed stunned by her frank summation. "I . . . I'd have agreed, had it not been for that phone call. That was one of the reasons I came tonight. I wanted to be sure."

Miranda thought back. "A particular phone call? I apologize, I'm not sure what you mean."

"That time we were . . . you know, we were flirting. I said I'd caught you in, and you said, 'in what,' and then . . ."

Truly puzzled, Miranda again tried to summon a memory of flirting with Zack on the phone.

"Well, anyway, you sounded so sexy that I nearly jumped in the car. I really wanted to connect with you."

"Miranda?" Zelda's voice cut through the conversation. "For heaven's sake! Hiding back here with Zackery, are you? I'm sorry, but I have a prospective buyer for you to meet."

Shoving her way past Zack, Zelda reached for Miranda's hand and pulled her back into the fray.

Cornelius had made it back to the gallery in ninety minutes. He'd practically shoved his parents out of the Durango when he'd deposited them safely at home, but they'd understood.

He reentered the premises inconspicuously, as the rooms were filled with guests who stood in small clusters in front of paintings or socialized while hors d'oeuvres were offered on trays.

Feeling more an observer than a participant, he thought it best to remain in the background till he could get his bearings. His original plan had been to keep his distance from Miranda for a while, leaving her free to enjoy her moment in the spotlight—and himself free to observe the various interactions.

It was now about two hours into the art show. The tuberoses were still fragrant, if slightly wilted, and Nicole had switched the music to a contemporary smooth jazz mix—he recognized Eddie Daniels's clarinet and Lee Ritenour's guitar. The evening seemed to be flowing on, with everyone apparently enjoying the high social whirl rarely celebrated in Milford-Haven.

He hadn't met Zelda, but he overheard her name and watched her move about the room like the proverbial cog in a well-oiled machine. But from what Miranda'd said about her, he wondered whether her passion was for the art or for the sales.

While Zelda had a smooth serpentine movement through the crowd, Nicole, whose French accent occasionally wafted over the hubbub of conversation, bounced from one patron to another, reminding him of a pinball machine. As Nicole raced to the desk for her catalogs, flitted back to customers and led them from painting to painting, Cornelius found himself suppressing a chuckle. Somehow, she also managed to spin on her high heels and balance trays of drinks and food.

Amusing as this array of art and humanity was, what he really wanted was a moment with Miranda. He needed to let her know he was actually here, even if she was far too busy for a conversation. After smiling his way through both gallery rooms, however, he hadn't spotted her. *If I know her, she's in that back room, taking a break, catching her breath, or even reviewing the guest list.*

As he started to make his way in that direction, he flashed back to their very first meeting—colliding, actually, right at the entrance to that little room, which he foolishly now thought of as "theirs."

He drew near, and thought he heard her voice. But as he arrived, he heard unmistakably a man's voice say, "Well, anyway, you sounded so sexy that I nearly jumped in the car. I really wanted to connect with you."

The words stopped him in his tracks. *She's in the back room with a guy telling her she's sexy?* He hardly knew whether to withdraw or to barge in to protect her.

Before he could decide, or even hear what *she* might have to say, he heard a rather shrill female voice say, "Miranda? For heaven's sake! Hiding back here with Zackery, are you? I'm sorry, but I have a prospective buyer for you to meet."

He pressed himself against the desk as Zelda dragged Miranda off. And that left him face to face with the guy who must be Zack. He stuck out his hand. "Cornelius Smith," he said.

Zack seemed nonplussed for a moment, then took the offered handshake. "Zack Calvin," he replied.

Zelda cast her trained eye around the room to assess what she might need to take care of next. *What, or who*, she amended.

She'd managed to get Miranda out of that back room. Even if she *was* having an important conversation with Zackery, this was hardly the time or place! She'd also continued tracking that Samantha woman, pleased to see she was occupied with other guests and not standing at Joseph's elbow.

Then she saw Russell Clarke arrive and was about to rush to greet him. He'd placed a hold on two of Miranda's paintings a few days earlier, and now it only remained to complete the sale of at least one.

She was surprised, though, when Joseph got to Russell first and the two greeted one another like old friends. While they chatted, Zelda held back for a moment, curious to see how the two men interacted. Though they were hardly familial, they seemed mutually respectful. *Of course . . . this makes sense. Russell is in shipping: Joseph is in oil; they must do business with one another.*

She tracked something else too, however. Despite having as much elegance and polish as Joseph, there seemed to be something vaguely sinister about Mr. Clarke. *Something I can't put my finger on.*

Last fall she'd concluded her first transaction with him—but taken a bit more than her usual percentage. *Just as it should be. I worked much harder than usual to complete that sale. Sometimes that's how it is with a demanding customer.*

Zack had greeted Russell Clarke and chit-chatted with him and his father for a few minutes. Now, however, he was beginning to feel he'd done his duty by Miranda and wondered how much longer he'd need to stay at this event.

He also wondered who this Cornelius Smith person was, and why exactly he'd made a point of introducing himself. If Zack didn't know better, he'd think the man was staking a claim on Miranda. But his shy—or possibly *not* so shy—former girl-friend—or *un*-girlfriend—didn't seem the type to already be seeing someone else.

On the other hand, she'd been far more outspoken and intentional during their brief conversation in the back room than he'd ever heard her be previously.

Women! Should he try to finish their talk? He did want to get to the bottom of that phone call. But certainly, this wasn't the place to try monopolizing her when she needed to stay available for prospective buyers. In any case, Zelda wouldn't allow it.

And really, was there anything more to say? Miranda had stated pretty clearly that their relationship, such as it was, had morphed into friendship. The thought brought an edgy depression. *Hate to admit it . . . I think I've become a fifth wheel here. If there's nothing more to discuss, why should I stay? Maybe I'm just bored, now. But dad's still enjoying himself.* Zack was about to hunt up some of those circulating hors d'oeuvres and maybe get a refill on his drink.

Just then he heard a laugh—a deep, infectious sound that effervesced through him more than the champagne he'd drunk earlier. *That's how Miranda laughed during that phone call!* Suddenly, his ennui fled, and he spun around to catch sight of her in *this* mood, the one he kept missing.

But the woman whose sparkling laugh now slid into a gasp looked at him with wide-eyed recognition. *Who is that??* He heard the question in his mind, feeling its urgency. *I have to know! She's looking at me as if we've met before.*

"Mer!" a familiar voice called from behind him.

He watched as Miranda rushed toward the woman and they embraced. He saw similarities . . . body type, hair color . . .

"Glad you finally got here!" Miranda continued.

"Sorry, I had a meeting with that local client that took much longer than I'd planned. You look great! And you've got a crowd, kiddo!"

The woman looked at him again, this time over Miranda's shoulder. Seeming to sense his presence, Miranda now turned around. "Oh, Zack, I'd like you to meet my sister, Meredith."

"Aha," he said before he could stop himself.

"Caught you in," the newly arrived sibling teased.

Damn! That's what I said during that call! He recovered in time to observe the formalities. "Great to meet you," he said, shaking her hand and noticing her firm grip. The puzzle pieces all began tumbling into place. *Surely this is the woman I talked with on the phone. It wasn't Miranda at all.*

As though she could hear his thoughts the woman—Meredith—blushed, making her even more attractive, if that were possible. Somehow her discomfort made him feel needed, as though he could help her past the awkward moment.

"Good to meet you, too." She covered her unease with a dazzling smile.

"It's great Miranda could have family here for her big show. Her work is superb."

Now he watched Miranda blush, smiling at the compliment. "Mer, would you like some champagne? I'll go get you some."

With that, Miranda fled, leaving Zack staring at Meredith, the sister, the mystery woman. Her eyes weren't green like Miranda's . . . there was more blue, making the irises look almost teal, like dark aquamarines. But it was the sense of play dancing in them that got to him.

"This should be interesting," he said.

He saw a faint trace of guilt cross Meredith's face, but it was quickly replaced by a gleam of defiance.

"Think you're up to it, Zack?"

"Born for it," he quipped back. *Where did that come from? I don't know, but I have to find out.* "Listen, while your sister gets your drink, why don't you come meet my father?"

"I'd be delighted," Meredith said, following where he led.

Cornelius bided his time for another forty-five minutes. By then, the alcohol had run out and the flowers had begun to droop. The few remaining guests seemed to be saying their good-nights. When he noticed Nicole tidying up around the edges, picking up stray glasses and putting away tossed-aside fliers, he knew it was time to find Miranda.

Seeing her standing alone—probably for the first time tonight—he walked over, took her hand, and led her to the famous back room.

When they arrived, he closed the door.

"Hey, you," he said, standing in front of her.

"Hey, you," she replied. Despite her evident exhaustion, there was an eagerness in her eyes. "You did come."

Then he grabbed her to him, and held her for a long moment. When he pulled away, he took her by the shoulders. "You're not still seeing Zack, are you?"

"No!" she proclaimed, then added in a quiet but firm voice, "No, I'm not. I think I made myself clear to him tonight."

"Good. Because as of now, you're seeing me. Are we agreed?"

"Oh God, yes."

Then he kissed her till she opened that beautiful mouth and let him in.

When she pulled away to catch her breath, she said, "I'm sorry it's been so crazy tonight."

"I figured it would be. Well, maybe not quite as crazy as it turned out," he added.

They both laughed, releasing whatever tension remained.

"Listen," he said, "I leave for Tokyo in the morning."

"Tokyo? Wow, you said some travel, but—"

"Short trip. I'll call you when I get back. If you really want me to, that is."

"I-I-if?" she asked, turning the whine into three syllables.

He smiled down at her. "Just checking. You're highly sought after, you know."

"Right. Well, *you* can seek after me. If you really want to, that is."

He would have laughed, but at this point he wanted her so badly he could hardly speak. "*When*, not *if*," he said in a deep voice.

And then, after one more kiss, he let himself out the back door.

Chapter 27

M iranda saw Zelda out to her car, where they promised to have a lengthy follow-up conversation dissecting every detail of tonight's show.

Happy, distracted, and weary, Miranda considered tonight's sleeping arrangements. She longed to climb into bed and drift off on dreams of Cornelius. But her sister had made the long drive to Milford-Haven to support her at her first major art show in town. Miranda could hardly turn her away and had fixed up the daybed in her studio for her.

"Thanks, Mandy," Meredith replied, shaking her head. "But I took a room at that nice little motel, the Belhaven."

"Mer, you know you're always welcome—"

"We'd stay up and talk all night. And frankly, I'm exhausted after that drive. I'll call you tomorrow to see if we can get together before I head north."

"Well, if you're sure," Miranda conceded.

The Calvins were hovering near the front door, overhearing the sisters. "Listen," Joseph began, "we're all—well, all but you, Miranda—staying at the Belhaven, and it's been a long day. How about if we all meet for breakfast? Miranda, you can recommend a place?"

Miranda looked around at their faces. "Mer, would that work for you?"

"Sure, as long as we meet by about 8:00. Then I can get on the road no later than 10:00."

"Works for me," Zack chimed in. "Dad?"

"Fine. So we have a plan. Miranda, will you meet us at the motel so we can follow you to a good breakfast spot?"

"Sure. I'll be at the Belhaven at, say, 7:45."

She watched as her sister climbed into her Beamer. Then she saw Zack give her sister a rather intense look. *What was that about?*

"It was a great show, Miranda," Zack offered.

"Thanks, Zack. And thanks for being here."

He nodded and a moment later, he drove away in his Mercedes, his father in his passenger seat, and Meredith following close behind in her own car.

Miranda stood there a moment longer. *Is there . . . did they?* But Nicole's voice rang out, interrupting her musings.

"Bonsoir, bonne nuit! C'etait merveilleux, tu sais? Fantastic, Miranda!" She waved, then locked the front door, seeming to have almost as much energy as she'd had at the beginning of the evening.

"Thank you so much for everything, Nicole!" Miranda managed a tired smile before walking the few steps around the side of the building to her car.

Delmar made a brief stop at Miranda's art show earlier, and it had proven to be more interesting than he'd anticipated. He'd made a point of arriving in civilian clothes and was, as usual, one of the only guests of color.

Miranda's paintings were not only spectacular, but evocative. In one of the gallery's rooms, a series of landscapes had been displayed, and each of them tugged at his heart. He'd never responded like that to images of mountains and coastlines, but he had begun to appreciate the Central Coast region's particular beauty. She captured the imagery, but also some sentiment the scenery held.

He'd said a brief hello to Cornelius Smith as he'd been hurrying out. Then he'd greeted Miranda, congratulating her on her show. Despite being surrounded by her fans, she'd broken away long enough to thank him for coming, and she'd introduced him to Zelda McIntyre. *Now there's a powerhouse. I saw her at the Calvin party but didn't meet her then.*

He'd said a brief hello to Joseph Calvin and met his son. Then he'd been introduced to Russell Clarke.

"Of Clarke Shipping in Morro Bay?" he'd asked.

"You've heard of our company?" Clarke had asked.

"Your firm is famous in these parts."

Of course, it made sense that the CEOs of a Central Coast oil company and shipping firm would be acquainted and possibly do business together. Del had refrained from asking about the house Clarke was having built here in Milford-Haven. He could play that card another time. After some brief, innocuous chit chat, he'd circulated for another few minutes. He'd been out of his element at such an event, yet he'd felt for two reasons, it had been a good idea to attend. First, he found it useful to get to know as many people in the community as possible. In this case, the community extended to points south—to Morro Bay and as far as Santa Barbara. Second, he felt it was good for local law enforcement to be visible in a supportive way.

There was one possible disadvantage that might accrue from his brief public appearance, and that was that now Russell Clarke would recognize him. Next time he stopped by Clarke Shipping to see Gladys, he might have to mind his manners.

He still had no clear idea if or how Russell Clarke was connected with the Chernak Agency. But the more pieces of the puzzle he could gather, the better chance he had of assembling it enough to see the whole picture.

Del had made another sweep through town, driving slowly past the now shuttered shops on Main Street and a few of the adjacent roads. He decided to circle back to Finders Gallery to make sure it was locked up properly for the night. He was just in time to see Miranda walking toward the parking lot.

Why is she alone? No one is seeing her home? "Hi, Miranda," he said after rolling down his window.

"Oh hi, Delmar. Thanks again for coming tonight."

"Glad I didn't miss it. Your work is something else. Mind if I follow you home?"

Miranda seemed startled. "You don't have to do that."

"It'd make me feel better," he countered.

She smiled. "Sure. Appreciate it."

He followed the taillights of her Mustang as they wound up the hill to her house. When they arrived, he waited till she stood in her open doorway, then waved goodnight.

Zack dropped his dad off at their motel, then explained he felt a bit restless and wanted to go for a short drive.

He navigated through the sleepy village, illuminated now only by streetlamps and a few commercial signs.

Cracking his window, he inhaled the cool ocean air and let the glimmer of waves play at the edges of his vision. *Meredith,* he thought. *There was a surprise. So like her sister, and so different.*

Her voice was similar enough for one to be mistaken for the other. Yet Meredith's was infused with an extra voltage of energy and lacked the silky calm of Miranda's.

Both women were knock-outs. But where Miranda always seemed slightly apologetic about her beauty, it was clear Meredith was at ease with hers. And where Miranda seemed often to shy away from life, Meredith evidently liked to pursue it.

The image of Meredith—her self-assured grace, the taunt in her blue-green eyes—sent a clench through his gut. *Attraction? Competition?* It seemed a tempting, dangerous admixture of both. *But meeting her did answer the very question I came to Milford-Haven to find.*

Here was a woman who had it all—beauty and brains, money and success. She didn't seem to need a relationship. Otherwise, she likely wouldn't have come to town by herself. *Is she too independent for me? Do I need to be needed? Was that the appeal of Cynthia?*

He felt the unmistakable desire to pursue Meredith. But how could he? First of all, he'd scarcely gotten beyond dating —or thinking about dating—Miranda, and now he proposed to chase after her sister? Secondly, they lived at two ends of the state. Well, that was an exaggeration. But it'd be a good five-plus hours to get from his city to hers, and that was without traffic.

Why am I thinking about drive-time when I don't even know the woman? He turned his car around and drove the short distance back to the Belhaven. But when he pulled into the parking space by his room, he saw Meredith standing in the open doorway a couple of rooms down from his.

"Mind if we take a drive?" Her voice was low but clear in the night air.

Heart thumping, he said, "Climb in."

Meredith pulled shut the door of his Mercedes and sat facing forward as Zack backed out of the parking space and turned onto the lane that followed the coastline. The ocean was calm and she was anything but.

I'm taking a big risk here. But what the hell? We're here in person. If I don't talk to him while we're face to face, I may never have the chance again.

After a moment, she said. "You flirted with me tonight."

"You flirted first," he hit back.

"I did. And I loved every minute of it."

Zack inhaled sharply and found a turnout at a small ocean overlook. He pulled to a stop, turned off the engine, and faced her. They stared at one another across the intimate space of his two front seats.

"That sounds good," he offered.

"But here's the thing," she said. "I got caught up in something once, and it's not going to happen twice. So I have two questions for you."

"Okay. Shoot."

"First, are you involved with my sister?"

Zack pressed his lips together and stared out his front windshield. "I toyed with the idea over the past several months. I don't mean I toyed with *her*, but I . . . I admired her. But the spark just wasn't there. Well, except in that phone call. I came tonight to chase it down, see if there was anything real. Imagine my surprise." He gave her a wry smile that had no hint of a smirk, or she'd have leapt out of the car. "She and I talked tonight. She says we're friends. I think she was being charitable. I'd be lucky to have her friendship. But there's nothing more."

Meredith could feel her shoulders go down an inch. "Okay. Good answer. Here's my second question. Would you want to be with me?"

Zack rocked back in his seat and put a hand through his hair. "Jesus. You don't pull any punches."

"No. I don't." She waited a moment, then continued. "Don't get me wrong. I like the flirting. But I'm . . . for obvious reasons, I had to keep it secret, and I'm tired of suppressing my feelings, tired of waiting. That may sound weird, but I've waited weeks. No, months, to talk with you again. And I knew this time it had to be face to face."

She turned to face forward. "I bet you have a . . . *busy* life in Santa Barbara. And I have a thriving business in San Francisco. I have no doubt both of us have been seeing other people. So, neither of us need further complications."

Zack gave a huff.

"If that's all this is." Meredith turned to face him again. "Are you interested in someone like me? I just need an answer, yes or no."

She worked hard to keep her breathing steady as she looked at his chiseled profile in the dim starlight. She knew she'd been wanting some fantasy version of him. But she had come to realize that she actually wanted *him*—not a fantasy, and not just an affair, delicious as that might be. With this man, it would have to be all or nothing.

She nearly stopped breathing all together when he turned to look at her. His eyes glistened, and she saw his pulse beating in his neck.

"I would love to be with someone like you," he said in a hoarse voice. "No. I would love to be with *you.*"

Meredith nodded her head and exhaled. "Then we'll take it step by step. Starting with breakfast tomorrow with your father and my sister."

Chapter 28

Cornelius waited till the big jet lifted off the runway, then reclined his seat. Though he'd have preferred a First Class cubicle, he and his long legs were grateful for the Business Class accommodation.

Saturday morning here . . . already Sunday across the International Dateline. The flight attendant stopped by his chair to offer a hot rolled towel, *oshibori*, according to Japanese custom. He loved Tokyo and found himself wishing he could share it with Miranda.

Good Lord, I've got it bad, he thought. Every time he was with her, the time together merely whetted his appetite for more. When could he get her alone? When could they stay up all night and talk under the stars? Would there, indeed, be any talking involved if he were with her all night? Not likely.

That art show was a zoo! Between Zelda treating her client like a steamer trunk she could push around, Zack cornering her in the back room—*our* back room—to tell her she was sexy, and her sister arriving and moving right in on Zack. *Yeah, I caught that. Did Miranda?*

He thought back to just a few months earlier, before he'd collided with Miranda at the gallery, before she'd painted the rope hanging down the escarpment, before he caught a glimpse of her at the car wash. . . . Just when, exactly, had he become a goner? *Probably back when the stars sang together.*

And yet . . . if only life could be simple, he whined. Somehow this distance—the chance to travel halfway around the world—was just what he needed.

He hadn't bargained for a competitive sister, a clueless, haughty ex, a domineering manager. And he hadn't even met the parents yet! Who knows what he'd be up against there. Was the mother anything like the sister? God help him. And what about the father? Not supportive of her art habit, according to her. On the other hand, his own parents would love her. *Love her. Do I love her?*

He did. Damn it. And he hated complexities. But that was like saying he hated entanglement. And that was the stuff of which the universe—his favorite aspect of the universe—was made.

Miranda had never felt such a longing.

Ever since the art show, she'd been cramming her days' schedules to capacity in her effort to overcome it.

The breakfast with Mer and the Calvins and Zelda on Saturday morning had been surprisingly civilized, even pleasant, except that she'd felt like the proverbial fifth wheel, which, in fact, she was.

Zelda and Mr. Calvin were nicely paired off. It seemed their relationship had been developing further than she'd realized. In their sartorial sophistication, they exceeded the more casual style of Milford-Haven, but if they noticed, they didn't mind. Between bites of the brunch special at Michael's Lighthouse

Tavern—a richly superb crab benedict everyone had ordered— Zelda laughed at his anecdotes and Joseph chuckled at her comments about gallery guests.

The real surprise was watching the interaction between Mer and Zack. Not that they flirted, exactly, but they had a kind of energetic match. They seemed to stumble over common interests, whether of market trends, business practices, or even classical compositions, as if shared sensibilities shouldn't be allowed between them. *Because they were worried about me.* But clearly, they couldn't help the evident overlap of sensibilities.

All four of them had offered praise and admiration for Miranda's painting—and Zelda practically gloated over the number of pieces that'd sold, which seemed to startle her sister. It did feel good to have the event behind her and to bask a bit in the appreciation. But every time she thought of the event, she was swept back to that moment in the back room with Cornelius.

After brunch, Mer had started her drive north to San Francisco, the Calvins had headed south to Santa Barbara, and Zelda had insisted she meet with her to go over every detail of the show: the list of guests, overheard comments, sales, upcoming commissions, and future shows. After Zelda left, Miranda made herself a bowl of soup, watched an episode of *Magnum P.I.*, and collapsed into bed early.

Sunday she had breakfast with Samantha, went for a long walk, and started reading a book about stars she'd once bought, as if that would support her sudden affinity with an astronomer.

Monday, Tuesday, and Wednesday, she painted feverishly and rode her bike up and down the hills near her house. By Thursday, she'd admitted to herself that not only did she now have an official boyfriend, she'd fallen for Cornelius in a deeper way than she'd realized.

Resisting the temptation just to daydream about him, she figured this time apart was a good time to think things through.

She put a favorite CD into her player and the evocative strains of Pat Metheny's "Are You Going With Me?" filled her studio. *The perfect question . . . whether I'm asking it, or he is.*

With the possibility of a serious relationship coming into her life, a sense of loss tugged at her over the potential interruption of her artist-life. *That's an exaggeration. I'll never stop being an artist. It's not only what I do, but who I am.*

That imagined loss had concerned her when she'd thought about Zack months ago, and she saw now that it was because of some sort of misalignment. Her sense of how life would be with Cornelius was entirely different: gain, not loss; enhancement, not competition.

She did have to admit he was distracting. *Why? Fascinating, handsome, fun, considerate, brilliant, intuitive, pays attention, stays in contact . . .* and those were only some of the reasons.

But would he expect her to stop or even curtail her career? Not any more than she'd expect him to stop being an astronomer.

As an artist, Miranda had cultivated a solitude that enabled her to work uninterrupted, to inhabit another zone where she could revel in the long hours of concentration required for painting. While the emotional noise of her upbringing had seemed to starve her, the quiet nourished her.

Ever since graduating from art school, she'd been fiercely determined to make a go of her career. She'd pushed her aspirations of having a family off into the future and struggled to accept the idea of balance in her life, assuming real mastery of her craft might delay or even possibly obviate the possibility of having time to devote to being a partner, a wife, a mother.

Now her perspective had changed. She'd found someone with whom she loved to *talk*, a man who understood her and expected her to do more, not less. When she entertained the idea of being with him, she felt they were in some ways already partnered. And while gazing into this rainbow of promise had always scared her before, now she found herself impatient for its arrival.

And there was something else. When she lay down each night, physically exhausted, an unfamiliar thrumming stole over her. She thought at first she might be coming down with something, though she didn't actually feel ill.

But there was a weight in her solar plexus, as though it were suddenly lined with gold. She did some Tai Chi exercises to see if that might rebalance the slight convergence of energy, but the sensation persisted.

When she got home from another bike ride Friday, her answering machine light was blinking. And there it was: a message from him. *I missed his call!* She replayed the message and did some figuring on the scratch pad by her answering machine. *He said he'd be flying tonight Pacific time, and Japan is sixteen hours ahead, so it's already Saturday morning there. He said it'd be a twelve-hour flight. So, he'll be arriving home midday tomorrow, I think.*

He'd explained that he'd drive from LAX to his parents' home, where he'd visit with them and do his best to sleep away the worst of the jet lag. Then he asked if she'd please put him on her calendar for an early dinner Sunday.

She wanted to scrub her house from top to bottom, polish every stick of furniture, trim the trees, cook the best meal of her life, and tie a bow around Shadow's neck. She figured she might tackle a modest version of that agenda the following day.

But as she lay awake Friday night and replayed his voice in her mind, the sensation in her body was as intense as if she were gravid. And then she knew why. Her womb had come awake.

She ached with a gentle throbbing that rolled through her like a wave each time she imagined the sound of his voice or remembered the sensation of his kiss. She breathed and let the next soft clench bring a quiet moan until she drifted into sleep.

Cornelius had been enjoying his time in Tokyo.

He loved both the city, and the country, though there was far more to explore of both. The professional reason for the trip was to give a lecture at Tokyo University's Institute of Astronomy, known as IoA, which had been established just eleven years earlier. Using the Kiso Observatory, built in 1974, he shared his presentation with a keenly focused group of students whose natural curiosity and intelligence were both a challenge and a joy.

His university hosts had offered all manner of excursions, most of them tourism that didn't appeal, but he accepted several invitations for the sake of decorum and local custom. The perpetual dilemma arose: to decline a gift was to insult; to accept a gift was to sign on for the obligation to give something of equal value in return. Accordingly, he now expected several people to show up for a tour either of NASA Ames or of the Lick Observatory, sometime in the coming year.

When he could, he escaped for some tourism of his own. He'd opted to stay at the Imperial Hotel, not far from the university and walking distance to several interesting spots as well as the Shinbashi train station. He spent an early evening perusing the Ginza with its kaleidoscope of neon, and at other times searched out small neighborhood eateries, and even braved a performance in the world famous Kabukiza Theatre.

The only problem with sampling these delights was that he missed Miranda at every turn. He kept imagining her reactions, predicting her preferences, envisioning her enjoyments.

They could explore temples and shrines in Kyoto, sink into the *onsen* hot springs in Hakone, gaze up at the giant Buddha in Kamakura, climb Mt. Fuji, and spend a weekend in Shimoda Beach at the end of the Izu peninsula.

But all that would have to wait. Meanwhile, from his room, he'd called his parents, not because it was strictly necessary, but because they got such a charge out of it. His dad would calculate the time change, his mom would ask what he was eating and whether it was raining. He gave them a quick update on his lecture, the students, the gracious hosts.

He also reported that Miranda's art show had been quite the social event and she herself a star because of her beautiful work. They once again told him how much they still enjoyed the one painting of hers he'd bought for them last Christmas, declaring that it completed their living room.

"When are we going to meet this young woman?" his father asked.

"Soon after I get home, if she's available," he'd promised.

"Oh, good. Well, be sure to invite her for dinner, dear," his mother added.

After the call, he made himself a cup of tea and sat in a chair that offered a view of the *tokonoma*—a small recessed alcove with a long, low table, a single piece of art, and an *Ikebana* floral arrangement.

He felt he'd done little else but think about Miranda for days. Though neither of them had said the words, he knew this was love, knew it as well as he knew his own name. The other thing he knew was how entirely mutual were these feelings. He saw it shine in her eyes, heard it in her voice. Was she struggling through it in his absence, or was she ahead of him, already waiting for him to catch up?

That moment when he'd declared they were dating and asked, "Are we agreed?" "God, yes," she'd answered, as if she'd been waiting years for him to say it. *There really is magic in that little back room at the gallery.*

What he hadn't divulged to his parents were his plans for this afternoon: a visit to a famous jeweler whose store was located downstairs. K. Uyeda had been established in 1884 by Kichigoro Uyeda, who learned English and started an art store for overseas customers. Now known simply as Uyeda, the store had long since become a preeminent purveyor of jewels, both nationally and internationally.

All this had been explained during a previous trip to Tokyo when one of his married colleagues had joked with him. "Someday, Ko-ni-ri-us-San, you will buy ringu for wifu, ne?" At the time it'd seemed the remotest possibility he could imagine. But now, he felt compelled to seize the opportunity.

Here he sat at perhaps the farthest geographic point away from her that he could. The distance itself, though agonizing in some ways, had been serving him well, as though it'd offered a focal distance on a star he needed to study. And now that metaphorical star looked to him like a diamond in the heavens, one he'd have to pluck and bring home to her.

He'd called ahead for an appointment with one of the sales associates and was met in the store by a Miss Saito, who bowed and led him to a chair in front of a desk.

"You would like to find diamond engagement ring," she began by confirming. "But not traditional setting. Is this correct?"

Her charming accent seemed to enhance her excellent command of English, and he appreciated that she'd paid attention to what he'd already mentioned on the phone.

"Accordingly, I have several rings for your viewing."

She brought out a tray lined in black velvet with grooves that held an array of sparkling pieces—so like his metaphor. Knowing the importance of courtesy, he looked at each. But he'd known immediately which one caught his eye.

"May I see this one?" he asked.

She pulled from the tray a simple gold band with a recessed diamond, the stone neither big nor small, but just wide enough nearly to fill the band. *This wouldn't snag her clothes, catch on her brushes, or be in the way as she paints.*

He sat holding it until Miss Saito asked, "Would you like me to model the ring for you?"

"Please," he said.

She slipped it on, and though this woman's hands were smaller, he was now able to picture it on Miranda's. He continued staring until Miss Saito spoke again.

"By the way, this may be purchased as a single ring. However, it is also part of a set with colored stones."

"Sorry?"

"I will show you."

She returned in a moment with a smaller tray, this one holding three bands that matched the original, but each had a different stone.

"Ruby, sapphire, emerald," she said, pointing out each.

Instantly, he could see these as an elaborate set, which her long fingers could easily handle. An emerald beside a sapphire beside a ruby—three rings designed to be worn side by side.

"Stacking rings," the jeweler explained.

He asked several more questions about sizing, shipping, price. And then he asked whether the colored stone rings could be held for him.

"Yes," Miss Saito confirmed. "We will keep for you."

For today, he bought the one with a simple diamond, and waited while it was placed in a small black velvet box.

"*Domo arigato,*" Cornelius said, confident in one of his few Japanese expressions.

"You are most welcome," Miss Saito replied, and they bowed to one another.

Chapter 29

M iranda did, in fact, polish her home and put a bow on Shadow, though it was a yellow one, in honor of spring. She'd managed to sleep Saturday night, though it'd been hard, knowing he was already in town.

But today was Sunday, and Cornelius would be picking her up at 4:00 p.m.—a few minutes from now—for a date to celebrate his homecoming, and the destination was a mystery. He'd said to dress for hiking, so they weren't heading out for a fancy dinner. *Will we end up here later? I don't care where we land tonight, as long as it's just the two of us.*

She heard his Durango rumble to her curb and flung open the front door.

"Hey, you!" he called.

"Hey, you!" she answered.

He practically ran up the walk to engulf her in a hug, which had her giggling, and she'd have fallen over backward, had he not had firm hold of her. He kissed her with more vehemence than tenderness, as though eager to take her somewhere. Still standing in the open doorway, he propositioned, "How about another sunset date?"

"I thought you'd never ask," she quipped, teasing him by repeating the phrase he'd used himself when he'd come to her house for lunch.

"Great. This time, we're going early to the location I have in mind. It's got a lot of trees that'll make it seem like twilight sooner rather than later."

She called to her kitty, who walked primly toward them. Miranda picked her up and said, "This is Shadow." The sleek ebony feline, evidently feeling quite fancy in her bow, uttered a polite, "Mow."

"How do you do, Shadow," Cornelius said with equal formality. "You're looking especially beautiful today," he added looking first at the cat, and then at the woman.

"You take care of the house," Miranda instructed Shadow, putting her down, then grabbing the backpack already resting on the floor.

As he drove them, he began to explain. "There's a piece of property I've loved since I was a kid. My pal Jameson and I used to climb around the old buildings and brambles when we were in grade school."

"It's great to have those places to explore when we're children. My sister and I used to do the same thing near Mount Tamalpais. Anyway, that's where we're going, to the special place you used to explore?"

He nodded. "And . . . there's more."

"Oh goodie," she said. "A secret."

He laughed. "I guess you could call it that, because at this point only Jameson and my folks know about it, and now you will."

"Wow. Buried treasure?"

"There's treasure for sure. And in a way, I guess it is buried under the aforementioned brambles."

"Curiouser and curiouser."

As they'd been talking, he'd driven out to Highway 1, then onto a narrow road on its western side that wound outward toward a point of land. She loved it out here, and her senses began to tingle as the area grew more familiar. Then Cornelius pulled to a stop and cut the engine.

"But this is . . ." she began.

"This is it," he confirmed. "The Tangle, everyone calls it. Abandoned by the family members who inherited it when they realized how much they'd have to spend to clean up the property and restore or tear down the buildings."

Through the mass of weeds and a few partially felled trees, she could just glimpse it—the small lighthouse she had first sketched. "But this is the place," she said again.

"Yes, this is the place."

"No, I mean . . . When I drove here for the first time, this is what made me stop, pull off the road," she explained.

"Sorry, what made you pull over?"

"The little lighthouse. I saw it through the trees, and I just . . . I recognized it."

"So. . . you'd been here before?"

"No, it was one of those artist intuition things."

"Like when you painted the rope on the mountain?"

"Yes. It was before I moved here. I drew a small lighthouse hidden behind some trees. So when I saw it for real, I could hardly believe it. I knew I had to find out more, and the nearest town, just down the road, was the turnoff for Milford-Haven."

"I always wondered what made you come here. And was that . . . was that the day I saw you at the car wash?"

"Right! that same day. You and Kevin spoke with each other, and I. . . . well, I thought you were so handsome." She felt her cheeks grow warm as she admitted to having noticed him back then.

"And we locked eyes for a moment."

"We did."

"Okay, back up a moment," he requested. "You're driving along, and you see the lighthouse. That lighthouse over there. And that's what makes you stop here."

"Yes. And . . . I trust those things, you know? It's. . . . Guidance."

"It sure as hell is." Cornelius had an intensity in his voice and his eyes seemed to hold some kind of wonder. "The thing is, there's more to the story. That's why I wanted to bring you here."

"The secret," she said excitedly. "Yes, I want to know."

"Come with me."

Of course, I'll come with you, she thought, as she watched him walk around the front of the SUV.

He took her hand as she exited the SUV. "Watch your step. The ground is more uneven than it appears in places."

Late afternoon light glinted off the water visible through the coastal pines, through which the golden rays slanted, lending a glow to the land. She inhaled the evening air, laden with the intermingled scents of ocean and pine, feeling a sense of belonging.

She turned to find Cornelius looking at her. "I know," he said, as though she'd spoken aloud.

All she could do was nod.

"Ready to see more?"

She nodded again.

They walked toward the lighthouse. "We can't go in. It's not stable, needs repair. But someday."

"Oh, wouldn't that be grand."

"Well, that's the thing. It will be."

"You said the heirs had let it go. So someone bought it?"

"Yeah, someone did."

"Do you know who?"

"I do, actually," he said with a sly smile.

"You? You bought it?"

Now a huge grin split his face.

"So . . . all this is yours?!"

He choked out a laugh. "Such as it is."

"But it's fantastic! It's amazing! I mean, it might take a while. And a lot of money, I suppose. But wow!"

He grabbed her hand again. "Before we lose the light, I fixed up a spot for us."

He led her south, keeping the ocean to their right, and as they progressed across protruding tree roots, hidden rocks and boulders, and masses of weeds, she glimpsed what seemed to be a mansion, then a cottage, then a pool. Eventually, a large tent came into view, illuminated from within by a pair of hanging lanterns. She peeked inside to see his sleeping bags zipped together and laid out with pillows and an extra blanket.

"Oh my," she said under her breath. The thought of being with him in that intimate space had her heart hammering. Once in the clenches with him, she wondered how she'd ever leave. That he'd been thinking along the same lines made her weak in the knees. She managed to say, "How absolutely lovely."

Cornelius watched as her face flushed and her breath caught. *She wants this as much as I do, if I'm reading her right.* "That's for later," he said, "if we decide to stay. For now, there's a spot closer to the water with a good view. And there's dinner. No grill this time, but I think it'll be okay."

He saw her eyes come up to meet his, and a sweet smile play across her mouth. *She's got her equilibrium back.* "Careful as we go."

He led her to the two camp chairs he'd set up, next to a small solar oven, in which he'd prepared a dinner of vegetables baked in foil.

"You've gone to such trouble!" She exclaimed.

He smiled and gestured. "Have a seat." He offered her a chilled bottle of peach iced tea he pulled from a cooler and took the seat next to hers. After taking a sip from his own bottle, he looked at the view and said, "Pretty, eh?"

"Breathtaking."

As evenfall arrived, they watched the clouds over the crumbling seawall, and she began to point out the many colors banded across the sky.

"Perse," she murmured.

"You need your purse?" he asked.

"No," she chuckled. "Spelled with an 'e'. It's a color. A very dark purple."

"Purple? Really?" he asked.

"Just wait a moment, you'll see it."

"Aha, you're right, there it is. Sort of a dark lavender."

"Exactly."

"And then where it's stitched together with that stripe of orangey peach? That's the real job, I think. Seeing what's actually there."

"In that case, we have exactly the same occupation."

"Oh, wow. Never thought of it like that."

"But it's more too," he added. "In astronomy it's not enough to see it. I have to actually read it."

"Read what?"

"Read the universe."

"Oh. Well, that shouldn't take long!" she quipped.

"I figure it'll take eternity. But since that's the amount of time we've been allotted, it should work out fine."

"You think we have eternity?"

"I'm sure we do. Nothing else would make sense."

She sat back to think about that for a moment then said, "Well, that goes along with my observations. I mean color, for example, is infinite. How can you get to the end of yellow?"

"Exactly," he said. "And, uh, speaking of work."

She giggled. "Were we?"

"Well, I haven't told you that much about mine. But it has several facets. One of them is this idea I had about finding planets. Actually, finding them is part of my job, but there's so much data to get through that the search could potentially take decades.

"I wasted some time trying to figure out how to get a super-computer or at least gain the use of one. But then it hit me. A lot of us now have personal computers, and we're not using them to full capacity most of the time. And to protect the screens, we run screensavers, which are tiny programs hardly grabbing any battery life or RAM."

She was listening politely, but a slight frown pulled between her brows.

"So," he continued, "what if the screensaver were doing computations while providing nice on-screen imagery?"

She turned to look at him now. "Like DOS running behind Windows?"

"God, you're quick. Yes, something like that."

"So if you had enough computers doing these computa-tions . . ."

"Exactly. You'd have the missing supercomputer."

"Brilliant!" She exclaimed.

He waited till each of them had a couple more sips and watched a few more colors smolder in the sky.

"Then there's the financial angle," he said quietly.

"Oh! I didn't even think of that. You developed the software and did the whole thing? Packaged it? Marketed it?"

"Yeah, we did," he confirmed. "I have a small team. And the marketing was mostly word of mouth."

"What fun! What do the onscreen images look like? I mean, if you need a painting of stars, let me know. If it would help," she offered.

The first thing she thinks of is how she can help. No wonder I fell for this woman. "Might have to take you up on that idea," he said. "For now, we're using NASA images from Hubble."

"Of course, you are! Oh, that's perfect. And you have some takers?"

"We do have some, yes."

"Takes time to build an audience. That's what Zelda is always telling me about my paintings. I do have a few thousand who get my mailings now."

"That's great. We do too,"

"A few thousand? That's wonderful!"

"Yeah. A few more than that, actually. It's a licensing thing. Doesn't cost much. But it adds up."

She peered at him with her eyes narrowed. "Does it?"

He took a breath. "Enough that I could buy this piece of land. Enough that I can get started on repairs."

Miranda choked on her drink and set the small bottle in the cup holder of her arm rest. He reached over to pat her on the back.

"Okay?" He asked.

"Yeah," she croaked.

"Yeah," he echoed.

"Wow," she said. Then after a moment she added, "Yay!"

He grinned at her. "Pretty exciting."

"Oh, Cornelius, I'm happy for you!"

He watched her as news of his success seemed to hit home in stages. *Hit home. Yes, with her here to share it with me.* "Thank you. That means a lot."

They sat looking as the sky changed again. Cornelius not-ed the moon was now visible at about twenty-five percent illumination.

"Slip of a moon," she said.

"Waxing crescent," he confirmed. "So. Hungry? Wanna hear plans?"

She smiled. "Yes! Yes!"

He served their foil packets on the tin camp plates he'd brought. As they unwrapped the vegetables, they started eating. "Jameson says the lighthouse is the heart," he said.

"Totally agree," she said, nodding as she took another bite. "This is yummy, by the way. Yes, the heart. So, the design ideas begin there, right? It's round and it rises. Bottom floor for kitchen? Next floor up for the master? It's not that tall, so . . . three floors?"

He noticed she'd stopped eating, caught up in visualizing the spaces. "You sound just like Jameson! I'll have to get you two together."

"Oh, I'd love that. I mean, if I won't be stepping on toes."

"You won't. We'll have dinner with him and Susan, his wife. You'll love her and vice versa. But we should walk the property together, too."

She put her flatware down and looked at him. "It's happen-ing, isn't it. Your home, the one you've always wanted."

"It is. And that's not all. We're happening too. Am I right?"

"God, I hope so."

He stood, put his plate down, put hers aside, and took both her hands to pull her up. "Done eating?"

She nodded.

She helped him as they worked quickly, efficiently, to store all the food items in the cooler. He locked it, and asked, "Can I hold you now?"

"Please."

Miranda saw that'd it'd grown quite dark in the shelter of the trees. She held one of his hands, and in his other he clutched a flashlight as they headed back to his tent. Once inside, the ceiling was high enough for them to stand. But as his arms came around her and his first tender kiss began, it was all she could do to keep her knees from buckling.

He took care of that by lifting her, then setting her down on the sleeping bags and stretching out beside her. The kissing deepened and intensified, both of them grasping, moaning.

His hands started exploring the soft layers of clothing she wore, then moved under them to find skin. She heard herself hum at his touch and felt him shiver when her hands reached under his flannel shirt to touch his back.

"I haven't told you about Tokyo," he managed to say.

"I meant to ask," she whispered.

"You want to hear about it now or later?"

I can barely hold back. But he's talking. "Something you want to tell me right away?"

"Something I want to ask you," he whispered in her ear.

She opened her eyes and looked into his, breathing hard. "Okay."

They rested on their sides, facing one another. He touched her cheek and asked, "Are we good, Miranda?"

"The best," she admitted.

"You're okay? You're not … I'm not making you feel … I just want you to feel. . . ." his words trailed off.

She took a breath, let it out. "You want to know how I feel?"

"I do want to know."

"Okay. I've never . . . I suppose I should be coy or something. But I can't. I've never felt like this."

He stroked her long, silky hair.

"I love talking with you," she continued, "love to hear how your mind works. You make me laugh, and I need that. You respect my work and you get it, you get what I'm after, what I'm up to. You're way ahead of me in some ways—"

He chuffed.

". . . and I love that challenge. And I think between us, we see three dimensionally, the way it takes two eyes to see depth. It's like that."

"Because I'm a scientist and you're an artist?" he asked.

"Well, yes. I like how that works. But also because you look up to the stars. Sometimes I think you look out *from* the stars, while I look at my earthly surroundings," she explained.

"You don't just look, you *see* what's around you, see it well enough to capture it on canvas and paper," he added. "And I lose track, sometimes, of what's actually going on right in front of me."

"And I get stuck in the weeds, lose the overview," she admitted.

He nodded. "Makes us a good team."

"Yes," she said quietly. She took a breath. "You asked how I feel. Well, I'm not afraid to say all this to you. I'm excited we're alive at the same time and living on the same planet. I'm not sure I can picture life without you, now."

He stroked her arm, looked into her eyes. "I know it's sudden. Or if not sudden, it's kinda quick. But it doesn't feel fast. Because it's deep."

"I know." She inhaled, feeling that now familiar pull in her solar plexus, wondering whether, if she put his hand there, he'd feel the wave roll through the long flat muscle. "I thought for so long you'd never come."

"I'm here," he said. He stroked her hair again, and her face. "I promised to tell you about Tokyo."

"Now?" She asked.

"I found something for you there."

"You've already given me so much! The flowers—how did you know I love tuberoses? And the dinners. And the lovely camp sites."

He smiled. "Just getting started." He rolled onto his back and reached into his pocket. "It's small, the thing I got you. But you might like it."

This man . . . so thoughtful. He got me a souvenir. I love this. I love him. She could feel her body start to hum for him again, growing impatient with their conversation, much as she was enjoying it.

"But it does come with a question."

He held something shiny and sparkly. When she focused, she gasped.

"Wanna marry me?"

Tears sprang into her eyes, and she began to laugh at the same time that she was crying. "Really?" She sputtered.

"Really. Really, really and for real."

She heard herself squeal. And then she said "Yes! I do! I will! I want to!"

By then he was laughing, and then he started to kiss her again. While he did, she stuck out her hand. "On!" She demanded.

"Yes, Ma'am!" He slid it on slowly, looking into her eyes as he did. "Perfect fit," he said.

"Of course, it is," she whispered.

Cornelius had felt tears come to his own eyes when she said yes. He'd envisioned this several different ways: on bended knee; in the shower; on a hike. But this had been perfect. Intimate, but not yet naked. It'd seemed too crass to bed her first and ask her afterward. If she'd said no, she could have left in dignified fashion. But, of course, she didn't leave. *She wants to be with me as much as I want . . . no, need . . . to be with her.*

They held each other, the new possibilities washing over and through them. He felt the shock of her acceptance, then the relief of it, the thrill of being intimate with her, then the awesome responsibility of matching her soul with his. He felt like a surfer catching a succession of waves, his board rock steady under his feet as they moved him powerfully forward.

He pressed the full length of her to him, feeling the alignment, and the heat. He began kissing her again, her response kicking him into a shuddering passion. His hands were everywhere—tangled in her hair, fumbling past fabric. "Can we get rid of these clothes?" he croaked.

"If we don't," she whispered hoarsely, "I shall explode."

"Oh good. Wait for me."

Miranda gasped out a pent-up breath when his mouth found her breast, then quivered through a first release when he kissed her tender parts.

But when he began slowly to slide himself into her, she felt her entire system flood. Clutching, gasping, groaning, she found she couldn't look away from his eyes, so full of the most intense tenderness.

"You don't have to be quiet out here, you know."

With that the feral growl that escaped her throat might have alerted other species, but there were no other humans nearby to notice. *There are no other humans.* That's how it felt to be with him—that the world itself had been made anew, with the two of them as its first inhabitants.

They paused there while he still filled her. Smiling down at her, he said quietly, "Perfect fit."

She started to laugh, lifting her hand to look at her ring. But then he began to move again, and he brought her to her next peak while he finally reached his own.

Cornelius, who regularly spent his nights under the stars, had spent a night of wonders. He'd been a marathoner, a coach, an avid student, even sometimes an observer as though watching this most significant turning point of his life.

She loves me! He didn't have to shout it, because the wind already carried the tune that rose from his property up through the tree branches, into the top of the lighthouse, out across the ocean, and up to the stars.

And soon it would be *their* property, *their* lighthouse, *their* everything. He'd never had so burning a desire to share what he had, what he knew, who he was. *Will she change her name? No. Miranda Jones is an established painter. What if we have kids?*

The thought made his heart swell. It also reminded him it'd been a good idea to bring condoms. "Thank God," was all she'd said on the subject, except to add that she'd made preparations at home.

That's when they'd discussed what to do next, deciding they deserved and needed a day of rest—and whatever else— at her place. They'd sneak home before dawn and keep the street-side blinds closed all day.

They had plans to make. They already knew they'd be in Alaska together next summer. *Will we be married by then?* Would Miranda want a fancy wedding, an elopement, or something in between? He felt certain their ceremony, whenever it might be held, would take place outside, in some natural setting, a mutual favorite. She'd bring her creativity to it, as she did everything. He'd likely go along with whatever she wanted.

They had this property to design and rebuild. The finances would certainly allow them to get started. *How long will all of it take? We should move forward with the lighthouse right away. Can we live at her place until it's ready?*

When would they start letting people know? His parents first, they'd agreed, because they could be told in person. And in a small town, word would spread fast. His folks deserved to top the list. Then her parents—though this would likely require a trip north because they would want to meet the man in question. She'd mentioned her Grandma Dorothy, who lives on the East Coast, and he didn't know whether notifying her grandparent would also require an in-person visit. Cornelius, resting on his back, pressed his lips together. *It'll be fine, she'd promised.* He trusted her in this and in every other matter he could imagine.

A couple of hours earlier, she'd lifted her head to say, "Don't leave me again, okay?"

"Never," he'd promised.

Then she'd looked at her ring by starlight and fallen back to sleep.

Cornelius inhaled as cool breeze drifted in through the open overhead window in his tent. The air felt soft, she'd said. He'd never thought of it that way.

It was *she* who was soft, her skin tender as silk in some places, smooth as satin in others. He felt himself stir to life at the thought of touching her again, and he reached for her, tracing the line of her shoulder delicately so as not to wake her. But he watched as a gentle curve pulled at her mouth, and he listened to her soft moan.

That did it. He wanted her again. Needed her. "Sorry, babe," he whispered. "Can't help myself."

"Good," she whispered back, sliding one arm smoothly up his chest to entangle her fingers in his hair.

Chapter 30

from Samantha Hugo's Journal
(Volume 49, maroon cloth cover)
Belhaven Hotel, Touchstone Beach &
Enchanted Forest, Hollow Beach

Finally, this mental health day has arrived! I took a wonderful upstairs corner room at the Belhaven, told nobody I'd be staying here, and feel blissfully unreachable.

Though I like writing in my cozy hotel room, I also like my custom of writing outside, so I grabbed a croissant and filled my thermos with coffee in the lobby. Now I'm sitting alone on the lovely deck that overlooks the shoreline.

By now, there's so much on my mind, it'll take me a while to write it out. Before I dive into my personal issues, I want to jot down my thoughts about Miranda's art show.

What a convergence it was! Of course, Miranda and her work were at the center of it. But it drew a diverse group of people together, and the threads of several lives seemed to cross-connect—my own included.

First, I have to say there's no question in my mind about Miranda having a new relationship. She's found someone she cares about, and it certainly appears to be mutual. They were either too busy, or too focused on each other, to notice me noticing them.

I've heard of Cornelius Smith, of course. He's been rather famous in town for years, the local boy who went to work for NASA. I know his parents slightly. Had I not been so distracted over the past few months, I might even have thought to introduce him to Miranda.

But that doesn't matter. They found each other. It may seem an unlikely match, the artist and the scientist. But now that I think about it, their two fields require a similar solitude, con-centration, and an individual sense of industry. I hope to spend time with them when they decide to socialize. Meanwhile, I feel so happy their journey has started.

I enjoyed meeting Joseph Calvin. If Zelda McIntyre didn't have her claws firmly embedded in him, I might have enjoyed getting to know him better. But she was like a bobcat circling her prey, when she wasn't busy scouting for sales of Miranda's paint-ings. Joseph seemed to enjoy the attention, so it's just as well.

Meeting his son Zack was probably the most interesting part of the evening for me, mostly because I'd heard about him for so long from Miranda and knew that at one point she thought they were heading for a relationship.

Honestly, I can't see how they'd ever have been a good match. His focus is business, something Miranda can hardly stand to talk about, which makes her grateful to have Zelda handling sales for her. More importantly, the fact that he lied to her—or lied by omission—allowing her to believe his career was in music promotion when, in fact, he's the proud vice president of an oil company, partnered with an even prouder father.

But there was another distraction for me, and that was Zack himself. I imagine he's about the age Gregory would be. And now that I know Gregory grew up in Santa Barbara, the two might have gone to school together, might even have become friends.

I'd have liked to ask Joseph about raising his son—one of the reasons I'd have entertained the notion of getting together with him. I didn't see much physical resemblance between the two men, but perhaps Zack resembled his late mother. If so, she might look a little like me in terms of height and bone structure.

And I'm stopping that line of thought in its tracks. If I start imagining any young man I happen to meet as being someone who knew my son, I'll drive myself crazy. I simply must continue waiting for Stacey Chernak to provide further information, unless it comes in via Delmar or another source.

I was rather fascinated to meet Miranda's sister. In their case, there's a lot of family resemblance, yet no one would ever confuse the two when they stand side by side. Meredith has something exotic in her looks. She has a sharpness and polish, rather than Miranda's fluidity. Meredith seemed quite focused on the Calvin men, from what I could see. Since she's a businesswoman herself, maybe something will click there.

I briefly said hello to Susan, of all people who seemed unlikely to attend the art show. And it was Kevin who brought her. I knew he'd helped Nicole and Miranda with hanging the show a week or two ago. He's always so helpful to anyone who asks.

But Kevin and Susan? Now there was a true "Mutt and Jeff" match, not only because they were the tallest and the shortest of the assembled guests, but because she's as sour as he is sweet. In any case, I was glad to see my assistant looking dressed quite nicely and behaving herself. And to be more charitable, I do hope she actually enjoyed being there as much as Kevin obviously did.

Sally was there, and she'd done an excellent job with the hors d'oeuvres, even if that's hard for me to admit. I still don't know why she rubs me the wrong way. But tonight, she arrived with a lanky, good-looking man in a wheelchair. He must be the veteran Miranda told me about, who was honored at that Doobie Brothers concert. Did he and Sally meet there? Or did they already know each other? I must say, she appeared more at peace or more even-tempered . . . something was different about her. And his was a soulful presence. Maybe I'll be able to talk with him one day. I even saw old Mr. Hargraves at the show. He seemed to arrive with Sally and her friend, but I couldn't tell whether they were together or not. Ralph Hargraves seemed to inspect some of Miranda's work very carefully. Who knew he was an art appreciator?

I'm glad for our little town that we hosted such a sparkling evening. I knew I was smart to hire Miranda to create our Environmental Planning Commission mural when she first came here. And if that helped her decide to make this her home, it seems to be a blessing all the way around.

I returned to my room, grabbed my backpack with water, journal and pen, and attached my folding camp chair. Of course, I headed to my favorite secluded beach. I was winded from the walk, but I'm settled in my chair and now it's time to start writing about my own issues.

What's on my mind is secrets. When I think about it, even the gallery evening was full of them. Zack kept a secret from Miranda; the relationships evident during the evening all seem to have been kept rather secret, too. Who knows what other undisclosed information circulated unseen?

Concealing information might in some cases be the same as lying. I read once that lying is a sign of higher intelligence, with dolphins being a good example. If an ant goes scouting for food on behalf of his colony, he reports back "yes" or "no" with no possibility of dissembling. But if a dolphin finds food and wants to keep it for himself, he can go back to his pod and report, "Nope, no food over this way," then laugh all the way back to his cache.

Is it a natural state for humans to maintain secrets? It certainly seems to be. It's the basis of gossip, as in, "I know something you don't, and by choosing how, where, and when to reveal it, I make myself more powerful." Bring that concept to a broader scenario, and we arrive at diplomacy; take it farther, and we have classified information that is the stuff of espionage.

In politics and in war, secrets are probably one of the most critical elements of failure or success. But what about in relationships? Among those we trust, we try not to conceal anything important about who we are and what we do. Are there times in an intimate relationship that keeping a secret protects the one we love? Or does it invariably do more harm than good?

No one I know has kept a bigger secret than I have. Since moving to Milford-Haven, people in town have never known I once had a son. More significantly, not even his own father knew. I made that choice so many years ago that it became more and more difficult to reveal.

Has that been a blessing for me? Professionally, probably so. Presumably, being unencumbered by a child left me free to complete my PhD and be taken seriously by those in a position to hire me. The assumption was made that I was putting career first, and that it might therefore be worth investing in me. In every professional field, there were resentful rumblings that women would take a coveted spot in an advanced program, a place that would otherwise go to a man. Then the woman would desert the career for which she had trained, leaving to get married and have children. Has this really changed? If I'd kept my child, would my career actually have suffered? Is a mother less worthy to be promoted than her childless counterpart? Society is still trying to answer this.

Over time, do secrets become more important? Or less so? Perhaps the circumstances that necessitated the confidentiality have disappeared as years pass. Perhaps revealing what was once unknown would no longer matter. On the other hand, some secrets seem to expand until they want to burst their seams. I think I'm approaching that point where there's a growing urgency, and an increasing gravitas to the matter.

Ever since receiving news that Gregory was adopted in Santa Barbara, my heart is resonating with a sense of proximity. Is it possible my son never left the region? If so, is this what actually brought me here to Milford-Haven in the first place? Just as I reach to embrace this notion, as though there really is a surety of guidance in this universe, I'm again swamped by guilt.

A mother is supposed to be sure and steady as a homing beacon in the dark, a lighthouse somewhere on the rocky shore of life. It provides a repeating signal at a fixed location. It's the child's assurance that he can always get to his safe haven.

Here I am writing in a journal, looking north to the Piedras Blancas Lighthouse near a place called Milford-Haven. Yet I was neither beacon nor haven to my child.

Though he didn't ask for it, what I did give my child was a secret. If a child comes up with his own secret, it's a shining inspiration, as hot as a shooting star burning a hole in his pocket. But when he's forced to carry a grown-up secret, it becomes a burden, robbing him of his inherent freedom, dampening his spirit, darkening his path.

Did my son carry this burden? Did he feel he dragged an invisible weight everywhere he went? Or did he actually have his carefree childhood, and has that enabled him to build a successful life somewhere? If he found me now, would he attain only an albatross around his neck? Or would it give him the chance to make sense of his own missing pieces?

I've often tried to answer these same questions about Jack, and now it seems more relevant than ever that I do. I haven't thought of him as the father of my child for years, but that, in fact, is who he is. What good or bad things might Gregory have inherited from his father?

What of Jack's own childhood? He was reared by a single mother. Granted, his father's abandonment was the involuntary absence of a soldier, but does that matter to the child psyche? His mother was everything to him, and even though long gone by the time of our marriage, almost an impossible ghost against whom to compete. She was absolute in her loyalty to Jack. But he viewed me as less loyal, construing my doctoral thesis as competition for his affections. He had high standards imposed upon a boy of six, that grew with him. Is this why he left me?

I remember his self-absorption, his seemingly impermeable super-fortified ego-armor. Sometimes, only dimly aware of having cut me to the quick, he'd show up for a faltering apology, and we'd wind up in the sack again, wild with passion, drowning both his guilt and my hurt. When we married, I assumed he'd outgrow this self involvement at some point, thinking it was one of the defense mechanisms only young men needed. But his stoic disregard for my feelings persisted. Now, I realize it was his own feelings he was disregarding. He seemed not to care at all that I left. Perhaps this was the ultimate masking of his vulnerability.

Who was that mythological character? Oh, yes—Narcissus, who fell in love with his own reflection. Teal affliction of the narcissist is that he looks everywhere for an adoring face and stops only when he finds one in the mirror.

I see now that I had more the opposite problem. I looked everywhere for those who criticized me and trusted no one who didn't. Was this why I chose Jack as a mate? Chose Susan as a secretary? Chose Sally as an adversary? If so, my friendship with Miranda is one of my only exceptions, but even there I attribute more of her kind admiration to our age difference and take her praise with a grain of salt.

I think the biggest secret is the one I've kept from myself. Do I dare write it down? I must because it's time to be honest. I loved Jack. I loved him so fiercely that it had to be all or nothing. I could never have been his friend, or someone he dated casually. My heart pounded at the sight of him and my knees went wobbly at his touch.

I always hoped he'd love me as fiercely but was afraid I never really penetrated that hard shell he carried. I could see he did care for me, and he was madly attracted. I think he convinced himself the only way to satisfy his craving was to marry me, perhaps in hopes his feelings would grow to match my own. Instead, his jealousy, unfounded though it was, swamped the love that had started to grow, extinguishing it like a sudden rainstorm deluging a campfire. It sizzled for a while but could never be reignited. Then it froze over in the winter of his discontent.

In my naivte, I always thought he'd be grateful to have found me. I certainly was. How could I not be? The man of my dreams had walked into that library one day, living and breathing the raw masculinity I craved, paired with soaring intelligence, vibrating appreciation for my physique, an irresistible sense of humor, and perfect timing.

In me he found his intellectual match, a passionate sex partner, and a good partner. After a suitable number of lonely or frustrating years, he had found me at last. Yet apparently he thought he would find better one day, or that he could take me for granted despite shoving me away emotionally. I was stunned at his ingratitude. I still am.

After Jack and I divorced, my disappearance from his life seemed not to faze him in the slightest, as far as I could tell. It was the first and, at the time, most wounding and horrible shock—to feel I'd meant so little to him that I'd faded without a trace. Perhaps it was my own invisibility that convinced me both to keep my pregnancy a secret from Jack and, ultimately, to give up my son. After all, Jack recovered miraculously from losing me. The wound healed so utterly that the knife seemed never to have entered the flesh. So it would be with my boy. I'd disappear without a trace, and good riddance. Without a scar, the boy would find a better mother, and the less known about that original sin, the better.

But in the assumptions we've made, both Jack and I seem to have missed the larger picture. He took a bitter view of life; I settled for a partial one, denying much of what and who I am. If I've learned anything thus far from my present turmoil, it is that healing is required.

Everything vital about someone's soul can be found locked in what they hold closest, hidden sometimes even from themselves. Perhaps this is why hearts keep secrets.

Cast of Characters

Joseph Calvin: mid-60s, 6'1, gray eyes, steel-gray hair, clean-shaven, lean, handsome; CEO of Santa Barbara's Calvin Oil; eligible widower; dates several women, including Christine Christian and Zelda McIntyre.

Zackery Calvin: mid-30s, 6'2, blue eyes, dark blond hair, handsome, lean, athletic; Vice President of Calvin Oil, works with his father; popular bachelor; dates Cynthia Radcliffe; becomes smitten with Miranda Jones, then with Meredith Jones.

Nicole Champagne: mid-20s, 5'5, brown eyes, brunette, chic dresser; runs Milford-Haven's Finders Gallery; sells Miranda Jones's and other artists' work with skill; originally from Montreal, Quebec, and speaks with a French-Canadian accent.

Stacey Chernak: late-40s, 5'6, blue eyes, blond hair, kind, submissive, speaks with a Swiss-German accent; married to abusive Wilhelm Chernak; works full time as Clarke Shipping secretary, and works part-time for Chernak Agency.

Wilhelm Chernak: mid-60s, 6', deep-set black eyes, silvered hair and beard, low resonant voice, a Swiss citizen who still carries an accent from his native Germany; capable of fierce and sudden anger; started the Chernak Agency, a service for locating adopted children; abuses his wife Stacey.

Christine Christian: early-40s, 5'6, aqua eyes, blond, vivacious, beautiful, intense; special investigative reporter for Satellite-News TV station KOST-SATV; lives in Santa Maria; frequent international traveler; dates Joseph Calvin; is being investigated as a possible missing person.

Russell Clarke: early-60s, 6'3, coal black eyes, dazzling white teeth, dusky skin, deceptively strong, by turns charming and stern, adopted, has unknown mixed lineage; owner of Clarke Shipping; Stacey Chernak's employer; business associate of Joseph Calvin; commissions Jack Sawyer to build him Milford-Haven's most magnificent seaside mansion.

Tony Fiorentino: early-40s, 6'4, brown eyes, black hair, athletic wheelchair paraplegic, recipient of Veterans Assistance Award; lives in New York City but is moving to Milford-Haven; high school boyfriend of Sally O'Mally in Arkansas.

Kuyama Freeland: mid-70s, 5'7, pale gray eyes, long white hair down her back, strong and graceful, unadorned, Native American, a Chumash Elder.

Ralph Hargraves: late-70s, 6', blue eyes, gray hair, a face seamed with smile lines, pleasant disposition; a fixture in Milford-Haven, owner of Hargraves Hardware.

James Hughes: early-60s, 5'11, brown eyes, thinning gray hair, soft-spoken with a mid-Atlantic accent; the fiercely loyal butler at the Calvin estate, Calma.

Samantha Hugo: early-50s, 5'9, cognac-brown eyes, redhead, statuesque, sharp dresser; Director of Milford-Haven's Environmental Planning Commission; Miranda's friend; Jack Sawyer's former wife; a journal writer.

Deputy Delmar Johnson: early-40s, 6'2, brown eyes, black hair, handsome, muscular, African-American; with the San Luis Obispo County Sheriff 's Department, assigned to the Special Problems Unit; originally from South Central Los Angeles.

Charles and Veronica "Veri" Jones: late-50s, parents of Meredith and Miranda, elegant members of Bay Area elite society; long-ago friends to Joseph Calvin and his late wife.

Meredith Jones: mid-30s, 5'8, teal eyes, medium-length dark hair, beautiful, exotic, shapely, athletic; San Francisco financial advisor; known as Miranda's sister; her secret identity is "daburu" or double Asian-Caucasian lineage as Miranda's half-sister.

Miranda Jones: early-30s, 5'9, green eyes, long brunette hair, beautiful, lean, athletic; fine artist specializing in watercolors, acrylics and murals; a staunch environmentalist whose paintings often depict endangered species; has escaped her wealthy Bay-Area family to create a new life in Milford-Haven.

Michelle "Shelly" Larrup: mid-40s, 5'6, hazel eyes, bobbed burgundy hair, well-toned dancer's body, flamboyant dresser; originally from Australia and speaks with the accent; owner of Shell Shock in Milford-Haven.

June Magliati: mid-40s, 5'2, brown eyes, dark brown curly hair, no-nonsense expression that goes well with her thick Brooklyn accent; Sally O'Mally's trusted friend and employee at the restaurant.

Will Marks: mid-30s, 6', dark eyes and hair, athletic build; VP at Clarke Shipping; contact of Zack Calvin's at Calvin Oil.

Zelda McIntyre: early-50s, 5'1, violet eyes, wavy black hair, voluptuous, dramatic and striking; owner of private firm Artist Representations in Santa Barbara; Miranda's artist's rep; corporate art buyer; has designs on Joseph Calvin.

Mary Meeks: late-50s, 5'2, warm brown eyes, mousy brown hair perfectly coiffed, trim figure, conservative dresser; loyal secretary at Calvin Oil, remembers every detail of Calvin business.

"Notes"(Ken Casmalia): mid-30s, 5'9, black eyes, shoulder-length black hair, lean, long-muscled, handsome, Native American; a musician whose band often plays warm-up for the Doobies; an enigmatic man who hasn't revealed his name and listens more than he talks.

Sally O'Mally: early-40s, 5'3, blue eyes, blond curly hair, perfectly proportioned; owner of Sally's Restaurant; owner of Burn-It-Off; born and reared in Arkansas; Miranda's friend; dislikes Samantha; secretly involved with Jack Sawyer.

Michael Owen: mid-40s, 5'9, blue eyes, black hair, slightly rotund; owner of Lighthouse Tavern.

Cynthia Radcliffe: early-30s, 5'8, amber-brown eyes, blond, shapely, gorgeous; passionate, petulant, persuasive; Santa Barbara social climber; Zackery Calvin's girlfriend.

Kevin Ransom: late-20s, 6'8, hazel eyes, sandy hair, strong jawline, lean, muscular; Foreman at Sawyer Construction; innocent, naive, kind; tuned in to animals; technologically adept; highly intuitive; has longings for Susan Winslow.

Jack Sawyer: mid-50s, 6', blue eyes, salt-and-pepper hair and mustache, barrel-chested, solidly muscular; Milford-Haven contractor-builder; Samantha Hugo's former husband; secretly dated Sally O'Mally.

Cornelius Smith: late-30s, 6'1, indigo-blue eyes, black hair, handsome, lean; grew up in Milford-Haven where his parents still live; a professional astronomer who works part time at NASA Ames and plans to build an observatory in Milford-Haven; a loner, an eccentric.

Gladys Wilson: mid-50s, 5'9, heavyset, long-limbed, short black hair, African American; Director of Safe Haven; a former victim of domestic violence whose wisdom and compassion now helps other victims.

Susan Winslow: mid-20s, 5'4, black eyes, long black hair, rail-thin, attractive but sullen, Native American; Samantha's assistant at the EPC; avid rock-star fan; victim of traumatic childhood; feels trapped in Milford-Haven; defensive about her heritage; toys with Kevin.

Milford-Haven Recipes
Miranda Jones's
Dill Gazpacho
(As prepared at her home for Cornelius)

Serves 4: *(2 servings to save for the next day)*

Ingredients:
     3 medium sized ripe tomatoes, chopped fine
     1 cucumber
     1 small onion, chopped fine
     ½ lemon - juiced
     ½ T Balsamic vinegar
     1 T olive oil
     1/4 c fresh dill
      salt & pepper to taste

Preparation:
Stir together in large bowl: tomatoes, cucumber, onion. Season
with lemon juice, vinegar, olive oil, salt, pepper.

Add half the mixture to VitaMix, blender, or food processor.
Puree till smooth, then return to bowl.

Add dill, cover, and chill for one hour.

Optional serving suggestion: Add dollop of plain yogurt and top
with a sprig of fresh parsely.

—Provided by Mara Purl, adapted from All Recipes

Milford-Haven Recipes
Cornelius Smith's
Baked Vegetables in Foil
(As prepared by Cornelius at his campsite)

Serves 2

Ingredients:.
  1 zucchini
  1 summer squash
  6 new potatoes
  1 medium sized onion
  Optional:
  1 can peas
  2 oz.mushrooms, sliced
  2 clovesgarlic

Preparation:
Cut all vegetables into bite-sized pieces; cut the onion into slices.
Mix in a large bowl with a drizzle of olive oil. Optionally add fresh
herbs, two cloves of garlic.

Lay out strips of heavy-duty foil about 14 inches long. Spoon half
the vegetable mixture into the center of each foil strip. Lift the
foil edges and fold together, then roll the open sides toward the
center to create a closed package.

If cooking inside, place on oven's center rack and bake for
30 minutes in a 375 degree oven. If cooking outside, place on rack
over coals, or on gas grill, and cook for 30 minutes.

Be careful when opening the cooked packages, as hot liquid will
have formed and can spill. Place the foil packet on plates before
serving.

—Provided by Larry Norfleet

Milford-Haven Recipes
Miranda Jones's
Custard with Berries
(As served to Cornelius)

Serves 2

Ingredients:
  4 c whole milk
  1 T vanilla extract
  1T butter
  4 eggs
  ½ c sugar
  3 T cornstarch

Preparation:
In a saucepan, place milk, vanilla extract & butter. Cook and stir over medium heat till simmering. (Do not allow to boil.)

In a bowl, whisk eggs, sugar & cornstarch together. (Keep whisking till sugar is dissolved.)

Place the saucepan over low heat again. Slowly pour in egg mixture, whisking constantly. (Keep whisking till custard thickens.)

Serve warm or place in covered bowl, cool, then chill if preferred.

—Provided by Mara Purl, adapted from All Recipes

Milford-Haven Recipes
Veri Jone's
Coquille St. Jacques
(As prepared by Veri and Pilar for Easter Brunch)

Preheat broiler – medium heat

Ingredients:
 ½ c dry bread crumbs
 5 T melted butter
 6 oz shredded Gruyere
 1 c mayonnaise
 1/4 c dry white wine
 1 T chopped fresh parsley
 1 lbsea scallops, cleaned & quartered
 ½ lb button mushrooms, slices
 ½ c chopped onion

In a small mixing bowl, toss bread crumbs with 1 T of melted butter. Mix well, set aside

In a separate small bowl, combine cheese, mayo, wine & parsley. Mix well, set aside

In a skillet, saute scallops in 2 T of melted butter over medium heat till opaque. Transfer to plate lined with paper towels.

Reheat skillet, cook mushrooms & onion in 2 T of melted butter until tender. Add cheese mixture, return scallops to skillet. Cook till cheese is melted.

Spoon mixture into individual ramekins or pour whole mixture into 11x7 baking dish. Spring top with bread crumbs mixture.

Broil 6 inches from heat for 2-4 minutes, or until browned.

Serve with crusty French bread to sop up buttery sauce.

—Provided by Marshelline Purl

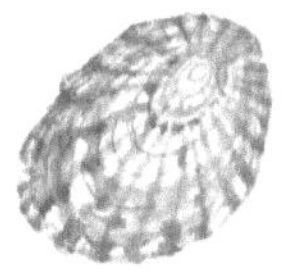

Prologue

Senior Deputy Delmar Johnson was not eager to read the journal of a dead woman.

Presumed dead, he corrected himself, hoping it wasn't so. He almost felt he'd gotten to know Chris Christian in recent weeks, watching videos of her special reports, piecing together elements of her interrupted life.

But all day he'd put off reading her journal—even to the point of lingering over dinner at the Bird's Nest. Now just outside the restaurant, he delayed for a moment longer before leaving, taking in the view.

The customary coastal chill of late spring was settling over the Central Coast as it prepared to bed down for the night, almost ready to pull a foggy blanket over its shoulders. Those hills do look like shoulders, he thought, still reveling in his good fortune at having moved here. *I'm a long way from South Central Los Angeles.*

He worried that his reflexes had slowed in an atmosphere no longer charged with nightly drive-by shootings. And he rejoiced that he could now go several hours thinking about something beyond survival of the fittest.

Gravel crunched under Del's boots as he crossed the parking lot, and he felt comforted by these surroundings, enjoying a still-new sense of belonging. Tempting though it was to head for his cozy studio apartment, he could no longer avoid his self-appointed task of reading the journal.

Though he'd had orders not to treat the missing reporter's case as an active one until—or unless—something concrete turned up, he was free to pursue whatever he wished during his time off, and he'd done just that.

As of yesterday morning, all that had changed. Hikers— lost while trying to make their way through a local canyon— had used an abandoned wreck of a car as their reference point when calling Park Rangers for help. When the car's plates had later been called in, they matched those of a missing woman: Christiana Christian.

After getting the hikers safely out of the area, the department had towed and processed the car. Though the forensics team were still going over the vehicle, what had come to light was that the owner's purse was not in the car. That seemed—at least for now—to lead to only one logical conclusion: Ms. Christian survived the crash, then crawled out of the damaged vehicle to find help.

The team dod discover a velcroed pouch under the carpet of the rear seat. In it was tucked the reporter's notebook, which proved to be a journal. She had kept several, and he'd read a previous one. Delmar imagined this diary contained some leads, or perhaps at least one smoldering clue. And it waited for him now, its information potentially hot enough to burn a hole through his desk.

Pulling into his assigned parking spot at the Central Coast Sheriff's station, he turned off the motor and let the Suburban begin to cool. As he stepped down from its high running board, he let the heavy door slam and heard all four locks respond synchronously as he pressed the remote and headed up the stairs to the front entrance.

The San Luis Obispo County Sheriff's office shared a building with the Department of Forestry, perhaps signifying that trees were every bit as important as people—a sentiment with which Del was beginning to agree. The two species stood toe to toe in a necessary symbiosis, each literally creating the other's air to breathe. Experimental programs in inner cities proved third-generation welfare families who'd never seen a tree began to overcome depression and hopelessness with the planting of a single sapling.

Del opened his office door, his gaze flying to the journal where it still waited, disproving his theory of spontaneous combustion. Still intact, the unprepossessing volume contained the full weight of what was almost certainly the last months of a dead woman's soul.

Lifting it, he ran his hands over the nubby, black synthetic-over-cardboard perfect-bound book. Like her others, it wasn't an expensive item—she hadn't chosen leather or raw silk for her memoirs. Yet it had a simple elegance about it—classy, understated, functional. He asked himself for the hundredth time whether or not he had the right to read someone else's private writings.

Of course, he could rationalize that it was his job to read it. Yet it surprised him what hesitance he felt. Perhaps it was the very nature of self-reflection that bothered him. Now he knew of at least two local women who wrote journals: Sally O'Mally and Chris Christian. There might be others. Do women tend to write the same sorts of things, or are diaries as distinct as the personalities of those who write them? What would happen, he wondered, if he started to write his own journal? He'd never done that much soul-searching, if that was its primary function.

And when it came to recording the daily events of life, they seemed far too mundane to bother. Of course, he kept a log of work-related activities, but that came with the job.

Could I write down personal thoughts—how it is to be one of the few African Americans living in a Caucasian stronghold? Or how I might feel about a particular woman? Involuntarily, he found himself resisting the idea of committing anything to paper. It wasn't so much the inability to frame his thoughts and feelings in words; it was that he didn't trust what would happen to the journal itself.

What was a private diary but a dangerous little emotional time-bomb that sooner or later was bound to go off? Full of betrayals, heartbreaks, and all manner of things best left unknown, it seemed to him a bad idea ever to keep one. Unless . . . unless something happened to the owner.

And here I am, the follower of clues. Thinking back to Christopher Darden's book, he remembered what the former D.A. had written—that Nicole Simpson had left those photos of herself battered and bruised . . . had left them for him. Did Chris Christian leave this journal for me?

Del sat in his desk chair and picked up the book. One of the last things he knew she'd planned was her dinner date with Joseph Calvin, which had been scheduled for Tuesday, October twentieth. He flipped to that page, hoping something written in her own hand would provide a clue.

Each page of the diary was devoted to a single day, with numerals indicating time printed down the left column. The capital letter "J" was written twice on that day, first, in the morning. The printed six a.m. numeral was circled and next to it a small heart and several hastily sketched stars were added. Eleven p.m. was also circled, the "J" appearing again, this time with a question mark.

Between the two, the six p.m. was circled. Opposite it was the cryptic notation "MM." He didn't really expect to find she'd named her own killer. Yet it was possible she did.

Del closed the diary. Logically, the next thing would be to read from the beginning, but he squirmed at the idea. Not only did he still balk at intruding too soon. He also believed there was more to her life than could have been captured in a layout of printed days with minimal notes added.

He thought back to his mother Ruby's practice of opening her Bible at random. "God will lead you when you let Him," she'd say. Though intellectually this made him feel foolish, as though he were following an old wives' tale, in his gut he sometimes trusted the old ways, and felt now was a good time to employ the practice. He flipped open a page. "Good date with Joseph last night. He still refuses to be called 'Joe.'"

What was startling in reading the words was their immediacy. Chris didn't seem dead at all, or even missing. Her voice was here-and-now in present time, and he felt transported not only back to that moment, but also into her particular reality as convincingly as if she'd taken his hand and walked him into her life. And in my dream last night, she did just that, walking me down a steep, densely treed forest, to a gully where her car rested at an unsafe angle. I'd bet my bottom dollar that's exactly where the hikers found it.

Shuddering at the thought, he reminded himself for the hundredth time that Chris wasn't necessarily dead at all. Yet he couldn't shake the feeling he might be trespassing on someone's grave.

Chapter 1

Like steam lifting off a cauldron of hot soup, morning fog rose above Milford-Haven and dissipated over the Pacific.

Snugged against the Central Coast's shore, the town threw off its blanket of cloud cover and rolled out of bed. It was only six a.m., yet already residents were walking along the beach, watering flowers, or sipping their morning coffee, taking advantage of the cool hours before afternoon sun again heated the day to a simmering point.

Miranda Jones awoke in a cuddle. Curled on her side in the dim pre-dawn, she felt the warm fur of her cat curled against her stomach, and the comforting thighs of Cornelius Smith pressing against the backs of her knees. This is perfection, she thought, reaching around to run her palm down the length of manly leg.

Cornelius made a soft grunting sound, which made her offer a soft moan which then inspired Shadow to utter a "Meh" as if completing a domestic chorus.

Miranda chuckled to herself, enjoying the little rustle that rippled through her family, and feeling utterly pleased that her nearest and dearest, Shadow and Cornelius, had adopted one another as though born to be together.

Born to be together. That's exactly how she felt about herself and her fiancé, her beloved, her intended, her one and only.

Time for them had become fluid. It seemed it had taken forever to find each other, but now it felt as though they'd been together forever. Yet, with multiple projects—their upcoming wedding among them—it seemed they were always busy, which made this time together all the more precious.

She lay there hoping for another few minutes of sleep, but the bright light of dawn crested over the edge of the high bedroom windows and her eyes blinked open. Sliding carefully to her side of the bed, she freed her arm from the covers and had to look again at the shiny ring sparkling on her hand. Then she looked across the pillow to the shiny face of her fiancé, then saw where sunlight was shining onto the objects in the bedroom she now shared with him. Life itself seemed shiny and new. She'd been smiling so much since last March, she was surprised her jaw didn't have a perpetual ache.

With summer having just arrived, one thing didn't seem so shiny: the chaos of their home. Though not even this could dim her joy, she did recognize that the list of tasks seemed to grow longer by the day.

Cornelius had purchased the land where their new home was being renovated. But until that rather large project was completed several months from now, they'd combined household belongings in her rental. He'd had a rental of his own in northern California, near his NASA Ames job. But since he'd made arrangements to continue working for them remotely, he'd been able to move back to Milford-Haven, where he'd grown up.

This house had worked perfectly for her when she lived here alone. A large enough master suite downstairs; an open concept main floor with a separate artist's studio for her. But Cornelius had clothes, furniture, books, more books, lots more books, equipment, and a desk. All of this had been crammed into her space but this was hardly satisfactory.

Just yesterday, they'd had the brilliant idea to ask Miranda's landlord whether they might also rent the adjacent house. Actually, the two "houses" were connected with a common wall, but the two dwellings were offset, which provided more privacy for each. The nextdoor space was designed for short-term rental and had been nearly always empty as long as Miranda had lived here, so she didn't think it'd be a problem to rent it themselves. Then Cornelius could have ample office space; they'd have room for guests; and Cornelius could even host some of his colleagues, should they need to meet in person. All in all, it seemed ideal.

Cornelius had offered to approach the landlord, and she appreciated that he'd volunteered to take on a task she didn't relish herself.

COLOPHON

The print version of this book is set in the Cambria font, released in 2004 by Microsoft, as a formal, solid font to be equally readable in print and on screens. It was designed by Jelle Bosma, Steve Matteson, and Robin Nicholas.

The name Cambria is the classical name for Wales, the Latin form of the Welsh name for Wales, *Cymru*. The etymology of *Cymru* is *combrog*, meaning "compatriot."

The California town of Cambria is named for its resemblance to the south-western coast of Wales, where the town of Milford Haven has existed since before ancient Roman times and is mentioned in William Shakespeare's *Cymbeline*.

The dingbat is the scallop shell, drawn by artist Mary Helsaple. The scallop is an active marine bivalve that moves rapidly by clapping its shell halves together. Found in seas all over the world, they are characterized by fan-shaped shells with radiating ribs and often have bright colors. This particular shell, with its large size and ridges, is the lion's paw scallop, of *nodipecten nodosus,* found along the Atlantic coast of North and South America.

The scallop has ancient symbolism. In ancient Rome, it is associated with Venus and with fertility. In Christianity, it is associated with the Apostle James and pilgrimages undertaken in his honor. The scallop is traditionally used to scoop water from baptismal fonts over the heads of infants and was chosen as the icon for this book because of its connection to a childhood rite of passage.

Each of the *Milford-Haven Novels* features a real lighthouse. The Point Conception lighthouse is hidden from view, restricted from public access, and shrouded in a history of mariners being thwarted by treacherous seas, making it almost a "secret" lighthouse. Though most of California's coastline races in a roughly north-south direction, along the Santa Barbara Channel, the coastline holds to an east-west direction. At Point Conception, where the coastline abruptly turns ninety-degrees, two strong currents converge at the point of land where the coastline turns sharply northward.

One of the earliest attempts to navigate these waters was made by Juan Rodriguez Cabrillo in 1542. In 1602 Sebastian Vizcaino attempted this part of the coast and named it Punta de la Limpia Concepcion. In 1835 the sailing ship *Pilgrim* was damaged and nearly capsized.

The original Point Conception Light was built in 1856, and its firstorder Fresnel was transported from France around Cape Horn. The light was activated on February 1st of that year and became the sixth lighthouse operating on the West Coast, situated sixty-five miles west of the village of Santa Barbara. The lighthouse was severely damaged in an 1857 earthquake but was repaired, and a fog signal was added in 1872.

It wasn't until 1881 that the lighthouse was rebuilt, at which time it was also moved lower down the bluff—resting at 133 feet above mean sea level—so as to be visible below low-hanging fog.

An iconic science fiction film, *The Monster of Piedras Blancas,* was filmed here—not at the Piedras Blancas lighthouse—in 1959 and provides a black-and-white tour inside and outside the structure (along with glimpses of an unlikely reptilian sea monster).

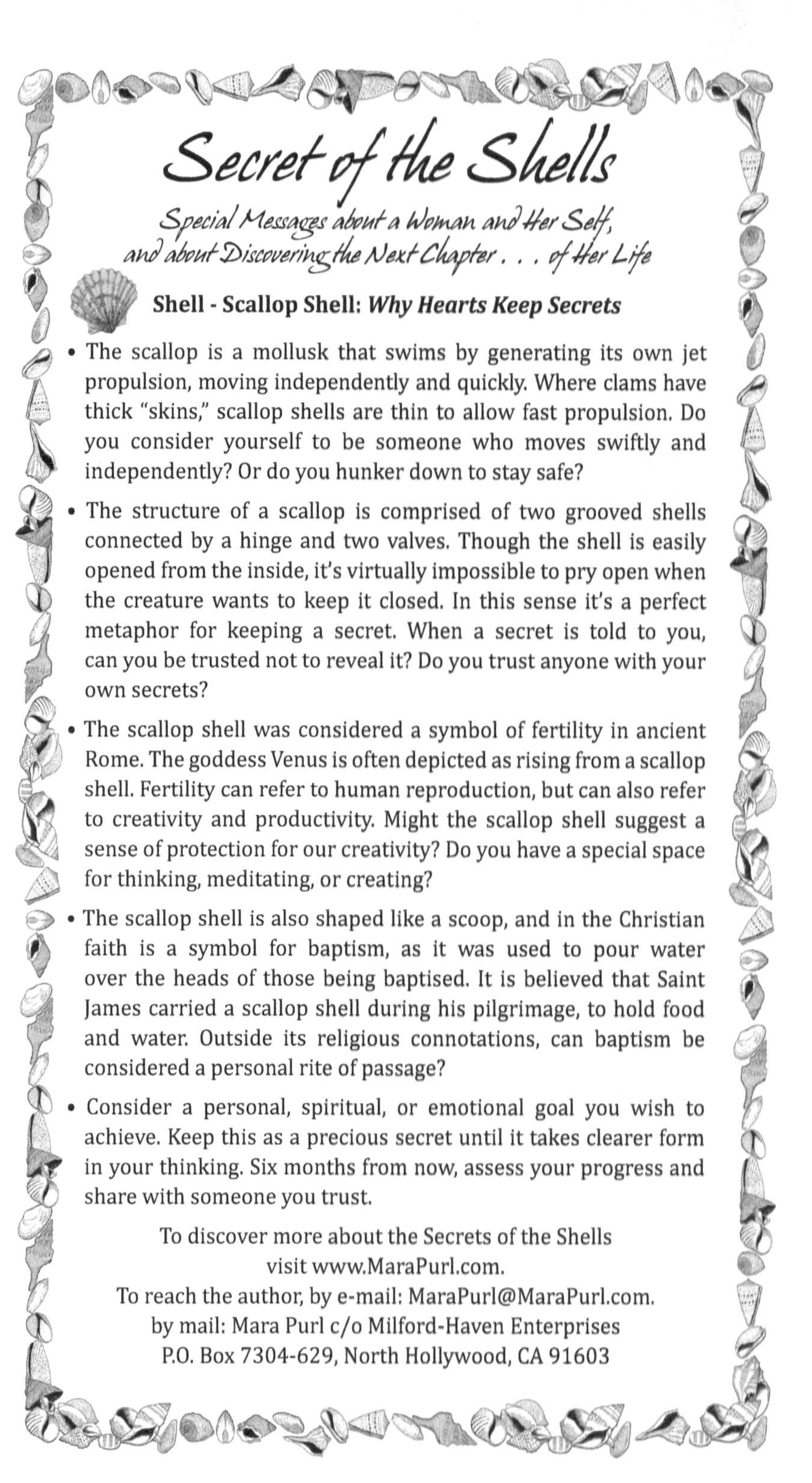

Secret of the Shells

*Special Messages about a Woman and Her Self,
and about Discovering the Next Chapter . . . of Her Life*

Shell - Scallop Shell: *Why Hearts Keep Secrets*

- The scallop is a mollusk that swims by generating its own jet propulsion, moving independently and quickly. Where clams have thick "skins," scallop shells are thin to allow fast propulsion. Do you consider yourself to be someone who moves swiftly and independently? Or do you hunker down to stay safe?

- The structure of a scallop is comprised of two grooved shells connected by a hinge and two valves. Though the shell is easily opened from the inside, it's virtually impossible to pry open when the creature wants to keep it closed. In this sense it's a perfect metaphor for keeping a secret. When a secret is told to you, can you be trusted not to reveal it? Do you trust anyone with your own secrets?

- The scallop shell was considered a symbol of fertility in ancient Rome. The goddess Venus is often depicted as rising from a scallop shell. Fertility can refer to human reproduction, but can also refer to creativity and productivity. Might the scallop shell suggest a sense of protection for our creativity? Do you have a special space for thinking, meditating, or creating?

- The scallop shell is also shaped like a scoop, and in the Christian faith is a symbol for baptism, as it was used to pour water over the heads of those being baptised. It is believed that Saint James carried a scallop shell during his pilgrimage, to hold food and water. Outside its religious connotations, can baptism be considered a personal rite of passage?

- Consider a personal, spiritual, or emotional goal you wish to achieve. Keep this as a precious secret until it takes clearer form in your thinking. Six months from now, assess your progress and share with someone you trust.

To discover more about the Secrets of the Shells
visit www.MaraPurl.com.
To reach the author, by e-mail: MaraPurl@MaraPurl.com.
by mail: Mara Purl c/o Milford-Haven Enterprises
P.O. Box 7304-629, North Hollywood, CA 91603

Why Hearts Keep Secrets

Reading Group Topics for Discussion

1. This is the third novel in the Milford-Haven series, and there are novellas and novelettes that are also part of the saga. Since this is the third in the novel pentalogy, it's the most entangled of the novels, with multiple storylines creating complexity. How do you feel about this?

2. Protagonist Miranda has been alone and often lonely throughout the saga so far. How do you feel about her finding her voice, resolving things with Zack, and recognizing the depth of her feelings for Cornelius?

3. The story focuses on artist Miranda Jones and astronomer Cornelius Smith. Do you feel it's realistic for people with such different careers to understand one another? Do you feel they're so right for each other that their romance is inevitable? What obstacles are they likely to face?

4. How do you feel about Sally O'Mally? Do you feel she waited too long to separate herself from Jack Sawyer? Were you surprised that Tony Fiorentino has moved to Milford-Haven? Do you think they can work out a relationship, even with the challenges each of them faces?

5. Deputy Delmar Johnson has a heavy workload at the Sheriff's Department, but on his own time continues to investigate the missing journalist Christine Christian. There is more of their story in the novella *What the Soul Suspects*. Is he doing a good job as a protector of Milford-Haven?

6. A protagonist should have some solid, recurring qualities, but also should grow and learn from her experiences. In this book, Miranda "finds her voice." What does that mean?

7. Were you surprised by Meredith's mixed heritage, which had mostly been a secret? What about her bold move toward Zack? Do you believe she might be able to inspire him to be more honest than he has been, if they begin a relationship?

8. Author Mara Purl has now won more than seventy awards for her series. Before then, she created a hit radio drama for the BBC. What do you consider to be her strengths as a writer? What other parts of her series do you wish she would write?

9. Why is this book called *Why Hearts Keep Secrets*? What are some of the secrets that are revealed? What are some that are not yet revealed?

To share or print these discussion points please visit:
http://marapurl.com/books/why-hearts-keep-secrets

Find yourself in . . .

Milford-Haven

Small town simplicities . . .
Global complexities . . .

"Where Jack, Zack, Miranda, Cornelius, Samantha, Rune, Meredith, Connie, Emily, Kevin, Joseph, Sally, Tony, Zelda, Notes, Susan, and Cynthia, are building, buying, painting, observing, planning, rehearsing, advising, traveling, reporting, cogitating, dominating, dishing, dealing, conniving, playing, sneaking, and seducing, respectively."

Subscribe to the Milford-Haven Podcast!
Enjoy the original BBC radio drama
with an all-star cast,
original music & sound effects,
plus Bonus Material!

Also available on CD or in downloadable formats

www.MilfordHaven.com

MARA PURL
Milford-Haven

Find Saga Chronology at
MaraPurl.com/Books

Mara Purl, author of the best-selling and critically acclaimed *Milford-Haven Novels, Novellas & Novelettes,* pioneered small-town fiction for women.

Mara's beloved fictitious town has been delighting audiences since 1992, when it first appeared as *Milford-Haven, U.S.A.*©—the first American radio drama ever licensed and broadcast by the BBC. The show reached an audience of 4.5 million listeners in the U.K. In the U.S., it was the 1994 Finalist for the New York Festivals World's Best Radio Programs.

Mara was named the Top Female Author for Fiction by The Authors Show, and to date, her books have won more than seventy book awards, including the American Fiction, Benjamin Franklin, National Indie Excellence, USA Book News Best Books, and ForeWord Books of the Year.

The *Milford-Haven Novels*, set in the late 1990s, capture the spirit of adventure and the soul of small-town life, interweaving the tales of three multi-generational women who find romance, friendship and success on California's gorgeous Central Coast.

Mara's other writing credits include plays, screenplays, scripts for *Guiding Light*, cover stories for *Rolling Stone*, staff writing with the *Financial Times (of London)*, and the Associated Press. She is the co-author (with Erin Gray) of *Act Right: A Manual for the On-Camera Actor*.

As an actress, Mara was "Darla Cook" on *Days Of Our Lives*. For the one-woman show *Mary Shelley: In Her Own Words*—which Mara performs and co-wrote (with Sydney Swire)—she earned a Peak Award. She has co-starred in multiple productions of *Sea Marks* and plays the title role in *Becoming Julia Morgan*. She was named one of twelve Women of the Year by the Los Angeles County Commission for Women.

Mara is married to Dr. Larry Norfleet and lives in Los Angeles and in Colorado Springs.

Visit her website at *www.MaraPurl.com* where you can subscribe to her newsletter and link to her social media sites.